LAINIE ANDERSON

KV-374-436

LONG FLIGHT HOME

Complete and Unabridged

AURORA
Leicester

First published in 2019 by
Wakefield Press

First Aurora Edition
published 2021
by arrangement with
Wakefield Press

Copyright © 2019 by Lainie Anderson
All rights reserved

A catalogue record for this book is available
from the British Library.

ISBN 978–1–78782–708–0

East Riding of Yorkshire
Library & Information Services

9 0 0 9 5 5 1 3 6 9

BEL

Published by
Ulverscroft Limited
Anstey, Leicestershire

Printed and bound in Great Britain by
TJ Books Ltd., Padstow, Cornwall

This book is printed on acid-free paper

9009551369

East Riding of Yorkshire
Library and Information Service

PD00328

SPECIAL MESSAGE TO

THE U
(registe
was establishe
diagnosis and
major project

- The Chi
Hospital, I
- The Ulve
Ormond S
- Funding
treatment a
Ophthalmo
- The Ulv
Institute of
- Twin ope
Ophthalmic Hospital, London
- The Chair of Ophthalmology at the Royal
Australian College of Ophthalmologists

You can help further the work of the Foundation
by making a donation or leaving a legacy. Every
contribution is gratefully received. If you would like
to help support the Foundation or require further
information, please contact:

THE ULVERSCROFT FOUNDATION
The Green, Bradgate Road, Anstey
Leicester LE7 7FU, England
Tel: (0116) 236 4325

website: www.ulverscroft-foundation.org.uk

SPECIAL MESSAGE TO READERS

THE ULVERSCROFT FOUNDATION
(registered UK charity number 264873)

was established in 1972 to provide funds for research, diagnosis and treatment of eye diseases. Examples of major projects funded by the Ulverscroft Foundation are:-

* The Children's Eye Unit at Moorfields Eye Hospital, London
* The Ulverscroft Children's Eye Unit at Great Ormond Street Hospital for Sick Children
* Funding research into eye diseases and treatment at the Department of Ophthalmology, University of Leicester
* The Ulverscroft Vision Research Group, Institute of Child Health
* Twin operating theatres at the Western Ophthalmic Hospital, London
* The Chair of Ophthalmology at the Royal Australian College of Ophthalmologists

You can help further the work of the Foundation by making a donation or leaving a legacy. Every contribution is gratefully received. If you would like to help support the Foundation or require further information, please contact:

THE ULVERSCROFT FOUNDATION
The Green, Bradgate Road, Anstey
Leicester LE7 7FU, England
Tel: (0116) 236 4325

website: www.ulverscroft-foundation.org.uk

LONG FLIGHT HOME

The First World War is over and air mechanic Wally Shiers has promised to return home to his fiancée, Helena Alford. But Wally never reckoned on charismatic fighter pilot Ross Smith, and an invitation to compete in the world's most audacious air race. A £10,000 prize has been offered for the first airmen to fly from England to Australia. Smith is banking on an open-cockpit Vickers Vimy, a biplane with a fuselage that looks ominously like a coffin. And who can resist a hero? Wally writes to Helena to say he won't be home for another year — and the love of his life is left holding her hand-stitched wedding dress ...

For Max

PART ONE

PART ONE

Chapter 1

ADELAIDE, 1968

Beer is my friend. Everyone's my friend at the Hilton pub on South Road. I'm 78. Old and lonely and shrinking. But when I drink, I'm young Wally Shiers again, and the world's at my feet. I drink and I talk. The regulars gather round, because January in Adelaide is stinking hot, the bar is cool and I always shout the Friday beers when I tell my tale. 'Start from the beginning, Wal,' they say, like this old cracked record could start anywhere else. They wait while I dab behind my glasses and silently give thanks that this story is mine to tell. And when glistening beers are cradled in strong hands around me, I rub the precious watch under my shirt sleeve and 50 years are gone, just like that.

★ ★ ★

NARRANDERA, 1914

At first I thought the kid was throwing rocks.

I quickened my pace, called out 'Oi!'. He stopped and turned to face me.

Not a sound. Not a soul around. Houses all closed up and hushed. You know those days? When the heat is like a hand holding everything down?

Then he took off, a flash of blonde hair.

When I reached the house, I stopped and leaned my overnight bag against the fence.

Jeez, what a mess, especially the window. The kid

3

wasn't throwing rocks. He was throwing eggs — and it's amazing how three or four eggs can splatter.

In the distance, there was cheering from the cricket match over on Cadell Street. The Narrandera boys must have got a wicket. It took me back to twilight as a kid, playing street cricket in the dust with my older brothers and their mates. So many fielders, dozens of them dotted down the road, and me way out back behind the wickie, desperate for a loose ball so I could have a throw. When the light was almost gone and someone's Mum yelled 'Inside!' my brothers would let me face the final over. And whoever had the ball would hurtle in like he was going to bowl the nastiest, fastest ball ever, and at the last minute he'd throw underarm and I always got a run. Always.

At the end of the day, there's only ever family. Remember that.

I stared down the empty road for a good long while. Then back at the house, expecting the front door to open. Willing it to open, really, so I could dob in the kid and be on my way to the cricket and then the pub and cold beer and banter with the boys.

Nothing. When the flies started to settle it was time to move, one way or the other, and I knew I couldn't leave it like that.

It was cooler on the porch, but the egg was already drying in yellow gobs against the red brick. I found a spot on the door frame that wasn't sticky and knocked as loudly as I could, wobbling the wet egg on the rattling fly-wire. I could smell the lavender hedge lining the verandah and eucalyptus sweating from the huge gum out back. I picked absentmindedly at a drop of yolk on the wire, flicked it over the lavender. I licked the flesh of my thumb and rubbed at another bit.

4

Waiting. Listening for sounds of life inside. From the branch of a bottlebrush, a magpie watched, beak open to the heat.

A whistle sounded way down the river and I imagined the Murrumbidgee washing over me, waking me up. I thought I'd miss the red dust when I left the mine in Broken Hill, but the Riverina suited me fine. Same open sky overhead, richer soil underfoot — if you were looking to grow stuff, that is, and not dig stuff out. I planned on growing stuff one day.

I looked back out to the road. Stared up at the sky. Not a cloud. For days it had been the same. Bit weird for November.

Nothing. Damn.

I walked around the back of the house. Hens rushed to the door of their coop, expecting to be fed. No such luck, ladies, cluck all you like. The tank was cool to touch, half-filled with water. I soaked my head under the tap, replaced my hat and then filled an old metal bucket. Whistling softly, I headed back to the front of the house.

'Hello? Can we help you?'

Coming through the garden gate, shielding their eyes from the glare, were two women with wide-brimmed sun hats. Mother and daughter maybe.

I put down the bucket and raised my palms. Funny how you can feel guilty when you've done nothing wrong. 'Sorry,' I said. 'Some kid threw eggs at your house. I was just getting water from your tank to clean it off. Hope you don't mind. Sorry, I'm Wally. Wally Shiers.' I was babbling. Embarrassed. For me. For them.

Their eyes moved from me to the porch, and I realised they hadn't noticed the egg. Too shocked by some

5

random bloke in their yard, I s'pose.

The older woman said something and I noticed a slight German accent. Now the egg made sense.

They stood there, taking it in. The mess. The meaning. The meanness of it all.

I could feel my wet hair steaming under my hat, sun burning the back of my neck. Poor women. They were tiny things too, neither of them more than five foot.

Finally the younger woman squared her shoulders and put an arm around her mother's back.

'Just some silly boy, Mother,' she said, head down, guiding her mum to the front door. 'Fred will be home soon. Let's get you out of this heat. I'm sure poor Mr Shy-ers is thirsty. Why don't we fix him a nice cool drink and he can be on his way.'

She returned with a glass of water. Slice of lemon. Light pink glass.

'Thank you Mr Shy-ers,' she said, surveying the splatter with pressed lips and anxious eyes. 'It was very kind of you.'

She had a nice way of saying Shiers. All 'shy' with a soft 'ers' on the end.

'Don't mind giving you a hand,' I said, staring into the glass between sips. 'We'll get it cleaned off in no time.'

We worked silently, for the most part, her on one side of the porch and me on the other, both careful not to meet at the bucket in the middle.

'I'm Helena Alford,' she said at last. 'Can't believe you're helping me scrub egg off our porch and you don't even know my name.'

'Nice to meet you, Miss Alford,' I said, allowing myself a quick glance. She was about my age, maybe a bit younger. And gee, she was little. I wondered how far her brown hair would fall down her back if she let it loose from that bun.

Silence again. The smell of grass drying, dying already. Her mother's soft footsteps on the floor-boards inside.

'Father was born in Germany,' she said a while later, without breaking the circular rhythm of her arm or shifting her gaze. 'Decades ago. Didn't even call it Germany back then.'

'Right,' I said. Poor things. Bloody kid.

'He's passed away now,' she said. 'Today I'm almost glad.' Her voice caught and I stole a glance, panicked she might be crying. She was biting her upper lip, wiping damp hair from her forehead with the back of a doll-like wrist.

I shook my head in sympathy. What do you say to that?

And I was disappointed when it was done. Almost thanked her for having me. Hadn't spent any real time alone in a woman's presence for years – forever really, if I didn't count my sisters.

I was fixing to leave, shy and stupid, when her mother stepped out onto the porch and asked me to lunch the following day.

'It would be nice to thank you properly,' she said. All soft skin and smile lines, like some older women get. 'You'll meet our Fred. I'm sure you'll like him.'

'I might even make a sponge,' Helena said then, her face brightening for the first time. 'Show you the proper way to use eggs.'

I'm not kidding – the sponge was the best thing I'd ever tasted. Icing sugar dusted on top, thin layer of strawberry jam in the middle. It was all I could do not to ask for thirds. Fred was just a year older than me and worked on one of the farms over in the Murrumbidgee Irrigation Area. I was doing some electrical work on the new homes out there, so we knew a few lads in common. That was good, broke the ice.

He was a funny bloke, ruddy face with messy brown hair and piercing blue eyes that always looked interested in what you had to say. Loved talking about cars and aircraft almost as much as I did – we'd barely had time to sit down before he was showing me his collection of Flight magazines, including quite a few copies I hadn't already read. He was positive the magician Harry Houdini had been the first man to fly over Australian soil in 1910, but I knew for a fact that a South Australian by the name of Custance had beaten Houdini by a day. By the time lunch was on the table, I was calling him Freddy Houdini and he was calling me Wally Custard, and I knew we were going to be best mates.

The house was pretty recent, Federation style. Their father John Alford had been a big landowner and builder and had done very well for himself. A couple of blokes I'd asked that morning had heard of him. You could tell they weren't poor, but they weren't too posh either. Church of England, so nothing silly. I'd been brought up C of E, too. The Alford's dining table had a lace cloth on it and Helena kept smoothing it down with open palms as she listened to me and Fred talk. She had light freckles on the back of her hands.

'You gonna enlist, Wally Custard?' Fred asked.

I knew it would come eventually.

'You can't ask him that,' said Helena.

I put down my knife and fork, glanced at the roast

8

lamb on my plate. 'That's okay. Fair question. I'll go if I have to, if I'm needed. Rather keep out of it for now, though. I'm trying to save up for a block out Leeton way. Seems there's plenty enough blokes lining up to fight. How about you, Freddy Houdini?'

'Same,' he said. 'Put a bullet in the Hun if I have to. And actually, I'd make a good spy with my bits of Deutsch.'

Helena threw her mother an exasperated look, but you could tell she adored Fred. They both did.

Later the three of us walked down to the irrigation channel. Fred wasn't silly, he wandered off a bit, skimming rocks as Helena and I sat on the bank, staring at the water. Corellas were making a racket in the gums.

'So you're buying a block,' she said ages later, still staring at the water. 'You think you'll stay?'

I picked a blade of grass and started splitting it as I watched her out the corner of my eye. 'Can't see why not.'

She smiled ever so slightly at the river, and I noticed a tiny dimple in her right cheek.

We both knew.

It was a couple of weeks before our first kiss. Didn't rush things in those days. We were in her backyard, putting the chickens away one Sunday afternoon a few hours before I caught the train home. I was bent over, sort of half-running around the backyard, mustering up the chooks all silly-like. Helena's beaming face was bathed in sunlight. I looked back at the house to see no one was watching, cupped her chin in my hand and kissed her on the lips. Then she pulled me behind the tank and kissed me back. That was that.

* * *

9

Any idiot can fall in love. The tricky stuff comes after.

I bought the block in Leeton in early 1915 — had enough for a down-payment because prices dropped after war broke out. Then I heard about a bloke in Sydney almost giving away a shipment of fruit trees. It felt like it was meant to be.

So there I was, just before Easter, in the second-class carriage of the overnight train to Sydney, reaching through the open sash window to hold Helena's hand. She was on the platform, looking towards the front of the train, waiting for the signal while we chatted softly about everything and nothing. We'd spent a lot of time together over summer and were fitting together nicely. I didn't like the idea of leaving her and the Riverina, even just for a night or two. Made me anxious. Made me stupid.

'Guess what,' I said, the idea hitting me just as the whistle blew and the train creaked into motion. 'You know what I'm going to do when I get back?'

'Plant orange trees with me?' she asked, as our fingertips were pulled apart.

'Well, yes,' I said, raising my voice as the train chugged away. I was leaning out of the window now to see her face as I said it: 'But I'm going to ask you to marry me, too!'

I can still see her face — the blue eyes round with confusion and delight and a hint of something else.

I fell back into my seat, laughing.

'You're a sly dog,' said the bloke opposite. 'How'd a fella like you win a girl like her, anyhow?'

I stopped, stared blankly out the window, Narrandera disappearing behind us in the dusk. Jesus, what

10

had I done? Was it anger I'd seen in her eyes? Reluctance? Disappointment? And what the bloody hell was I doing, asking the most important question of my life as a train rolled away? To this day, I still can't believe I did it.

The train got me into Sydney Central around eight o'clock the following morning. It had been a night of little sleep and much anxiety, and I was wholly unprepared for the punch in the face that was Australia's biggest city.

Away from the quiet banks of the rolling Murrumbidgee, it was suddenly clear that Australia was at war. Impatient. Unsettled. Itching for action.

I'd never felt so out of place, so obviously an outsider. The city was rowdy with strong chiselled lads in Australian Imperial Force uniforms, all shaking hands and slapping backs and bending over adoring sweethearts.

'Hey mate, you signing up?'

If I heard it once that morning, I heard it a dozen times. With each new query, I offered a friendly wink and carried on my way to the meeting point with my nurseryman, stomach churning and desperate to return to Narrandera and its 180 degrees of soothing, open sky. Can you imagine how stupid I felt, shopping for orange trees while every other bloke my age was headed to fight the Hun?

And then it happened — my run-in with the Sydney copper.

'Oi, young feller,' the officer said. I'm not joking, the bloke was nearly seven foot – tall as a tree. Dark stubble, brooding eyes, black hair greying at the temples.

'Yes, sir?' I said, distracted, dishevelled and decid-

11

edly little in the shadow of this hulking man. 'I'm just on my way to buy orange trees. Train's leaving this afternoon.' I must have sounded like a lunatic.

'Never mind that, son,' he said, shoving a postcard at me. 'I've got a job for you.'

Lord Kitchener, Minister of War, with his accusatory finger and bushy moustache was staring out from the card in my hand.

'I thought we already had too many volunteers,' I said, knowing immediately what it meant. 'What do you need me for?'

'Don't take it personally, lad,' the officer said. 'You can never sign up enough men in a voluntary force – got to get you all trained up as ready reinforcements.'

'But I've already got a job,' I said. I wasn't upending a life that was just beginning because I'd met a random old copper in the street. And you couldn't be forced into a volunteer army. 'I'm an electrician out with the Murrumbidgee Irrigation Scheme. We're growing food for blokes at the Front.'

He rested a giant mitt on my shoulder and for a second I thought I'd convinced him. 'Listen son, it's normal to be scared,' he said, tightening his grip ever so slightly and allowing a hint of contempt to enter his voice. 'The bigger lads will look out for you.'

'Fear's not stopping me,' I said, meeting his gaze. I was no coward. I was five foot four inches, the shortest man in most rooms, shorter even than Charlie Chaplin if you can believe that. But there's no height limit on courage. I'd stood up to bullies like him all my life, and I knew there was only one way to loosen his grip and end the conversation: I jollied him along, played the charmer and said what he wanted to hear.

'Good lad,' he said, but I was already out of earshot, putting maximum distance between us.

When I'd gone a few blocks I found a bench in a sad, dusty little Sydney park and sat for a while to collect my thoughts, away from the jostling crowds and bragging soldiers.

I didn't want to enlist. I suppose that sounds lily-livered, but good things were happening for me. I'd just branched out with my own sparky business. I'd bought the block. Me and Helena had plans. And her mother treated me like a son. My own mum had died years back and I didn't realise how much I missed her until Mrs Alford gave me one of her little lady's bear hugs. I wanted to be an electrician with a Riverina fruit block. I wanted to be a husband, a dad, with little people running around my legs.

A bloke about my age slumped down on the bench beside me and put his head in his hands, just as I'd done a half-hour before.

'Looks like you ran into the same copper I did,' I said. 'Did he tell you to enlist, too?'

The bloke looked puzzled and pointed to his coat lapel and a brass badge no more than an inch wide. Surrounding the Australian Coat of Arms were the words 'Volunteered for active service. Medically unfit'.

'They knocked me back,' he said. 'That's the second time now. Reckon my heart and lungs aren't up to the job. I had TB as a kid.' He stared into the distance for a moment, then snapped himself out of it. 'They'll get desperate soon enough, then they'll take me.'

I studied my hands. 'Why are you so keen to fight a war on the other side of the world?' I asked.

He turned to me. 'You think this isn't our war?' he said. 'You think the Hun will stop at France and

Britain? If everyone had your attitude, the Germans and Turks would be sailing into Sydney Harbour by Christmas. And there'll be no one left to back us up. Will it be your war then?'

He rose abruptly and left me to my bench. When he'd taken a couple of steps he turned back and spat, 'God help your mates if they're ever in strife.'

I called out a lame 'Sorry, mate ...'

I tried to clear my head. I was so thirsty.

You know, that was the only day of my life I felt small.

Chapter 2

NARRANDERA, 1915

I took a deep breath and opened the Alfords' front gate as quietly as I could. Damn thing still creaked. How many times had I told Fred to oil those hinges? By the time I'd taken the few steps to the verandah, Helena had already thrown open the door and was standing there beaming.

'Welcome home, Mr Oranges,' she said. 'I've been counting the seconds since you left.'

She saw me hesitate, saw the look on my face, and straight away knew something was wrong. Thought I'd changed my mind about the wedding.

'What's the matter?' she asked, her face fallen.

'Everything's fine, love,' I said, reaching out for her. 'It's just that when I was in Sydney they made me enlist. An old copper practically forced me.'

We were still in the doorway, half in, half out, and she gave me a little shove backwards onto the verandah. 'What?' she asked, folding her arms in front of her chest. 'What do you mean you enlisted?'

I rubbed my forehead. 'I had to, love. They're making everyone sign up. You should have seen it. Every bloke my age was in khaki.'

She stared at me with a fierce intensity. 'I thought you wanted to be an electrician with a Riverina fruit block, Wally. I thought you were going to ask me to marry you.'

'I still do, Helena. I still am.' I rested my hands on

15

her shoulders and pulled her toward me.

She shrugged me off. 'So when do you leave?'

'No word on when we embark for the Front,' I said, and hesitated before adding, 'But I'm wanted back in Sydney day after tomorrow.'

She looked at me in disbelief. 'The day after tomorrow!' she repeated, raising her voice.

I glanced into the street, praying the neighbours weren't in earshot. She looked like she was going to cry, so I opened the door and put an arm around her shoulders to guide her into the hallway.

'Is everything alright, Helena?' Mrs Alford called from the kitchen. For a horrifying moment I thought she might come out, but then Fred said: 'No, Mum. Leave it.'

The hallway was painted a dark green and the light was always dim, but there was still no avoiding the photograph of Mr Alford. Proud white beard. Demanding glare. 'I am John Alford,' it seemed to say. 'And who are you?'

I turned my back on him and took hold of Helena's hands. 'Helena, darling, I'm sorry,' I said quietly, hoping the others couldn't hear. She'd started to cry now, in soft little sobs. 'I'm sorry for enlisting, Helena, I'm sorry for what I said at the station ...'

'So I'm right,' she interrupted with a defiant look. 'You didn't mean it.'

'I meant every word,' I whispered. 'I just wish I hadn't said it from a moving train, especially given everything that's happened since. I'd give anything to take it back and ask you properly without this bloody war hanging over us.'

She was quiet for a long while, biting her lip, then slowly shook her head. 'There's no point thinking

16

about marriage now,' she said.

'Actually,' I said, 'lots of couples do it. Blokes heading off to the Front figure their sweethearts might as well be listed to receive a widow's pension if the worst happens.'

She let out a wail and Mrs Alford appeared at the end of the hallway, clutching a tea towel anxiously. I looked desperately from mother to daughter before Fred poked his head out with a 'sorry, mate' grimace, before gently tugging his mum back into the kitchen.

'Oh love,' I said, pulling Helena in tightly. 'That was a daft thing to say. Nothing's going to happen to me, okay?'

I smoothed down her hair until she stopped crying. 'Only two things matter – that I love you, which I do, and that you love me.'

She pulled back from my chest and offered a weak smile, her eyes sad and wet, her nose red and shiny. 'Love you … I do.'

'Well then,' I said, 'this war won't last forever, and when it's over I'll be on the first ship home.'

'Promise?'

'Promise. Before you know it, I'll be at the altar in St Thomas's, watching as you walk down the aisle.'

Then I went down on one knee, fumbling for the imitation diamond ring I'd bought instead of orange trees in Sydney. 'Miss Helena Alford, will you marry me?'

* * *

They threw a little farewell party for me, before I caught the train the following day. I'd met her family over the summer – older brothers and sisters all mar-

17

ried, but not far away. Nice people. And always lots of 'em, noisy, with a crop of kids underfoot.

I wore my Light Horse uniform, looking nothing like those other chiselled lads I'd seen in Sydney. The woollen jacket itched my neck. The felt slouch hat was too tight on my head.

Helena promised there'd be no speeches but Fred stood on a chair anyway. Said he was proud to call me a friend; was glad Helena had found someone almost as short as she was.

When they'd done three cheers, Helena said, 'And when Wally comes home, we're getting married.'

Well, that raised the roof. Nearly put out my back with all the slapping.

Helena and I managed to duck off together for an hour before the train left. We walked arm in arm over to East Street like there wasn't a care in the world, and I felt a bit proud with Helena all lovely in her best green frock beside me. The uniform did make people look at you differently. Blokes would give a nod of respect and ladies wished me well. It was embarrassing at first — no one ever noticed me before — but I got used to it.

'Maybe the war will be over soon,' Helena said. 'We can just return to before.'

I tugged at the collar of my uniform. 'I just don't know, love. I can only promise to keep my head down, which shouldn't be hard for a shorty like me, should it? And whenever I'm not pointing my gun at the Hun I'll be thinking of you.'

I was trying to keep things light, giving her waist a little squeeze when I spoke.

'And one day we'll start a family,' she said. 'Little cousins for all the others.'

18

I'd seen the way she nursed her baby nieces and nephews, or sat on the floor with her head bent over a game of dolls or toy soldiers in a circle of nippers. I turned to face her, pushing my slouch hat back from my forehead and wrapping an arm tightly around her back. 'Yep, one day we'll have a whole brood of 'em. Girls who all love to bake sponge cakes.'

We had a nice long kiss, right there in the street down from the pub with the late afternoon sun warming our faces. We didn't even stop when the hollering and whistling started through the pub window.

Later at the train station, Helena's mum held me close, all rose water and soft cheek, and she whispered, 'You're family now. Be careful, Walter.'

* * *

SYDNEY, 1915

I don't remember spending a lot of time with my father as a kid. He was a plasterer, and when he wasn't working he was either eating dinner or exhausted, or both, and us kids were seen and not heard.

Dad was a decent man, never raised his hand to us, or to Mum, and only ever drank when the house was full of aunts and uncles and Mum's Irish ditties. I do remember him sitting me down once, on the old brown velvet settee in the front room. Must have been around the time I went to work for Mr Frazer the market gardener, but I was still at Richmond Public School because I remember tugging at the bottom of my grey school shorts, embarrassed and keen to get outside to the kids kicking the footy.

'Not everyone can be the winner, Walter,' he said.

19

'But there's plenty of room in the world for hard workers.'

I can't have been more than 12 or 13. Not a kid anymore, but a long way from being a man. 'Yes, Dad,' I said, relieved I wasn't in trouble. And he ruffled my hair and it was over.

One night, years later, my brothers and I got to reminiscing about Mum and Dad over a few beers, and realised we all got the same speech on that settee. The old man hated formalities, but he chose those words wisely.

Take the army. They weren't looking for anything special from blokes like me. Keep working. Keep your chin up. Keep out of trouble. And looking back, I s'pose the life suited me fine. I never minded a bit of routine or being told what to do, and I'd never lived posh. I liked the tucker too, for the most part, and the camaraderie.

But there was this one bloke, Sergeant Patrick Copping.

Copping was meaner than a red-back. He was a Boer War vet with a white puckered scar on his left cheek. He said it was from shrapnel; got it from some big siege when a handful of Aussies held out against the Boers. Reckoned he'd met Breaker Morant, too, but I say he was full of the stuff we mucked out of the stables.

I joined up with the 4th Light Horse Brigade and my first day was at Liverpool training camp just outside Sydney. Some recruits turned up for training with their own horses, but most of us had to be matched with government mounts called Walers.

And that's when I met Copping.

I wasn't used to the humidity in Sydney and I

remember my nose was itchy from damp hay and horse sweat. The horses were tied up to a long line of rope on one side of the yard and us blokes were on the other, a bit like blokes and girls eying each other off from either side of a dance hall. We'd been standing around for hours. Drizzle turned to blinding sunlight, turned to drizzle. My nose was running. My jacket was a lead weight. My eagerness to get a horse had given way to dread churning in my guts every time this bloke Copping swept his eyes past me to some other bigger, stronger recruit.

You know that feeling when big kids are picking out their teams for cricket or footy, and the youngest or weakest kids are always last? You can either beg for selection or stand there powerless, and either way you look like a right dope. That's what this was like.

At 25, I had years on some of the blokes invited across the yard before me, and I knew Copping's kind by the way he made every man grovel before stepping across to meet his horse.

It took most of the morning – three long hours – until only two of us were left. The young bloke beside me was called Bernie, a thin, shy chap, all arms and legs. He was shaking and fidgety. I worried a bit for him.

Copping's small, nasty eyes finally found me. 'Done much ridin'?' he asked, spitting out the words like he already knew the answer. Nasty blokes always mistake shortness for weakness.

The best horses were long gone. 'Yes, sir, I can handle myself on a horse just fine. But I'm told this young bloke is a champion in the saddle. Might as well sort him out before you bother with me. Sir.'

His eyes narrowed as he stepped forward. Without

21

taking his eyes off me, he growled softly at Bernie, 'Off you go then, son. Take the chestnut on the left.'

Bernie bolted to collect a saddle and join the men paired with their mounts. 'Walk, you dumb bastard!' Copping hissed at him. 'Don't startle the bloody horses.'

Copping came close, like those sorts of blokes always do. Close enough for me to smell tobacco and Pears soap and a hint of stale beer. He used a thumbnail to scratch at something between his front teeth.

'Name.' It was more a challenge than a question. He was a head taller than me and twice my bulk in muscle. Keg on legs. A vein throbbed at his temple, just beneath his slouch hat.

'Walter Shiers, sir,' I said, nice as pie, back straight and eyes forward like they taught us in the Barrier Boys' Brigade, my old cadet group back in Broken Hill.

'Age?'

'Twenty-six next month, sir.'

'Old enough to know you're no fucking hero, then, Shiers.'

'Yes, sir.'

He marched me across to the remaining horses. 'Light Horse is no place for a man who can't ride,' he announced to the other recruits. 'It's a danger to every soldier in the regiment.'

There were two horses left. And I'm not kidding, one looked a canter away from the glue factory. Bare blotches of skin on its neck, barely able to lift its head. To my relief, Copping stopped at the other one, a bright-eyed, bay beauty with a large white diamond on its forehead.

'You heard of Walers, Shiers?' he asked, scratching

22

the horse behind its ear. 'They're named after this great state of New South Wales. All the Light Horse regiments use 'em 'cos they're tough as nails. Where you from, Shiers?'

'Born in Adelaide, sir.' The other blokes were watching intently, waiting.

'Croweater,' he said slowly, his lip curling. 'Should have known.' The sweet smell of manure was turning my empty stomach.

He looked up, like he was searching for something in the sky. He ran his hand slowly down the back of the horse and made like he was going to smack its rump. Frightened me. He shook his head, smirking.

'This is actually a bloody fine horse, Shiers,' he said finally.

I stepped forward to take the reins, glad the game was over. But as I cleared my throat to say 'Sir' he cut me off.

'So we might have to save him for a soldier who knows a horse's arse from its head.' He stepped between me and the animal. 'You can have Bobby.' He nodded toward the nag. Someone sniggered.

I took a deep breath, doing my best to hide the disappointment as I looked over to Bobby. And then I did the worst thing possible. I hesitated.

A nasty smile spread across Copping's face. He looked at the waiting men and said, 'There's always one sloppy sheila holding up the crowd, eh boys?'

'Yeah, hurry up, Shiers. We're gonna miss lunch,' said one.

'Fuckin' Croweaters,' said another.

'He thinks he's too good for Bobby, boys!' said Copping, stepping close and pressing a forefinger into my chest. 'A Croweatin' private should count himself lucky to score any nag from New South Wales. Get on with it!'

I quickly collected my saddle and blanket from the stable manager before Copping could have another go, then walked across and held my hand to Bobby's lowered mane.

'Looks like it's you and me, old mate,' I said quietly. He nuzzled my breeches and I felt a surge of pity for the pair of us.

'Right then, men. We're done here,' said Copping as I set my kit down, completing the line of horses, men and gear. 'Head to the mess for some tucker, but be back here for drills at two o'clock.'

As we turned to walk off he said, 'Not you, Shiers. This yard needs mucking out. Get it cleaned up.'

I missed my lunch, but truth is I was happy to stay back with the horses for a bit. When I was a kid, I'd never dreamed of owning a horse and such a fine saddle, or wearing all the new kit and the boots and the belts. I felt sad for my parents. Wish they could have seen me.

I wanted to spend a few minutes with my new horse, too. The stable manager had some tea tree oil and I added a few drops to a bucket of water, gave the horse a rinse down to relieve the heat rash and it bucked him up no end. I introduced myself to Bobby, told him about Helena and the Riverina, let him know I'd look after him. Might sound daft, but the best horseman I ever knew always talked to his animals, made them feel safe and special. Willy Martin, his name was, taught himself to ride as a nipper on a station outside Broken Hill — nothing he couldn't do on a horse's back, saddle or no. He was a funny bloke, too, always daring us other Barrier Boys to try new tricks when the horse trainer had his back turned.

By the time Copping came back with the others, I had my jacket off and sleeves rolled up and was helping the stable manager unload hay.

'Are you a Light Horseman or a stable boy, Croweater?' Copping asked when he saw me. His stood with his legs apart, arms folded. The other men were lined up behind him, silent and staring.

My heart sank. 'Light Horseman, Sir.'

'Well, untie your horse, race to the bottom of the yard and clear that jump on the way back. No saddle. No reins.'

'No saddle?' asked one of the other blokes.

'Quiet,' Copping snarled. 'You think the Hun's gonna wait till you're all saddled up to attack, you soft bastards?'

I eased Bobby out of line and warned him I was coming aboard, grateful for the time I'd had to cool him off. Grabbing a fistful of mane in my left hand and steadying myself with the right, I threw myself up and over his back, finding my balance after a wobbly second or two as Bobby adjusted to the weight. Without thinking, I smiled and looked over to the men. To my surprise most smiled in return.

'Don't get cocky yet, Shiers,' Copping said. 'My wife can sit on a horse. Doesn't mean she can fucking ride. You fall, you're out.'

My stomach lurched, but I told myself it was fair enough. If I couldn't rise to a 400-yard challenge in Sydney, what use would I be on a battlefield? Then I prayed like no Shiers has done before or since.

Leaning forward, I gripped Bobby's mane with both hands, squeezed my thighs and made a 'K-K' sound in my cheek to move him forward. We were a good fit right from the get-go, Bobby and me. Walers are bred small and stocky, with bags of heart. We gained speed and reached the bottom of the paddock quickly. Turning was tough — my left hand lost grip and I almost slipped down his right flank before throwing myself forward to rebalance and tighten my thigh hold. We took the log with me lying low against his neck and returned to the yard victorious.

A couple of blokes started to cheer, but they were silenced by a look from Copping. Didn't matter though. I'd done it. I'd shown the bastard good and proper.

I dismounted, hoping no one could see the shaking in my knees.

★ ★ ★

We trained in Sydney for two months before shipping out to Egypt.

Copping was on my back every chance he got: if I fumbled reloading my rifle; if he couldn't see his reflection in my boots; if Bobby strayed slightly out of formation. All stupid stuff that said more about him than me. A couple of the blokes took to running a book, offering pretty good odds on how I might set him off next. But hatred's not so funny when it's close to home.

Helena came to see me twice, with Freddy Houdini as chaperone.

The first time was when I had leave, which happened to be May 17th, my birthday. They arrived on the overnight train from Narrandera. It was a beautiful day, cloudless skies and a gentle breeze, and I think we were all a bit giddy about meeting in Sydney.

There was lots of chatter about the Alfords and my army mates and my block back home — Fred was keeping an eye on it for me.

'You're not much of a block owner, Wally Custard,' he joked. 'A thousand weeds and not one bloody fruit tree.'

We ate ice-creams for morning tea in Hyde Park then caught the tram to Bondi Beach and sat on the sand for hours. Fred wandered off in search of supplies for a picnic, while Helena and I stayed watching the sea.

'Bit wider than our river,' I said, cupping white sand in my hand. It was the first time we'd seen Bondi Beach: the sand and surf and sea and sky. Lots of khaki, too — looked like half the AIF had a sweetheart on the beach that day. Sitting there in my own uniform with my own girl gave me a warm feeling of belonging that I'd never felt before.

Helena scooped some sand and let it fall through her fingers onto the back of my hand, and we watched as the grains trickled away.

'If only you had to cross the Murrumbidgee to go to war, and not the Indian Ocean,' Helena said. 'You could come home every night.'

Then she laughed and said, 'I realise it's not quite as simple as that, but you know what I mean.'

'I know what you mean,' I said, watching a steamship move across the horizon.

I lay back on my elbows, taking in the line of her neck and shoulders under her white blouse, and wisps of hair escaping from under her hat. You didn't see much skin in those days. You didn't need to. For a long while we were silent, enjoying the sunshine and the drifting voices of nearby couples on the beach. I'd almost dozed off when she asked, 'Do you ever feel scared, Wally?'

I thought about it for a bit. 'No, it's all too unreal. Sometimes in training drills I try to imagine what it'll be like coming face to face with the Hun, but the picture sort of breaks up before anything happens.' I reached out and touched my palm to her shoulder-blade. The soft cotton was hot to touch. 'I worry more about you – about being so far away.'

She drew our initials in the sand a few times, still with her back to me, and then spoke in a voice I could barely hear. 'Freddy Houdini's going to make himself disappear for a couple of hours when we get to the hotel.'

I twirled a strand of her hair around my finger until her brother returned with the food.

★ ★ ★

'Have you got your enlistment papers?' Helena asked. 'Your pay book?'

'For the hundredth time, yes, love,' I said, patting my kit bag and smiling to compensate for the impatience in my voice.

It was four weeks since our day on Bondi Beach, and despite my protests, they were back in Sydney to see me off.

The wharf was crowded and chaotic – families cheering and crying and cajoling, Red Cross volunteers rattling collection tins, stall holders selling stationery and socks and anything that might separate a soldier from a few bob.

'Jeez, you'd think it was a sporting carnival,' Fred said, looking around and shaking his head. He fell

28

forward as he was shoved in the back again by folks from a large, loud family farewelling their boy with speeches and laughter and slaps on the shoulder.

Made our party seem all the more small and sad.

And truth is, I was impatient. I'd spent two months fretting about this farewell and now I just wanted it over. I wanted to put it behind us, to be on my way. I wanted to get caught up in the excitement of the adventure ahead, the mates I'd meet, the places I'd see.

The family beside us started pointing and we looked up to see a horse suspended high above the crowd in a canvas harness.

'Oh God, it's Bobby,' I said. We all stared silently as the animal swayed against a sky dark with rain. The Vestalia was a seconded merchant transport vessel, not a defence ship built to carry troops and mounts, so they were hoisting the horses up over the side to be lowered straight into the hull. And I can tell you there's nothing more unnatural and unsettling than a horse dangling in thin air – the spine curved into a freakish 'n' shape, the legs hanging limp, the neck absurdly long and low. Without his feet firmly on the ground, Bobby was a picture of misery, defenceless and dejected. And there was such a sense of pathetic inevitability about it all that for the first time I felt terrified at the thought of being marched onto that ship.

An officer's whistle sounded and we were called back into line.

Fred and I shook hands and he gave me a half-empty pack of his favourite smokes as a parting gift. 'No one's gonna waste a bullet on a little bloke like you, Wally Custard,' he said. 'You'll be back before I've got your fruit block clear of weeds.' Then he reached out and punched my shoulder before stepping just far enough away to stay in sight of Helena while we said goodbye.

Amid the commotion and tears and shouts of a thousand farewells, Helena and I stood silently, hands locked. We'd been together seven months now. There wasn't much that hadn't been said.

'Love you I do, Helena Alford,' I said, kissing her gently and touching my forehead to hers.

'Love you too, Wally Shy-ers,' she said. 'Now get on that ship. The sooner you leave, the sooner I'll have you home.'

I squeezed her hand and turned away, weaving through the crowd to get back to the men. I was proud of her for keeping it together. Proud of us both.

I noticed Copping standing over by the wharf's edge, with a fine-looking older woman and a young lad who seemed to be crooked at the middle. The boy's legs were twisted and he leaned on walking canes.

Copping had one arm tucked around his wife's back, and he was using his free hand to wipe his son's tears as he talked softly to them both. As I passed by I briefly caught his eye, before he looked away, distraught. It was one of the most moving things I've ever seen: that mean bastard bent over his crippled kid. There's a reason for everything, isn't there?

We marched onto the Vestalia and were directed to our designated area below decks, a narrow mess room with ceiling hooks for hammocks. The air was already thick with the smell of horses and hay and too many sweaty blokes per square foot.

When the ship's horn eventually sounded our departure, I bolted out of the room, dodging around men and scrambling up stairs to get a good vantage

30

spot at the rail in front of an army of taller blokes. Rain was falling steadily now and the wharf was a sea of black umbrellas and frantic faces searching for men they'd maybe never see again. Just in time I spotted Helena. She was waving madly with one hand and wiping away tears with the other, crying and laughing with Fred and doing her best to put on a brave face. Her eyes locked on mine and she went perfectly still. As the ship pulled away from the dock, I gave her a jaunty salute and she pressed her fingers to her lips.

Chapter 3

ADELAIDE, 1968

'What was the war like, Wal?' asks one of my young bar mates like he's checking on a cricket score. I wink at the other old blokes who know the answer, and tell him, 'The short answer, son, is that it was bloody hot. Freezing cold. Lonely sometimes, even in a crowd of your best mates. Many days were boring. Many were sad. A few times it was terrifying, but for me it was never hell. I've spent a lifetime feeling guilty about that.'

★ ★ ★

AUSTRALIA TO EGYPT, 1915

It took around six weeks to sail from Australia to Egypt. I'd never been on a ship before and I can't say I enjoyed it. Cruel really, expecting a man to find his sea legs while sailing around Australia's southern coast in winter. I never did find mine. Some days I'd cling to the rails, almost willing the rolling waves to take me as I surrendered another meal to the sea. Even when we crossed the equator and the sea mirrored the sky, I didn't come good. The ship stank of men and horses, sick and sweat and shit, no matter how much we scrubbed the decks.

I was homesick for Helena. I hated that I could never get a second to myself. I hated that everyone around me was so chummy while I was so out of sorts and

32

always desperate to be swinging silently in my hammock at lights out. Bobby coped better, bless him. I don't know what I'd have done if he'd got crook and I had to watch him go over the side. Copping left me alone too, for the most part. Though there was the time he made me stand to attention somewhere near Kangaroo Island and then had to wear my breakfast on his khakis. A small victory for South Australia.

You probably think I ended up in Gallipoli or France. Most people assume that. But I never got far from Egypt.

We arrived in late July 1915 and spent the first couple of months in a camp near Heliopolis, north of Cairo — not quite in the shadow of the pyramids, but close enough to see them on a clear day.

Huge British and allied camps ringed Cairo. They were like bustling cities, with each division assigned its own suburban block of golden sand. We had our own mess tents and latrines, and whitewashed stones lined the streets. Egyptian hawkers set up any place they weren't kicked out — you could get your hair cut or your photograph taken or buy a cheap souvenir or tobacco for the price of peanuts.

We slept in round, conical bell tents, eight to a tent like spokes in a wheel. The horses were always lined up just out back. Now I think about it, everything around us was meticulously designed and planned, but us troops looked like tramps a lot of the time.

We trained eight hours a day, six days a week. Marched into the desert for miles, teaching our bodies to handle the heat and our eyes to spot the enemy in the flat white haze.

Because there's no cover in the desert, we taught the horses to lie down in front of us for protection. We'd even shoot over their prone bodies; I'd hum *Keep the Home Fires Burning* to keep Bobby calm as I fired my Lee-Enfield at targets 100 yards away. Every instinct must have told that horse to bolt, but he always stayed put. Loyalty on four legs, he was.

After the disastrous Gallipoli landing in April, the campaign dragged on for eight months. Us reinforcements in Cairo were there to top up the numbers as the casualties mounted on the other side of the Med. In August alone, over 2,500 Australians died, and that's when they tapped my regiment for volunteers.

One of the officers who'd seen me feeding the fish from Sydney to Cairo laughed when he saw the look on my face. 'Am I right in thinking you'd prefer to keep your feet on dry land, Shiers?' he asked.

'I'll go where I'm needed, sir,' I said.

But they had too many volunteers in the end. Besides, I was aiming to be promoted to driver, and there wasn't much call for lorries on the beach and cliffs of Gallipoli. There was no call for horses either — they all stayed in Egypt.

Must have been around then that I first climbed the pyramids. I remember it well, because young Bernie was still there. A whole gang of us caught a tram and then rode donkeys to the base of Cheops, where archaeologists fussed over ruins and Egyptian cameleers shouted 'You ride, Aussie good!'

After the climb we sat up there for a bit, looking down on the chaos of Cairo beside the orderly training camps, and the Nile River with its strange cloak of green. Felt like we were up with the pharaohs.

'Makes you feel insignificant, doesn't it?' said Bernie. He was a teacher back home, not long out of

34

training college. Always had his gangly neck bent over a book.

I touched my palms to the giant limestone block beneath me, trying to get my head around the mechanics and the manpower needed to create something so substantial in the sand, thousands of years before.

'Ever stopped to think that maybe we're the slaves of today?' Bernie asked, nodding his head toward the hundreds of troops marching in perfect formation in the distance.

'Fair go, Bernie,' said one of the other blokes. 'No one put a gun to your head. How's that pay in your pocket?'

'Yeah, I s'pose,' Bernie said. 'Just makes you wonder, is all.'

I gave him a little bump with my shoulder, kept my voice low. 'You'll be fine, mate. Me and Bobby'll look after Patch till you get back. Just do as you're told. Don't be a hero.'

'Ha! Not much danger of that,' he said. I knew he was fretting about leaving his horse. About the horror stories we'd heard.

They left for Gallipoli the following week.

★ ★ ★

The rest of us in the ammo reserve stayed camped in Heliopolis, marching out to endless training drills, target practice, desert trench building. When our mates arrived back from the Dardanelles after the Gallipoli evacuation, Bernie wasn't with them. Shot dead by a sniper a week before the withdrawal. He was left behind on that desolate stretch of peninsula with over 8,000 other Australian lads.

35

I went out to Patch when I heard about Bernie, whispered the news, scratched behind his ears while I smoked my pipe and watched the stars. I should have been there, helping Bernie keep his head down.

I was still with Patch half an hour later when Copping found me. He stood there staring with his usual look of contempt, and just when I thought he was going to say something foul he reached into a sack and held out an envelope.

'Here's the post, troops!' he yelled. 'Come and get it!'

I held the envelope and the faint smell of lavender almost made me weep. Still does to this day, after all the scented letters Helena wrote to hurry me home to her front verandah.

I rubbed Patch's muzzle and wandered over to the light of the mess tent to read. 'To my darling Wally' is how they always started. 'Love you I do' is how they'd end. In between was everything and nothing – a weekly roundup that always left me as sad as it did happy.

Patch was allocated to a young cavalryman in need of a new horse. He was a nice lad, a jackaroo with a ready smile from Western Australia. Bernie would have liked him.

★ ★ ★

By the end of January 1916 we were attached to the 1st Light Horse Regiment, headed south down the Nile Valley in search of Senussi tribesmen armed by the Turks to cause strife out of Libya.

Action at last, or so I thought.

Imagine riding a hot, tired horse into white, blister-

36

ing nothingness, and that's what the next four months of desert patrols were like.

Some days the temperature got upwards of 110 degrees, so we did a lot of our patrols by moonlight. I didn't fire a single shot at a Senussi Arab — didn't even spot one before we were hauled back up north to Kantara, east of Cairo.

Our next job was helping to defend the Suez Canal. Didn't fire a shot there either, not even in the Battle of Romani where the Light Horse turned back a major Turkish advance on the canal. Not much of a soldier, eh? But I drove a lorry that resupplied ammo, and also managed to get a lot of shot-up and shattered lads out of harm's way. One bloke had both legs torn off in a blast — kept crying out that his feet were on fire.

After that battle there was a big sale of deceased officers' clothing. All of us stood around haggling over dead men's stuff to raise money for their relatives. Death gets impersonal in wartime.

It wasn't long after that I got a really good look at my first warplanes. Mesmerising, they were – two tiny Fokker monoplanes like the ones that caused the deadly Fokker Scourge in the skies over the Western Front. They were the first aircraft with the machine gun synchronised to the propeller, so the pilots could shoot out in front.

I heard them before I saw them — a hum far off in the distance, and I didn't think much of it because the Brits were often out that way doing reconnaissance. The hum became a loud buzz and you could see the afternoon sun glinting off something on board. Too late we realised they were headed straight for us, and there was a great panic and cries of 'Take cover!'

37

as bullets strafed the camp. I dived onto the sand, praying not to be hit, and within what seemed like seconds the planes were making another pass. Two bombs hit within moments of each other: huge blasts that roared in my ears before a shock wave smashed over me. For a split second, nothing, and then sand and stones and God knows what else rained down. I stood groggily, scraping blackened sand from my face and almost gagging on the foul, burning stench in my nostrils and the back of my throat. Men were running in all directions and yelling and I saw scores of horses strewn across the sand. Bobby was one of them. I sprinted and found him on his side, a huge gash from his shoulder to his flank, bits of rib sticking out.

'Bloody hell, Bobby,' I said, sinking to my knees beside him. I knew I had to get my rifle, but his eyes were so wild and terrified I couldn't leave him.

'That Waler's been fucking good to you, Croweater – he deserves a quick send-off.' It was Copping. I didn't look at him. I forced myself to get up.

'You want me to take the shot?' he asked.

I nodded, and as he raised his .303 to take aim, I knelt and hummed *Keep the Home Fires Burning* one last time to my old mate. The crack of the rifle was so close, felt like it went straight through me. Copping reached down and roughly squeezed my shoulder before he walked off to silence other splintered animals.

Chapter 4

EGYPT, 1916

'Good night, lads. God bless.' The padre strolled along the line of bell tents, and as he passed the glow of each tiny crackling campfire his face was briefly lit up in the darkness.

He was a young Catholic priest from the Queensland bush, and had served with the boys in Gallipoli. During the evacuation in December 1915, the last soldiers were ordered to wear socks and old rags on their feet so the Turks wouldn't hear them leaving. The padre told the men their fallen mates wouldn't hear them leaving either, and could sleep on in peace. It helped a lot of blokes to cope, that did.

By October 1916 I was serving with the 1st Double Squadron near the Suez Canal. Us Double Squadron blokes had been deemed 'surplus to requirements' in the main Light Horse units, and had the job of guarding the canal while most of the Anzac Mounted Division pushed east to drive the Turks out of Palestine. Most of the Australian force was long gone from Egypt to the Western Front, after a brief stint recuperating from Gallipoli. Poor bastards.

Our camp had been hit by yet another blinding Sinai sandstorm earlier that day and the lads were restless and resentful after rebuilding their tents and retrieving a mob of horses that had taken flight with the dust.

As the padre's orange silhouette grew faint in the

39

distance, a soothing calm descended, like it always did in his wake.

I'd been out with my mate Westy in the lorry all day, collecting supplies from Kantara, and it was well after dark when we finished the final run and were making our way to the mess tent.

'Y-Y-Y-You religious, Wal?' asked Westy. I could tell he was weary from a day at the wheel. Westy was a driver like me, and only ever stammered when he was tired. He'd been an apprentice tram driver back in Melbourne. Loved a chat. Loved his tucker. Loved the Saints footy team. I liked him a lot.

'Me, religious? Not right now, I'm not — I'm starving. Bet we've missed out on chops.'

I was right, too. A tin of bully beef and a lump of bread was the only food in the offing.

'Never been religious, really,' I said, taking a seat at an empty table. 'Mum was Irish Catholic but Dad wanted us kids raised C of E. Neither of them had much heart for it, though.'

I didn't mention my brother Bill. Didn't trust myself to talk about it to anyone yet — about how he'd died in a shitty trench at Pozières and left a wife and four littlies. What kind of God turns a blind eye to the Somme?

Westy pushed the corned beef around his plate, mopping up the oil with his bread and licking his lips like it was the best thing he'd ever tasted. 'D-D-D-Dad says football is the only religion a m-m-m-man needs, especially when Saint Kilda are winning,' he said. 'M-M-Mum likes church though — says it's the only time of the week she gets to sit d-d-d-down.'

'S-S-S-Sounds like s-s-someone needs b-b-b-bedtime.' The taunt came from a neighbouring table, and a few men sniggered.

I gave Westy a look that said 'ignore them', but he was staring at his plate. I knew how much he hated his stutter for the weakness it implied. Cruel that a stammer could still define a bloke who'd taken out three snipers at Gallipoli.

'My mum was the same,' I said. Westy didn't have any brothers or sisters, and he was fascinated that I'd grown up in a house with 12 kids. I launched into a yarn about the sleepy lizard us boys kept leaving around the house one summer to scare the wits out of our sisters. Then Mum got sick of the screaming and threatened to chop its head off with her meat cleaver. I told him about us sleeping four to a bed, two up and two down, and the night Bill farted 23 times under the covers before Mum got out the meat cleaver again. My voice caught when I mentioned Bill, but I forced myself to smile. He was four years older than me – my favourite from the minute I could focus.

'Mum was a trooper, really,' I said. 'And always busy, like a top that won't stop spinning. But you could take any friend into the house and she'd bring out the biscuit barrel and ask 'How's your ma?' and 'Watcha up to now?' like she had all the time in the world.'

Westy laughed his throaty laugh. 'What I wouldn't do for a b-b-b-biscuit barrel right now,' he said, shoving the last bit of bread in his mouth. 'G-G-God I miss jam drops.'

'Cream sponge,' I said, picturing Helena with a smudge of flour on her forehead. 'And Mum's raisin walnut biscuits, fresh out of the oven – heaven on a plate.'

We walked outside, pausing briefly in the doorway

to light our pipes, and wandered back to the tent in silence. I had a head full of Mum: how she always demanded your first kiss in the morning and your last kiss at night; how she called me her 'Angel Walter' because I came along four months after the first baby Walter died at the age of two, and I was his spitting image; how I spent the day of her funeral trying not to cry in front of the others, but still bawled when I saw her face all ghostly white in the casket. I was in my early teens then, and remember Dad putting his arm across my shoulders. It was the only time he ever did that.

The family moorings came a bit loose when we lost Mum, but I guess that's just how it is when you're settling into a new kind of normal. I'd moved up to Broken Hill after that, lived with my oldest brother, Jack, and his new missus, Ellen, until they had so many nippers they couldn't spare the room.

Jack helped me get a foot in the door at the North Mine and later I did some schooling to become an electrician. I joined the Barrier Boys' Brigade and won a footy premiership with them, and a swag of medals in gymnastics. Some called it progress when those cadet corps and brigades were phased out. Wouldn't have become half the man I am without the Barrier Boys.

Westy and I reached the tent and settled down to finish our pipes beside the dying fire, just as the other boys were turning in.

'Hey Wally,' called Bruce from inside the tent, 'Y'hear they're recruiting for the Australian Flying Corps? You're always on about planes.'

'Yeah,' I said. 'We heard that from the lads down at Kantara today. I'm thinking about putting my hand

42

up. There's gotta be jobs in aviation after the war.'

'They're after a different breed of man than you.' Copping's voice came out of the darkness; we could just make out the glow of his cigarette as he walked past our tent. 'They want elite Light Horse recruits, not just blokes making up the numbers.'

I started to call out after him, but what do you say to that? When you know every man within 20 feet is listening, judging? I took a deep breath and said, 'I can but try, Sergeant. I can but try.'

Westy looked fit to kill. 'Does that b-b-b-bastard ever let up?' he muttered.

'Water off a duck's back, Westy,' I said, wiping a hand across my face to hide the embarrassment. I cursed myself for sounding so keen before I weighed up my chances.

A voice from inside the tent said: 'Honestly, what the bloody hell would Copping know about the Flying Corps?'

'Yeah,' piped in Westy. 'He still thinks c-c-cars are a p-pp-assing fad.'

★ ★ ★

The recruiting officer scanned my AIF papers. 'We're not a big outfit yet, Shiers,' he said. 'So I'll be frank. I'm not taking on many lower ranks today. What do you think you'd bring to the Flying Corps?

I toyed nervously with the slouch hat in my hands. 'I'm a bit of a jack of all trades, sir. Been doing mainly signalling and driving work just lately, but figured you might need some extra mechanics for those planes?'

'I see. Any formal training?'

'Formal? Ah, no, sir.' I watched him jot something

43

down in his note book. Black mark probably. 'But I've been messing about with water pumps and engines ever since I got my first job back in Adelaide. Being mechanical is being methodical — that's what Mr Frazer taught me in the market gardens.'

'Mr Frazer was correct,' the recruiting officer murmured, putting down his pen and taking another look at my forms. 'I see you've been promoted to driver. You must know a thing or two about engines, and a number of Light Horse officers speak highly of your ability to fix just about anything that's broken. For every man we put into the air, there's nine men on the ground, Shiers — methodical workmen who keep our planes flying and our pilots alive. And the Barrier Boys, eh? Heard only good things. What took you to Broken Hill?'

'My oldest brother was working up there on the North Mine, sir, helped me get a start. Eventually got my electrical tickets.'

'Close family,' he said, making another note in his book.

Then he asked about other jobs I'd held down before the war. Wanted to know where I'd been to school, what sports I'd played. More notes went into his book and I felt my confidence rising. By the time he asked what I knew about aircraft, I was really quite enjoying myself. Of course, I only knew what I'd read in papers and magazines, but that was true of most blokes back then. Christ — the Wright brothers had only made the first powered flight 13 years earlier. My own brothers and I climbed onto the roof when we heard, sat staring at the sky and dreaming of flying to England. I told the recruiter bits and pieces that I knew — about hot air balloons being used to spy on

44

the enemy in the American Civil War, about the magician Harry Houdini being one of the first men to fly in Australia, and the fact we were the only country in the British Empire to demand its own separate Flying Corps in the war.

Eventually the recruiter held up both hands. 'Follow me,' he said, throwing down his pen.

He led me outside to a dusty Triumph Model H, its rear wheel belt sagging in the dirt.

'You've got 60 minutes to get this machine purring,' he said. 'Tools and spares are in that box.' And then he turned on his heel and headed back inside his tent.

An hour later, I was testing the engine a final time and thinking how best to clean the grease from my hands, when the recruiting officer reappeared.

'Mr Frazer certainly did make you methodical, Shiers,' he said.

I grinned. 'Best service she's had in Egypt, sir,' I said.

'Only service she's had in Egypt, Shiers,' he said. 'You'll find your way around an aircraft engine in no time. When we shipped out of Melbourne in March, most of us had barely swung a propeller. We're all learning on the job.'

I grabbed a fistful of sand at my feet to scrub the worst of the grease from my hands. 'Thank you, sir,' I said. 'Do you mind if I ask a favour? Can you show me around that two-seater?'

'The old BE2?' he asked. 'Dog of a plane – no match for the Fokker or the Aviatik. No guts when it's climbing. Slow in the air. Decent for reconnaissance and photography but impossible to intercept the enemy. 'Fokker fodder', they call it.'

It was the most beautiful, perfectly formed object I'd ever seen. I ran a hand along the smooth wooden blade of the propeller, goosebumps forming on my arms, and walked slowly around the wing to the rear pilot's cockpit and down the fuselage. It smelt of engine oil and wood and lacquer heating in the sun. It felt solid and powerful under my palm. Alive somehow. Waiting.

'I read about a British general who tied his plane to a tree after landing, just like his horses,' I said, almost to myself.

The recruiter smiled. 'It's remarkable, the number of men who mention horses the first time they get up close to a plane. And it generally bears out that a man who can handle a horse seems to instinctively know how to work with an aircraft. It's no accident that we're recruiting cavalrymen from the Light Horse.'

And you know, it really was like walking around a horse and feeling the urge to run your hand from its head down its back. The nose, the tail, the sheer energy of a machine that could defy gravity and propel a man into the clouds. Horse power.

Back at camp, the blokes took one look at me and knew I'd got in.

'You b-b-b-bloody b-b-b-beauty Wal,' said Westy. They all threw their hats in the air and started clapping and hollering. Even Copping offered a begrudging nod of respect.

★ ★ ★

The following morning, with my kit bag over my shoulder, I caught a lift to Kantara for Flying Corps training. I had the back of the lorry to myself, and it

46

was one of those rare moments in war when a man gets a few hours alone, to think about where he's been and where he's going.

After an hour on the road I suddenly panicked that I didn't have my enlistment papers and pay book. As I frantically rifled through my bag I thought about Helena on the Sydney wharf. She'd have a good laugh if I'd lost them.

Mrs Alford's two knitted brown balaclavas fell out of the bag, and finally I found my papers where I left them — bundled with a little pile of Helena's letters, tied with twine. I felt a rush of affection for both women, untied the loop knot and opened the most recent envelope.

September 6th, 1916

My darling Wally,

Fruit block first! I've double-checked with John and he says it's no trouble at all to keep an eye on it now that Fred's away.
He's got a fencing mate who owes him a favour so they're going to fence it off and get some goats in there to keep the weeds down until you're ready to put trees in. Aren't my brothers lovely?
I've been seeing quite a bit of John of late – we're working together on the Conscription Committee. I'm not liking our chances of a 'Yes' vote, I'm sorry to say. Can you believe they're calling it the 'Blood Vote' now? I had a half hour 'debate' with Mrs Allen in the middle of East Street the other day, she's adamant her sons shouldn't be forced to fight a war on the other side of the world. Missing the point somewhat,

47

don't you think? I just can't fathom that people living happily and safely home here can turn their backs on those of you fighting for our freedom. I'm not going to start on that again, Wally, because it makes me too upset. We're doing everything we can to get it passed in New South Wales at least.

It's so quiet here now with Fred gone – I miss his Flight magazines strewn about the place and the smell of his cigarettes on the front verandah. It's quite maudlin some days really, but we do our best to keep busy and our spirits high. Fred would be in France by now – we're hoping for a letter any day to hear he's safe and settling in as well as can be expected. The stories from the Somme are frightful aren't they? Those poor men. We're worried sick that's where Fred will end up. Mother's got fingers of fury knitting balaclavas and socks to keep you both warm over the northern winter. I keep reminding her that you're in a desert and you've only got one head – but she insisted I post another balaclava anyway. You know you can just share them with the other boys. She'd love that, bless her.

We saw dear young Alec Smart yesterday, the butcher's son. Poor fellow had half his leg and right hand blown off at Gallipoli. He sat there in a corner of the shop, staring into space while his father told us how lucky he was. He didn't look lucky – he looked lost. Mother came straight home to bake him a sponge to cheer him up. If only it were so easy. Promise me you'll try to stay out of harm's way, Wally. And I don't mean to sound melancholy. It's just such a shock sometimes, seeing these boys who went away so full of adventure, now back home and so broken.

Mother and I are forever thinking up ways to raise money for the Red Cross. The oven seems to be on night and day for trading tables, and Mother's always out back scolding the chickens for not laying fast enough. I don't tell her how frustrated I feel sometimes, with everyone over there in the thick of it and me home here baking cakes and selling patriotic buttons to 'do my bit'. But you know I raised 20 pounds last week, just selling the latest patriotic buttons door to door. It's quite the craze to collect them. Who'd have thought something as insignificant as a button could help the war effort? Go little buttons!

Well I best run to catch the post before the YMCA meeting. We're planning a picnic down by First Beach to raise funds for the families who've lost loved ones.

Love you I do,

Helena

P.S. I forgot to mention the swallows nesting in the creeping rose out by the back door. Three chicks have finally hatched – they're ever so cute, but noisy! If I stand on a chair I can see their little upturned faces squawking for their mother, but the adult birds get so frantic I daren't do it too often.

Stay safe, my darling.

I sat for a good long while staring out the back of the lorry, watching the dust rising in its wake to a rich blue sky.

Helena hadn't known about my Bill's death when she wrote that letter. It sometimes took six weeks for post to get from her to me, so our news was always overlapping at sea.

Bill in a grave. If he even had a grave. I wondered about my other brothers at the Front, Dick and Arthur and Alfred, and if they were still alive. And now Freddy Houdini was over there too. They'd all been condemned to serve in France and here I was, on my way to a new job, waving back to cheeky kids splashing around in irrigation channels.

Don't think I didn't know how lucky I was. Made me crook in the guts sometimes.

I wondered if Mum was watching over us all and whether Bill was with her now. And I thought about that time she was tucking us boys into bed, and I'd asked her why we didn't go to church on Sunday like all the other families.

'A good soul doesn't need a church pew to prove it,' she'd said dismissively, avoiding my eye. But just as she was about to close the door behind her, she came back in and sat on the side of the bed.

'Listen to me, boys,' she said, reaching out to touch my cheek and looking one by one at me and Bill and Alfred and Arthur, with the quilt tight against our chins. 'All my life I've had people telling me to believe in God. I've always thought it was more important to make sure God believes in me.'

Chapter 5

EGYPT, 1917

I scooped a mouthful of beans, self-consciously wiping the sauce from my chin, and took another look around the mess tent.

'I can't believe this isn't the officer's mess,' I said, nodding at the two blokes playing cards in the small lounge area to the side. I could smell meat roasting, bread baking.

'Yeah,' said Ando, a chatty aircraft rigger who was showing me around. 'The ranks all chip in for a decent mess. It's a Flying Corps thing. Our tent's almost as good as the officers'. Except for the quality of the booze.'

My seat was a wooden crate, but the table had a white cloth on it, and there were candlesticks wedged into old wine bottles. The plate of fried eggs, sausages and baked beans on buttered toast was the best meal I'd eaten in nearly two years since leaving home.

The air was cool too, despite the blanket of heat outside. Reminded me of Narrandera's better pub dining rooms: the soothing quiet, the familiar whiff of old beer and cigarettes. I'd taken Helena out to lunch once, when we hadn't been together long, but so many people stopped to ask about her mother we decided not to do it again. I hadn't realised how popular Mrs Alford was — turns out she'd nursed just about every sick woman and child in the district.

The far end of the mess opened out to the canteen

and I could see two lads peeling potatoes, talking and laughing with another bloke washing dishes. I envied them. Settled in. Mates. Not a new chum on his first day of a new job, all nervous and desperate to please. That first-day feeling never gets easier, no matter how old you get.

'You ready to check out the aerodrome?' asked Ando, rising from his chair.

I took a last swig of tea and grabbed my kit bag, nodding my appreciation to the kitchen lads as I followed him to the door.

It was March 1917 and I'd just arrived at Kilo 143 on the overnight train from Kantara. My first day with No. 1 Squadron, Australian Flying Corps. 'Kilo 143,' said Ando as we headed outside. 'Exactly 143 kilometres east of Kantara and the Suez Canal.'

It was only 9 o'clock in the morning but already the light was blinding. Three machines buzzed in to land and I shielded my eyes from the sun to watch, cursing myself for not getting more sleep on the train. The railway followed Egypt's northern coastline toward Palestine, and I'd sat up most of the night with my face out the window, sucking in the salty breeze as we passed allied camps bathed in ghostly blue moonlight, and small naval vessels just offshore, defending against attack from the sea.

'Throw your kit bag in here, Wal.' Ando ushered me into a bell tent and I was hit with steamy, stale air. 'You'll be dossing down in here and working over on the other side of the landing field,' he said. 'We march over each morning and we're marched back at night — unless a plane's really busted up, then we keep working until it's fixed.'

The aerodrome was a flat stretch of sand running

pretty much to the sea. Half a mile across the dirt strip stood three huge khaki canvas aircraft hangars, 70 feet wide with gently curving roofs that looked stark against the flat horizon. Each hangar belonged to a 'flight' — A Flight, B Flight or C Flight — and each flight had six aircraft. So the squadron had 18 aircraft and 18 pilots, a dozen or so observers and around 220 ground crew. Maybe 250 people all up.

'Jeez, they're massive,' I said, pointing to the hangars.

'Yeah,' said Ando. 'You'll fit six aircraft in them easily. Egyptian labour crews put 'em up mostly, but I once saw a pilot attach the canvas to the back of his plane and fly the covering right over the frame. Boy, did he cop a roasting.'

A BE2 took off and we walked toward its cloud of dust, while Ando pointed to the series of smaller tents and canvas workshops running in a line beside the hangars — headquarters, the instrument workshop, the armoury where bombs, ammunition and weapons were prepared. As we neared the large assembly tent, Ando showed me inside a mobile workshop built on the tray of a lorry. Think of a well-stocked, spotless garage on wheels and this was it — lathes, drills, grinders, generators, tool chests, lighting, you name it.

'Hey Ando, I've been looking for you!' The shout came from a man standing in front of a hangar. 'We need you in here.' When we reached the great mouth of the structure I saw a dozen men working on three aircraft. One of the mobile workshops was parked in there too, its side canvas rolled up to reveal the tools. 'Give us a hand with this fuselage,' the same bloke called. 'It's bloody ripped again.'

Ando looked at me apologetically. 'Sorry Wal, I'd better get to work. The transport depot's behind the far hangar. Just ask for Bushy when you get there. He's a ripper bloke. Good luck, eh?'

I thanked him and promised to shout the beers soon, before heading in the direction of the depot. As I passed the last hangar I noticed it was empty of men and housing a little single-seater I hadn't seen up close before. Without thinking, I ducked inside for a quick look.

It was one of the Martinsyde Scouts I'd heard about — nice clean lines, two Lewis machine guns. A heavy leather flying jacket was laid over the side of the cockpit, like the pilot had just popped away for a minute. I checked no one was coming, and ran a palm along the soft brown leather. I'd always wanted one of those jackets.

Right that second it happened: three quick bursts of machine-gun fire.

Shit! I sprinted for the nearest cover, like we'd been trained in the Light Horse, diving behind a hoisted engine at the back of the hangar and knocking the wind out of myself in the process. The dirt floor had been hosed down to settle the dust, and now I was covered in mud. Somehow I'd ripped my shirt.

I crouched, listening hard, blood pumping in my ears. The air was thick with heat and the smell of engine oil. Deathly quiet.

The vast hangar was almost empty and I looked around desperately for something to use as a weapon. In the dirt 10 ft away I spied a spanner, and scurried over to grab it before returning to my hiding spot.

There was movement at the front of the hangar and I tightened my grip on the handle.

'Oi!'

I crouched lower behind the engine.

'Oi, mate!' it came again, calm as anything this time. 'You might want to get out of this hangar. That machine gun fire is a Hun air-raid warning. They'll be aiming for your arse in here.'

I poked my head around the side of the engine.

'I reckon you'd be a new bloke,' he said, bending to scratch a lanky leg as he spoke. 'Is there a body with that head?'

I dragged myself out of my hiding place and walked toward him, wiping mud from my face with a torn shirt sleeve.

'G'day,' he said, grinning. 'Jim Bennett. Everyone calls me Benny.' He nodded at my spanner. 'I see you've found my missing spanner.'

'Um, yes.' I gave it to him and he tucked it into a back pocket before thrusting out a large hand to shake mine. Then he turned to scan the sky, hands cupped over his eyes to shield against the glare. 'Looks like a Hun recco to me,' he said, pointing out two tiny specks in the distant sky. 'But let's not chance it, eh? We'll be in all sorts of trouble if Dicky hears we're not in the trench.'

He led me quickly toward the end of the airstrip, to a trench filled with men hunkered down, helmets on.

'You one of the blokes attached from the Light Horse?' asked Benny over his shoulder as I tried to keep up. 'And I didn't catch y'name ...'

'Yeah, Wally Shiers,' I said, lengthening my stride. Second-class air mechanic. First-class idiot. 'Sorry you had to come get me.'

'Don't worry about it,' he said. 'You'll get used to air raids. The Germans are getting more aggressive in

55

the air. Mostly they're recco missions, to see if we've got any new aircraft or moving further east.'

When we reached the side of the trench, the murmur fell away. Heads turned. Eyes stared. I studied my boots.

Benny put a hand on my shoulder and said, 'Gentlemen, I'd like you to meet Wally Shiers, our new air-raid specialist.'

Everyone laughed. A few gave mock cheers. We jumped into the trench and a young bloke inched his backside over and gestured for me to sit down, offered me a cigarette.

'How are ya, Wally? Frank McNamara.'

I could see he was a pilot, from the wings pinned to his open jacket. 'Thanks very much,' I said, taking the cigarette. 'Nice to meet you.'

For a few minutes I sat silently, enjoying the smoke and absently picking the drying mud from my shorts. The men were discussing a cricket match coming up against the Army Post Office boys, and jobs that needed doing on different machines: a smashed spar, dodgy spark plugs, controls crippled on a BE2. It struck me that the pilots and mechanics all sat about together, enjoying their smokes and yarning away as mates. It wasn't like that in the Light Horse. It was always clear who was boss.

I plucked up my courage and turned to McNamara. 'So what's it like up there?'

He can't have been much more than 20. Cheeky-looking bloke. 'Wonderful,' he said, crushing his cigarette underfoot. 'Especially when you cut the engine and you're like an eagle and all you can hear is the wind whistling through the wires. I'll take you up on a stunt sometime.'

56

'Really?' I said. 'Thanks!'

Word came that it was safe to get back to work. I thanked McNamara again for the smoke and headed toward the lorries at the other end of the airstrip.

I didn't see him again during the war. A couple of days later I overheard Benny telling blokes in the mess that he'd been badly wounded and sent by train to the military hospital in Kantara.

'They were bombing a railway junction near Gaza,' Benny said. 'Seven of our machines in all, flying in a line at 50 ft. They reckon McNamara's last shell exploded early, right under his seat, and that's why he's got so much shrapnel in him.'

'Shit, I hope no one pays for that,' said one of the other men. A mechanic or an armourer could be court martialled for negligence.

'Frank McNamara's certainly paid for it,' said Benny tersely. 'So Frank's got blood pouring from wounds in his arse and his legs, and then he sees Captain Rutherford's been forced to land with engine trouble. Rutherford's got a whole bloody cavalry unit of Turks breathing down his neck. The other pilots start strafing the Turks to keep them at bay, while McNamara lands his Martinsyde. He's bleeding like a stuck pig but he's aiming to rescue Rutherford!'

'Bloody hell!' I said.

'Rutherford climbs onto a wing and holds onto the struts for dear life, but the plane is so overbalanced that McNamara crashes on take-off. So they abandon the Martinsyde, set it on fire so the Turks can't have it, and stumble back to Rutherford's two-seater.

'McNamara shoots at the Turks with his pistol while Rutherford fixes the engine. They finally get the thing going and McNamara flies 70 miles and lands

57

it back here. When we run to the plane, he swears like a trooper and passes out. Never seen so much blood in my life. Can't believe he survived.'

I remember thinking maybe Copping was right: pilots were a different breed of men. McNamara won a VC for that, the only Australian airman to win the highest honour for bravery in World War I.

We heard later that he'd had a severe reaction to an anti-tetanus shot at the hospital and nearly died. While he was still unconscious, they packed metal hot water bottles around his body to keep him warm, but one burnt the skin right through to the bone on his heel. That's what got him sent home.

★ ★ ★

I was classed as an 'Air Mechanic' from the day I finished my training, but truth is most ranks were aircraft mechanics in the Flying Corps. Some blokes were fitters, working on the engines. Some were riggers, tending to the frames. Armourers looked after the machine guns, ammunition and bombs. And then there were the photography specialists and instrument repairers, who'd often been watchmakers back home.

My job in the early days, much to my frustration, was still 'Driver Wally Shiers', transporting men and supplies along dusty roads to airfields and army camps.

I settled in fine though, busy with the squadron's next move east to Rafa. I had my own Wolseley lorry, and worked round the clock transporting stores to the new aerodrome. The closest I got to the aircraft some days was hearing the fitters' yarns in the mess – or watching Huns drop bombs on the camp. We counted

40 bombs one night. A few of us took to sleeping in sandhills a couple of miles away for a bit. They called us the 'Desert Column'.

One morning, a couple of months into the job, Benny found me sweeping half the Sinai desert out of the lorry tray. 'G'day, Wal. Watcha up to?' he asked.

I leaned on my broom and gave him a look that said 'stupid question'. Sandstorms were the bane of everyone's existence in camp. 'What's up?'

'We've had a truck break down to the east while they were scouting a new aerodrome,' he said. 'Have to go repair it. Mind giving me a lift?'

I parked the broom, jumped out the side of the tray and opened the driver-side door.

'I'm taking that as a yes,' Benny said, putting his toolbox in the tray and climbing in the passenger side. 'Shouldn't be too much wrong with the engine. The blokes just had to hightail it because a Hun plane was spotted in the air.'

As I drove out of the camp, two recco planes roared off overhead and pointed their noses east. 'Nasty business with No. 14 Squadron,' I said. The day before, two Royal Flying Corps machines had collided over their own aerodrome and another had been shot down behind Turkish lines. Six British airmen dead.

'Yeah,' Benny said, looking straight ahead. 'To be honest it's nice not to know the pilots personally for a change. I'm sick of picturing dead blokes.'

You know, all through the Great War we used no parachutes. They were considered too bulky for the tiny cockpits. Besides, the top brass didn't want their machines being abandoned too hastily mid-air. One in six British and allied airmen died, making their odds of surviving even worse than a soldier in the trenches.

59

Makes you wonder how many blokes might have survived given the option of jumping clear.

Benny and I drove in silence for a bit, elbows resting on open windows. I had *Keep the Home Fires Burning* in my head. Made me think of Bobby, and how much he loved bread crusts.

The road ran parallel with the coast, and as we passed over a small rise we saw a couple of mine trawlers at work just offshore.

'I stowed away on a ship as a kid,' Benny said. He sounded weary. Sad almost.

I shot him a glance. 'How'd that finish up? If I ran away to sea, my dad would have tanned my hide.'

He smiled. 'Yeah, I thought I was in for a good belting too, but by the time Mum and Dad heard from the ship's captain in Fremantle they were just glad I was alive. I missed my sisters so I caught the next boat back to Melbourne.'

I eased down a gear to slow the lorry as we passed a gang of Egyptians labouring for a British officer. Thousands of Egyptians worked for the British Army during the war, moving camps, building roads. Happy fellas, for the most part, always waving when I passed. 'What made you stow away?'

'I was apprenticed out of school as a bloody printing compositor. Hated every minute of it, so I took off with nine pence in my pocket. When I got home, Dad managed to get me into motor engineering. That's how I got straight into the Flying Corps.'

He was quiet for bit, then added, 'Good bloke, my old man. Should have told him that more.'

I noticed him wince as he spoke. 'You alright, Benny? You don't look too great.'

He took a deep breath, exhaling loudly, ducked his

head out the window. 'Been feeling a bit crook in the guts to be honest. Just needed to get away from that hangar for a bit, I reckon. Bit of clean Egyptian air should do the trick.'

We turned off the road and started weaving our way slowly around small mounds and scrubby bushes, eventually sighting the abandoned lorry. 'Stay alert for stray Turks or Arabs, Wal,' Benny said, leaning forward in his seat. 'Don't want any surprises.'

The stranded Wolseley had been stripped of its canvas awning, but otherwise it was untouched. I knew my way around the engine but Benny was my superior so I stood sentry, rifle loaded, keeping one eye on him and the other on the surrounding desert. The midday sun was fierce — I was grateful for my slouch hat.

Benny opened the bonnet and began inspecting the engine. Next moment he was squatting on the ground beside the front wheel, arms folded across his middle. 'Benny?'

'Sorry Wal, I'm gonna have to rest up for a bit. My guts won't stop cramping. Head feels like it's going to crack open.'

'Jeez mate,' I said, crouching beside him and noticing his face all pale and clammy. 'We've got to get you back to camp. It's too hot to be crook in this sun.'

He shook his head. 'I'll just sit in the shade for a while. Got too hot. I'll be right in a minute. Can't leave this lorry here — the Turks will thieve it or the bloody Arabs will torch it.' He put his head between his knees and started retching.

I stood there for a minute, looking around from one empty horizon to another. 'Get this into you,' I said, shoving my water cannister into his lap. 'Even if you feel like throwing it back up. I'll take a look at the engine.'

It didn't take long to work out the problem — sand in the fuel line. But Benny was getting worse, and soon he had it coming out both ends, poor bugger. There was no way he could get behind a wheel, so I laid him under the canvas shade in the tray of my truck.

I reversed up to attach a tow-line to the other lorry, but it was up to its axles in sand and I couldn't get it to budge.

In the end there was only one thing to do: drive back to the Egyptian labour crew we'd passed earlier and see if I could borrow some workers with shovels.

I found the young Tommy in charge. He listened to what I needed while we walked around the back of the lorry to take a look at Benny. He was in a bad way, lying on his side with knees pulled up, wet through and stinking in the heat. Some of the Egyptian blokes had crowded around, and I'll never forget one of them pulling off his headscarf, climbing into the truck and gently putting it under Benny's head.

Then the Tommy officer said, 'You'd best get the corporal back to your squadron. We'll sort out the other vehicle.'

Benny was sick for months, in and out of hospital with enteric fever. Lots of blokes went down with it, especially the lads from Gallipoli. But good old Benny took the trouble from his sick bed to recommend me as a fitter when a spot came up. Within a month, in the middle of 1917, I was remustered as fitter and turner, finally getting my hands dirty on those aircraft engines. If there'd been a solid roof to climb when I heard the news, I'd have gone up there with a beer to stare at the sky and toast my brothers.

Chapter 6

PALESTINE, 1917

It was barely light when I reached the beach. I closed my eyes, hoping the salty sea air would take me back to the white sands of Adelaide. But a gull cried overhead, and gulls don't sound the same north of the equator. They sound exotic, sort of mournful. Australian gulls squawk. And I had a pang of homesickness for squawking gulls, and my big brother Jack, and the smell of gum trees, and Helena, and her mum's house clean as a whistle, and everything about life before the war.

It was a relief to find the beach deserted. I'd barely slept — tossed and turned for hours until one of the other blokes in the tent finally told me to piss off out of there and let him get some rest before sun-up. So I pulled on my shorts and shoved the letters in my pocket, praying the news would be different when I read them again.

It was July 1917 and we'd advanced into Palestine. We'd set up near a town called Deir el Belah, knocking together an ingenious little aerodrome, with the tents and hangars mostly camouflaged from the air by trees and bushes. The city of Gaza was just a few miles up the coast, and the town of Beersheba was 30 miles inland. Both were fortified by the Turks and their main defensive line ran between the two. Our pilots were charged with taking aerial photos of the entire 30-mile Ottoman line so detailed maps could be drawn up ahead of a planned British ground offensive. Bastard Hun pilots were charged with stopping the recco missions of course, and their planes were still superior to ours. A number of our boys had been shot down and killed. Weighed heavily on all of us.

I walked down to the water's edge and gave my face a splash. Felt good. Then I retreated a little way up the beach and took a seat in the sand, pulling out the envelopes and holding them side by side: Fred's scratchy fist beside Helena's beautiful flowing script.

Fred first, I decided. Poor old Freddy Houdini. What a mess. He had gonorrhoea: the dreaded red plague. A month and a half in hospital with daily washouts up his old fella, then straight back into the trenches.

I stared out at the blue of the Mediterranean. Here I was on a quiet beach, out of harm's way, enjoying the war most days, if I was honest — especially now I was working on aircraft engines and in the thick of it at the aerodrome. The guilt nagged at me.

I re-read Fred's last few pitiful lines:

… I had to tell someone, Wal. Sorry. The other blokes in the battalion can't stand me. They reckon I'm a slacker. I didn't choose to get trench fever or gassed. I certainly didn't sign up for bastard VD. I shouldn't have gone absent without leave for those few days — I know that now. Would break Mum's heart if she found out. But everybody does it. Well, everyone with any sense. I don't think I'm going to get through this, Wal. I can't imagine ever getting home. I can't tell Helena. Can't even bring myself to write to them. Could you do it for me Wal? Say you've received a

note and all is fine. Tell them I'm busy and paper is scarce in the trenches. Tell them I've seen a bit of England and the countryside is beautiful, Mum will like that. Tell them I love them. But promise you won't say anything about the clap, Wal. It would kill Mum to know how pathetic I am. And if I don't make it home take good care of them. Please. I'd do anything to be sitting beside the Bidgee river right now. If I try hard I can picture every gum tree at Yabby Flat. Sorry to sound so pathetic. Hope this finds you well, old mate. Think of you often, my old chum Walter Custard. Goodbye.

I looked at the page for a long time afterwards, wondering what to do, where Fred might be now. Whether it was too late. The letter was written a month back. Anything could have happened.

I opened Helena's envelope, the faint smell of lavender making me smile. She'd have been smiling too, when she pressed the flowers between the folds of paper.

May 30th 1917

My darling Wally,

We've just received your letter about finally joining the men at No. 1 Squadron. We're so proud of you, my love, and all you've achieved in this dreadful war. Your work sounds wonderfully important and we're so happy you're safe, for the most part, in the aerodromes well behind the front line. These machines really are making a difference in the war effort, aren't they?

I was hoping to tell you some news of Fred but I'm afraid there's still nothing. It's been months now. We did finally get official confirmation that he'd had mild trench fever. Why they'd write to tell us he'd been wounded in action, with no other details, is beyond me. You can imagine we were out of our minds at the possibilities of that. I suppose mild trench fever was good news in the circumstances. Mother's worried sick as you might expect and it's all I can do not to fret, too.

I tell her we'd hear news if things were dire. That's true, isn't it, Wal? If something bad happened to him we'd receive word, wouldn't we? But there's no point dwelling on it, as I tell Mother constantly. Especially when there's not a thing we can do except keep up our letters to him, sending him our love and strength to stay safe.

There's talk of another vote on conscription. The committee is regrouping, Marg Little says there's a meeting next week. I can't believe anyone can vote 'No' when tens of thousands of you are already over there in desperate need of reinforcements. But it's getting harder to convince people in the street when we hear so many stories of death and defeat. And many feel that our boys are simply cannon fodder too, of course. I can't help being worried about the impact of a second vote on the town. It got very fierce last time, almost tore the district apart. Everyone knows someone who's died. Others have sons or brothers or friends who've spent three Christmases away and they can't bear the thought of another year apart. That all makes some people feel more strongly in favour of conscription, and it has the opposite effect on others. My feeling is that we simply can't sit on our hands

*and expect to win this war. Not enough men are step-
ping forward to do what's right, so I can't see a way
forward to victory without conscription.*

*Oh, I'm rather maudlin today, aren't I, Wal? I'm
sorry about that. I had meant to write and talk about
lovely things to cheer you up over there. It's just all so
maddening. You know one of the arguments against
conscription is that men are needed at home to do the
work that women cannot? And that's despite what
we've seen in England. I even read that women are
working in the British aircraft and ammunition factories now – they probably helped to build the planes
being flown by your boys. Australian women are perfectly capable of working in offices and factories and
driving farm machinery. Australian men just don't
want us to!*

*I promise to stop now! Here's something I know will
make you smile. Shirley brought dear little Hazel over
for a visit the other day. You probably don't remember
Hazel – she was just a tiny thing at your farewell
lunch. She's two now and quite delightful. Such a joy
to Mother. I was doing some baking and she was desperate to help, but before I could pop her up on a chair
she'd reached up and pulled at a half-empty bag of
flour and upended it all over herself. She near raised
the roof howling from the fright, but my she did look
funny. Just like a little white ghost. Mother had to sit
down, she was laughing so much. It was just the tonic
we needed. I took Hazel outside and gave her a good
shake and a wipe down under the tank tap, and she
sat very quietly on Shirley's lap after that, waiting
for a biscuit to come out of the oven. Dear little thing.
To think this horrible war has been going her entire
lifetime.*

I'll go now, Wally. The train's due and I'm rostered on with Marg to rattle the Red Cross tin on the platform. Wish you could see me in my uniform. I think I look rather fine.

Love you I do.

P.S. Did I tell you that two of the swallow chicks survived? They're well out of the nest now. Makes me happy when I see the family swooping around out back. Can't wait to create our own little nest.

A gull cried mournfully and I put my head in my hands, knowing I needed to get back.

I stood to leave and noticed another bloke just up the beach. He was standing perfectly still at the water's edge, his undershirt in his left hand. He was taller than me but scrawny — looked like he needed a good steak. Sandy hair, thin on top. I'd met him briefly earlier in the year with some Light Horse boys passing through Kantara. Ross Smith was his name. He'd been a lieutenant then.

'Morning, sir!' I called out as I quickly walked past. I wasn't supposed to be alone on the beach and I wasn't in the mood for a reprimand.

He turned. 'Ah, hello there. Thought the beach was empty.'

I nodded and smiled, kept on my way. 'Sir.'

'I know you,' he said. I stopped, took a breath. Here we go.

But he walked up the beach to shake my hand. 'Shiers, isn't it?'

'Yes, sir. Wally Shiers. We met once at Kantara. You were with Johnno and Alf from Broken Hill.'

68

'That's it! When did you move across?'

'Joined the squadron in March. Been on transports mainly. Finally just got remustered to fitter a few weeks back.'

'Good for you. I can't tell a spark plug from an oil filter.'

We laughed and both looked out to sea. I wondered if he felt the same longing to dive in and keep swimming.

'Beautiful, isn't it?' he said. 'Almost makes you forget why we're here.'

I cleared my throat in agreement.

'I'll walk back with you,' he said, pulling on his shirt. There was a tattoo of a butterfly on his upper left arm. I wondered why he had it.

I let him lead the way along the narrow track through the scrubby dunes. Up ahead we saw four recco machines roar into the sky and head east. It was always east.

'Shiers, am I right in thinking you're a South Australian too?' he said over his shoulder.

'Yes, sir, born in Adelaide, but I worked on the North Mine in Broken Hill for a few years.'

'Ah, that's it.'

'You're from up that way too, aren't you?'

'Sort of. As a kid I grew up on Mutooroo, a big sheep station right on the border with New South Wales, not far out of Broken Hill. But I did all of my schooling down in Adelaide. My brothers and I boarded at Queen's.'

From the way he spoke, I'd already guessed he'd gone to a good school. He was posh, but not posh, if you know what I mean. Hint of a Scottish accent. The Broken Hill boys told me he'd started out as a regular soldier but earned a commission at Gallipoli. Born leader but not cocky, they'd said. Great bloke.

'Remind me, Shiers,' he said, stopping to turn, 'didn't you know someone working on the conscription campaign in Australia?'

'Yes, sir.'

I was surprised he remembered so much of our brief conversation back in Kantara — we couldn't have talked for more than five minutes. But he was the type of bloke who gave you his full attention, took everything in, made you feel like there was no one else he'd rather be talking to. 'I was just reading a letter from her actually,' I said. 'Looks like there'll be another vote soon.'

He nodded. 'My brother Keith is working as a scrutineer for the Australian government in London – making sure the soldiers vote.' He turned away to continue walking. 'I hope that miserable lot back home help us out with a 'Yes' vote this time,' he said, his voice low. 'They can't sit on their hands and expect us to win this war.'

'That's funny, sir,' I said. 'My friend Helena wrote exactly those words.'

'Ha!' he said. 'Clever girl, your friend. Pretty too?'

I laughed. 'Yes, sir. So you're a pilot now?'

'C'mon, Shiers, no one says 'sir' around here unless they're talking to the CO. But yes, as a matter of fact I just returned from pilot training this morning. Finally got my wings.'

That explained why I hadn't seen him in the workshop these past months. 'Congratulations. What rank are you now?'

'Still lieutenant. Hoping to make captain one day. And thanks, I am rather bucked,' he said.

70

We'd reached the edge of camp and he turned to shake my hand. 'Great chatting again, Shiers. See you over at the workshops after breakfast. Say hello to that clever girl of yours.'

He headed in the direction of the officers' mess, but then he turned and called, 'Have you been up for a stunt yet, Shiers?'

I shook my head. 'No, sir!'

'We'll go up some time!'

I waved and jogged across to the mess for breakfast with the other mechanics. Then I wolfed down my sausage and eggs so I had time to write three very brief letters before we had to fall in and march across to work.

The first letter was to Freddy Houdini, telling him to keep his chin up and not lose hope. I told him plenty of blokes said you hadn't served in the AIF unless you'd spent a night in a brothel and caught the clap. I promised I'd write to Helena and that his secrets were safe with me.

The second was to Helena, telling her that I'd heard from Fred and he was fine but exhausted like all the poor devils in France. I told her I'd met a new pilot, Lieutenant Ross Smith, who'd already made a name for himself in the Light Horse, and how amazed I was that he remembered me. I said he'd promised to take me up for a stunt. Just before I sealed the envelope I added that she was wonderful, and I couldn't wait until the war ended.

And finally I wrote to my younger brother Dick with the 10th Battalion in France. I told him my future brother-in-law was doing it tough and if there was any way he could make contact I'd appreciate it, being so far away as I was. I gave him Fred's details with the

55th and hoped for the best.

Later that morning I was grinding a couple of valves in a mobile workshop when Lieutenant Smith found me. 'Shiers, I'm going on a quick flight to check the ailerons on No. 6775. The BE2e is hardly the most exciting aircraft, but if you're working on these machines you really need to have the experience of flying in one. Do you have time to come along?'

'Yes, sir,' I said, quickly tidying up around the lathe, putting the valves to one side and jumping off the side of the lorry. Every fitter, or 'engine-man', was assigned to a particular aircraft, and one of the lieutenants had flown mine to Cairo for a few days so I was less pressed than usual.

We walked to the plane and he handed me a leather coat, helmet and goggles. 'You'll be surprised how cold it gets up there,' he said. 'Have you got a handkerchief for the oil?'

I nodded, excitement growing now as I clumsily tried to manouevre my arms into the heavy leather. Benny was watching and came up behind me to casually lift the coat by the shoulders so my arms could slip in. He thumped me on the back and said, 'Have fun, mate. Try not to lose your breakfast.'

Lieutenant Smith nodded to my rigger friend Ando, who was standing by to turn the propeller. 'Right lads, let's go.' He hoisted himself into the rear cockpit and I stepped up onto a wing to climb into the front observer's seat. I'd sat in a BE2e inside a hangar before, but still felt the thrill of settling in. The observer's cockpit was basically a lacquered timber box, less than three feet by three feet, with padded leather lining around the opening rim and a leather cushioned seat with a wicker back. There were no controls or instruments in

72

front of me, only a couple of thin copper pipes coming out of the front timber panel and passing along the sides of the cockpit to the instrument panel in the pilot's cockpit a few feet behind me. The upper wing of the biplane was directly above, and straight ahead was the engine with its four-blade propeller. I slipped my arms through the leather shoulder straps on the back of my seat and pulled the goggles over my leather helmet.

'Contact!' yelled Ando.

'Contact!' yelled the Lieutenant.

The R.A.F 1A engine roared to life and I was whacked by the prop's backdraught. And even though I'd marvelled at the deafening, grunting power of those eight cylinders a hundred times before, knowing they were about to lift me off the ground was something else. I grinned at Benny and Ando as the plane taxied forward. Lieutenant Smith gunned the engine, and we quickly picked up speed from a bouncing canter to a gallop to a smooth clip. I curled my fingers around the sides of my seat and took a deep breath, noticing for the first time the engine oil spitting onto my goggles and face. And then, with the weirdest feeling of my stomach being sucked backwards and down, we lifted off the ground. I wiped the goggles with my handkerchief and strained forward to see the ground dropping away and our shadow bouncing across the earth. The engine eased to a droning roar and all around me the wires whistled. The fierce vibrations of the engine took a bit of getting used to, especially knowing you were sitting in little more than a wooden coffin lined with lacquered fabric. But it was smooth and fast. Faster than anything I'd been in. Faster than anything on earth.

With the machine climbing steadily, the Lieutenant turned us west toward Egypt. We passed over a Light Horse camp with its perfect rows of white bell tents and lines of tethered Walers, low enough for me to make out Westy and a few of the other lads. To my right, the sparkling blue Mediterranean ran to the horizon, dotted with tiny fishing boats, patrol vessels and hulking transport ships. Fringing the coast was a patchwork of crops bisected by dirt roads linking tiny walled villages and larger towns, and out to the left the Sinai Desert dunes began and never ended. Everything looked so clean. So perfect. So peaceful. I wished my brothers could have seen it. It was probably the greatest gift I ever received in my life.

When we reached 5,000 ft, the Lieutenant did a series of banks and turns and dives to test the ailerons. I could see why so many observers became pilots. The urge to take the controls and test myself against the machine grew with every sweep of my stomach. It wasn't until we were nearly back over the aerodrome that I realised we were home.

'Well, Shiers, what did you think?' the Lieutenant shouted when we'd alighted. He'd taken off his leather helmet and his thin sandy hair was sticking out at all angles.

My ears were ringing, I could barely hear him. 'Incredible, sir!' I shouted back. 'Now I know what they mean by deafening silence!'

'You get used to it!'

'I loved every minute! Thank you, Sir!'

The Lieutenant began a rundown with Ando, suggesting they take a little more slack out of the aileron controls. When Benny asked how the engine was, the Lieutenant replied, 'Splendid, Bennett. Thank you.'

I wavered a second before I spoke. 'If you don't mind me saying, sir, I think it might be worth checking the valve mechanism. Just sounded a little off when we were coming in to land.'

Lieutenant Smith raised his eyebrows. 'Ha! Corporal Bennett knows I'm hopeless with engines, so I'm happy to defer to an expert.' As he walked off he tapped me on the shoulder and said, 'Good work, Shiers.'

All that day back in the mobile workshop, I felt rather chuffed with myself, thinking about my flight and the Lieutenant tapping me on the shoulder and the three letters I'd sent off that morning. I pictured Fred and Dick meeting up in some little French village or back in London perhaps. Getting to be mates, looking out for one another.

Late that afternoon one of the blokes came by with news of yet another British offensive on the Western Front. And it suddenly struck me that Fred and Dick might already be dead.

* * *

PALESTINE, CHRISTMAS EVE, 1917

It's surprising how quickly you get sick of rain, even after months of wishing the skies would open. By Christmas Eve 1917 we'd endured three days of determined drizzle. Not enough to down tools, but enough to get every man down.

We hadn't been camped long at El Mejdel in Palestine. Beersheba had been taken in late October, and the British had also occupied Gaza and Jerusalem. The mounted charge into Beersheba by the Light Horse lads was already a legend across the allied camps.

In the skies above, our boys had played an important role keeping Fritz out of the air and off the scent of preparations and troop build-ups below. And every flight for reconnaissance or photography or bombing or strafing Turkish ground forces was followed at the very least by a maintenance ritual – if not an all-night engine overhaul.

Flying was finished for the day and Benny had a few of us getting the planes under cover. Most of us groused as we pushed the wet wooden frames, lamenting the weather and another Christmas at war.

Benny urged us to look on the bright side. He wasn't a particularly religious bloke, but he appreciated the novelty of being a stone's throw from Bethlehem on Christmas Day. 'If you can't get into the Christmas spirit this year, you're probably going to hell,' he said, giving me a wink. When one of the other blokes suggested we might be there already, everyone laughed. 'Mind you,' said Benny, 'I reckon those poor buggers in France might argue the point on that.'

I thought about Fred's last letter, thanking me for putting Dick in touch. They might have caught up if Fred's VD hadn't returned so viciously, sending him back to hospital with 'a screaming purple scrotum the size of a cannon ball'. Dear old Freddy Houdini. Even with inflamed balls he was counting his blessings to be on the safe side of the Channel.

Late afternoon a breeze picked up, gentle at first. We thought it might move the clouds on for Christmas Day and all cheered up. When the message came through that an officer had gone missing on the way back from a neighbouring British aerodrome, most of the mechanics were sent out to join the search. A few dozen of us stayed back to finish sheltering the aircraft.

As the afternoon wore on, the breeze strengthened into an unpredictable gale that drove stinging squalls of rain.

'Gotta move it now, fellas!' Benny yelled over another angry gust. 'Every plane we don't get in here is a plane we might lose.'

Wire wing struts began to scream and ping. Wooden frames creaked and cracked. Tarps lifted from cockpits and flew like ghosts into the sky.

'Keep clear of those wires!' someone warned. Everyone had heard horror stories of men losing eyes to highly tensioned struts breaking under strain.

Soon we were staggering like drunks against the wind and horizontal rain. 'Look out!' Benny yelled, as two RE8s pirouetted on their noses before flipping onto their backs.

We had four planes safely in a hangar by then, and as other blokes returned from the search party we rushed to tether the remaining aircraft with ropes and pegs. But the ground was too soft and pegs wouldn't anchor. A huge gust caused another RE8 to flip, its linen fuselage splitting with an almighty crack.

I grabbed Benny's arm and yelled into his ear: 'What if we used lengths of tarp as tethers and our own body weight as anchors?'

He thought for a second and gave a thumbs-up. We ran into the hangar to grab the longest lengths of tarp, yelling at other men to follow our lead as we struggled into the gale toward the remaining planes. In the last of the light, Benny and I twisted our length of tarp to strengthen it, lashed it over the fuselage near the tail and each wrapped an end around our waist.

Then we hunkered down back-to-back in the mud to hold the plane firm. Two pairs of blokes followed suit to help anchor our aircraft, while others took care of the remaining machines. As everyone settled into the mud, I buried my face in my knees to rest my eyes from the stinging rain.

'T'was the night before Christmas,' I thought as I sat catching my breath, drenched to the skin, ears ringing. It was three years since my first and only Christmas Eve with Helena, but I remembered it like yesterday. Sitting in the sixth pew of St Thomas's on Larmer Street, down the road from the Narrandera Hotel where I'd spent a drunken lonely night the year before. I was tired from fitting electrical wires in one of the new houses over in Leeton and only half listening to Rev Rawling's sermon – something about war and sacrifice and God's will. Then Helena rested her fingers on mine on the wooden pew between us, shifting slightly in her seat so the folds of her skirt fell over our hands. It felt like a bolt of electricity had passed between us, and when I gave her a sideways glance she was staring straight ahead with a face of pure devotion.

For hours, Benny and I huddled there in the pitch black, mud rising against our legs as the wind and rain howled and the plane strained and screeched to get free. It was miserable. I played the Helena game, blocking out everything but memories of our time together. There was our first ride on the Triumph motorcycle I'd bought in pieces from a bloke who'd crashed it. The night we played euchre past midnight, when me and Fred paired up and used an elaborate system of winks, throat clearings and head scratches to steal tricks. Clearing the back fence line of thistles and sour sobs one Sunday afternoon to plant Helena's vegetable seeds for summer.

I must have fallen asleep, because when Benny nudged me in the back, it was deathly still. The wind had died, the rain had stopped and to the east a tiny sliver of light marked the horizon. Tired blokes stood and stretched around us. We'd saved a few planes, but the tarmac was still a forlorn sight, with aircraft tossed about and torn apart.

We dragged ourselves up and made the long trek to the tents. 'Christ almighty,' groaned Benny at the site of our collapsed tent.

'Worry about it later,' I said. 'Right now brandy, sleep.' So we trudged over to the mess and cajoled a swig of brandy from the cook. 'Merry Christmas lads,' he said, pouring two generous shots.

Then we walked back to the hangar and curled up under canvas to grab a couple of hours' sleep.

The mess was near silent when we walked in for breakfast. Blokes all exhausted, dishevelled, starving. 'Did we find Lieutenant Matheson?' I asked, remembering the search party.

No, he hadn't been found. The flooded wadis – what the Arabs called the desert creek beds – made the hunt too difficult. A search party was headed back out after breakfast.

I collapsed into a chair as someone put a tray of sausages and eggs and strong coffee in front of me.

'And here's your Christmas post, Wal,' said one of the lads. 'Postie made a special delivery.'

I shoved a whole piece of toast in my mouth and gave him a noise of thanks and two thumbs up, as he placed a small pile of envelopes and a package in front of me.

Over breakfast I quickly read the cards from my brother Jack and sisters Liz and Mary. Jack was proud as punch because two of his sons had won footy premierships in the junior colts in Broken Hill. Liz sent a message from Dad, too. He was still living in a boarding house in Adelaide; had crook hands from all those years working with wet plaster, but was happy enough. Loved talking about my promotion to the Flying Corps, apparently.

I saved Helena's package for later. And it was many hours later. First we had to clear away the wreckage and salvage what parts we could, fix up the camp and hang our belongings out to dry in the hangar. Lieutenant Matheson had been found dead. He'd wandered for miles and died of exposure. He was a great bloke. So polite. So bloody young.

When I finally tore the package open I found a sprig of lavender, another balaclava from Mrs Alford, a light blue handkerchief embroidered with a tiny gum tree in the corner and a small, slightly crushed box of Cadbury chocolates.

All lovely, but it was the letter I craved. Words from home. Sweetness from my girl. And it did start sweetly enough, saying how thrilled she was about my upcoming promotion to 1st Class Air Mechanic, throwing in a bit of gossip about her sisters and news that John was trialling a couple of citrus varieties on the block for me. But there was an edge to her words I'd never noticed before, and by the end there was no hiding her feelings.

… I know it's my job to write letters of sweetness and light, dear Wally, but I just can't pretend today. I can't bear that you're away for another Christmas. I can't

80

bear the thought of another year like this. And Fred could be dead for all we know. The only news we get of him is from you now. Why is it that he can confide in you but not his own sister? But perhaps you're glad to still be away, Wally, conquering the Holy Land with all your new friends. Swimming in the sea on your days off, climbing pyramids, visiting exotic places. You certainly seem close to Lieutenant Smith these days. Your letters are filled with more of his news than your own. There, I've said it. Aren't I ghastly today. I can't stand myself like this. Come back to me. Merry Christmas. I'm sorry.

Love you I do,

Helena

We'd just got the tent cleaned up, and it was all I could do not to tear it down again. How dare she! Sitting in her pretty little room, with her fine little stationery set. She had no idea.

The officers had invited us all to Christmas dinner, as was the tradition, so I put on a cheery front as we walked across to their mess.

'Congratulations on the promotion, Captain Smith,' I said as I entered. He was already nursing a large glass of whisky. Slapping me roughly on the back, he wished me Merry Christmas and loudly told the officers around him that it had been my idea to use human weights to anchor the aircraft in last night's storm. With Helena's words in my head, his praise and camaraderie embarrassed me to my core.

I sat quietly, resenting her more with every mouthful of tomato cream soup and roast beef and plum pudding dessert. Through beers and smokes I replayed those sentences in my head. And when the boys started singing Silent Night, I took a generous glass of whisky back to the tent, tore some pages from an unused diary and said what I thought.

25th December 1917.

My dearest Helena,

Well that's a Christmas letter I won't soon forget. I'm sorry you're unhappy my sweet girl, but it's hardly peaches and cream on this side of the world either. I can only hope you're feeling more like your old self by the time you read this letter.
To Fred first. He writes to me because he thinks I understand what he's going through. I don't, of course. I can't even begin to imagine what life in the trenches is like for him, or my own brothers who haven't already been killed in that hell hole. I eat three cooked meals a day, surrounded by my 'new friends'. In France, their friends rot beside them, the same corpses blown up again and again, night after night in no-mans land. I feel guilty every day for being here and not there. We all do. But we've been asked to do a job and that's what we do. That's all we do, except the odd Sunday when, yes, I go for a swim to break the monotony, or ride a donkey to the nearest town to look for some little souvenir or trinket to show I'm thinking about you. And as for Lieutenant Smith, he's actually a Captain now. Just been promoted to Commander of C Flight. And rightly so. I write about him because there's nothing else to write about, unless you want me to fill the pages with how I've been grinding

valves or cleaning spark plugs? My life is boring. His life is not. The top brass down here say he was the best aircraft observer they'd ever seen before he trained for his wings. He got the Military Cross for helping to rescue a British pilot behind enemy lines, actually stood up in his observer's cockpit and knocked off the Turks one by one with his revolver to hold them back. He got shot in the face over Beersheba, needed three weeks to recover from the bullet that went right through his cheek and knocked out some teeth. The man's a hero, the first pilot in the entire Australian Flying Corps to score a victory against the enemy, and you people back home don't even know his name. You all know Manfred von Richthofen though, I bet. Makes me sick. Captain Smith's younger brother Colin died recently at Passchendaele. Did I tell you that? You're free to cry and grieve about death back home. We're expected to keep a stiff upper lip. The Captain heard the news and got back in his plane to take aerial photos. So forgive me for writing about my friend. At least, I assume we're friends because in the middle of everything, he sometimes stops to ask how I am, or to ask about your work on the conscription referendum. Would you prefer I had no friends, Helena? Would you rather I sounded miserable and bored to make your life more bearable?

I was just getting started when Benny burst through the flap of the tent. 'Jesus, Mary and Joseph, it's Christmas mate! What the hell are you doing writing letters when the officers have opened their liquor cabinet?'

I looked down at the letter, words swimming.

'Put it away Wal,' Benny said, stumbling roughly against my shoulder. 'If it's worth saying, save it for tomorrow. We're bloody crusaders in the Holy Land. Tonight we drink.'

★ ★ ★

PALESTINE, BOXING DAY, 1917

I woke up face down and fully clothed under my blanket, with a throbbing headache and a vague recollection of writing to Helena. The tent reeked. Mouldy socks, cigarette ash, stale alcohol. I turned my head on the pillow, groaning with the effort, and saw everyone else still asleep, snoring. Groping around on the ground beside my camp bed, I found the loose diary pages. And as I struggled to decipher my own sentences, one thought kept coming to mind: thank God I hadn't sent it.

I rolled onto my back, laid an arm across my eyes to dim the light. That's the worst thing about tents — always light from first dawn. Helena deserved better than this. She just wanted the war over and me home. How could I blame her for that? And she wasn't stupid — she'd know I wasn't hating this war. She'd know I wasn't desperate to get home.

Jesus, two and a half years, and I was enjoying myself more now than when I left. What did that say about me? About Helena and me? Did I love her? Yes. Never looked at another woman. But could I go back to life in Narrandera? Probably not, in truth.

I groaned into my arm. Shit. I thought about all those new houses I'd worked in before the war, fixing the electric wiring to new bare walls. It churned my guts. I wanted to be up to my elbows in engine grease, standing by as an aircraft roared to life. Maybe get my wings one day. Helena knew I wasn't the same man who left in 1915. She worked it out before I did, bless her.

I slowly rubbed my temples, then propped myself up on one arm and grabbed the diary and pencil, writing across a single blank page.

26th December 1917.

Dearest Helena,

Love you I do, my darling girl. The war will be over soon and our life will begin. I'll be home as soon as I can. Promise. Get that wedding dress ready.
Your Wal

Chapter 7

ADELAIDE, 1968

One of my young friends leans forward on his bar stool. 'Smith – I know that name,' he says, looking pleased with himself. 'Smithy, wasn't it? Smithy and his Southern Cross?' I sigh and drink the last of my beer, placing the empty schooner on the bar for a refill. I look across to the small television in the corner. The news is on, and they're showing pictures of an Apollo spacecraft, the kind the Yanks want to land on the moon. Makes me wish I was 50 years younger, but lots of things make me wish that. I turn to the young lad, and shake my head. 'No son, you're thinking of Charles Kingsford Smith,' I say. 'I'd be a rich man if I had a quid for every time I've heard that. I'm talking about another bloke entirely. Captain Ross Smith. Just so happens he was cursed with the same surname.'

★ ★ ★

PALESTINE, 1918

Captain Ross Smith. He was fearless in his Bristol Fighter that final year of the war. Peerless too. Just ask anyone. Scored 10 of his 11 victories in that one machine. If the ground forces were under fire from above, they'd raise their fists to the skies and shout, 'Ross Smith'll get you, bastard!'

86

And those same blokes would always ask 'What's Ross Smith like?' when they heard I was with No. 1 Squadron.

'Nice bloke,' I'd reply, trying to sound casual. 'Takes you up to his rank when he's speaking to you, if you know what I mean. Maybe because he started out at the bottom like the rest of us.'

But he was nothing like the rest of us, and everyone knew it from the top brass down. When aerial photos were needed before some new advance on the Holy Land, he was usually the bloke they tapped on the shoulder. He said growing up in the South Australian outback helped to sharpen his eye on the terrain.

When a single Handley Page bomber arrived from Britain, its 100-ft wingspan dwarfing every other aircraft on the Eastern Front, it was Captain Smith who flew her. He started the final campaign of the war in Palestine, General Allenby's Battle of Armageddon, by dropping sixteen 112-pound bombs from the guts of that giant Handley Page, right onto El Afule. The Turks never recovered.

He was fearless, yes, but never reckless. I've never known a man so methodical. Often we'd see him sitting in the shade with his head in some manual, or writing letters — he was always writing home to his Mater, as he called her. He had a lot to write home about. Barely a week went by when he wasn't mentioned in despatches or awarded some new decoration.

He was the most decent man I ever met, but he wasn't above the thrill of killing. He joked that downing Fritz was good sport, but it was much more personal than that, especially after his brother Colin died — you could tell by the way he cursed any Hun who fled a fight in the air.

He flew Colonel Lawrence sometimes too, the bloke who became famous later as Lawrence of Arabia. I met Colonel Lawrence a few times — was surprised to find him as short as me. Apparently he had a handshake like a wet fish, but he was clearly brave, or mad, or both. Anyway, even Colonel Lawrence admired Captain Smith — he wrote in his famous book how they were eating breakfast one morning at his desert camp, and between mouthfuls the Captain started up his plane and shot down Germans. He was always doing things like that. Made flying and fighting and killing look as easy as eating porridge. After the war, every man I met from the Flying Corps said his proudest memory was knowing Captain Smith. Got to the stage I could hardly bear the sadness of it all.

* * *

Some people don't believe in luck. I do. A bloke can improve his odds with hard work, but every now and then you need the dice to roll your way. In May 1918, one of the better air mechanics in the squadron was forced out of action for four weeks with a bad case of 'eruption face', a nasty skin rash that affected lots of blokes in the desert and forced them into hospital isolation. Joe Bull's angry blisters coincided with the formation of a special British air detachment, called 'X Flight, RAF', formed to work in the desert with Colonel Lawrence and his Arabs. They were getting hammered by Hun planes at that point, so the idea was to offer air support while they advanced on key Turkish positions from out east. A couple of British officers were selected for the job and No. 1 Squadron was asked to provide the ground crew.

Captain Smith knew Colonel Lawrence quite well by that stage, and he recommended Benny as well as me and two other lads.

What a bloody adventure. We went as far as we could by ship up the north-eastern arm of the Red Sea, and then loaded our tools onto camels and trekked 70 miles out into the rocky desert hills near a place called Ma'an in southern Palestine. That's where Colonel Lawrence's mate Prince Feisal had his camp at the time. As our camel train came over a rise at sunset, we saw all the tents stretched out across the desert plain — sky and sand the colour of burnt orange and thousands of Bedouin fighters in robes and headgear all rising as one to watch as we entered camp.

Made me glad I'd never sighted one of those angry Senussi Arabs on patrol with the Light Horse. 'Keep to yourselves until the machines arrive in the morning, lads,' one of the British officers had warned us. 'Our new friends will warm to us when their aircraft arrive.'

He was spot on. You've never seen anything like it when those BE12a machines landed out of the sky. Chanting, dancing, waving silver daggers, firing shotguns. They called the planes 'Tiyaras' — apparently it meant 'female flying things'. And they couldn't get enough of them. We'd be trying to work, checking the spark plugs or the fuel lines and there'd be a hundred of them crowded around, furiously discussing each move we made. I never could understand a word they said, but I liked their strength, their resolve. Always watching, sizing things up.

Anyway, it was a short-lived mission. The BE12a was designed for reconnaissance, not combat, so even I could have told the Brits they'd be of little practical use. The powers that be soon realised it made more sense to patrol the skies with No. 1 Squadron's aggressive Bristol Fighters flying out of Ramleh. So after a month or so we packed up and headed home. The officers reckon it did the trick in impressing the Arabs, though. It helped convince them they were on the winning side.

Did the trick for me and Benny, too – we became known as two of the squadron's top mechanics. 'There's nothing you two can't fix with a screwdriver and a shoelace,' one of the British officers said, and he told the COs as much when we got back. So when the giant Handley Page bomber arrived from England, Captain Smith had me and Benny assigned to it.

★ ★ ★

'Shiers!' the batman yelled, struggling to be heard over the roar of a Bristol Fighter starting up nearby. When I looked down he cupped his hands over his mouth and yelled 'Telegram!' and waved his thumb toward the HQ tent.

Shit. That could only be bad news. I jumped out of the lorry tray — we needed to get up high to work on the twin engines of the gigantic Handley Page — and ran across the airfield. I stretched my neck and shoulders as I went, tired and stiff from a shift that started well before sun-up. I looked up at the lightening sky, wondering how far north the Turks had been driven by now.

The news had to be about Fred. No Shiers would pay for a telegram, no matter how bad it was. I took off my hat as I walked inside the HQ tent, and smiled my thanks as the sheet of paper was handed to me.

It was the first telegram I'd ever received. FRED SHOT ARM LEG CHEST. ALIVE. HELENA.

So there it was. Fred had finally been cured of VD after another five lousy months in hospital, and now he'd gone and collected three bullets. At least this would get him home without a dishonourable discharge. At least he wasn't dead.

There was nothing I could do for either of them, and there was too much going on to think about it, so I jogged back to the hangar, stopping at the airfield to let Captain Smith rumble by in his Bristol Fighter. He gave me a thumbs up as he passed and I stood there for a few moments watching as he charged along the dirt to lift off. Funny how war can be the making of some men, and the undoing of others.

I wondered how many more airfields there'd be before it all ended and I could go home to Helena.

It was September 1918 now and we'd been at Ramleh aerodrome for the past four months, preparing for General Allenby's autumn assault to finally drive the Turks out of Palestine. Allenby was a genius at bluff and diversion. I'd hate to have played him at cards. He had dummy camps created to hide the build-up of thousands of troops on one section of the front. He even used fake horses made of canvas. Dozens of tractors dragged huge wooden logs in the dirt to stir up massive columns of dust and create the illusion of cavalry movements.

The Flying Corps' main job for most of the year had been photography, bombing work and aerial combat, to drive the Hun out of the skies. For eight days before the offensive started, not a single German machine crossed the British lines to see what the ground forces were up to.

And then, two nights earlier, Captain Smith had started the campaign in the Handley Page, bombing the central telephone exchange and railway station at El Afule to destroy Turkish communications. The Handley Page was built to be 'a bloody paralyser of an aeroplane' and that's exactly what it was. I'll never forget the night it took off under a full moon to bring on Armageddon.

'Oi, Shiers!' yelled Benny from beside the Handley Page. 'Could use a hand over here!'

I saluted as I ran. 'Yes, Sergeant!'

It was Sergeant Jim Bennett now. He'd been promoted in March, even mentioned in despatches by General Allenby for 'distinguished and gallant services and devotion to duty'. We razzed him a lot about that, but there wasn't a mechanic in the squadron who wasn't proud of him.

'Everything alright, mate?' he asked as I climbed into the lorry tray beside him.

'Fred's in a bad way,' I said. 'Three gunshot wounds. Helena and her mum'll be beside themselves.'

'Bugger,' he said. 'But he'll be in good hands back in Blighty, Wal. Think of the nurses fussing over him. Won't be long and he'll be home.'

Within an hour we got word from a recco crew that a massive column of Turks was trying to retreat through the narrow Wadi Fara gorge toward the Jordan River. Our boys had bombed escape routes front and back, leaving the entire Turkish 7th Army trapped. They were sitting ducks, thousands and thousands of them. Motor transports, teams of horses and wagons, gun carriages. And no Hun air support.

As fast as we could get one plane checked and refuelled and reloaded with 112-pound bombs and machine-gun ammo, another one landed. And every time a plane took off, someone would yell 'this is for Jacko' … 'for Bluey' … 'for Jimmy' … 'for the boys at Gallipoli' … 'for Beersheba, you bastards!' There wasn't a man in the squadron who hadn't lost a brother or cousin or friend in the war, and we all tasted vengeance that day. We ran between aircraft like our lives depended on it, loaded bombs in double time, didn't catch breath for fear of missing the action.

Early that evening, when all the planes were back on the airstrip, Benny and I and the other lads were making our way to the mess to grab a quick meal when I noticed Captain Smith and Lieutenant Sutherland around the side of a hangar.

The sky was turning a great smear of pink and we were all elated, knowing the day was a turning point. I told the lads I'd catch them up and jogged off to congratulate Captain Smith. Benny tried to grab my arm and pull me back, but he was too late.

Lieutenant Sutherland was leaning against the side of the hangar. The Captain had his back to me, hands on his hips. As I got closer I caught Lieutenant Sutherland's words.

'Did you see their faces?' he said. 'Did you see it all?' He was taking deep breaths as he spoke, snot running from his nose. To my horror I thought he might be weeping. 'All the blood? All the panicked horses running straight off the cliffs, legs flailing, all those legs? Did you see the white flags? That wasn't war, Smith … it was sheer butchery.'

He doubled over and threw up.

For a second I stood rooted to the spot, too shocked to speak. Too close to back away. And as Lieutenant Sutherland wiped his mouth with the back of his hand, he saw me and turned his head away.

I cleared my throat. 'Everything okay, Captain? Can I fetch the Lieutenant some water?'

He didn't turn to face me. His voice was icy. 'If I wanted water, First Class Air Mechanic Shiers, I'd ask for it.'

As I turned away, I heard the sound of retching and Captain Smith muttering: 'Buck up, old son. It's the big show. This is how we end it.'

When I caught up with the other lads, Benny must have noticed my mortified look. 'Don't take it to heart, Wal,' he said quietly. 'Been a long day. The pilots have been ordered to go back and finish the job tomorrow.'

They reckon the dead stretched for miles and miles. Thousands of Turks and horses, shredded and minced by two days of relentless bombing and strafing by our boys and the Brits.

Once the job was done, pilots were ordered not to fly back over the area — top brass didn't want them seeing what they'd done and going soft on the enemy.

Every night since joining the Flying Corps, I'd sat with the other mechanics after dinner, thinking up ways to make the machines more efficient. Talking about how aviation had changed war forever. How it would change the world. That night, no one said a word.

Within eight weeks, the Turks had surrendered and the war was over in Europe.

Chapter 8

ADELAIDE, 1968

You get thrown into war when you enlist. It's immediate and intense. Moving on afterwards isn't nearly so straightforward, because there's no set routine, no one issuing orders. It makes war a hard habit to break. Maybe that's why I went to India with Ross and Benny — so I didn't have to start thinking for myself.

★ ★ ★

CALCUTTA, 1919

I found two empty leather armchairs near the back of the room, waved across the sea of white heads at Benny and took a seat. A young Indian waiter in a crisp white uniform presented a generous tumbler of whisky on a silver tray. 'Chivas Regal, sir,' he said. 'Compliments of Brigadier-General Borton. Enjoy your evening at the Bengal Club.'

I returned his bow awkwardly in my seat as I took the glass and relaxed back against the soft leather, tugging at the collar of my uniform. A rattan ceiling fan circled slowly above me. The air was thick with sweet cigar smoke and warm leather, and somewhere a string quartet played something classical and complicated. I moved slightly in my armchair and the waiter suddenly reappeared with a shallow box of neatly arranged cigarettes, cigarillos and cigars. I took

95

my time, trying to guess the most expensive cigarillo, thinking Benny should hurry up so he could have one too.

A tall elderly Sikh with a magnificent turban and white suit appeared at the waiter's elbow, gently taking the cigar box and dismissing the younger man with a tiny nod.

'May I suggest the Indian Trichinopoly Cigarillo, sir, for a slight taste of cinnamon and chocolate.' The Sikh opened a palm to the top corner of the box. 'It is very popular among the gentlemen.'

I'd worked with Sikhs on the North West Frontier. Their discipline fascinated me — the work ethic, the honesty, the humility. Big strapping lads, though. You wouldn't mess with them.

I selected a cigarillo and leaned forward to let him light it for me. 'Thank you, sir,' I said. He gave me a respectful nod, like I was the richest bloke in the club.

The room was quite incredible. I wished Helena could have seen it. A vivid tiger skin lay on the timber floorboards near my feet. A stuffed peacock was hung on the white wall behind me — a spectacular fan of shimmering feathers. On other walls were framed photographs of fine India buildings and the Delhi Durbar of 1911. King George V and Queen Mary sat crowned and robed under the shade of a tiny dais, surrounded by tens of thousands of subjects and Indian troops in full military get-up. I wondered if they felt like I did when a crowd of 300,000 watched us land on the Calcutta racecourse: fascinated by the sheer mass of people, but bloody terrified by it, too.

The bar was teak — everything was teak really, or leather or rattan or stuffed. Along one side of the room, huge white shuttered doors opened to a terrace lined with potted palms, with tall bamboo torches lighting the lawn beyond. Everywhere, men in black evening suits were clustered in small groups, smoking, murmuring, debating. I remember feeling so in awe of it all, and so utterly out of place, and wishing I knew how I was going to get home.

Benny threw himself down into the armchair beside me. 'That's quite enough questions about Captain Smith for one day,' he said. 'Jesus, they can't get enough of him, can they?'

The young waiter reappeared with a Chivas for Benny. 'Thanks, mate!' Benny said, before leaning over to chink our glasses. 'Here's to us, Wal, and our amazing bloody adventure — it's been good while it lasted.'

It had lasted nine months, ever since the war ended in Palestine and we'd flown a giant Handley Page out of Cairo to Baghdad and onwards to Delhi and Calcutta.

Major-General Salmond, who'd commanded the British flying forces in the Middle East during the war, had wanted to inspect his men further east and establish air routes for Empire. Captain Smith and his RAF mate Brigadier-General Amyas 'Biffy' Borton were only too happy to do the flying. They became the first pilots to fly from Cairo to Calcutta. Eventually, they hoped to fly the Handley Page all the way home to Australia.

By the war's end, Benny and I had clocked up scores of hours working on Rolls-Royce Eagle VIIIs — the twin engines that powered the Handley Page. No one in Palestine knew more than we did, so Captain Smith had asked us along to keep the big bus in the air. We'd done that and more, travelling by ship all the way from Calcutta down to Timor in the Dutch East Indies, scouting possible landing strips for the rest of the route home. In the process, General Borton and the Captain had almost died in an explosion aboard the fuel-laden Indian mail ship Sphinx. But when we returned to Calcutta to collect the Handley Page, we learnt she'd been seconded for a new war against the Afghans on the North West Frontier. The three of us Aussies were sent up there for a few weeks, too, helping out the Brits in No. 31 Squadron with their little fleet of Bristol Fighters.

We survived another war, but the monster Handley Page didn't. Some silly bugger had her out in a storm, crashing her into a mountain and destroying our plan of flying her on to Australia.

So by August 1919 we were back in Calcutta, with no wings and no hope of arriving in Australia as conquering airmen. The evening at the Bengal Club was General Borton's way of saying 'bad luck chaps and farewell'. He was headed home to England in the coming days and we were waiting to board the first ship back to Sydney.

'Can't believe it's all over,' said Benny, idly tearing at a palm frond until he remembered where he was.

'Is the Captain still smarting about losing his Handley Page?' I asked.

'Yeah,' said Benny. 'And losing the chance to fly Biffy down to Australia in time for the Melbourne Cup.'

General Borton had taken us all to the Viceroy's Cup when we first landed in Calcutta. Back then it was one of the biggest horse races in the world. Captain Smith even got to know the Viceroy. He wanted to return the favour and take the General along to the big race in Melbourne.

Benny looked across at me. 'Be good to get home though, eh Wal? What's it been for you now — four years?'

I twirled the whisky in the bottom of my glass. 'I'm not really sure where home is, Benny.'

He leaned across and thumped my leg. 'Mate — we've been over this a thousand times. Since the war ended, the mail service has gone to shit. I've only had a couple of letters from my sisters since Christmas, and they write every bloody week.'

I leaned back in the chair, wiping a hand down my face. 'Jeez, Benny, I hope you're right.'

I'd received only one letter from Helena in the past nine months. It was written on November 12th 1918, the day after the war ended in Europe. It had finally found me in Calcutta, a full seven months later. The envelope was an ugly mishmash of crossed-out addresses, but the letter inside was wonderful. Joyful. Hopeful. I carried it in my jacket pocket and could recite every word.

November 12th 1918

My darling Wally,

I still can't believe it's true. I can't believe this war is finally over and you and Freddy Houdini are coming home. Thank God, Wal. Thank God.
I've been up all night having a high old time in East Street – the party is still going on over there. I can hear it from inside the house. It's quite mad. And you'll never guess how it all started. It was after midnight and the church and fire bells started ringing

furiously and we could hear rifle shots and sky rockets blasting out all over town. The word is that Bill from the Argus newspaper had the post office lads intercepting and decoding any telegrams which might be carrying news of the Armistice. So suddenly they haul the Mayor out of bed to officially tell us the war is over! What a lark! Mother got the fright of her life, but when the church bells didn't stop ringing we knew it could only mean one thing. Oh Wally, we stood there clinging to one another in the hallway, sobbing and laughing and listening to those wonderful bells ring out. It was glorious. Then I helped Mother to quickly get dressed and we went out to the front yard and followed everyone streaming into East Street. There were hundreds already there, hugging and dancing in the moonlight, clapping and singing and waving flags. I so wish you and Fred had been there. It was the most incredible moment of my life. The speeches went on all night and they're still going! Mr McCaughey from North Yanco Station made the funniest speech. He said the plane he donated to your No. 1 Squadron was court-martialled for cowardice for continually breaking down when approaching the enemy! I'm sure you already know all that, but it was quite hilarious the way Mr McCaughey told the story.

It's right on lunchtime now and I've been up since midnight. I've just popped home for a quick nap and I'll take Mother back later. I'm feeling very weary, and you can barely hear a word in East Street, what with kids banging kerosene tins and the Narrandera marching band playing. The hotels are doing a roaring trade and making such a racket. Every now and then an entire bar empties of people and they all weave along East Street in procession and then weave back inside the bar again to their drinks. I've never felt such an overwhelming feeling of happiness. Of course a lot of the speeches are about sacrifice too. They're saying as many as a hundred men from the district have been killed. Poor Mrs Dixon lost two sons and two brothers. Bless her. How could you ever get over that? I don't know what I'll do with myself now it's over – until you get back of course and we can get busy making plans.

And now I've got something to tell you. On my way home just now I walked over to speak with Reverend Rawling at St Thomas's. I wanted to get in before all the other girls. He's had quite the rush of appointments already. So my darling Wally, we're due to be married on the second weekend in April. That should give you plenty of time to get home and settled back in, don't you think darling? And it will be almost four years to the day since you enlisted and we were parted, so I thought it was the perfect weekend to celebrate starting our married life together. Oh Wally, won't it be wonderful! I can't believe it's true.

Love you I do, love you I DO!

Helena

There was just one small problem. The very same day she'd written that letter to me, I'd written to her saying I wasn't coming straight home. After three years away at war, I was staying on with Captain Smith — maybe for another year.

And I hadn't received a single word since.

No response to the embroidered Egyptian cotton

napkins I sent from Cairo. No response to the pink pashmina shawl I sent from Delhi just after Christmas. No response to the pretty silk pincushion and little blue china bowl I sent from Singapore.

Nothing but silence. The Army Post Office blokes at the Calcutta barracks were sick of the sight of me. For weeks I'd appear at the door and they'd yell out, 'Nope! Nothing!'

The Sikh returned, refilling our glasses before offering the magical cigar box and lighting our chosen cigarillos.

'I could get used to this,' Benny said, leaning back and drawing deeply on his cigarillo.

I took a mouthful of whisky. 'I think I've really stuffed up, Benny,' I said.

He looked at me. 'Now, mate,' he said, taking a deep breath. 'I'm going to say something blunt about Helena, because nothing seems to be sticking in your thick skull. She's heading toward 30, right?'

I nodded. 'She's 27.'

'Well then,' he said. 'With all respect to Helena, it's not like a whole lot of blokes are going to be beating her door down. Not when so many lads have been lost at war and there's so many women to choose from. Think about it — she's all yours!'

I sat for a minute, processing what he'd said, staring at the black stripes of the dead tiger. I was nearly 30 too. Who the hell would want me if she didn't?

I leaned forward, slapping my thighs to snap myself out of it. 'Thanks for that, my brutally blunt friend!' I said. 'Anyway, I'm bloody sick of thinking about it.'

I took a deep drag of my cigarillo, exhaling toward the ceiling fan, and asked, 'What's the first thing you're going to do when you get to Melbourne?'

102

'I'm hoping the football season hasn't finished by then,' he said. 'Because I plan to drink a dangerous amount of Victoria Bitter while watching the Saints win a flag.'

Made me think of my old driver mate Westy from the Light Horse, and the way he used to stutter when we'd been out on the road all day. I wondered if he'd made it home.

There was a small cheer near the bar and we watched as Captain Smith and General Borton walked in. Men crowded around the pair, shaking their hands and clapping them on the back and vying to order their drinks. Calcutta had never seen a plane before we'd arrived in our great green Handley Page, with its 100-ft wingspan and thundering engines. It's hard to describe the impact that formidable bomber – and its pilots — had on people.

'Have you noticed how men seem to like Captain Smith almost as much as women?' I asked.

'Yeah,' Benny said. 'Women want to bed him and men want to be him. Lucky bastard.'

'Can you imagine him settling down with a woman, though?' I asked.

Benny shot me a puzzled look. 'One day maybe,' he said, drawing on his cigarillo. 'Apparently at one stage during the war there was a girl in Adelaide keen on settling him down.' He exhaled and continued, 'I think the idea of going back to normality scares him shitless. I mean, the bloke was a junior storeman in some city department store before he enlisted. Now look at him!'

'Harris Scarfe,' I said. 'That's where he worked back home.'

'Yeah, that's the one,' said Benny. 'I heard a motor

firm's just offered him a couple of thousand quid to stay on here in Calcutta, too, but he knocked 'em back. Can you imagine him being stuck behind a desk?'

A dozen people were crowded around the Captain. We couldn't hear what he was saying, but whenever his lips stopped moving a roar of laughter erupted.

'Before the war, I used to read about men trying to set flight records in flimsy old crates,' I said. 'People were fascinated. A couple of my brothers went to see the first exhibition flight in Adelaide. The crowd rushed in to get close to the plane and the propeller took a kid's hand off.'

'Jesus,' said Benny, screwing up his a face.

'It's the same with the Captain – they're fascinated by him. Not so long back, these old blokes would have sat in here arguing whether powered flight was even possible.'

Arriving out of the sky was a hell of a way to make an entrance. But that wasn't the only reason people were drawn to Ross Smith. There was his war record. Eleven kills. A chest full of decorations. Bullet scars on his cheek and forehead. And there was something about him being Australian, too. Very Australian, very athletic and very young – he was still only 26. He spoke beautifully and was educated enough to fit right into the richest crowd, yet he was still always Ross Smith. Boy from the bush in South Australia.

Just then, the Captain caught my eye and waved a folded newspaper in the air. The next second, he and General Borton were pressing through the crowd toward us.

'Benny,' I said quickly, 'Biffy advancing.'

We stood smartly, hands behind our back.

'Oh for pity's sake, gentlemen, at ease,' said Gen-

104

eral Borton. 'The Captain has some rather thrilling news. Let's see if there's a table on the terrace.'

We all followed him outside, Benny and I exchanging a look on the way. 'Thrilling news' could mean anything coming from Biffy Borton. He'd said the same thing before dispatching us to the desert on the North West Frontier.

Brigadier-General Amyas Borton was the very picture of a charming British gentleman. Monocle. Moustache. Lots of back slapping and 'Jolly good!'. He wore a fixed expression of quiet amusement, like he knew something we all didn't. And maybe he did. His grandfather had been the governor-general of Malta and a knight, and his father was a retired lieutenant-colonel and country squire on some rolling estate with its own village south of London. Biffy had risen quickly through the ranks of the Royal Flying Corps, surviving a shocking bullet wound through the jaw in a dogfight over France to eventually be given command of the Palestine Brigade — including our No. 1 Squadron.

No one really knew how he'd earnt his nickname. I heard once that during his time with the Black Watch militia in Scotland, he'd taken to giving disobedient blokes a bit of biffo. Apparently it was less fuss than writing a report. And he certainly didn't stand on ceremony in Palestine. Parading was banned on his aerodromes. 'We are at war,' he'd say.

'When we are through with that, then we can 'fall in' and look nice.' There was time for tennis though, and golf, and flying back to Cairo for grand dinner parties at Shepheard's Hotel. He referred to us No. 1 Squadron lads as 'my Australians', like he was just so damned proud of us. He knew we all called him Biffy behind his back, too; 'Jolly good,' he'd said when he heard. You couldn't help but like the man.

We found four rattan armchairs around a low teak table and sat down, the General on my left and the Captain on my right. Biffy ordered four whiskys and four Black Tiger cigars with his usual exuberance, before leaning back in his chair, smoothing down his thick black moustache with thumb and forefinger, and nodding for the Captain to begin.

Captain Smith leaned in, grinning, and threw the folded copy of the *Sydney Morning Herald* on the table. 'Lads, you won't believe this, but our government has announced an air race from England to Australia.'

'What?' said Benny, picking up the paper and quickly scanning down the page for the headline.

'Read it out, Sergeant,' said General Borton.

Benny read: 'By air. Australia from Great Britain. With a view of stimulating aerial activity, the Commonwealth government has decided to offer a prize of ten thousand pounds for the first successful flight to Australia from Great Britain on a machine manned by Australians.' He kept scanning: 'Competitors should be required to supply their own machines and to make all other necessary arrangements in connection with the flight.'

He looked up. 'Ten thousand quid!'

'Benny, can I take a look?' I said, and when he handed me the paper I checked the top of the page for the date. 'This race was announced back in March. We're in August.' For a fraction of a second I hoped we were too late.

'Quite right, Wal,' the Captain said. 'I've cabled London and Sydney to clear a few things up. But I think it's a fair bet the race hasn't begun yet, or we'd

106

have heard about it.'

'But wait a minute,' said Benny, 'why would the Australian government hold a race? And offer *ten thousand* pounds?'

'Same reason the British government asked us to survey landing strips between India and Australia,' said Biffy, biting on his cigar. 'We've seen what these machines can do in war. Think what they can do in peace. Trade. Defence. Passenger travel. Think about it, old boy — it's all about strengthening Empire.'

He sat back and stroked his moustache. 'I'll bet you all a guinea that your odd little Prime Minister, William Hughes, was flying between London and Paris for the Versailles talks and got a taste of the world from the skies. Probably quite like to fly home himself.'

I sat forward. 'Alcock and Brown received ten thousand pounds in prize money for their first flight across the Atlantic in June. Must be the going rate.'

Benny slapped a hand on the table. 'All this time we've been aiming to fly home to Australia, and now the government wants to give us ten thousand bloody quid to do it!'

We laughed, and Biffy caught the waiter's eye. 'Four more whiskies, man,' he said as the Sikh approached. 'No — bring the whole damn bottle.'

The Captain had been sitting back quietly, and now he lightly tapped his fingers on the table. 'There wouldn't be too many Australian pilots with the confidence to fly eleven thousand miles.' He paused. 'And make it home in one piece.'

'That's our Ross!' said Biffy. 'Already sizing up the competition!'

'Eleven thousand miles?!' said Benny.

'Roughly,' the Captain said. 'I'd need to work out

our landing spots and measure it all up. The longer the better, though, for us. There were some damn fine Australian pilots flying over the Western Front by the end of the war — but hopefully the distance will deter a few of them.' You could tell his mind was already racing. 'I reckon we'll be up against maybe a dozen teams at most. They'll all have flown over Britain and France in the war, but no further. None of them know the route from Cairo right down to Australia like we do. If we can get back to England in time, no one will beat us.'

'And don't forget, Ross old chap,' said Biffy, drawing on his cigar. 'I've already shaped the air route from Britain through Italy and Greece and down to Cairo. We've got the jump on that section too.'

The Captain leaned over to chink Biffy's whisky tumbler. 'Here's hoping the rules allow you to come along, General. You're almost an honorary Australian these days.'

When Biffy laughed, his whole body shook. Not for the first time, it struck me that he was only a few years older than me.

'Too right,' said Benny. 'Us four — we'd be unbeatable! That ten thousand pound cheque's already got our name on it.'

Ten thousand quid was more money than I could fathom. Back then I earned nine shillings, or less than half a quid, a day. It would have taken me 60 years to earn a sum like that.

'Never mind the money,' the Captain said. 'How about being the first men to cross the planet in a plane?'

He raised his glass, leaned forward in his chair and said, 'Chaps, we're going to win this race — and then

I'm flying to Adelaide to see my mum.'

We all raised a glass to that, and then Biffy and Benny and the Captain threw themselves into planning. How we'd get back to England. Where we'd land along the route. Who we'd approach about a plane.

John Alcock and Arthur Whitten Brown had crossed the Atlantic in a Vickers Vimy twin-engined bomber. If he couldn't get a plane out of Handley Page, the Captain would talk to Vickers. Biffy already knew a chap at the company – a bloke he'd flown with during the war.

I listened and tried to take it all in. Ten thousand quid. The chance to make history and be a hero. But it meant going to Britain. And London was just about as far away from Helena as it was possible to get.

Captain Smith leaned toward me. 'Wal, grab your whisky. Come for a stroll.'

I stood and followed the Captain away from the cigar smoke and onto the lawn. There was a rich smell of frangipani, and kerosene burning in the bamboo torches.

The Captain nudged at a fallen white flower with his boot. 'The Viceroy's wife told me frangipani is a symbol of immortality in India,' he said. 'Even when they've been removed from the soil, they can still flower and grow leaves.'

'Gee,' I said. But he didn't get me out here to talk about flowers. 'Captain, I understand if you'd rather take another mechanic on the race. I know you had many other fine blokes working for you in Palestine — Joe Bull for one. You've got to do what's best for you.'

He held up a hand. 'Wal, an aircraft is only as good as its mechanics, and there's no matching you and Benny on these big twin-engine buses.' He paused to take a mouthful of whisky. 'I want to talk to you about Helena.'

'Pardon?' I said.

'Wal, I know I've asked a lot of you these past nine months since the war, but Benny told me you missed your own wedding.'

I frowned, embarrassed. 'Don't worry about that, Captain.'

He took another drink. 'All things being equal, it should take about a month to fly from Britain to Australia. If we can ship out for London quickly from here and secure ourselves an aircraft, I reckon I can have you home in four months at the most – in time for Christmas.'

I looked at him in the dim light, wishing I had even just a fraction of his conviction.

'But let's not be naive about this,' he said. 'We've both seen the jungle between here and Australia. No landing spots for thousands of miles. No rescue party. It's a risk I'm willing to take — but then, the only woman waiting back home for me is my mother. It sounds to me your Helena is worth living for.'

'She is,' I said, nearly choking on the words.

'Well then, I want you to think very carefully. The decision has to be yours, because if we do this I'll demand your absolute commitment.'

We stood quietly for a while.

I tugged a frangipani flower from a nearby branch, and as the pungent sweetness washed over me I thought back to Helena in our Sydney hotel room.

She'd asked me to close my eyes while she undressed, and before I knew it she was tucked up in the narrow single bed, with the covers under her chin and a big, silly smile on her face.

'How come you get to watch me undress?' I'd asked, sitting on the side of the bed to tug off my boots.

'Lady's prerogative,' she'd said, biting her bottom lip as she reached out a smooth, white arm to gently rub my back.

Shadows flickered on the bare walls from a single candle.

Her dark hair was loose against the cream pillow. I'd leaned over to softly kiss her, and she'd put her hand behind my neck and pulled me in tight.

Then she'd pressed her lips to my ear and whispered, 'Get a move on, Private Shy-ers.'

I sighed, tucking the frangipani flower in my pocket before taking a sip of whisky.

I'd come too far and risked too much to go home now.

'I'm in, Captain,' I said. 'And you know you can always count on my total commitment.'

'Thank Christ, Wal,' he said, looking up. 'Just look at the size of that sky. I'm going to need you lads to get me through it.'

Chapter 9

ENGLAND, SEPTEMBER 1919

For the first time in four and a half years I'd been ordered to sleep in, but there was little chance of that. I was in England, land of kings and castles, staying at Biffy Borton's family estate, Cheveney. It even had its own name, like it was a person.

I couldn't remember the last time I'd woken in my own room, free from a dawn chorus of Benny's farts. Instead there was birdsong: shrill whistles and tweets and rat-a-tattats. In the distance a rooster crowed.

I pulled the quilt higher and surveyed the room. I was in the servants' quarters, not far from the garage. The room was only tiny but it was bright and white, from the walls to the floorboards to the quilt and the chair. Only my filthy kit bag was out of place. My nose crinkled at the sight of it in the corner. 'Don't give up on an old mate so quickly,' I told myself. *'That kit bag will follow you home. Nothing else here will.'*

The night before, Benny and I hid in a stuffy broom cupboard deep in the stern of a ship while we waited for Biffy's orders on how to smuggle ourselves onto the Southampton docks and into Britain. 'Just walk through the galley and down the services plank,' Biffy had told us. 'Don't talk to anyone, don't explain anything. The ship's captain says the less everyone knows, the better. Turn left in the first alleyway and stay out of sight until my car appears. We'll see you back at

Cheveney and worry about the paperwork later.'

We'd waited and waited, and just when we were getting desperate the headlights appeared. And we'd bundled ourselves and our kit into a Ford motor car fit for King George.

'Heads down,' the chauffeur ordered as we turned a corner and drove past milling Tommies.

We shrank down to the floor, heads almost touching, and Benny whispered, 'Bloody hell, Wal. Welcome to Blighty!'

I rolled onto my side in the bed, making a cocoon of the thick quilt, and stretched out an arm to run my finger along the floorboards. No dirt floor. No dust. No rocking of a ship or seasick guts.

The late-night supper of sausages and mash had settled me down already, just as Edie said it would. Dear old Edie. It was past midnight when we arrived, but Biffy's family cook still insisted on preparing us supper. She'd hugged us when she said goodnight, too, said it was a blessing to have young men in the house again. Four Cheveney workers had been killed in the war — two blown up in the same week at the Somme.

I rolled myself tighter still inside the quilt, thinking about Helena and wondering if she'd received my letter yet about entering the race. Over many glasses of rum on the voyage from Bombay, Benny had convinced me there was still hope. And anyway, we'd be heroes soon. What woman could deny a hero? My mind wandered to what Helena and I might buy with my share of the £10,000 prize money. A nice little home. A garage business in Sydney, maybe. *'Don't get ahead of yourself, Wal,'* I told myself. *'Pride comes before a fall from the sky.'*

113

I looked out the window and saw blue sky through the leaves. A tractor started up and way off in the distance a cow mooed. I sat up, scratched, and opened the door a crack to find a pile of freshly laundered clothes folded on the floor. Still warm. Edie again. My clothes smelled of lavender and home. I hoped Helena was as excited about our future as I was.

It was chilly outside, despite the clear skies. To get a full view of the house, I had to walk quite a way back. The lawn was bigger than Narrandera cricket oval, with a lake down the far end lined with oaks and pines and silver birch. There were even two miniature cannons. I'd expected the wealth, but the colour shocked me. The England I imagined as a kid was grey. Towering factories billowing smoke. Grand civic buildings surrounded by cobblestones. Grey and urban, not tranquil and green.

Cheveney was magnificent. Two-storey in the Tudor style. It had high-pitched roofs, but it was homely too — lived-in somehow — maybe because it was all so higgledy-piggledy. It had clearly been built in stages, with panelled gables of varying sizes rising to the sky above grand picture windows. Ivy covered the right wing and a covered courtyard out the front was filled with worn wicker chairs arranged casually around a central table. You could imagine the parties that went on out there: dapper men, beautiful ladies. I knew I'd never join them.

I was standing there with arms crossed, counting the chimneys, when an elderly man came striding across the lawn, waving a finger at me. There was no doubt he was Biffy's father. He had the same wide forehead and hair slicked back from a middle part, only the hair was white and thin. Similar moustache,

114

only bushier. Same height, only thicker-set. I immediately thought I was in trouble — I should have known better than to stand on the grass. But before I could move, he'd grabbed my hand and was shaking it with purpose. Same energy as Biffy, too.

'Ah, you'd be one of my son's men from Australia,' he said. 'Colonel Arthur Borton. Welcome to Cheveney.'

'Nice to meet you, sir,' I said. 'I'm Wally Shiers. Thank you for having me.'

He looked back toward the house. 'So what do you think of the old place, eh? Bit worse for wear after the war.'

I followed his gaze. 'It's magnificent, sir.'

He smoothed down his moustache with thumb and forefinger, exactly like Biffy did. 'Yes, the Tudor style is impressive. Elizabethan, technically, the original farmhouse on the left at least. Parts of the building date back to the fifteenth century. Let me show you around the lake.'

He walked briskly, firing questions about my war service, the air race, the Captain and Benny. He listed off various trees and plants in the collection, bird species too. He told me about his oldest son Arthur, who'd won a VC in Palestine. Told me he couldn't be more proud of his sons. Made me wonder if my own dad ever spoke that way about us boys. I hoped so.

When we got to the other side of the lake, the Colonel stopped and pointed out the vast hedges fringing either side of the estate.

'Lost four of our workers in the war, Wally. Brave young lads, every one. Don't know how I'll ever get the yew hedge tidied up.'

I thought about my little room down the back of

115

Cheveney. It probably belonged to one of those blokes once.

'I know a thing or two about gardening, sir,' I said. 'Feel free to use me while I'm here.'

He clapped me on the shoulder and beamed, all white moustache and crow's-feet. 'I think we're going to be fine friends, young Wally.'

On the walk back, he prioritised jobs that had been neglected around the garden, and after a bowl of porridge with Edie, I was back outside attacking a hedge a mile long.

Captain Smith and Biffy were working on securing an aircraft for the race and Benny was in the garage. I'd bet him a pound he couldn't keep his hands off that Ford for more than 24 hours and, lucky for him, old Tom the chauffeur was happy to share.

I spent the morning alone with my shears, dreaming about the race, life's possibilities, Helena, Bondi Beach. Must have been around midday, when I was drinking a glass of water, surveying the small section of hedge I'd tamed throughout the morning, when the Colonel called out from the house and waved me inside.

'Take a break, Wally,' he said as I removed my shoes in the mud room. 'I'll tell Edie to send the housemaid with some sandwiches. And there's quite the parcel arrived for you.'

I looked down at the bench and saw a package wrapped in paper, tied with string. 'Helena,' I said without thinking.

'Helena, eh?' said the Colonel. I felt my face go red. 'I'll leave you to it.'

'Thank God,' I thought as I sat down. And I suddenly felt exhausted. After all these months she'd finally found me.

When I turned over the parcel, I saw Fred's handwriting. Not Helena's.

I untied the string and tore open the paper and there was no hint of lavender. Only my own letters returned unopened. My package with the linen napkins was there. So were the packages with the pashmina shawl and the silk pincushion. I rummaged through the pile, feeling increasingly hopeless as envelopes dropped to the ground at my feet, and finally I found a letter addressed to me from Fred.

July 6th 1919

Wally old friend,

I hope this finds you well. This is a bastard of a job, but it's not fair to leave you in the dark.
Helena says it's over. She doesn't think she can ever trust you again. She won't listen to reason. For months I've tried to explain everything you did for me while I was sick, but she won't hear it. I'm afraid she hasn't opened one of your letters since you wrote to say you were staying on to fly to India with Ross Smith. She says you can have them all back. She gets furious if I press her on it, and then Mum hears and gets upset too, and that's the last thing we need because Mum's crook, Wal. She beat the influenza but she's not the same. It's like the light's gone out of her. Rarely leaves her bed. And I can't even bloody help to lift her because my left arm's useless. Her bedsores would make you weep. Helena's exhausted looking after us both. I spent years wishing I was home and now I'm back and it's shit, Wal. You should see the way people

look at us blokes who fought for king and country. Only place I feel normal is in the pub with the others. How am I ever going to get farm work again with a crook arm? Be better off if that Hun bastard had shot straight and killed me good and proper. Anyways, Wal, I'm sorry it didn't work out with Helena. I don't know what else to say. Bloody wish you'd come home, but if the shoe was on the other foot I'd have stayed too. There's nothing here for us now.
Take care, Walter Custard. Let me know what you're up to.

Freddy Houdini

Fred's letter was dated July and the package had been redirected from India. So they didn't know I was in England or planning to fly home in the world's greatest air race.

Not that it mattered. All was lost. I slowly piled up the letters and wrapped them up again in the brown paper.

Denny the housemaid arrived from the kitchen with a tray of sandwiches and lemonade. 'Gosh, Wally, you're popular,' she said with a sweet smile when she saw the package. And suddenly I was homesick. What was I doing here, on the other side of the world? Trimming hedges like some damn country squire? What a fool. Ashamed, I covered the package with my arm and cleared my throat.

'Yes, it's always nice to get news from home.'

I took the sandwiches outside and hid them deep inside the hedge.

PART TWO

PART TWO

Chapter 10

ADELAIDE, 1968

Someone yells for the television in the corner to be turned up. There's a news story about the Vietnam War. 'Get you another beer, sweets?' asks Delvene behind the bar. She's a good sort, our Delvene. She lost her first husband in New Guinea. I glance up at the telly — women are marching against the war in Washington and LBJ's wringing his hands again. 'Boys,' I say, drawing them back in. 'In Palestine we knew exactly who the enemy was. Johnny Turk. Fritz. But in London — that's where it got tricky.'

★ ★ ★

ENGLAND, SEPTEMBER 1919

'Welcome to a Borton breakfast tradition, chaps,' Biffy said. He waved us into two vacant seats at the round mahogany table. 'Dad reads out a snippet from the *Morning Post* and those of us feeling so inclined make an attempt at verse.'

Confused, I looked across the table to Colonel Borton, who poked his head briefly from behind his newspaper. 'Morning, gentlemen,' he said brightly, returning to rifle noisily through the pages.

Beside him, his wife Mrs Laura Borton had her chair pushed back and was almost completely hidden behind a large shaggy black poodle sitting upright on her lap. She peered around the dog to smile, before continuing to pull burrs from its coat.

Benny shifted uncomfortably on his seat beside me.

Ten minutes earlier we'd been sitting in the kitchen, drinking tea from chipped mugs and discussing the relative merits of the Ford, the Lancia and the Austin in the garage. Then Denny poked her head around the door, saying Colonel Borton requested our presence for breakfast. 'Oh God, no,' Benny said under his breath. We quickly rose, tucking in shirts and smoothing down hair, before following her along a sloping corridor to the dining room.

Biffy reached for the teapot. I was still getting used to seeing him in civvies, and I'd never noticed so much Brilliantine on one man's head. 'Help yourself to tea, lads,' he said. 'Ross is on the telephone.'

'Yes, do make yourselves at home,' said Mrs Borton in a soft English accent. 'Denny shan't be long with breakfast.'

I'd met Laura Borton and her shaggy poodles Banshee and Marmaduke in the garden the previous afternoon. She'd come out to do some weeding while I was trimming the hedge. Nice lady. Tall. Elegant despite the holes in her brown cardigan. She'd converted the village institute into a hospital during the war, to care for 'the Colonel's cripples', as she called them. Denny had told me later she was actually Biffy's stepmother. She'd married the Colonel after the death of his first wife, though she'd known the family forever.

I sized up my china teacup, its red pastoral scene matching every piece of crockery in the room. In the middle of the table was a careful arrangement of silver centrepieces, delicate painted pheasants and a splendid glass fruit bowl. Any one of those items would

122

have been worth more than my annual salary. Carved wood panelling lined the walls and an oriental rug lay underfoot. I glanced up at the exposed wooden beams, easily two feet thick.

'Impressive, what?' Biffy said, startling me. 'There's graffiti on beams in the attic dating back to the seventeenth century.'

He pointed to a large oil painting of a formidable-looking man with muttonchops and full military regalia. A picture of wealth and power. 'And that's dear old grandfather General Sir Arthur Borton, Governor-General of Malta, Knight Commander of the Order of the Bath, St Michael and St George.' He sipped his tea. 'Became quite the mouthful, really.'

I noticed the old Colonel glance up from his paper to nod at the portrait. 'One can't beat the panache of the red coat,' he said.

Biffy chuckled. 'Scarlet tunics would have been a tad foolhardy in the Sinai though, eh Dad?'

Denny came around a green baize screen hiding the servants' entrance to the kitchen, carrying two white serving platters: fried eggs and grilled tomato piled on one, bacon and sausages on the other. The plates looked so heavy, it was all I could do not to jump up and take them out of her hands. She moved around the table and we served ourselves, before she left the platters warming above small burners on the huge oak sideboard.

I realised I was starving.

Suddenly the Colonel cried out, 'Aha, this one's just the ticket! Are we all at the ready?'

He smoothed his newspaper before him: 'A Mr Day of Coventry is due to wed a Miss Week of Maidstone. A Mr Day. A Miss Week. Marriage.' Then he began

123

jotting notes in its margin with a tiny nub of pencil.

Biffy leaned back in his chair, rubbing his chin, deep in thought. A notepad and pencil sat untouched beside his place setting.

I looked at Benny, who made a face of mock terror as he sipped his tea. The china cup looked ridiculous in his huge brown hands.

Something moved on the floor next to Mrs Borton and I realised the other family dog, Marmaduke, had been asleep at her feet. She whispered to the dog and he settled again.

'Any takers?' the Colonel asked, after a minute or two of furious scribbling. I'd seen enemy soldiers look less combative at Romani. 'Wally?'

He was looking right at me.

'Um.' God, I'd never written a poem in my life. My mind raced to remember the clues. A Mr Day. A Miss Week. Marriage.

'I'll give you another minute, son,' the Colonel said.

The room fell silent. A clock was ticking. No. Two clocks. Ticks and tocks slightly off.

I could hear Banshee panting on Mrs Borton's lap. The dog was hot – it needed to run outside on the green lawn. I knew how it felt.

A teacup rattled into a saucer.

A Mr Day. A Miss Week. Marriage.

Had it only been a day since Fred's letter? Felt like a year. Mum flashed into my head. Her face in a white coffin. Scarlet lipstick. Red coat.

Helena's face looking up from Sydney wharf. Black umbrellas. Rain. A punch in the guts.

A Mr Day. A Miss Week. Marriage.

Marriage. Gone. Gone to sit at this table. To fail. To

124

feel like a fool. No, to feel like an old fool.

Where was that boy from Sydney wharf, the one who promised marriage? Where was he?

He was gone. Gone four years ago. Four years. Not days. Not weeks. Not marriage.

'There once was a man called Day ...'

It was Benny, my friend.

'Speak up, man!' the Colonel cried excitedly.

Benny cleared his throat.

> *There once was a man called Day,*
> *Who was handsome in his own way.*
> *He met a Miss Week,*
> *Kissed her pretty white cheek,*
> *And she swooned, or so they all say.*

Biffy rapped his knuckles twice on the table in appreciation, and Benny grinned sheepishly.

'So you're a limerick man,' the Colonel said, smoothing his moustache. 'Unconventional, sir, but nicely played! Now – Biffy?'

'Not so much as a single line, I'm sorry to say. Got a head full of air race. Same as Wally here, I suspect.' Biffy smiled at me and nodded.

I looked at my hands in my lap. He had no idea.

'And how about you, Dad?' Biffy said. 'Come on, out with it.'

The Colonel seized his newspaper and sat upright in his chair, clearing his throat loudly.

> *One Day the more, one Week the less,*
> *But let time not complain,*
> *There'll soon be Days enough*
> *To make a Week again.*

125

His whole body shook as he laughed.

Mrs Borton smiled and patted the Colonel's arm. Biffy applauded, leaning across toward me and Benny: 'Dad can be rather obscure on occasion, but if the newlyweds have seven children they'll make a week. Get it chaps?'

'Ahhh!' Benny said. We clapped, too.

'Bravo, Dad,' Biffy said, shaking his head in admiration. 'You're in fine fettle this morning.'

I picked up my cutlery as the door opened and Captain Smith strode in looking miffed.

'Well, that went well,' he said sarcastically, dropping roughly into his seat. He glanced at me and Benny. 'Morning, men.'

He rested his elbows on the table, rubbing his forehead with his fingers.

I quietly returned my knife and fork to the plate, waiting. Benny's stomach grumbled.

Sunlight streamed into the room from the large French windows. I could see out to where I'd trimmed the yew hedge yesterday.

'More bad news, old chap?' Biffy asked.

'I'm afraid so,' the Captain said. 'The Australian Imperial Force has got wind that we've arrived in Britain.' He looked across at me and Benny. 'You two have been ordered to appear at headquarters in London tomorrow afternoon. They want to check your papers are in order. And they want to see me separately.'

Papers? I had no papers from India – none of us did. And nothing to prove that the Acting Sergeant's stripes on my sleeve were legitimate from my stint with the Brits on the North West Frontier. I could just picture some furious brass hat in the AIF tear-

126

ing strips off me, not to mention the three stripes I'd stitched on by candlelight in a tent in Risalpur.

A knot twisted in my guts. That's all I needed — to be sent home in disgrace.

'Bah!' said Biffy. 'You'll square things in no time, old chap.'

I always envied Biffy's optimism. Made me wonder if he'd ever been told 'No'.

'Please begin, everyone,' said Mrs Borton, scooping the dog off her lap and pulling her chair to the table.

I picked up my knife and fork, and hesitated before asking, 'How'd it go yesterday, Captain?'

He took a long sip of his tea. 'First of all, from now on lads, it's Ross. I know we're still in uniform, but the fighting's over and the squadron's long gone. Ross is fine.'

'Okay … Ross,' I said, feeling slightly stupid. I glanced across at the Colonel, but his head was buried again in the Post.

'Sure, Ross!' Benny said through a mouthful of egg.

'Thanks, fellas,' Ross said. 'And I'm sorry to say yesterday's trip to London was rather challenging on a number of fronts.'

The Royal Aero Club, responsible for administering all air races in Britain, had confirmed what we'd anticipated: Biffy was ruled out of the race on account of not being Australian.

Worse, the RAC had confirmed five teams were already entered and set to depart for Australia within weeks.

The final blow had come after a courtesy visit to the offices of Handley Page, where Biffy and Ross had been unable to convince the aviation managers to hand over a new machine for the race.

Ross reached into a jacket pocket and pulled out a small leather notebook, placing it open on the table so Biffy, Benny and I could see it.

'Right, you two,' he said, pointing at the list. 'Here's tomorrow's mission. After you've sorted your papers with the AIF, you're to visit the Chevrons Club. I want you to find out everything you can about these five pilots and their machines. We need to size up the competition.'

The Chevrons Club was for petty and non-commissioned officers from Britain and allied nations, and popular with Flying Corps NCOs. Which was all well and good, providing the AIF let me keep my stripes. Without my Sergeant's insignia, I wasn't an NCO and I wouldn't be getting into the club.

But Ross was in no mood for a debate, so I shut my mouth.

Biffy lit a cigarette, settled back into his seat and nodded to the open notebook on the table. 'Right, who are we up against?'

'First on the list, Captain Cedric Howell in a Martinsyde A1 biplane,' Ross said. 'Two-man team. Rolls-Royce Falcon engine, 275 horsepower. One of the fastest single-engined aircraft in the war.'

'Cedric Howell is an Adelaide boy,' I said.

'Cedric Howell is also a jolly good pilot,' Biffy said. 'Flew with the Royal Flying Corps over France and Italy during the war. Claimed nineteen victories. Single-handedly took on a formation of fifteen enemy machines and brought down five of them. Quite remarkable.'

'Howell will be a tough adversary, no doubt about it,' Ross said, scratching his chin. 'How about the Martinsyde machine? You blokes worked on Tinsydes

128

during the war — how would you rate them for long flights?'

'Good stamina,' Benny said. 'Absolutely reliable.'

'Right-o,' Ross said. 'Second, we have Captain George Matthews in another two-seater biplane: the Sopwith Wallaby. Rolls-Royce Eagle VIII engine, 350 horsepower.'

Benny whistled. 'Lordy — 350 horsepower is one big engine.'

'Matthews is another South Australian,' Ross said. 'I met him a couple of times with the Light Horse at Gallipoli. Last I heard he was with the AFC in France.'

Biffy exhaled. 'The chaps at the Royal Aero Club say he's been working at Sopwith with good old Harry Hawker since the war.'

'Oh gosh,' Mrs Borton said suddenly, looking up from her crossword. 'We all adore dear Harry Hawker.'

Australian airman Harry Hawker had become famous for crashing his Sopwith into heavy seas during the race across the Atlantic Ocean just three months earlier. He and his co-pilot were missing for a week, with all hope lost, when suddenly they turned up alive in the Outer Hebrides. They'd been pulled out of the water by an old tramp steamer bound for Scotland, with no radio on board to wire the news. Hundreds of thousands turned out to welcome Hawker home to London's Kings Cross Station — cries of 'coo-ee' apparently rang out like air-raid sirens. Within weeks the race was won by two Brits: John Alcock and Arthur Whitten Brown.

'Poor old Alcock and Brown,' Biffy said. 'I imagine their victory was almost an anti-climax after all the Hawker hoo-ha.'

'It was, rather,' the Colonel said. 'But they got their

knighthoods. And I'd wager King George has something similar in mind for the winners of the air race to Australia.'

'Imagine being that famous,' I said.

'Not sure if I'd like it,' Benny said, smearing butter on a slice of toast.

'Right, gentlemen,' Ross said impatiently, smacking a hand on the tabletop. 'Next up is a four-man team led by Lieutenant Valdemar Rendle and Captain Hubert Wilkins. Blackburn Kangaroo. Rolls-Royce twin-engine Falcon, 250 horsepower.'

'Wilkins!' I said. 'Another South Australian. Might as well call it the South Australian air race. Do you know him, Ross? He's from up bush, too, isn't he?'

'Only know what I've heard. He was one of our official war photographers. Won an MC for rescuing wounded soldiers.'

'Incredible young man, by all accounts,' Biffy said. 'Got a bar to his MC for taking charge of an American unit that lost its officers during the Battle of the Hindenburg Line.'

'Pretty sure he hasn't got his wings though,' Ross said. 'You lads know anything about Rendle or the Blackburn Kangaroo?'

'No, sorry,' I said.

'Nope,' Benny said, taking a bite of his toast.

'Lieutenant Roger Douglas,' Ross said. 'Two-man team in the Alliance Endeavour. Single 450-horsepower Napier-Lion engine.'

He looked at Benny and I.

'Nothing,' I said.

Benny shook his head. 'Four hundred and fifty horsepower! Strewth, that's a monster.'

The Colonel spoke up. 'Alliance had an aircraft

130

entered in the race across the Atlantic. Withdrew for unknown reasons.'

'It's an amphibious aircraft,' Biffy said. 'Enclosed cabin. Solid reputation for long-distance flying.'

'Interesting,' Ross said. 'The ability to land on water will be a definite advantage. Okay, finally there's a Lieutenant Raymond Parer, but no aircraft confirmed as yet.'

'Never heard of him,' I said.

'Me neither,' said Ross. 'That's it for the Australian competitors. Bit of a motley crowd. We've got four-man teams in bombers and two-man teams in single-engine biplanes. We've even got a seaplane. This race is sounding like something out of Jules Verne. They've all been at liberty to take off for Darwin since the eighth of September, so we can expect any one of them to start soon.'

'Pity we don't have a plane, then,' said Benny.

'Yes,' said Ross. 'And we have another fly in the ointment, by the name of Etienne Poulet.'

'Etienne Poulet?' I said. 'I remember reading about him before the war — he was famous for looping the loop. But he's French!'

Ross leaned back in his chair and crossed his arms. 'Etienne Poulet is indeed a Frenchman. Apparently he's planning to fly from Paris to Melbourne in a week or two.'

'In what?' I asked.

'In a Caudron,' said Ross. 'He's crossing the planet in a Caudron biplane pulled along by two 80-horse-power engines.'

'One hundred and sixty horses!' scoffed Biffy. 'That's out-and-out madness!'

'Maybe,' Ross said, 'maybe not. They've said he's

131

ineligible for the ten thousand pound prize, but we're told the Australian government is offering every assistance, including arranging fuel and landing places.'

'What?!' I said.

'You're kidding!' said Benny.

The Colonel looked up from his paper. 'Poulet is quite the chap. Means 'chicken' in English, and the man is anything but.'

The newspapers had been filled with tales of Poulet's exploits for months. He had a swag of French aviation records and had test flown more than a thousand planes during the war. He'd also been a mate of the great French airman Jules Védrines, who'd spent the war flying spies in and out of enemy territory. After the Armistice, Védrines had landed his plane in spectacular fashion on the roof of the Galleries Lafayette department store in Paris. He died in a crash soon after — while planning a flight from Paris to Melbourne no less. Poulet was now determined to carry out the flight in his friend's honour and raise funds for Védrines's grieving widow and children.

'Well, well,' Biffy said.

'Poulet might not be eligible for the money,' said Ross, 'but it sounds like he's certainly capable of stealing the glory.'

Biffy crushed his cigarette in a bronze ashtray and rose from his chair. 'Qui n'avance pas, recule,' he said. 'Who does not move forward, recedes. Onwards to London, chaps.'

★　★　★

Benny and I stood on the pavement outside AIF headquarters. We'd caught the train up from Kent and

132

were waiting for our appointment. It was ten months since the Armistice, but there was still no shortage of slouch hats on the streets. There hadn't been enough ships to get everyone straight home. Australian lads filled their days with vocational training or lectures or lurking among the Delilahs in the streets south of Westminster.

We were ten minutes early, so we leaned against the wall, smoking nervous cigarettes and chatting with a couple of amputee corporals. They used to be wheat farmers south of Perth.

'They reckon Bram Stoker lived around here,' said one of the corporals. He pointed with the stump of his arm. 'Down that way.'

Benny was watching a couple of women hurrying past, their long skirts swishing. There was rain on the way. 'Who's Bram Stoker?' he asked.

'He wrote Dracula,' I said.

'Ahh. Never did get round to reading that.'

An old bloke with a black satchel yelled, '*Daily Mail*! Get yer *Daily Mail*!'

I drew on my smoke. 'Hey Benny, I've been meaning to say thanks for getting me out of a hole this morning.'

He cocked an eyebrow. 'What hole?'

'You know, the Colonel's little poetry competition.'

'Jesus! Don't remind me.'

'Least you managed to string a few words together. I sat there like a bloody mute.'

'Yeah, well the Colonel's not getting another verse out of me. Unless you think Mrs Borton would appreciate 'The Old Man from Devizes'.'

I laughed. 'Whose balls were two different sizes!'

Benny mimicked the Colonel's blue-blood accent:

'One it was small, And no use at all, The other was huge and won prizes.'

One of the corporals guffawed so loud he startled the newspaper seller.

We stood watching the passing cars and carriages, listening to the occasional whistle of barges over on the Thames and the corporals trying to memorise Benny's limerick. The wind was picking up and a Union Jack flapped noisily overhead.

An Austin pulled up alongside us and I was shocked to see Biffy's chauffer Tom at the wheel.

'Eh?' said Benny, startled. 'What's Tom doing here?'

The rear door opened and out sprang Biffy in full military uniform. Benny and I stepped forward in surprise while the corporals snapped to attention.

'Not too late am I, chaps?' asked Biffy, looking at his watch.

'Um, no, sir,' I said. 'Not at all.'

The corporals exchanged a glance. They'd probably never seen a monocled British brigadier-general.

'Jolly good,' said Biffy. 'Follow me.'

We quickly crushed our cigarettes underfoot and turned to follow him inside. Benny slapped one of the amputee lads on the back: 'Good luck, Corporal Devizes,' he said.

We were led down the centre of a vast hall filled with desks, scores of busy office women stopping to stare as the Brigadier-General marched past, his footfalls echoing on the timber floor.

As we were ushered into a tiny office, my stomach churned. Behind the desk was an Australian major with a handlebar moustache, round-rimmed glasses and a large frown.

Biffy didn't even give him time to stand.

134

'Morning, Major,' he said. 'Acting Sergeant Shiers and Sergeant Bennett have travelled from India to Britain on attachment to the Royal Air Force at my urgent request. They were under my command in Palestine and their service records are impeccable. The AIF should be damned proud of them, as I am. I consider it entirely unnecessary to apply to India for their documents. They'll give you the particulars.'

When the Major opened his mouth to speak, Biffy said, 'Good chap.' Then he turned to nod at me and Benny. 'Gentlemen, I will be waiting in the car.'

With that I was Acting Sergeant Shiers. No questions asked. And in half an hour our paperwork was signed and we were back in the Austin, with Biffy insisting Tom drive the long way to the Chevrons Club to give his guests a good look at Whitehall and Buckingham Palace and Westminster.

'I've left Ross at my club,' he said. 'He's making a telephone call to Vickers Aviation. With any luck he's secured an appointment for this afternoon.'

I sat beside that powerful man in the back seat, as he pointed out squirrels and told us about the 13-tonne bell named Big Ben, and felt a bit overwhelmed. 'Sir,' I said, clearing my throat, 'I want to thank you.' 'No need for thanks, Wally,' he said with a wave of his hand. 'It was nothing.' Maybe to him.

Chapter 11

At the Chevrons Club, the first beer didn't touch the sides.

'Thank Christ,' said Benny. 'Same again, Sergeant Shiers?'

'Don't mind if I do, Sergeant Bennett.'

I leaned back against the bar. Men were gathered in quiet groups around the six snooker tables. Lots of Brits of course. A few Canadians with their brass maple-leaf badges at the collar, South Africans with their springboks and Australians with the rising sun. Just boys, most of them. The older blokes — men my age — were either back home or dead, pushing up poppies in Flanders Fields. All these young blokes had filled their shoes in the final stages of the war.

Benny handed me a beer and leaned an elbow on the bar. 'So, I take it we're not talking about the package that arrived from Narrandera yesterday?'

I sipped my drink. 'Nothing to talk about.'

I avoided his eye, trying to sound casual.

'Shit, Wal. Did she …?'

'Nah, all good.'

'Bloody women, eh?'

'And what would you know about women, Benny?' I teased him, trying to shift the attention.

He laughed. 'Mate, I sold some of the first Hupmobiles in country Victoria. There's more than one way to test independent suspension.' He turned to look out over the tables. 'Now, Sergeant, ready to do a recco?'

We took our beers and casually walked between the tables, listening out for anyone mentioning aircraft or the Flying Corps. Rain was rapping on the windows. The room was gloomy except for six pools of light cast by shades hanging low over the green baizes. We discounted a group of South Africans, and a few Australian infantrymen discussing the trenches at Verdun. Three other Australians were sucking on big cigars in the back corner. One of them caught my eye and winked as he curled his mouth around his stogie. 'Too young, too silly,' Benny muttered. 'These blokes might be better game.'

We stood watching as two sergeants — an Australian and a Canadian — worked artfully through the colours, and just as the Canadian potted the black ball to win we heard him mention the Avro 504.

'You beauty,' said Benny under his breath, before chalking his name on the board. 'G'day — the name's Benny!'

Ralph Heffernan was an air mechanic from Nova Scotia. Friendly bloke with a wide gap between his front teeth. He'd spent the war with the Royal Flying Corps in Folkestone, not far from London. Turned out he knew Sergeant Thomas Kay, the mechanic on the Sopwith Wallaby entered in the race.

'Kay just got his wings, actually,' said Ralph, lining up a long shot on a red ball. 'He's assistant pilot and navigator, as well as mechanic on the Sopwith.'

I raised my eyebrows at Benny. Kay's skills left us for dead. 'Handy bloke to have around,' I said.

Ralph took his shot. Balls scattered in all directions. 'Handy at the bar, too. Kay can slam down four pints in under sixty seconds.'

I noticed the three young Australian blokes wandering over with their cigars.

'Can I play the winner?' asked the lad who'd winked at me earlier. He was gaunt and gangly, no more than 21. His two mates looked the same age. One was big. Arms like Christmas hams.

'Sorry, mate,' I said. 'I'm next. You need to put your name on the board.'

He walked over and chalked his name: 'Snowy'.

Benny moved slowly around the table. 'Hey, Wal, remember that Yorkshireman at the Calcutta barracks? Used to stand on his head and drink a pint with no hands?'

'I remember you trying to copy the trick and nearly opening your neck on broken glass,' I said.

'Yeah,' he said, grinning to himself while he sized up his next shot. 'So why are you still in Blighty, Ralph?'

'Stayed on in the Special Reserve while I get my wings,' said the Canadian. 'A buddy and I are using our demob payouts to buy a couple of Avro biplanes and ship 'em back to Halifax.'

'Benny, go the pink,' I said.

'Yeah, hurry up!' said the gangly kid, Snowy. He was cheerful enough, but his two mates let out rude grunts of laughter.

Benny stopped and leaned against his cue, staring at the young bloke. 'You right, son?' he asked.

'Sorry, boss,' Snowy said brightly. 'No offence.'

Benny turned his attention back to the table, and I walked over to chat to Ralph. 'How much they asking for one of those Avro biplanes?'

'Forty quid.'

'You're kidding!' Benny said, before smacking the pink ball into the corner pocket.

'Forty quid?!' I said. 'For a two-seater biplane? Including the engine? I could buy five Avros and still have change!'

'The *Aeroplane* magazine's full of ads,' Ralph said. 'You two would be mad not to buy a couple and ship 'em back.'

Benny took aim at a red ball near the middle pocket. 'Nah,' he said. 'The only plane we need is a twin-engined bomber.'

'Why d'you need a bomber?' It was the Snowy kid again.

Benny turned around, startled.

Snowy was still all smiles.

'Ummm,' Benny said, 'I'm having a chat with my friends here, mate. That alright with you?'

Snowy sipped his beer. 'Yeah, course. But I thought I heard you talking about that air race to Australia.'

Benny blinked. 'And?'

'Well, we reckon it's all bullshit.'

'What's all bullshit?'

'The race. Pilots were ready to start back in June, but here we are three months later and no one's left the ground.'

'Know all about it, do you? Your hands look too clean to be a mechanic, and I'm sure you're not expecting us to think you're a pilot.' Benny rolled his eyes and returned to his shot.

Snowy took a long pull on his cigar. 'I'm not a pilot,' he said, through a cloud of blue smoke. 'But a good friend of mine is. Charles Kingsford Smith. You've probably heard of him.'

Benny didn't look up. 'Nope,' he said, and drove the red into the pocket.

'I've heard of him,' said Ralph. 'Is he in the race?'

'Not any more,' said Snowy. 'Because the Australian government keeps delaying the start date and introducing new rules.'

'What new rules?' asked Benny.

'Navigation, for one. Kingy's been dumped from the Blackburn crew because he doesn't have navigation experience.'

Benny looked at me and back to the kid. He was losing his patience. 'It's a race over eleven thousand miles, not a bleedin' egg-and-spoon race. You need rules. How old's this Charles Kingsford Smith, anyway?'

Snowy jutted his jaw and narrowed his eyes. 'He's 22 and won the Military Cross over in France. So you can fuck off with your egg-and-spoon races.'

A couple of heads turned at the nearest snooker table.

'Look, Snowy,' I said, 'sorry about your mate. But it's got nothing to do with us, okay?'

'Well, that's what I've been trying to figure out,' he said. 'Haven't you blokes just arrived from India?'

Benny stepped forward, frowning. 'Yeah. And?'

'Well, word is the government's been holding up the race on purpose. They don't want it to start until some bomber pilot gets back from Calcutta.'

Benny's voice was like steel. 'And?'

'And, so, who's your pilot?'

I looked from Benny to the kid. 'Captain Ross Smith,' I said.

'Yeah,' said Snowy, turning to smirk at his mates. 'Ross Smith. That's the one.'

Christmas Hams piped up. 'You're the reason they've delayed the bloody race!'

'Christ, I've heard everything now,' said Benny.

A crowd was forming and I was suddenly aware I could only hear rain.

'Snowy,' I said. 'When exactly did they delay the race?'

Christmas Hams sneered. 'June!' He had a neck like a bull. 'Way back in June. Crews were wanting to fly out and they were told no one could leave London until September the 8th.'

Snowy pointed his cigar at me. 'Our mate Kingy's on the bones of his arse after waiting around for months on no pay. So they changed the rules and he's lost his plane and a chance at the prize money.'

Someone in the crowd spoke up: 'Yeah and don't forget Bert Hinkler! He had his name down ages ago, and he's been forced out, too.'

'What?' I said. I looked at Benny, blindsided. What the hell was going on?

'See?' said Snowy, with a cocky grin. 'I reckon the British Air Ministry and the Australian government have been planning this all along. Sounds like they're clearing the field for your bloke, Ross Smith. They've backed in their own horse.'

'This is bullshit,' Benny said, shaking his head in disbelief. 'They're hardly clearing the field. There's five pilots with their names down to compete!'

'Just so long as one of them beats that bloody Frenchman,' yelled someone from the back.

Everyone laughed – me included, and mostly with relief. My heart was thumping.

Snowy sucked at his cigar and appealed to the crowd. 'So we think it's okay for Ross Smith to get special treatment?'

'What special treatment?' asked Benny, exasperated.

'Brass hat treatment.' Snowy curled his lip into a sneer. 'Does the name Brigadier-General Borton mean anything to you?'

'We were in India with him. How is that an advantage?'

'You were scouting fucking airfields all the way down to Australia! Of course that's an advantage!'

Benny was stopped in his tracks for an instant. He looked at me, a flicker of doubt on his face.

'Mate,' he said at last, drawing a deep breath. 'We – have — no — advantage. We don't even have a fucking plane!'

'Yeah,' said Snowy. 'But you'll *get* a plane because Ross Smith is the chosen one. And then you've got the inside run all the way home.'

Christmas Hams folded his beefy arms. 'The Australian government gave Ross Smith all the time in the world to map out his route and get back here to the starting line. I'd say that gives you fellas a pretty decent advantage.'

The crowd murmured its agreement and Snowy threw his hands in the air, shouting: 'I'd say Ross Smith has rigged the England to Australia Air Race!'

Benny lay his cue on the table and walked to within inches of Snowy. The room fell silent again. 'If the name Ross Smith comes out of your mouth one more time, I'll put my fist in it.'

I watched Christmas Hams, shifting my weight in case I had to jump in. 'Come on, fellas,' I said quietly. 'Anyone swings a punch and we're all banned.'

Benny kept eyeballing Snowy. A vein bulged in his neck. 'Belting my old mate here would be worth it.' But then he shrugged and turned away. 'Now, whose shot is it?'

'Fuck you,' Snowy said. 'I know what I know.'

'Actually, you don't know shit, buddy.' It was Ralph, the Canadian.

Snowy scoffed at him. 'Fuck you too.'

Ralph stayed calm. 'If you'd read anything about the race, you'd know they delayed the start while they got permission to fly through countries along the route. No point in flying all the way to Siam and then getting shot out of the air.'

'Like you'd know, Gappy,' said Christmas Hams.

Ralph ignored him. 'That diplomatic stuff takes ages. And then there's the fuel and oil. That all needs to be shipped along the route for the crews when they land.'

Snowy shook his head. 'Rigged!'

'Mate,' I said, 'Ralph's right. The countries beyond India are nothing but jungle. Believe me – we've just come back from there.'

The crowd watched intently.

'It's not like flying from London to Manchester,' I said. 'There are no airfields, or Royal Air Force chaps standing by to refuel your plane. It's jungle! Not a white man for thousands of miles! There are no landing strips — they need to be cleared. There are no fuel supplies — they need to be delivered.' I pointed at the window. 'And you see that rain? That's nothing! The monsoons in the Far East run from June to September. You try to fly through them and you'll die. That's a pretty good reason to delay an air race.'

'Monsoon?' Snowy snorted. 'A monsoon wouldn't stop Kingy!'

'Oh yeah?' said Ralph. 'Why don't you ask your mate Charles Kingsford Smith why he was really dumped by Blackburn? I've heard it's got something to do with the planes he crashed for insurance money.'

Benny looked at Snowy. 'Hah!' he grunted. 'Sounds like your mate should've stuck to his egg and spoon.'

The crowd started laughing. Snowy laughed too, and then made like he was moving to shake Benny's hand. Only he dropped his shoulder and lunged. Benny was too quick. He dodged sideways and slung a sharp right hook to the jaw as the kid passed.

A roar went up across the snooker room. Snowy went down like a shot kangaroo.

The duty manager pushed through the crowd. 'Gentlemen! Gentlemen! What's going on here?'

Benny shrugged. 'Poor bloke must have tripped. You right there, son?' he asked, helping Snowy up. 'Oopsadaisy.'

Snowy's mates dragged him off to a corner as men returned to their games, boisterous now after the dust-up.

'Jesus, Benny, nice hook,' I said. 'Didn't know you could box.'

'Second runner-up, Victorian schoolboy championships 1908.' He rubbed his knuckles. 'I need a beer.'

One or two men slapped Benny on the back as we returned to the bar. 'Good luck with the race, you blokes,' someone said.

We shouted Ralph a beer and settled into three tub chairs. 'So,' Benny said as we raised our glasses, 'who's this Charles Kingsford Smith?'

'You blokes might not want to hear this,' Ralph said, 'but everyone seems to love him. He lost two toes in a dogfight over France and ended up in Britain as a flight instructor. Some call him brave, some call him reckless, but the boys over at Eastchurch called him King Dick, on account of his speed at bedding women.'

Benny snorted into his beer.

'Brass hats hated him though,' Ralph added. 'Always had him in their sights for doing some crazy stunt over the airfield or playing his banjo at all hours. He was big on poaching, too. Shot his game from the air before landing to collect it.'

'Is it true about the insurance money?' I asked.

'That's how the story goes. He and a mate have been barnstorming for ready cash and their planes were going down like flies.'

Ralph had a training session at Hendon early the next morning, so he finished his beer and shook our hands. 'Be safe, fellas,' he said. 'That's one helluva long flight.'

Benny lit himself a smoke and flexed his right hand.

'So what do you reckon?' I asked.

'Christ,' he said, running the other hand over his face. 'No way. We were there that night in Calcutta when Ross learned about the race. We were there!' He took a long swig of his beer and looked straight at me. 'It's the fucking Captain, Wal!'

'Yeah,' I said, letting out a deep breath. 'But the other pilots think we're cheats before we've even got off the ground.'

'What a mess,' said Benny, clenching his jaw.

I leaned back in my chair, rifling through my pockets to find my cigarettes. 'Do we tell him?'

'I've been asking myself that too,' Benny said. 'You know what he'd say: you can't plan a defence if you don't know your enemy.'

★ ★ ★

145

Benny had decided to tell Ross in the car that night on the drive home to Kent, but changed his mind when he sensed the mood in the back of the Austin.

Ross had not had a good afternoon. He hadn't even succeeded in arranging a sit-down with Vickers to ask for an aircraft. He'd called from Biffy's club to arrange an appointment and they'd given him a flat 'No' on the phone. Said they'd received enquiries from a number of experienced Australian pilots in recent months and the answer hadn't changed. So he and Biffy had spent the next few hours drowning their sorrows in whisky, and mapping out Plan C. By the time we were out of London I could hear all three of them snoring on the back seat while I kept Tom company at the front.

So we told him the following morning, sitting under the verandah.

Ross stared from Benny to me and back at Benny, like he was hoping the news might change if he waited long enough. It was the first time in two years I'd seen him speechless. Confused. Wounded. Mortified, now that I think about it. And so young. I'd never stopped to consider our ages before that moment. I was 29, senior to him by three years.

Without a word, he got up and walked across the lawn toward the lake. Just before he was out of earshot I heard him say, 'How did I not see that coming?'

I'm sure he found it doubly insulting because he'd volunteered to help Biffy provide a briefing to all the other race competitors on everything we'd learned about the route between Cairo and Timor.

Two days later we were in London again, Benny and me sitting at the back of a room filled with officials from the British Air Ministry, the Royal Aero

146

Club and the Australian government.

We got to see some of our air race competitors, too. Cedric Howell was there with his mechanic. George Matthews and Ralph's mate, Thomas Kay. Valdemar Rendle. Roger Douglas.

Ross and Biffy's debrief was gratefully received. They outlined things like terrain and weather conditions, approximate flight distances and fuel requirements, where best to land along the route and the names of key officials on the ground who'd offered assistance in various countries, some under British control, some not. Afterwards the pilots all agreed not to race until mid October, to allow more time for landing sites and fuel supplies to be organised.

When the official proceedings were over, Ross asked for a few minutes alone with the competing crews.

'Now, gentlemen,' he said when the brass hats had filed out, 'I've heard some allegations since return-ing to England that seriously reflect on my character. Claims have been made that the race is rigged in my favour – that the start was delayed to allow me to do a full recco of the route and get back here to compete.

'I'm not suggesting any of you are responsible for these claims – I have no doubt they were made by lesser men than you. But I want to state that I'm no cheat. Until very recently, before the race was even announced, it was my intention to fly from India down to Australia, to ensure my good friend Briga-dier-General Borton became the first man to fly the entire route east from Great Britain to Australia. Not very patriotic, eh, giving the honour to a Tommy? But it's the truth.

'Make no mistake. Now that I'm here, I plan to enter the race and I plan to win – for my brother Colin buried in France, for the dozens of good friends I've lost, for the five out of eleven lads from my cricket team who'll never see Adelaide again. Every one of those boys will be with me in the cockpit, flying home to Australia, and by God they won't see me cheating.'

Around the room, men nodded and murmured.

'Now,' said Ross, looking at the group and folding his arms, 'don't suppose any of you know where I can get my hands on a half-decent aircraft?'

Chapter 12

A young boy came tearing over the gate and I stepped back, startled. Ross and Benny laughed and the Colonel waved his walking cane like he was warding off an animal. 'That's quite enough, young man!'

'Sorry, mister,' the kid said, big blue eyes staring out of a dirty face. 'Playin' hide 'n' seek.' His dark hair was cropped so close you could see patches of scalp.

'Oi, Robbie,' a woman called. 'Yer s'posed to be 'elpin', luv. Watch yer sister.'

Without a word Robbie scrambled back over the gate, scooped a curly-haired toddler in his arms and ran back to the women.

'Wouldn't you have loved this as a kid?' said Benny, leaning on the gate. 'Swapping the city for this every summer?'

We stood watching the hop-pickers for a bit. Scores of women were plucking light-green hop cones off long leafy vines and tossing them into hessian sacks stretched over wooden frames like bathtubs. The trailing hop plants grew over wire trellises 15-ft high, making it look like the pickers were working in long green alleyways. Towering above the other workers were men on high wooden stilts, lifting the hop vines off the wires.

We'd heard all about the 'hoppers' from Mrs Borton. Tens of thousands of workers, mostly women and children, migrated from London each summer to work in the hop fields of counties like Kent. They earned good wages but they also gave their kids a couple of months away from the factory smoke and grime of the East End. Hopping work was so prized among poor families it had became known as the 'Londoner's holiday'.

'You mind yourselves now, lads,' the Colonel had warned us. 'Most of these women are away from their menfolk and like to take 'hop husbands'. We've seen farm workers get themselves in all kinds of strife when the real husbands turn up at weekends.'

Many of the workers had babies in their arms, and tiny tackers running underfoot letting off early morning steam. Some wore colourful silk scarves to protect their hair from the sticky hop cones. It was one of the prettiest sights I'd seen in years.

I shoved my hands deep into the pockets of the Colonel's old hunting jacket and brought out a penny. Maybe it was my lucky day.

'Let's not dillydally, chaps,' called the Colonel as he strode off down the lane. 'Wilson's waiting near the top woodland with the guns. And pheasants wait for no man.'

Benny lengthened his stride to catch up. He still looked odd in civvies. We all did. I'd borrowed a hunting jacket and rubber boots from the Cheveney mud room. Underneath I wore a new wool suit and striped blue shirt tailored for a few quid in India. I'd bought my Herringbone flat cap on sale in Maidstone a few days earlier. Mrs Borton said it looked rather snappy.

'Wal, mate,' said Ross. I don't think he'd ever called me mate. 'I need a quick word while we've got a minute.'

'Sure, Ross,' I said. We were walking past the Colonel's brick hop kilns, their conical roofs pointing to the sky.

'I just want to warn you that Biffy's luncheon up in London today is the last roll of the dice.'

I nodded.

It was the end of September, two weeks since Benny's scrap in the Chevrons Club, and we still had no plane. After Vickers rebuffed Ross, Biffy had launched a counter-offensive. He'd scheduled a formal luncheon with Vickers company chiefs, including Brigadier-General Caddell, who'd returned to civilian life after serving alongside Biffy in Egypt. Then Biffy brought in the heavy artillery: Major-General Salmond, who was back briefly in Britain from Cairo. Salmond was by then one of the most powerful figures in the newly formed Royal Air Force, and only too willing to expound on the pioneering flight he made from Cairo to Delhi with one Ross Smith. To Biffy's way of thinking, taking Major-General Salmond along to the luncheon was the ideal way to enlighten Vickers on Ross's credentials as a long-distance pilot, and persuade them to loan us an aircraft.

Ross chewed his lip. 'If Biffy doesn't come through, Wal, I might be forced to go with a smaller aircraft.'

There it was. It had crossed my mind too, this last fortnight. I just hadn't let myself dwell on it. Race competitors Cedric Howell and George Matthews had both assembled lean, two-man teams. One pilot, one mechanic who also acted as navigator. Ross would too, if it came to that. And if it came to that, I was out.

'Don't worry about it, Ross,' I said, managing a smile. 'I understand. I thought it was odd that you hadn't appointed a navigator. No point, is there, if you're down to two men?'

'It's not my preferred option, Wal,' he said. 'You're a damn fine air mechanic. But Benny's been with me

151

from my first day in the Flying Corps, you know? He's like family — my bloody mother even sends him Christmas presents.'

'I know, I know. It's okay.'

'But if the worst does happen, we'll get you on the first ship back to that girl of yours. You'll probably beat us home – be a newlywed for New Year's!'

I tried to force out a laugh. 'Maybe.'

Facing the prospect of not making it into the race, I was too ashamed to tell him Helena had broken it off. Besides, he didn't really need to know.

Women started singing in the field, the children chiming in with their small voices.

> *Oh, they say hopping's lousy*
> *I don't believe it's true*
> *We only go down hopping*
> *To earn a bob or two.*

I plucked a leaf from the hedgerow and tore carefully down the veins as we walked. Lucky penny, my arse. Then I took a deep breath and squared my shoulders. Buggered if I wasn't going to enjoy the Colonel's shoot. He'd been talking about it all week – his way of thanking me and Benny for overhauling his cars and fixing the electricity plant that powered Cheveney.

'Do you ever miss Australia, Ross?'

'I miss Mutooroo — Dad's sheep station,' he said, pulling out his cigarettes and offering me one. 'There's something about the Australian bush that binds you to it.'

Ross stopped to light our smokes. 'My brothers and I used to head out on our own, hunting kangaroos and rabbits. Colin was too young to chase down roos but Dad gave him a penny for every rabbit scalp. We'd hide in the scrub and whisper while we waited for something to move. I miss that.'

He drew on his cigarette and we walked in silence for a while, listening to birds twittering in the hedge-rows. 'You know,' he said, 'all through the war I couldn't wait to get home to Mutooroo. Now part of me's dreading it. I reckon that's where it will hit me that Colin's really gone.'

I thought about my brother Bill, buried at Pozières. Then I pictured us as kids, all tucked into our one bed with him going crazy if any of us touched his feet. So of course we always did, just to set him off. 'Do you have any sisters, Ross?'

'Just one,' he said. 'Janet. She only lived a month, died before the rest of us were born. How about you?'

I nodded. 'Plenty. Mum was Irish.' I liked making Ross smile. His mouth went a bit lopsided and his eyes crinkled.

We'd caught up to the others by then, waiting for us at a gate. 'Colonel,' Ross called, 'did I tell you my dad's sheep farm is three thousand square miles?'

'Good God, man,' the Colonel spluttered. 'That's not a farm, it's a bloody country!'

The shooting party bagged a dozen pheasants before noon. I'd never been a bad shot. My brother Jack taught me when I was a nipper, shooting tins with Dad's .22 down on the flats of the Torrens. But when it came to fixing one of those cheery pheasants in my sights, I didn't have the heart for it. Not after the last four years. I was happier to help with beating to drive them out. At lunchtime, Mrs Borton arrived with a picnic basket and set out dishes on blankets under an oak tree. We ate Scotch eggs and sausage rolls and drank strong tea, and the Colonel told us how, during the war, they could hear the shells exploding on the Western Front from here.

On the walk home to Cheveney later that afternoon, we passed the hop-pickers enjoying the sunshine outside a row of old tin sheds. A group of women sat by a campfire, chatting while toddlers slept in their arms. The air was rich with the smell of wood smoke and vegetable stew. A little kid ran up the lane and fell against his mother, bawling his eyes out and saying something about being called a 'bug crusher' by the local kids. His mum put an arm around his shoulder and kissed his nose, whispered in his ear. My mum used to do that. One day – I must have been about six – I was bawling about being called Wally Wingnut again by the other kids at school, and she whispered in my ear: 'They're teasing you about what's on the outside because they don't know what's on the inside yet. You keep being my kind little man, and you'll be just fine.'

The Colonel waved his cane toward the ramshackle buildings. 'You know, they all move into exactly the same sheds every year,' he said. 'And they do so in exactly the same order as their terraces in East London. Curious creatures.'

At Cheveney, we took ourselves around the back to the mud room, with its whitewashed walls and low wooden bench opposite a long row of hanging coats and scarves and winter caps. Me and Ross and Benny were sitting on the bench, pulling off our boots and talking about the shoot, when Mrs Borton poked her head around the door. 'Ross,' she said, 'Biffy has asked that you call him at his club.'

Ross took a deep breath, arranged his gumboots

neatly under the bench and walked through the door.

Benny and I sat there, neither of us wanting to move. I pulled the penny out of my pocket. 'Heads or tails?'

'Tails never fails,' said Benny.

I flicked the coin into the air and slapped it down onto the back of my hand. I groaned. 'Heads.'

Benny leaned back against the stone wall, closed his eyes and folded his arms over his chest. I didn't ask if he and Ross had discussed getting a smaller aircraft. I didn't want to know.

A clock chimed five in the hall, and a tractor returned to the sheds outside. Banshee and Marmaduke ran into the mud room, a snuffling, tumbling ball of soft black fur. I ordered them to sit, and kept them still by tickling them each behind an ear.

Finally, Ross walked through the door. 'You blokes got any plans for tomorrow?'

We shook our heads. I held my breath.

'Good, because there's a Vickers Vimy sitting idle at Weybridge, and she can't wait to meet you.'

Chapter 13

ADELAIDE, 1968

'Gee, Wal,' says Delvene from behind the bar, 'that hop-picking sounds lovely.' The pub's emptied out, so Delvene's enjoying a shandy and listening in. One of the young lads asks me to rest up a bit while he goes to the dunny, so I sip my beer and chat to a couple of RSL mates along the bar. 'Y'know, there were only 500 aircraft in service when the Great War broke out,' says one. 'By the end, France and Britain were building 30,000 every month.' Delvene chips in: 'And women built lots of them!' My word they did. I smooth down the bar mat with a wrinkled hand. 'Yep, that war changed everything.' It changed how men killed. It changed how men looked at women. It changed how women looked at everything.

★ ★ ★

LONDON, OCTOBER 1919

I couldn't help but compare her, and she didn't stack up. Too plain. Too stubby-nosed. Too thin around the middle. She looked like the slightest nudge might snap her in two. My first instinct was to turn and walk away.

'My God, Benny,' I said. 'Not her.'

He folded his arms and scuffed the cement floor with his boot. 'Well, mate, it's not like there's a whole lot of choice.'

156

'But fancy trying to fly this to Australia,' I said. 'She'd never last half the journey.'

'Well, okay,' he said. 'But you're going to have to tell Mr Mountain Man over there.'

My God, Rex Pierson was huge. I could see him deep in conversation with Ross on the other side of the fuselage, and he had to be nearly seven foot. His thumbnails were the size of pennies and he had a voice like a foghorn. Pierson was the chief designer of Vickers Aviation and had just been awarded an MBE for his service to Britain during the war. He was also our ticket to Australia.

I forced myself to look again at the Vickers Vimy biplane.

She was apparently the most advanced bomber in the world. So maybe it was just the time and place. It was Sunday afternoon and we were alone in a vast industrial shed the size of an English football pitch, with raked ceilings made of iron and glass soaring 30 ft overhead. Shoved into a corner was our aircraft, looking forlorn and forgotten. In fact the whole place seemed redundant, with only a few other aircraft bodies in varying stages of construction.

The Vickers Vimy came too late for war. She'd been designed as a heavy bomber, for either anti-submarine duties or for night-bombing raids on German cities in retaliation for the bombs that killed 1,500 Brits on home soil. But the Armistice was signed as she was coming off the production line, and contracts had dwindled from a thousand planes to just a hundred. Then three months earlier, Alcock and Brown flew a Vimy into the record books across the Atlantic, and suddenly everyone had heard of them. Even so, I wasn't convinced.

157

I ran my hand across her under-wing, feeling the knots of the threads holding in place the linen, which was coated in a plasticised lacquer, or dope, that hardened over the fabric.

'She's not pretty, is she,' Benny said quietly.

'Nope,' I said, shaking my head and hoping our voices weren't carrying to Mr Pierson and Ross.

The Vimy had none of the dashing good looks of our old Handley Page. Her fuselage was a crate 40-ft long, tapering from her strange pulpit-like nose to her twin-winged tail. There were three open cockpits: one in the nose where a gunner would have stood; a second directly behind for the pilot; and a third about 12 ft further again where midsection guns were once mounted. Both the over-wing and under-wing were 68 ft, much less impressive than the 100 ft wingspan of the Handley Page. The only thing going for her were the twin Rolls-Royce Eagle VIII engines, supported by thick vertical struts either side of the pilot's cockpit. Each was fitted with a 10 ft, four-blade wooden propeller.

'She looks like a bathtub with wings,' Benny said.

'More like a casket,' I muttered.

We stood for a while, hands on hips. 'Okay,' I said finally, taking a deep breath. 'No point worrying about things we can't change. How can we modify this bus so it doesn't kill us?'

Four hours later we had pages and pages of scribbles. By then Ross was sitting in Mr Pierson's office at the back of the shed, discussing logistics for the race.

'So what do you think, men?' he asked, rubbing his hands together. He looked ready to jump in the cockpit and leave today. 'Isn't she a beauty?'

Benny's eyes widened. 'Um, we've got a few minor

158

modifications, Ross. Can we have a quiet word?'

Mr Pierson waved us into empty seats. 'Please take your time, gentlemen,' he said, as he shut the door on his way out.

Without saying a word, I handed Ross my notepad. He read the first page and stopped. 'You want to strip the entire plane back to its frame?' he said. 'The wings and the tail fuselage — stripped right back?'

'Yes, sorry,' I said, glancing at Benny. 'And we want to replace all the tacks with screws.'

Ross pointed the notebook angrily at me. 'The Vimy is a new, superior aircraft — and you want me to tell Rex Pierson to start again? This is absurd.'

'Ross,' Benny said, 'she's been designed to make a few flights to Germany and then come home for an overhaul. We need to get her into the air every day for 30 days. And in some places she'll be lucky to get an oil change.'

'All the vibration, all those changes in temperature,' I said. 'She won't make it.'

Ross tossed the notepad onto the desk and sat fuming.

'Okay,' he said at last. 'There's no point going through the rest of that list until we ask Rex if he'll strip his machine for us. And whether he can get it done before bloody Poulet's eating Christmas dinner with the prime minister in Melbourne.' He ran a hand through his hair before snatching up the notebook. 'Wait here.'

Benny pulled a face like a guilty kid, and I waved him to stop in case we started laughing. I looked around the office. Aircraft manuals were arranged in bookcases and a blueprint was spread over a drawing table. The desk was almost empty except for pad of paper, a pen, four pencils and a maidenhair fern.

'Right gentlemen,' Mr Pierson boomed as he returned to the room. 'Ross tells me you'd like the Vimy stripped.'

I coughed. 'Would that be possible, Mr Pierson?'

'Call me Rex,' he said. 'My father's Mr Pierson. He's a rector up in Norfolk, and a rector I most certainly am not. We can strip the plane. It's a fine idea, given the journey you're about to undertake. How many women do you want?'

Benny frowned. 'Women?'

'Men still do the specialist mechanical work, of course, but we had 25 girls dedicated to the build of each and every machine,' Rex said. He looked at our blank faces. 'Shortage of men during the war! You can have as many girls as you'd like.'

Benny looked at me and raised an eyebrow. 'Will 25 women do you, Wal?'

★ ★ ★

It was seven o'clock in the morning, right on dawn, crisp and clear. We were running laps of the Brooklands motor-racing circuit, and I could see Ross out in front on the wide cement track. He was always out in front.

Hundreds of starlings were singing in huge pines down one side of the circuit. Their whistles and trills made me feel I could take on the world. I couldn't wait to tell my brother Jack I'd tested the circuit at Brooklands. He'd laugh that I'd done it on two legs instead of on four wheels. I could almost hear him: 'Trust you to do things arse-about!'

As young blokes, we'd read about motoring and aviation records being broken at Brooklands. The

160

circuit had opened in 1907 to test British cars at a time when the French were winning all the laurels. Aviation and motor manufacturing companies had sprung up around the track, and one of those companies was Vickers. The huge Vickers Sheds with their rolling doors opened right onto the famous Railway Straight.

Then 1914 came along and all manufacturing at Brooklands was requisitioned by the war office. By the end of 1918, the race track, 100-ft wide with huge banked turns, was in a sorry state after being used as a thoroughfare for heavy defence vehicles.

Car racing was due to start again in early 1920, and labourers were busy with repairs. Part of me was sorry we were going to miss it.

'Come on, men!' Ross called over his shoulder as we started our second lap of the circuit. 'Bennett, pick it up! I can hear you wheezing from here!'

Benny clutched his sides and tried to curse, but couldn't find the breath.

I quickened my pace and turned to run backwards beside him. He scowled: 'Bugger – off.'

Turns out Benny hated exercise. Loathed it. Cursed it. Cursed everyone in sight, too.

I smiled and turned back around, settling into my old rhythm – breathe in for two strides, breathe out for two strides. I relaxed my shoulders and kept my stomach firm and slightly pushed out, like I was being pulled forward by a rope tied around my middle. I'd done a lot of running with the Barrier Boys in Broken Hill, but it had been years since I'd really stretched out my legs for more than 100 yards. Felt good to be blowing out the cobwebs. I promised myself I'd run up the 30-ft sloping banks when I got a bit fitter.

Today, I just needed to finish.

Ross was 40 yards ahead, and the sight of him heading into that huge banking turn on the white cement track was so remarkable I almost stopped to watch. I pumped my arms like pistons. An image of Fred Alford popped into my head. Damn! I needed to respond to that letter. I wondered if his arm was any better, or if he'd had any luck finding work. I hoped Mrs Alford was alright. Every time I sat down to write, I'd just stare at the page before screwing up the paper. Responding made it real. If it was real I had to deal with it. So I ignored it, just like we'd been trained to do in the war. We all saw what happened to blokes who felt too much, too often. The poor fellas went mad. I'd blocked out Helena just like that, because I didn't want to go where the hurt would take me.

The Vickers Sheds loomed up on my right. Ross was already doing sit-ups beside the track.

'Well done,' he said as I pulled up and doubled over to catch my breath. 'I reckon it'd pay for us all to give up the cigarettes for a bit, but I got too cranky last time I tried.'

'Speaking of terrible moods,' I said, turning to watch Benny coming down the track. His army shorts were hanging off his hips, his undershirt had holes in the seams under the armpits, his red face was twisted like an old shoe.

'Ha!' said Ross. 'Leave him to me.'

Benny flopped onto the grass, spitting up phlegm. 'These bastard boots …'

'Yes,' said Ross, springing upright. 'I'll see if we can't come up with something a little lighter on the foot.' He sprang upright. 'Right lads, fifty push-ups!'

Benny groaned.

162

'Make that 60 push-ups. Followed by 60 sit-ups and 60 star jumps.'

'Right-o,' I said, dropping to the ground and counting out loud to needle Benny.

'From tomorrow we'll be doing 80 of each,' Ross announced. 'We won't get through this air race if we're not fit.'

Ross was right. We'd seen the strain on his body during the flight to India. Piloting the Handley Page was a Herculean task. To keep the plane level, he was constantly pulling against wires and cables to move the rudders and ailerons. Some days his neck and shoulders were so cramped he could barely get himself out of the cockpit.

The 11,000-mile race to Australia would be even more gruelling. For our part, Benny and I would be doing engine maintenance and repairs overnight, most likely without the help of decent equipment to lift machinery in some of the more remote landing spots. We needed to be fit.

After push-ups, I was about to start my sit-ups when I noticed four women coming around the side of the Vickers Sheds. They were dressed in white shirts and black knee-length skirts over woollen stockings. I recognised them, too – one of them had been showing Benny a quick way to strip the Vimy fuselage yesterday.

'Hey, Benny,' I said under my breath.

'What?' he grunted, his face like thunder. His push-ups were pitiful.

I nodded toward the women, who'd started doing stretches. 'Over there …'

'Jesus, it's Joan,' he muttered, straightening his back.

Ross had started his star jumps, oblivious to the women. 'First thing this morning we'll talk to Rex about extra fuel capacity,' he said. 'Wal, what do you think about some kind of compensator between the front and back fuel tanks?'

'That would make sense,' I said. The women were doing torso twists — I heard a couple of them giggle and wished I hadn't stripped down to my singlet. My shorts felt like big old bloomers. I'd lost a bit of weight, and nothing looks more pathetic than a small bloke in oversized clothes.

'I want to keep the fuel more evenly distributed along the length of the aircraft,' Ross continued. 'That way I won't have to wrestle with her so much in the air.'

'How about we rig up a system that automatically pumps the fuel between tanks as they empty?' I said. 'That'll keep the levels consistent and the plane won't end up too nose-heavy.'

Benny made reasonable work of his sit-ups. He must have caught the eye of one of the girls as he stood to do his star jumps, because he called out 'Morning!' in a cheerful voice.

'Morning!' they called back. Their voices rang out through the autumn air of Brooklands. Sounded lovely.

Yesterday, we had 25 of them staring at us. The Vimy had been moved into the centre of the main construction shed and the male and female workers had been told to gather around. The women certainly looked like a workforce in their matching brown work coats and bonnets, and it was the first time I'd seen women wearing trousers. I guessed most of them were in their 20s, and unmarried. They lived in the Vickers

164

boarding hostel up behind the sheds.

Once, there'd been hundreds of women rostered to keep the production lines running 24 hours a day, seven days a week. But redundancies had cut their number to the bone. The hostel was largely empty now — home only to a skeleton crew and, as of a few days earlier, us three blokes.

Rex Pierson had asked for quiet before introducing Ross as an Australian war hero and Benny and me as mechanical geniuses. I'd stared at my boots most of the time. Then Ross made a little speech, his voice echoing in the great empty space, and the women looked at him like he was a movie star. He said it was a great honour to work with the company that had built the very aircraft that had crossed the Atlantic only three months earlier. He said the Vimy's days of record-breaking were not over, and they all cheered when he said we'd take a photo of a kangaroo beside the Vimy in Australia. Then the woman in charge, Miss Dickson, walked over to introduce her team leaders. She was taller than me. Had broader shoulders, too.

'Done,' I said, finishing my last star jump. It felt good that I'd beaten Benny.

'Breakfast!' said Ross. He led the way toward the hostel, mumbling about needing better maps so he could confirm flying distances and fuel requirements.

The women were jogging slowly on the spot, their black skirts lifting and falling, lifting and falling.

'I'll be with you in a sec,' Benny called after us, tightening his belt and rolling his shoulders. 'Might just do some final stretches.'

They knew their stuff, those Vickers women. So did the men concentrating on the inner workings — fitting the Rolls-Royce engines, the fuel and oil lines, the instruments and gauges.

The company had come a long way since the first Vickers aircraft, an airship 512-ft long that broke its back on the inaugural flight. It was a story you couldn't forget: dubious workers had christened the poor airship the Mayfly, because they thought it may fly, but it may not. An Admiralty inquiry later ruled the whole thing had been the work of a lunatic. I was glad things had changed since 1911.

The job of stripping back the Vimy took us days, and it was incredible to watch the frame being revealed as the fabric was peeled away. Made you realise this flying caper really was a miracle. Some of the frame was steel, but most of it was lightweight tubing rolled from sheets of spruce. Miss Dickson said the spruce wood was native to a tiny strip of land on the Pacific coast of America.

It was different working with women, more calm and happy, somehow. I liked the constant buzz they made, quietly talking as they bent over their work.

Once the Vimy had been stripped, the girls got to work re-covering the plane in Irish linen. They sewed together long strips of linen on machines, then affixed the fabric to the aircraft with thousands of tiny knots of waxed cord. Then they shrank the fabric over the frame with nitrate dope.

More than half a dozen thick coats of dope were applied to make the fabric weatherproof and protect it from sunlight.

The dope fumes were awful. Miss Dickson made the girls drink lemonade at regular intervals, as a tonic I suppose. Often, me and Benny went outside when it got too bad. It was the only place we could smoke because the dope was so flammable. More and more,

Joan seemed to be out there, too.

Joan was from Elephant and Castle, south of the Thames. Nice girl, tall, with green eyes and red hair trimmed into one of those new shorter styles. She and Benny really got on. She'd said: 'D'ya really see kanga-rews in the streets of Melbourne, Benny?' and he'd say, 'Jeez, Joan, your Souf London accent's a larf. Say 'kangaroo' again.' Then she'd say his accent was funnier, and round and round they'd go. She laughed every time Benny opened his mouth, so of course he did it often. Wasn't long before he was smitten, and I was happy for them both.

Jack Alcock was testing the new amphibious Vickers Viking by that stage, and he often stopped by to offer advice. He was Sir John Alcock now, thanks to his record-breaking flight, but we just called him Jack. He was quiet and unassuming, nothing like you'd expect, and he got on like a house on fire with Ross. You could hear a pin drop whenever he was in the shed. Eyes followed him everywhere.

While the women were re-applying the fabric, we were doing things like adding extra fuel tanks inside the fuselage. The fuel pumping system we created worked a treat. We also split the rudder cables into sections, so if a cable frayed on the way to Australia we wouldn't have to replace the entire 30 ft.

It was clever the way Vickers had instrument gauges installed onto the sides of the engine cowlings. That way, we could all sit in our cockpits and monitor the engines — water temperature, oil pressure and revs per minute. Benny chose to be responsible for the port-side engine — that's the left side, facing forward. I had to look after the starboard engine.

They were good times. Exciting times. We lived and

breathed that plane. Even slept right beneath her, some nights, when we worked so late it was almost morning again. And slowly it felt like she was becoming one of us. A British bomber with an Australian heart.

Then came the 14th of October, 1919.

It was the day Etienne Poulet departed Paris bound for Australia and we were left reading about his courage and his sacrifice and his plans to fly the route Ross had mapped out with Biffy.

We were working on the Vimy's rudder when Rex Pierson came in waving the telephone message from Biffy: Poulet planned to be in Australia in 25 days.

I looked around at all the bits of our machine lying on the cement floor. We were weeks from being ready, and that's if everything went to plan. Ross was as frustrated as the rest of us, but he was too good a leader to say anything that lowered morale.

'Etienne Poulet might have a head start,' he called out, hushing the whispers and the cursing, 'but he doesn't have a twin-engine, British-built Vimy!'

Jack Alcock said he heard the cheer on the other side of Brooklands.

* * *

Be kind. That's the only advice Mum ever gave us boys about women. One rule. Two words. She said if we couldn't get that right, no other advice would help.

When Shirley Hopkins walked down the path, all shiny lipstick and soft curves under her grey coat, I quickly jumped out to open the car door.

'Whoa. Easy fella,' said Benny from behind the wheel. Joan giggled and thumped his arm.

It was Sunday and Ross had given us the afternoon off. Benny had wangled a car from the Vickers garage and talked me into spending the afternoon with him and Joan and her best friend, Shirley Hopkins. The two girls had worked together at Vickers until the lay-offs after the war. Joan said Shirley simply adored Australian servicemen, and was dying to meet me.

Shirley and I settled into the back seat, while Benny asked Joan for directions to the river.

'Next right,' said Joan, 'then a left.'

'Say 'roight' again,' said Benny, teasing her as he changed gears.

'Benny!' she said, hitting his knee. 'I can't keep saying 'right' or we'll go the wrong bloody way!' Her laugh was deep and throaty. It gave me a little pang in my chest, like I was a kid again, longing for something.

I leaned back in my seat to smooth my hair without being obvious. Shirley was studying the pink polish on her nails, stretching out her fingers in her lap. The backs of her hands looked red and sore.

Joan and Shirley started chatting about people they knew at Vickers. I looked out the window, listening as their strange accents filled the car.

We passed some kids standing around a busted wooden billy cart. One of them was screaming his head off, clutching a bloodied knee while his mum knelt beside him, licking a handkerchief and dabbing at his leg.

'So Shirley ...' I said, taking a deep breath to stop the wobble in my voice, 'what do you do in Weybridge?'

'What do I do?' she asked, staring out the window and tucking her hair behind her ear. It was blonde and wavy, cut into the same short style as Joan's. 'You

169

mean, what do I do since I was laid off by Vickers after 'elpin' Britain to win the war?'

'Shirley, don't start,' said Joan. 'Wal's just makin' conversation.'

I blushed beetroot red.

'Sorry, Wal, it's been a long day,' said Shirley, turning to look at me. She had the same south London accent as Joan. When she said 'Wal', the L sounded like another W. 'I'm a housemaid at the Lincoln Arms — makin' the beds, cleanin' behind the bar an' all that.' She was in her early 20s but her smile made her look older. 'At Vickers I had me own team of doping girls. I did, you know. BE2s were my favourites.'

I nodded and tried to offer an encouraging smile. 'The BE2 was a ripping little plane,' I lied. The BE2 was a dog. Fokker fodder. 'Reliable workhorse, eh Benny?'

Benny grinned in the front seat. I felt my face starting to go hot again, so I shut my mouth and looked out the window.

We were near the river now. A fours team was gliding over the water, their oars in perfect time. I pictured the Murrumbidgee, the brown water swirling and swollen after winter, the gums all ghostly grey across the way, knotted and gnarled and alive with bossy galahs. Helena's small white hand drawing circles in the river sand.

'Pull up over there, Benny,' said Joan, 'and we'll lay the blanket on the bank — near that gap in the weepin' willows.'

Benny had brought a few long-neck beers, and the girls got all giggly making sure no one was around before they had a swig. I was a bit shocked when they did it. I couldn't see Helena drinking from a bottle

170

in a million years. But it was fun, sitting there in the soft autumn sunshine, leaves on the ground, passing around the bottle and sharing cigarettes. It was the first time I got a real sense of what life might be like when me and Benny put the war behind us.

Shirley laughed at a couple of things I said. Touched my leg once when she spoke to me. It felt good.

Two mallards waddled toward the water, pecking the grassy bank as they went. 'Hey, boys,' said Joan. 'Wot's the name of that funny animal you've got in Australia? Bit like an otter, with a face like a duck?'

'I reckon you mean a platypus,' I said.

'That's it!' said Joan. 'Plat-eee-pus. I studied them at school.'

'Awww, say that again for me,' said Benny.

'Plat — eee — pus!' said Joan, leaning over and kissing him on the lips three times as she said it.

'Have you ever seen a plat-eee-pus, Wal?' asked Shirley.

'No, I've never seen one,' I said, shifting slightly on the blanket. Benny was whispering into Joan's ear. 'I'd like to see one though. They're supposed to be very shy.'

I took a swig of beer, watching the mallards drifting downstream.

'Right-o,' said Benny, flicking away a cigarette and rising to his feet. 'Me and Joan might go for a little stroll.'

'No worries,' I said.

'Have fun,' said Shirley.

We watched them walk off, arm in arm, Joan's head resting on his shoulder. Benny had left me the final beer and I opened it before offering Shirley the first swig.

171

Neither of us spoke for a while. A man and woman walked by on the opposite bank, his arm draped around her shoulders. Their voices carried across the water to us, where we sat among our willows. In the distance, I heard a car door open and shut.

'What's it like to fly a plane, then, Wal?' Shirley asked, handing me the bottle. When she wiped her lips I noticed her nail polish was chipped.

I thought for a moment. 'No one's ever asked me that. It can get very cold, and you'd think it would be quiet but it's really noisy. Not just the engine, but the wind racing past the struts and wires.'

'No, silly,' she said, drawing on her cigarette. 'What does it feel like?'

'Oh,' I said. 'I don't reckon I can describe it. Everything just seems small.' A ladybird landed on my trousers. I laid my hand flat and let it walk onto my palm. 'It does make you feel different. More peaceful maybe. Like your troubles are far away.'

She touched my arm, offering to share her cigarette. The ladybird opened its wings and flew off. 'You got a sweetheart back home, Wal?'

I felt my chest tighten when she said it. 'Not sure,' I said, taking the cigarette. 'I did have.'

'What happened?'

I took a drag and exhaled slowly, thinking about that parcel from Fred. 'She was expecting me home after the war, but I flew to India instead.' I flicked some ash onto the grass. 'I reckon she got sick of waiting.'

'Gor, Wal. I'm sorry. What's 'er name?'

'Helena.' I coughed and tried to remember when I'd last said it. 'Can't blame her, I s'pose. After all those years.'

Shirley was quiet for a moment. 'My sister had a feller over in France. Johnnie. We all loved 'im. Three years she carried a torch, and he went and got killed at Cambrai just before it all ended.'

She laughed and said, 'Silly sod,' but her eyes were welling up. 'We're not sure our Norma will find herself anyone to marry now.'

I handed her my handkerchief. 'Thanks, Wal,' she said, wiping her nose and dabbing her eyes. 'Norma said later that all the nights of waitin' and worryin', never knowing if Johnnie was alive, were almost as bad as hearing he'd died.' She sighed. 'Maybe your Helena just didn't have any more nights left in 'er.'

She leaned across me to take back the cigarette, smelling of perfume and face powder and malt from the beer.

I thought about Helena on Bondi Beach, sitting close, my hand on her back. The promises we'd made that day. That night. Mum would be ashamed of me. I hadn't been kind.

'Cheer up, Sonny Jim,' Shirley said, gently knocking my shoulder. 'Do you think it would 'elp if you kissed me?'

'I don't know.' The water was turning dark in the late afternoon. 'Maybe.'

'Okay, then,' she said. 'I'll make you a deal, Wal. I'll let you kiss me, if you take me up for a flight before you leave.'

'I'll try!' I laughed, brushing her leg as I took the cigarette. 'But I'm not a pilot. I'm a mechanic.'

'Oh,' she said, stiffening ever so slightly. 'Oh, I thought … Joan said …'

'Did she say I was a pilot? That's funny.'

'Yeah, funny,' she said. But I noticed her pull away.

I took a long drag of the cigarette then flicked it away, hoping she hadn't seen the engine oil stained into my hands. I stood up, looked for a stick and threw it in the river, watching for ages as it disappeared downstream. Helena had been so proud of me when I joined the Flying Corps, back when I was just a driver. I picked up another stick and hurled it as far as it would go.

I shot a look at Shirley. She was looking at her hands, scratching the red skin.

'I'm sorry, Shirley,' I said.

She smiled and sighed. 'Don't be silly. I'm the sorry one. I'm just tired of being me.'

I sat back down beside her, took a swig of the beer that was too flat now. Shirley reached out and touched my cheek, and for a second I thought she might kiss me after all. 'Go 'ome, sweet Wal,' she said. 'Go 'ome and get your girl.'

Chapter 14

I got crook not long after that day by the river. Woke up all snotty and sneezy and straight away Miss Dickson banished me to bed with an extra blanket and a gargling solution of salt and potash. Tasted like salty soap and it made me gag, but I figured anything that awful had to be good for me. I protested that I was okay, but Miss Dickson was being protective of her girls. The Spanish flu outbreak was over, but it had killed more than 200,000 Brits since the end of the war. Everyone seemed to know someone who'd died. Laura Borton had told me at Cheveney how she'd heard of four women playing bridge one night, and in the morning three of them were dead.

As I walked back to my room from the hostel dining hall, feeling lousy and sorry for myself, I muttered a song I'd heard often since arriving from India.

I had a little bird,
It's name was Enza.
I opened the window,
And in-flu-enza.

It was one of those kids' rhymes that sticks in your head, and I was still humming it to myself two days later when I was back at work with Benny. One of the Vimy radiators hadn't been running too flash, so we were replacing it with a spare that'd been taken out of Jack Alcock's Vimy before the aircraft was put on show at the Science Museum in London.

We had the radiator set up on a bench beside the Vimy and were running final tests when Ross walked up and said, 'Men, I've got someone I'd like you to meet.'

Beside him was a lieutenant in a RAF uniform. He was almost exactly the same height and frame as Ross with the same thin face, but with distinctly dark features instead of Ross's green eyes and sandy hair.

'Lieutenant Keith Smith, meet Sergeants Jim Bennett and Wally Shiers. Lads, Keith's my brother. He's going to navigate our way home.'

Benny was pleased as punch; started pumping Keith's arm like it was a petrol bowser. 'Pleasure to meet you, finally,' he said. 'Call me Benny. This here's Wal.'

I stood there wiping my hands with a rag, hoping Benny's enthusiasm hid my own disappointment. 'Nice to meet you Keith,' I said. 'Excuse me for not shaking your hand. Had a nasty cold.'

Keith fixed his black eyes on me. Didn't say a word.

'We're being extra cautious,' Ross interjected, 'in case the Spanish Lady's taken a liking to him.'

Keith was still looking at me. Felt like he was staring at my insides and didn't like what he saw. 'You sure you're well enough for this flight?'

It sounded more like an accusation than a question, and I was so taken aback I coughed.

'Wal's good as gold,' said Benny, whacking my back. 'Dr Bennett's prescribed more whisky.'

'Hmmm,' said Keith. Then he turned and surveyed the girls working on the Vimy. 'I hope these women know what they're doing, Ross?' he said loudly. Rudely. 'How many stitches per inch on the linen?'

I glanced at Miss Dickson, working nearby. Her

neck was flushed. I could hear the dope suddenly getting slapped on a little harder, a little more quickly.

'The women know exactly what they're doing, Keith,' Ross said. 'But I wouldn't have a clue. Let me introduce you to the wonderful Miss Dickson before you cause a walkout.'

As he strolled off to do the introductions, Ross called over his shoulder to me and Benny. 'You'll get used to him fellas,' he said. 'He's the blunt one.'

Keith didn't bat an eye. You could tell he'd been hearing it all his life.

Later on, me and Benny were outside having a smoke with Joan.

'It's not right,' I said, tapping angrily at my cigarette to drop its ash. 'Should be Pard.'

'Bit difficult when Pard's already back in Western Australia, Wal,' said Benny.

'Who's Pard?' asked Joan.

Pard was Ernest Mustard, Ross's observer with No. 1 Squadron and the handiest man I'd ever met. We used to joke that you could give Pard three inches of copper wire, a couple of terminals and a pocket knife, and he'd knock up a wireless set. He was the best observer over the Eastern Front, too. The brass hats couldn't wait to get their hands on his recco reports or photographs — they'd send someone sprinting whenever he landed. Anyone who'd witnessed the Smith-Mustard combination knew it couldn't be bettered.

Even by Smith-Smith.

'I hear what you're saying, Wal,' said Benny. 'But Pard didn't want to come to London and that's that. Besides, Ross wouldn't have asked Keith if he wasn't up to the job.'

177

I took a drag of my cigarette as we huddled together under an alcove, out of the misty rain. My head was throbbing. 'We don't know anything about Keith.'

'I know that he and Ross are close. So be careful what you say,' said Benny.

'Did he even fight?' I asked.

'He tried to enlist a couple of times in Australia but was knocked back on medical grounds. Varicose veins, I think. He had an operation and then paid his own way to England to sign up with the Royal Flying Corps. Instructing, for the most part.'

'So he didn't see active service?'

Benny rolled his eyes. 'Jesus Wal, give the bloke a go. Our war was hardly hand-to-hand combat with the Hun.'

I rubbed my temples, feeling guilty now. 'Maybe I just got off on the wrong foot.' I'd read that at one stage during the war, young pilots arriving at the Front were only expected to last two weeks. The death rate for instructors was even worse.

'This'll cheer you up, Wal,' said Benny, stubbing out his cigarette underfoot. 'Keith sailed from Australia to Britain on the RMS *Medina* and she was torpedoed by a German U-boat off the coast of Devon. Sank like a stone and rumour has it a whole heap of Indian treasures went down with her. Passengers escaped into lifeboats with nothing but the clothes on their backs.'

'And that's good news because …?'

'Well, Ross reckons Keith's got nine lives,' Benny said, turning to pull the door open for Joan. 'So I figure we'll all survive the flight to Australia so long as he's in the plane.'

On the walk back through the huge shed to the

Vimy, we passed a disused office where Ross had temporarily set up Race HQ. Large maps were strewn across a desk and drawing table. I could hear Ross and Keith talking inside, so I paused for the slightest moment. 'You know, Ross,' said Keith, 'I worked with some damned fine Australian air mechanics up in Yorkshire ...'

At the sound of our footsteps, Keith turned sharply and locked his black eyes on me, before taking a step forward and closing the door without speaking.

My heart was galloping. I looked at Benny and he shrugged his shoulders.

'Did you hear that?' I said when we were back by the radiator. Way above us, rain began to tap against the glass ceiling.

'Mate,' Benny said. 'It's nothing. Let's just get on with this.'

'But surely Ross wouldn't ...'

'Wal!'

Wasn't even half an hour later when Ross walked over and said he and Keith were leaving to catch the 4 pm train to London and wouldn't be back until the following evening.

'Anything we can help you with, Ross?' asked Benny, rubbing his brow with the back of his hand.

'Just dull stuff, Benny. Keith wants to introduce me to a couple of blokes.'

Benny nodded, frowning. 'Any word on Poulet?'

'Nothing, which makes me think he hasn't landed near any RAF bases yet, or we'd have received a wire.'

I cleared my throat. 'Jack Alcock's radiator is ticking over nicely, Ross.' At the back of the shed, Keith was in deep conversation with Rex Pierson. 'The old bus is starting to take shape.'

179

'Excellent lads!' Ross was already turning away. 'See you tomorrow.'

We watched as he returned to Keith and slapped him on the back as they stood chatting and laughing with Rex Pierson. The rain was pelting down now. It was almost as dark as night in the shed.

I started coughing and Benny said, 'Aw Jesus, Wal, you gotta stop coughing over everyone.'

Ross and Keith disappeared out a side door. I coughed again. 'Just go!' Benny said angrily, throwing a hand in the air. A few women looked up. 'Go back to bed, Wal. And drink that bloody whisky I got you.'

I trudged back to my room in the drizzling rain; my little song making me miserable.

> *I had a little bird,*
> *It's name was Enza.*
> *I opened the window,*
> *And in-flu-enza.*

I woke the next morning in my Vickers hostel room, feeling better than I had in days.

'Good to see you, old mate,' Benny said, jumping up from the breakfast table when he saw me enter the dining room. There were dark rings under his eyes. 'Sit down and I'll get you some gruel and a cuppa.'

Neither of us mentioned Ross or Keith. Back in the shed, we helped the blokes finish assembling the new fuel tanks inside the fuselage, and then kept ourselves busy weighing the spare parts we'd need for the engines. Jack Alcock's Vimy had weighed seven tons fully loaded, but Ross wanted to get our machine down to six and a half tons. One of the workers remarked that our Vimy was nothing but a flying fuel

180

container, on account of the petrol tanks stretching down the fuselage. 'Mark my words,' he said, 'if you blokes crash land, we'll hear it from here.'

Late in the afternoon Miss Dickson tapped Benny on the shoulder and said Ross had asked to see us both in his office.

That shed had never felt bigger. With every step my legs felt heavier.

I heard laughter as we got closer to the office. Benny was just ahead of me and when he reached the open door he said, 'What the heck?'

Ross was standing in the middle of the office dressed head to toe in new khaki flying overalls, a leather cap and fur-lined goggles. Keith was wearing a leather flying cap, too.

'Look at these, lads!' said Ross, his eyes staring out from his goggles. 'Sidcot flying suits! Keith worked up in Yorkshire with some blokes who know Sid Cotton. Yours are there on the desk.'

Sidney Cotton was an Australian bloke who flew with the Royal Naval Air Service during the war, before the British naval and army flying services were merged into the Royal Air Force. He invented an airtight cotton suit to fit over his uniform and keep himself warm in the freezing skies over Europe, with layers of fur and silk stitched in under heavy cotton. It was Hun sport to take out a British pilot and capture his Sidcot suit. The Red Baron had the design copied.

'Strewth, my own lucky leather flying cap,' said Benny, running his fingers over the leather. 'I've been wanting one of these since Point Cook.'

'Thank you very much, Keith,' I said. The fur collar was softer than a camel calf I'd patted at the base of the pyramids.

'Don't thank me,' Keith said without a hint of humour. 'Ross sealed the deal. He's the one with the charm.'

Ross peeled off his overalls. 'I'm buying us all dinner at the Hand & Spear and you two can fill Keith in on the Vimy. He doesn't trust a word I say about anything mechanical.'

It was still raining outside and the pub smelled of damp wool and steak-and-kidney pie and crackling pine on the open fire. There were low ceilings with thick beams and you could see where people had reached up and run their hands across the smooth, shiny wood over the years — perhaps centuries. We found a table out of the way and Ross went to buy the pints. Benny and I were just settling into our chairs, watching a plump, smiley waitress delivering steaming plates of pie and mash to other tables, when Keith pulled out a notebook and pen. He drilled us on what changes we'd made to the Vimy, what spares we were taking and what we were planning to do if this or that went wrong. Each time we spoke there was a pause while he finished noting the answer. We'd sit there, in awkward silence, looking across at Ross talking to locals with our beers sat beside him on the bar.

'Whose idea was it to strip the plane right back?' Keith said, putting down his pen. 'It's cost my brother a lot of time.'

Benny hesitated. 'Um. It was both of us — we thought ...'

'It was mine,' I said, holding Keith's gaze.

He leaned back in his seat and looked around the room. 'Well, it was the right decision,' he said. 'Quite a nice pub, isn't it?'

Benny stretched his arms and exhaled loudly. Felt

like we'd been through a school examination.

Ross finally returned, and I took a long sip of beer.

'Gee, Keith, you've got even more like Dad,' said Ross, nodding at the open notebook. 'His station records were more thorough than the Holy Bible.'

'Yes, they were,' Keith said. 'Wool clip. Sheep numbers per paddock. Total income. Expenses, capital and running. Miles of fencing. Miles of water pipe laid.'

'Wonder how old Perseverance is faring,' said Ross. He looked across to me and Benny. 'Dad's favourite dam — took him ten years to build.' He sipped his beer, deep in thought. 'Remember that flying fox we rigged up in the gum out the back of the shearing shed? Can't believe Colin didn't kill himself on it.' He let out a funny noise, sort of half laugh, half sob, and reached across to briefly squeeze Keith's shoulder. 'Be good to get home, eh?'

Keith closed his notebook and ran a hand over the black leather cover. 'Yes, it will,' he said. Then he turned back to Benny. 'Tell me more about the fuel system – I gather it's gravity-fed from the upper wing?'

In fairness, he understood the workings of an engine far better than Ross. It was clear he was going to be an asset to me and Benny, another practical mind to work through any problems.

'Which one of you is oldest?' asked Benny.

'Keith is,' said Ross. 'By two years.'

I tried not to look surprised.

'Ah,' said Benny.

'Keith's got classic Celtic features,' said Ross. 'Makes him look younger.'

'Ross has the gift of the gab,' said Keith. 'Makes him sound older.'

'Ha!' said Benny. 'I reckon you've both said that

before.'

'Once or twice,' said Keith.

The waitress arrived with our dinner: huge plates of crusty pie, creamy mash and green veg. For the first time in days I was starving.

'Hey, Keith,' Ross said, picking up his knife and fork. 'Been meaning to tell you, Wal's girl back home worked on the conscription campaign.'

Keith looked skeptical. 'Which one?'

'Both,' I said, reluctantly lowering my cutlery. 'She was on the conscription committee in Narrandera in 1916 and 1917.

New South Wales voted 'No' both times, unfortunately. I couldn't believe that.'

'It was worse in South Australia,' said Ross. 'We had the highest 'No' vote of any state. Lousy lot.'

'Your girl must be a courageous woman,' said Keith. 'The two votes were highly acrimonious back home. Communities turned on themselves. Rallies were often violent. I trust she was never injured?'

'Nothing like that,' I said. My cheeks were burning. She never told me she'd been caught up in any violence, and I never asked. I pictured the darkened streets of Narrandera at night, Helena walking home alone from an angry meeting in East Street with no one there to protect her. She must have been scared sometimes. I forked some hot pie into my mouth. It scorched my throat as I swallowed it down.

'Keith helped with the campaign here in England,' said Ross to Benny.

'Only the second vote in '17,' said Keith.

Ross rapped the table with the handle of his knife. 'Which should never have been needed. All those slackers who refused to do their duty. Humiliating!

The Kaiser must have been ...'

'Ross,' said Keith. 'We won the war, remember?' He took a sip of beer and leaned back in his seat. 'Most diggers over here voted 'Yes' in both plebiscites. The men thought it was only fair that others did their bit to fill the spaces left by the dead and wounded. That said, there were plenty who didn't want their mates to see the horrors they'd seen, or hear the screams they'd heard.' He forked some pie into his mouth. 'It was hard to argue with that.'

We ate in silence for a bit, and I wondered if there'd ever be a time when quiet moments weren't filled with the ghosts of dead brothers and fallen mates.

'I'm glad you're here, Buck,' said Ross.

Keith smiled briefly, revealing his bucky teeth. 'Me too, Froggy. The alternative's lousy.'

★ ★ ★

I stretched out as far as I could reach and manoeuvred my shears along the top of the hedge. Marmaduke and Banshee ran circles around the bottom of the stepladder and I was worried they'd knock it out from underneath me.

'Be gone, scoundrels!' the Colonel bellowed, before turning his ruddy face up toward me. 'What's this Smith brother like?'

I watched the dogs bound across the lawn, feeling the warmth of the Sunday sun on my face. It was nice to be back at Cheveney. Nice to have clear skies for a change. Nice to be invited, too. Ross had seen Biffy up in London and told him I'd been crook, and soon afterwards Mrs Borton had telephoned Vickers to say they were sending a car to collect me for a day of restorative soups and sunshine. When I volunteered to do some hedging, Mrs Borton protested but the Colonel nodded his head vigorously. 'That's the way, lad. Get the juices flowing.'

Keith Smith wasn't an easy man to describe. He wasn't easy to like, really, but maybe that's because I always compared him to Ross and he always came up short.

'Keith's good with maps,' I said finally, stepping down off the ladder to move it along a few feet. 'Benny says he's meticulous, too. It's a weight off Ross, knowing the navigation is sorted.' I made sure the legs were steady before climbing again. 'They've divided the route into four stages, with six or seven landing spots in each. London to Cairo. Cairo to Calcutta. Calcutta to Singapore. Singapore to Australia.'

The Colonel had his own set of shears and was clipping away brutally at the lower half of the hedge, with Mrs Borton following in his wake to clear up the mess. 'Good show,' he said. 'And how about that Poulet, eh? Down in Italy already, I hear.'

'I know,' I said. 'It's a worry. Ross says Matthews and Kay are likely to set off in the Sopwith Wallaby sometime this week too – maybe even tomorrow. We need to get a move on.'

The Colonel had stopped clipping and was filling his pipe with tobacco. 'Biffy says you take one short-cut with an aircraft engine and you pay twice later. Perhaps with your life. Steady as she goes, son.'

I found my balance at the top of the stepladder and began levelling the next section.

Over in the enormous kitchen gardens behind the hedge I saw a solitary magpie, with his round white belly, smart black waistcoat and long tail. Brit-

186

ish magpies looked so proper compared to our big, knockabout maggies back home.

'Mrs Borton,' I said, 'can you please tell me that magpie rhyme again?'

'Well,' she said. 'The one I grew up with was …

One for sorrow,
Two for joy,
Three for a girl,
Four for a boy.
Five for silver,
Six for gold,
Seven for a secret never to be told.

The Colonel looked up at me. 'How many can you see?'

'Just the one,' I said.

'Salute him, lad. Quickly now! Bad luck otherwise.'

I looked back into the kitchen gardens and saluted the bird, adding quietly 'G'day Banjo'.

As a kid I'd had a pet magpie called Banjo. My brother Jack reckoned there'd been too many mouths in the nest and Banjo had been kicked out before he could fly. He had the softest feathers. Used to curl up on my lap like a kitten, until his wings got strong and he flew away. Whenever I saw a magpie back home after that I thought it might be Banjo. And I couldn't hear a crow's caw without wishing it was a magpie's warble.

It didn't seem real that we were just going to start the Vimy's engines one day soon and fly away like Banjo did. Home to Australia. Rex Pierson had shown us a newspaper clipping from the New York Times that said Christopher Columbus didn't take one tenth of the risks the air pioneers would face on the race to Australia. It said we'd be throwing the dice at death. I didn't ever think about it like that, though. Not with Ross.

I pulled a piece of paper from my pocket and handed it down to the Colonel. 'I've been meaning to show you this, sir. Maybe you've heard it before?' I'd written the poem out with a view to reading it aloud, but was too embarrassed to have a go, now it came time to do it.

The Colonel held the page away from his face, trying to decipher my handwriting. 'What's this? Oh, my word.' He turned to wave Mrs Borton toward him. 'Laura, you'll want to hear this …'

'Ahh,' I said. 'There is a curse word in it, Mrs Borton.'

'Nothing I haven't heard before,' she said, tutting, as she moved in closer and bent to tickle the dogs behind the ear so they'd sit still beside her. I stepped down a couple of rungs to lean my elbows on the top of the stepladder, looking at them both below me.

The Colonel patted his chest, arranged his glasses and was about to begin when he looked up and said, 'What in blazes is an 'ack emma', Wal? I'll think we'll need to know.'

'Ah yes,' I said. 'During the war it was a signaller's timekeeping term for 'a.m.', so it also became slang for an 'air mechanic' like me.'

'Good Lord,' said the Colonel, returning his gaze to the piece of paper and clearing his throat.

The gallant young airman lay dying, and, as under the wreckage he lay,

With the ack emmas standing around him, these last parting words did he say:
Take the cylinders out of my kidneys, the connecting rods out of my brain;
From the small of my back take the crankshaft, and assemble the bastard again.

Laura clapped. 'Did you write that, Wally?' she asked.

'No,' I said, shocked she thought it was possible. 'One of the observers at No. 1 Squadron came up with it. I could never write anything as good as that.'

'Bah!' The Colonel said, tucking the piece of paper in his jacket pocket and striking a match to re-light his pipe. 'Anyone can write poetry. Words and application. That's all it takes.'

It was late afternoon when we finished the yew hedge and stood back to admire the job I'd started weeks ago on my first morning at Cheveney. The Colonel pointed to long shadows running across the lawn to the east and said I'd be following them soon on the flight home. 'Godspeed to you all,' he said, and I was touched by the pride in his voice.

Mrs Borton offered me my old room for the night but I was keen to get back to Brooklands ahead of Ross's training session in the morning. While I waited for Tom to bring around the car, she brought out a small package and asked me to give it to Ross. 'Open it,' she said, touching my arm.

'It's for all of you. For luck.'

'Marmaduke!' I said, when I saw his little face.

It was a perfect replica of a tiny mascot pilot that Biffy had installed on our Handley Page. We'd all felt his loss when the bomber was destroyed in India.

189

This little fella looked exactly the same: about six inches high, seated with his hands clutching the steering sticks, and a tiny two-blade propeller out front. His uniformed body and head were made of carved, painted wood, complete with flying cap and goggles.

'Marmaduke II,' Mrs Borton said, scratching the ears of Marmaduke the dog as she spoke. 'I thought we should have another one made for the Vickers Vimy to help guide you all home.'

'Better than those silly stuffed black cats Alcock and Brown took across the Atlantic,' the Colonel said.

'He's perfect,' I said, rubbing Marmaduke's flying cap with my thumb. 'Ross will love him.'

Chapter 15

'Matthews and Kay have taken off!' yelled Ross from the back of the shed, before disappearing back to the telephone in Rex's office.

A murmur rose around the Vimy. 'Hush, ladies!' Miss Dickson said firmly. 'Let's just get these boys in the air.'

'Damn,' muttered Benny under his breath. 'We can say goodbye to the bloody money, then.'

Under the race rules, crews had 30 days to reach Darwin and win the prize money. It was the 21st of October, which meant Matthews had until the 20th November to get there. Poulet was slowly but surely working his way east across Europe, too. We'd just heard he was in Albania.

So the clock was ticking, loud and fast.

The Vimy was still weeks from being rolled out into the sunlight. The paint job wasn't done. The electrics weren't finished either. Jack Alcock's test flights needed to come after that, and then we had to get Ross confident at the controls.

Our chances of victory were getting slimmer by the day.

Ross strode up with Keith close behind. 'Okay, so I've been on the phone to Biffy and the Air Ministry. It appears Matthews could be headed for Germany.'

'Germany?!' said Benny. 'That's not on the official route! I thought the Air Ministry said we had to head south to Italy and on to Egypt?'

Ross shrugged his shoulders. 'I know. But flying

over northern Europe is actually a more direct route. It's a risky venture with the weather at this time of year, certainly not a risk I'm willing to take. But maybe Matthews thinks he can steal himself a few days if he gets clear skies?'

Benny looked up into the glass ceiling. 'Please God, let it snow.'

I followed his gaze.

Except for that hedging day at Cheveney, the weather had been shocking for the past week. Blanketing fog. Raging winds. Pelting rain. We were all hoping it would clear before the Vimy was ready for testing and take-off.

Keith nodded. 'The approaching winter certainly seems more fierce than the last two years. If Matthews gets caught in Cologne, it will buy us time. Otherwise he's going to be tough to beat.'

'And I hate to say it,' said Ross, 'but those Sopwith blokes know how to design a decent machine.'

They'd been building the Wallaby in the Sopwith sheds on the other side of Brooklands. We'd seen it out for a test flight, but the aircraft had been a closely guarded secret until the company released an article in *Flight* magazine. She was the largest single-engined aircraft ever built, with adjustable seats so the pilot and navigator could sit well up above the fuselage, or drop right down to be fully enclosed out of the weather under a sliding roof. A canvas sheet separating the two airmen could be removed to create a single cockpit. And there was a complete set of dual controls for both men, so Thomas Kay could fly the plane when Matthews needed a rest.

'How did Matthews's departure go from Hounslow?' asked Benny.

Under the race rules, all planes had to depart from Hounslow Aerodrome east of London, or the Calshot Seaplane Station on the south coast of England. It was a pain for us because we wanted to fly direct from Weybridge. Instead, we had to detour a few miles up to Hounslow to get five official race seals added to the plane just before departure. Those five seals had to be intact when we landed in Darwin to show we hadn't switched aircraft or converted the Vimy too drastically.

Ross crossed his arms. 'There was a large crowd of press. Matthews made a big show of carrying the first airmail from England to Australia. It was a letter from King George V to Governor-General Munro-Ferguson.'

I looked down at my filthy hands and began wiping them with a rag, feeling sick that the Vimy was still stuck in a hangar.

'Matthews circled around the aerodrome for nearly half an hour for the photographers,' Ross said. 'And then Harry Hawker joined them in his little Sopwith fighter and escorted them all the way to Dover.'

'Christ,' said Benny, running a hand through his hair. 'Hawker doesn't mind getting his face in the newspapers, does he?'

'It's business,' said Ross. 'Hawker is a Sopwith man. He told reporters the Sopwith's reliability and cruising speed should see Matthews and Kay overtake Poulet in no time. Hawker is smart – he knows this race is all about selling planes. It's time we got smart about publicity, too.'

Keith raised his hand. 'I know a man in London who can help with that. Bloke by the name of Murdoch.'

'Can I checking the spelling of your surname please, Sergeant

Shiers?' the reporter asked.

'Sure,' I said. 'It's S-H-I-E-R-S.'

'Sounds like 'fliers',' added Benny, 'because we're going to be the first fliers home to Australia.' He pointed at the reporter's notepad. 'Write that one down.'

I elbowed Benny in the ribs to shut him up, but I couldn't blame him for being excited. It was hard not to be. The press had finally started paying us some attention, and within days we'd be departing for Australia.

It was the 9th of November. Two days earlier, 20 of us blokes had pushed the Vimy out of the Vickers shed and onto the gloomy tarmac for her first test flight with Jack Alcock. When we turned over the engines, Ross yelled into my ear, 'Listen to that deep-throated song of contentment and gladness!' It made the hairs on my arms stand on end.

Felt like an eternity as Jack taxied her down the runway with her engines roaring, and when her wheels left the earth we all leapt into the air, too, cheering with relief and excitement. By early afternoon, Ross was at the controls with Jack, while Benny and I were suited up in the open rear cockpit, looking down on Mother England in all her green-hedged glory. We pointed out the road to Kent and Cheveney, the Hand & Spear pub in Weybridge, the spot by the River Wey where we'd spent the afternoon with Joan and Shirley. It was the first time I'd been in the air since India, and it felt like home, among the squealing bracing wires

194

and the booming Rolls-Royce engines.

'What do you reckon, lads?' Ross had said afterwards. 'Solid as a rock, eh? Engines are running perfectly.'

'Yep,' said Benny, pulling off his flying cap. 'I wouldn't have believed it a few weeks ago, but she's a beauty.'

The only thing delaying us now was the delivery of fuel and oil to the more remote aerodromes. Shell had agreed to arrange the distribution of petrol along the route for all competitors, and Wakefield provided the oil. The 30-day schedule didn't allow for any time being wasted while supplies arrived.

Ross and Keith had spent a lot of the past week travelling up to London, too, meeting with an Australian correspondent by the name of Keith Murdoch. I think Murdoch took one look at Ross and knew if any pilot was going to make it home to Australia, it was him. They both had Scottish parents, and that seemed to count for a lot. Ross agreed to send cablegrams from along the route back to Murdoch at the United Cable Service based out of *The Times* offices in London. His special messages were to be published in the Sydney Sun, the Melbourne *Herald* and a lot of other papers, too.

Ross got Benny and me to write down a few particulars about our experiences before and during the war, and a day later we were presented with press biographies that made all four of us sound like war heroes. Keith was described as a 'pilot of unusual ability'. Benny's work experience in Melbourne made him sound like he invented the combustion engine. And mine was even better, suggesting I'd rapidly gained promotion in the Flying Corps and '… owing to his

195

ability and resourcefulness he was on many occasions sent out in the desert to bring in crashed or damaged machines, which was at times a most difficult and arduous task'. I didn't say anything to Benny, but we both knew Ross must have provided those details about me. Made me feel 10-ft tall reading it.

So Keith Murdoch was helping to make us famous, and Benny and me could never quite tell if it was for his benefit or ours. Maybe it was a bit of both. At any rate, a lot of journalists suddenly started asking a lot of questions. And Keith Murdoch was always there in the background, with his serious face, black woollen coat and smart grey trilby.

'So Sergeant Shiers, when do you think you'll depart for Australia?' asked the reporter from *Flight* magazine.

'I'll leave that one to Captain Smith,' I said, pointing toward the Vimy. 'He's the man in charge.'

We were outside at Brooklands, dressed to the nines in our AIF and RAF service uniforms for a series of press interviews and photographs with the Vimy. It was a miracle the rain had stayed away – Benny was fond of noting storm clouds had been overhead ever since Keith Smith arrived.

The press photographers asked us to all line up together in front of the plane. I straightened my spine, placed my feet slightly apart, held my hands behind my back and tried to look interesting, just like Ross had told us to do.

'Nice-looking aircraft,' called one of the reporters standing behind the press photographers. 'What does the G-EAOU stand for, Captain Smith?'

'It's a registration, you dunce,' called another reporter.

'Like a car,' said another. 'G stands for Great Britain.'

'Actually,' said Ross, glancing back at the huge white letters painted along the dark-green fuselage and wings. 'We think it stands for 'God 'Elp All Of Us'.'

A roar went up, and the pressmen scribbled furiously.

'Knew they'd like that one,' Benny whispered.

When the photographers had the pictures they needed, about half a dozen reporters began firing questions at Ross.

'So, Captain Smith,' said a bloke with a black trilby with a little white feather, 'Prime Minister Billy Hughes has sent a cable to Captain Matthews in Germany, advising him to never mind the thirty-day time limit. It seems the duration doesn't matter, so long as an Australian reaches Darwin first. What do you say to that?'

'That's a very good question,' Ross said. 'The Prime Minister's attempt to take the pressure off Captain Matthews is honourable. None of us wants to see foolhardy flying leading to injury or death.'

George Matthews and his Sopwith Wallaby had been snowbound near Cologne for weeks now. The alternate route had turned out to be a disaster for him.

'However,' Ross continued. 'I believe — and I know George Matthews would agree with me — that we have an obligation to the aircraft companies sponsoring us to show the potential of these planes. We also have an opportunity to show the world that timely air travel across the planet is now possible due to advances made during the war.'

'So the thirty-day time limit should stand?' asked the reporter.

'That's a question for the Australian government,' said Ross. 'But in my opinion, thirty days is achievable.'

'Do you think Matthews should be disqualified,' another reporter asked, 'for flying over former enemy territory against the express orders of the Air Ministry?'

'No,' said Ross. 'Where's the sport in beating someone through disqualification?'

'Captain Smith,' began another, raising his arm, 'do you reckon you can survive the Blazing Trail?'

Eleven British aviators had died attempting to deliver aircraft to Egypt since the war. Our old mate Colonel Lawrence of Arabia was one of the lucky ones to survive a crash. He was on his way back to Cairo when his plane crashed in Rome a few months earlier, killing the pilot and observer and leaving Lawrence with concussion, a broken collarbone and badly bruised ribs. The route had become so littered with crashed, burning machines it was now known as the Blazing Trail and an inquiry had been set up. It wasn't lost on Ross, me or Benny — and many others in aviation — that Biffy's successful 1918 flight from London to Cairo in the Handley Page had probably made the route look far safer than it really was.

Ross scoffed. 'I think it was Captain Douglas who said he'd rather fly six times around the world than six months against the Hun.' He looked at me and Benny and Keith. 'We've all stared down death. We know the risks. We're as confident as we can be of success.'

Another reporter, in a grey flat cap, shot up his hand. 'Just before he took off, Captain Matthews told us he was carrying a repeating rifle so that any hostility on the part of savages could be answered with a suitable argument. Will you carry a weapon, Captain Smith?'

'My Webley & Scott pistol is never far from my side,' Ross said. 'But if we can cope with a British press pack, I'm sure we'll have no trouble with a few savages.'

The pressmen laughed again.

It was odd standing beside him at times like this. On one hand, you wouldn't want to be anywhere else, but on the other you were very aware of being a lesser man — you were no Ross Smith, and never would be. Keith must have felt it too. The older, junior brother. Yet there was no envy, no resentment that I could detect. Nothing but mutual respect, and a greater bond than I shared with any of my brothers. I admired Keith for that.

'But really,' asked the reporter with the black trilby, 'is there any aircraft in the world capable of the eleven thousand-mile journey to Australia? Let alone in thirty days?'

'If the weather doesn't work against us, we'll get there in thirty days,' said Ross flatly. 'But you're correct. Everything will need to go to plan. And it's not just the weather. The racecourses in the Far East are dangerously short for landing a plane of this size. And apparently the Suda Bay aerodrome on Crete is presently flooded, so there goes the easiest route across the Mediterranean. We'll take advice on that from our RAF friends in Italy.'

Ross glanced at his brother and Keith stepped forward. 'That's it for now, gentlemen. We've got quite a lot to finalise before take-off in the next few days.

Thank you for your time.'

'Yes, thank you, chaps,' said Ross. 'But it would be remiss not to mention the men and women of Vickers Aviation. They are a credit to Great Britain and it has been extremely gratifying to observe their work.' He rubbed his hands together. 'But Keith's right, we best get back to it. There's a certain Frenchman who's getting a bit ahead of himself.'

★ ★ ★

I removed a pair of overalls from the back of the chair and sat down, my nose wrinkling at the faint smell of engine oil and feet in Benny's tiny hostel room. A bare hanging light bulb was just bright enough to show a faded picture of King George V hung over a perfectly made bed. A small wooden table was empty except for some personal documents and a notebook stacked neatly beneath two pencils.

'God, Benny, you're like an old woman,' I said, glancing into the open cupboard at his polished army boots beside a little tower of washed and paired socks.

'If you're looking for God, he's down the hallway in room 214. I think the Queen of Cairo scared him off.' Benny was kneeling on the floor, rifling through a fat kit bag. He flicked a postcard at me and it flew under the desk.

'Ah yes,' I said. 'The Queen of Cairo.' It was Benny's favourite bare-breasted beauty from the Wasser, dark hair flowing down her back. 'Good to see that shawl is still keeping her knees warm.'

I rested the postcard on my knee and lit myself a cigarette, looking around for an old teacup or saucer to use as an ashtray.

'By the wastepaper basket,' said Benny, pointing to a chipped white enamel mug on the floor by the door. 'Don't make a mess.'

I sucked on my cigarette, remembering rowdy days off with mates in Cairo. The museum. The mummies. The zoo. The cheap beer that made your guts churn for 24 hours afterwards. 'Seems like years ago,' I said.

'Yeah,' said Benny. 'Years ago and yesterday.' He took back the Queen of Cairo and placed her with a neat stack of exotic cards on the bed. 'This is the pile I'm not giving Joan.'

We'd weighed the Vimy earlier that day with a full fuel load, as well as our spare parts and tools wired to the inside of the fuselage. She'd still come up too heavy for Ross's liking, so he'd asked for the 100-pound radio to be removed from his cockpit and told us to ship home everything but our uniforms and flying gear.

'Old Keith's a funny one, isn't he?' said Benny, continuing to pull odds and ends out of his kit bag and line them up neatly on the bed, 'Trying to tell us we couldn't take the bloody chewing gum?'

'I know,' I said. 'How'd it go again?' I adopted Keith's low, plummy voice. "I do not chew gum!"'

'Ha!' Benny shook his head. 'Notice he didn't have a problem with the weight of his new camera.'

Two boxes had arrived that morning. One was from Kodak Ltd — they'd just announced a £1,000 photography competition as part of the race, and were sending every competitor a new box camera and film. I'd borrowed a mate's camera a few times during the war, and Benny had his own box at one stage before sand got through it. So we both fancied ourselves as possible contenders for the £1,000 prize. And we both loved all the free stuff we were getting.

The second box was 100 sticks of spearmint chewing gum sent to every crew by William Wrigley Jr, the American businessman who'd made his gum famous by supplying the British and her allies during the war. Rex Pierson said he'd read somewhere that Wrigley had once sent a free pack of gum to every name in every telephone book in America.

Benny and I were in charge of finding storage spots for everything on the plane, so when Keith wasn't around we fished out the bag of emergency rations and shoved the gum in with the Bovril beef extract, Bourneville chocolate, bully beef and biscuits. We had some fishing line and a few hooks in there, too. Ross said they might come in handy if we got stranded like Robinson Crusoe.

'Mate,' I said, reaching across the bed and picking up a small yellow bowl with tiny white and blue flowers. 'Where did you find all this stuff?'

'Rasilpur,' Benny said. 'You know – that one-toothed bloke with a stall near the RAF barracks. You mended his table that time.' He took the bowl out of my hand and returned it gently to the bed. 'I'll give that to Joanie.'

I ran my hand over the little red book of photographs from Genoa. We'd stopped in Italy on the voyage from India, and both bought a copy. There must have been a dozen souvenir spoons lined up on the bed. Letters from Benny's parents and sisters. A silk purse. A napkin from the Chevrons Club. Matchboxes. A pheasant feather from the Colonel's shoot. A tiny porcelain doll. A painted tile from Italy.

'Where'd you get the South African collar badge?' I asked, pointing to the brass springbok.

'At the Chevrons Club that night. A bloke at the bar was selling them for two bob apiece. Good, eh?'

'Hmm,' I said, flicking through the Genoa souvenir book. I glanced across at him, still kneeling on the floor. We'd all just had haircuts and the short back and sides made him look thinner in the face; younger than his 25 years. 'So what's happening with Joan?'

'Dunno,' he said, without looking up. 'We both know there's no point making any promises.'

'Yeah,' I said, exhaling a cloud of blue smoke. 'Does Joan want you to come back to England?'

'Maybe.'

'Would she move to Australia?'

'Yeah, maybe.'

There was a knock at the door. Biffy was on the telephone and wanted a quick word.

'I'll go,' I said, pointing to the stack of cards. 'I'm sure there's room on the Vimy for Miss Cairo.'

I strode down the hall to the hostel manager's office, thinking of the last time I saw Biffy. He and the Colonel were standing to attention in the drive at Cheveney, saluting as we drove off to inspect the Vimy.

'G'day, sir,' I said.

'Good evening, Wal,' he said, and I felt a little pang of sadness, or affection maybe. 'I'm afraid I've been called away up north to inspect one or two RAF bases. Might miss the big departure.'

'That's okay,' I said. 'Thanks for everything, sir.'

'Now, Wal, I'm damn glad Ross has got you and Benny in his corner. Keep your wits about you. Err on the side of caution after India. I couldn't be more proud of you all.'

'Thank you, sir.'

'Dad and Laura have become quite attached to you, Wal. Fine work you've done at Cheveney.'

'I received a letter and some photographs the other day from Mrs Borton. Please thank her for me.'

'Jolly good, old chap. You must come back and see us one day. You ...'

He cleared his throat and neither of us said anything for a second or two. 'Now, if you don't mind, I'll need a quick word with Benny.'

'Of course,' I said. 'I'll just go get him. Goodbye, sir.'

'Good luck, lad. Godspeed.'

I rested the receiver on the desk and ran back down the hall.

'Is he wishing us good luck?' asked Benny, surprised that Biffy wanted a chat with him, too.

I shook my head, feeling a tightening in my chest. 'I think he's saying goodbye.'

204

PART THREE

Chapter 16

ADELAIDE, 1968

I pause for a minute, like I always do, right before the race. 'The 12th of November 1919 was the most important day of my life, boys,' I say, reaching out for the scotch that Delvene's poured for me – like she always does, right before the race. 'It was a year and one day after the Armistice, so the first day of no more looking back at the war. It was the day we took off for home. And it was the day I decided there was more to life than being Ross Smith's mechanic.'

★ ★ ★

OVER FRANCE, NOVEMBER 12th, 1919

Boom.

Boom.

Boom.

The plane shuddered and dropped 20 ft, and I snapped awake, smashing my head against the side of the cockpit. Maybe I'd blacked out when Ross started climbing to escape the stormfront over France. I ached to my bones with cold.

I couldn't feel my feet at all, and the roar of the engine and the sickly stench of dope and petrol made my head hurt.

I scratched at the ice on my goggles with my leather mitt, already hating the useless padded flipper, but my stomach heaved so I rushed to get my head outside the cockpit before spewing porridge and chocolate and coffee. I don't know where it went.

Emptying my guts made me feel better. I pushed my goggles up and squinted ahead at Ross and Keith, grey shadows in the swirling snowcloud. Ice had started forming on the rear edges of the wings and there was a little white lump of ice on the fuselage just behind Ross and Keith. Marmaduke II. The freezing gale felt like tiny shards of glass cutting my eyeballs and skin. Then the plane lurched to port and I fell back into the fuselage across Benny and vomited again, mostly water this time. I groped around and settled back on my own side of the cockpit, bashing my head against the shifting spanner I'd fastened with wire into the corner.

Benny moved his knees over as I eased myself down, rubbing my head with the stupid mitt. The space was originally designed for one bloke standing to man a machine gun. The opening wasn't much wider than a 44-gallon drum, really, and we were perched on two eight-inch wooden bench seats built opposite each other along the walls of the fuselage. There were fuel tanks between our aft cockpit and the Smith brothers up the front, and there was a thick sheet of plywood between us and the tanks. The plywood had a square of leather padding where we could lean our heads, and we sat facing each another with knees knocking. Sometimes when the plane shuddered I was sure I could hear the sound of sloshing petrol. It terrified me.

I squeezed Benny's knee to say sorry for landing on him and for the vomit everywhere. It was a year since we'd flown from Cairo down to India, and I'd forgotten how miserable it was not to be able to talk, our voices drowned out by the roaring engines and squealing bracing wires. I'd forgotten how much I hated bloody airsickness, too, and I'd never had it as bad as this.

But then, I'd never been at this kind of altitude before. I reckoned we were getting close to 9,000 ft now, maybe more. Benny was lucky. The higher we got, the more he slept. I was cursed by always being half-awake, obsessed with how crook I felt, certain I'd never feel well again, praying it would end.

We'd designed our cockpit so we could both slump down out of the gale when the weather was really bad, with one of us curled up against the front plywood with its leather padding, and the other stretching his legs toward the tail of the plane. Benny was slumped with his head and shoulder against the front plywood, his arms folded across his chest and his legs sort of twisted and stretched out toward the tail. The bits of his body under the opening of the cockpit were covered with an inch of snow and ice. The fur collar of his new flying suit already looked matted and frozen.

I'd only seen snow for the first time a day or two back. It was great fun then. I hit Benny fair in the back of his head with a snowball bigger than a fist, and when he caught me he stuffed half the snow in Weybridge down the back of my shirt.

I hated snow now. Cursed the stuff. I hunched myself into a ball and wedged my mitts between my legs, jamming my toes against Benny's bench opposite and leaning against the front plywood to brace my body against the lurching and shuddering and falling of the plane.

Boom.

Boom.

Boom.

The engines roared their perfect tune. Thank Christ. Thank Christ for Rolls-Royce engines.

The plane lurched again and my guts lurched with it. I threw up over myself. It was only thin bile now and it felt warm on my chin before it froze. I didn't wipe it off. I didn't care. I couldn't think straight.

Mum came into my head and I felt a pain deep inside my chest. I forced her away again. Not now, Mum.

Tried to sleep.

I came to with brilliant sunshine pouring into the cockpit. We'd got above the clouds so the ride was smoother, but it was still achingly cold.

Must have been dreaming about Keith because he was in my head, now. Funny old Keith. He was the most British Australian I'd ever met, yet I'd never seen him so happy as when he was leaving Britain. Laughing. Joking with the press blokes. Even turned his camera on them from the cockpit. Benny said Keith must have had one too many cups of coffee, but I reckon he was just chipper to get away, like the rest of us. I wondered if he and Ross had made a pact to be happy for the press photographers, so their Mum would have those final memories if anything happened on the flight home. Ross was the kind of man who'd think of something like that.

We got a personal message from the heir to the throne, Prince Albert, wishing us good fortune on our 'sporting attempt'. Mum would have been tickled pink. And a copy of The Times newspaper was stowed for special air delivery to Governor-General Ferguson in Melbourne.

Then there was the official weather report: 'Totally unfit for flying.'

Ross had warned us it might say that. He also said he'd ignore it. Matthews had taken off weeks ago now, and we'd all had a gutful of hearing about 'plucky Poulet' and his handy head start.

Apart from the press, there wasn't a big crowd to see us depart. Rex Pierson was there, and a few of the Vickers blokes. Keith Murdoch. Some RAF men and Royal Aero Club officials who stuck the five seals on the Vimy. Our spirits were high when we finally took off at 9.05. Ross rose above the fog to 2,000 ft and we circled three times over Hounslow to make sure the engines were running smoothly, then he set a compass course for Folkstone and the English Channel. Biffy had asked us to look out for Cheveney, and by rights we should have passed close by, but it was too cloudy over Kent and we missed it. Near the coast the view cleared and we waved farewell to Britain and her magnificent white cliffs as we headed across the choppy waters of the Channel. We weren't far off the coast of France when we saw it – a towering bank of angry storm cloud that looked as solid as the Great Dividing Range.

I inched up my goggles to squint at my watch, taking deep breaths to try to quell the airsickness. Quarter past twelve. We'd been in the air for just over three hours. I looked across at Benny, still slumped and twisted. I hoped he hadn't frozen to death on day one. That would make him really cranky.

Every inch of me was stiff and screaming, but the sun on my face felt good so I wriggled around to kneel up on my bench for a look outside. It was a wondrous sight: the Vimy's tiny shadow dancing across towering, puffy cloud formations under the widest, bluest sky. I considered waking Benny – seemed wrong not to share something so beautiful. But then Keith stretched his arms in the cockpit ahead and must have sensed me out the corner of his eye, because he turned to give me the quickest smile and nod. He bent back over his work, and I pictured him studying his Admiralty compass and calculating the speed and the wind drift. He was marking tiny lines at 15-minute intervals on the map to determine our likely flight path.

Ross was unmoving, as solid and resolute as tiny Marmaduke II, screwed onto the fuselage behind him.

Mist began to engulf us and I noticed large bits of ice suddenly whipping off the propeller blades and crashing against the wire shields positioned either side of the front cockpit to protect Ross and Keith. The semi-circular shields were only a foot or so high but Jack Alcock said they were lifesavers in icy weather. Watching those Smith boys bent to the task, mist swirling and ice crashing around their ears, I felt pride and gratitude swell in my chest.

The Vimy lurched again, and I hunkered back down in the fuselage just as the plane dropped 10 ft. For five minutes we were tossed around like an empty bottle on an angry sea. I covered my ears to deafen the racket of engines, the heave of straining wood, the scream of struts and the slosh-slosh-slosh of petrol. I promised God I'd be a better man if everything just held together to get us down. I lifted my elbow and retched what was left of my stomach down my jacket, wondering if I'd live to clean it up. I was freezing and hot and suffocating. Couldn't breathe. I tried to rest my head but it kept banging against the fucking shifting spanner.

Boom.

Boom.

Boom.

'Wally!'

For the first time in months I heard Helena's voice, clear as day. Like she was sitting right there in the cockpit with me. 'Wally!' My eyes snapped open, but my goggles had iced over again. I wondered if it was like this under a frozen river, daylight so close, so far.

I pressed my chin into my chest, and shut my eyes to block her out. She wouldn't go. 'Wally!' Helena – in a wedding dress. In a chapel. Alone.

What had I done to her?

I'd put her second. After everything I'd promised, after all the months and weeks and days she'd waited, I'd stayed away. I hurt the only girl I'd ever loved.

I pictured her face, confused and sad as she read my letter. The look of hurt as she explained to her Mum that I wasn't coming home. Sweetly, patiently enduring Mrs Alford's sympathy, but desperate to be alone. Folding a wedding dress that she'd been making since 1915, putting it in a drawer to stay hidden, along with her sadness and shame.

Why had I never pictured that look of hurt?

My head banged against the shifting spanner and I let out a sob as I retched down my side.

Bang. Fool.

Bang. Fool.

Bang. Fool.

Fool! You think Ross Smith's going to give a damn about you when this is all over? If it's ever over. If you live.

At the end of the day, there's only ever family. Mum told you to always remember that. But you don't have a family because you gave it up.

You don't deserve Helena. You never deserved her.

I don't know how long I sat like that, ashamed and hating myself with a fury more fierce than the storm over France. Then someone shook me roughly by the shoulder and I heard a distant voice. 'Wally!' And it was Benny and the Vimy was banking and I scrubbed at my goggles and stretched up to see the plane swooping into a wide spiral through a gap in the clouds. Far below was farmland and a small town blanketed in snow. Benny was gesturing triumphantly: you beauty Ross and Keith!

He pointed at his wrist to show me his watch. Three o'clock. We'd been in the air for six hours. I felt like I'd aged 60 years.

When we got beneath the storm clouds, we headed away from the town over pretty countryside for maybe 40 miles, and in the distance I saw aircraft hangars in a sea of white. It was supposed to be Rome. That's where Ross had told the press blokes we were headed. But it sure didn't look like Rome. Did it even snow there?

Who the hell cared where it was, because we weren't falling, we were landing. I wasn't going to die. And I had an idea that just might get my girl back.

Chapter 17

LYONS, FRANCE, NOVEMBER 12th 1919

The airfield was coming up fast. We sat facing one another in the tiny cockpit, knees knocking, and tried to brace ourselves against the impact. When the Vimy's wheels hit the snow, we were hurled forward and my shoulder smashed the rim of the cockpit just as the propellers hurled a wave of white over the plane. We came to a stop and I sat there for a second, coughing and trying to work out if anything was broken. Then Benny was laughing and slapping the side of my knee and my ears were ringing.

'Bloody hell!' He was yelling. 'Bloody hell! What a lousy few hours!' He pulled up his goggles and started shovelling snow out of the cockpit with his mitts.

'How would you know?' I said, easing my screaming joints into a standing position. 'You slept through most of it!'

'You lads right?' Ross shouted as he and Keith stood and eased themselves out of the front cockpit.

'Yes, Captain!' I yelled out of habit.

The hot engines stank, hissing and sizzling in the cold, wet air. It was mid-afternoon and gloomy with twilight.

I hoisted myself up to sit on top of the fuselage, and noticed half a dozen blokes in the distance, approaching from the airfield hangar. 'Hey Benny, d'ya hear the racket in the starboard engine?'

'You reckon it's the exhaust manifold?'

'Yep. Day bloody one.'

Only one of us could climb out of the cockpit at a time. I left Benny trying to regain the use of his limbs and dropped down from the plane into snow a foot deep. After rubbing the blood back into my legs, I walked stiffly over to Ross and Keith standing near the front of the plane.

'Wal! Good to see you,' said Ross, wincing as he reached out to pat my shoulder. 'Sorry, mate. That was unpleasant.'

'Wasn't too bad in the back,' I lied, noticing an ache in my chest as I wiped frozen porridge from my flying suit. 'I didn't know it snowed in Rome.'

Keith raised an eyebrow. 'Rome be buggered, Wal, we're in Lyons.'

'Ah, that makes more sense,' I said, looking across the open fields.

I stepped toward the starboard wing. 'Just going to take a look at my engine.'

'Yes,' said Keith, eyeing the engine warily. 'Something's not right.'

'You think Wal doesn't know that?' Ross said impatiently, removing his flying cap. His hair was wet with sweat. He looked bone-weary, like he'd been in the fight of his life.

'Found a spare manifold!' yelled Benny from the back cockpit. 'In here if we need it.'

Ross groaned as he tried to move his head from side to side. 'Never flown in anything like that.' He rubbed his right shoulder. 'Jesus, what a silly ass.'

Keith glared at him. 'Enough now. We're fine. The Vimy's fine.'

Ross glared back. 'I realise that,' he hissed. 'I landed the damn thing.'

216

Across the snow I could hear French voices as the men got closer. I hauled my stiff bones onto the starboard wing, careful not to slip on ice and snow or touch the hot engine, and examined the manifold on the side of the cowling. 'Yep, she's cracked alright.'

'Dammit,' said Ross. 'Day bloody one. Vickers needs to know about that.'

'Can you fix it?' Keith asked.

'Of course he can bloody fix it,' Ross snapped. He turned, wincing with the effort. 'Benny! Where are the tarps? They're not up in the front cockpit where they're supposed to be.'

There was silence for a second or two.

'Benny!' Ross roared.

'Sorry, Ross, they're back here,' called Benny, his voice muffled inside the fuselage.

'Get 'em out,' said Ross. 'These cockpits need to be covered before it snows again.' He clapped his hands to keep warm. 'We'll worry about the manifold in the morning. Too bloody cold now. Be getting dark soon, too.'

I looked at the two brothers. Their eyes were thin slits in red welted skin.

Out of nowhere I pictured my brother Jack. I'd seen him look exactly the same once, the time he took on six-foot Davey McArdle in Broken Hill. Jack lost two weeks' pay at the mine for fighting, and his terrified kids thought he looked like a monster. He'd still said it was worth it. 'Only fools pick on people who are different,' he'd said, 'and cowards watch while they do it. I couldn't let it stand.' I'd never admired him more.

I eased myself off the wing of the plane and stood beside Ross. 'You took your goggles off,' I said.

'Yeah, they kept freezing over,' he said, dabbing at

his raw eyes. 'Gauges froze. Food froze. Everything bloody froze.' He winced again as he put his hands on his head and stretched his back. 'It's got to get easier,' he said, almost to himself.

Not since the war had I seen men look so crushed.

'*Bonjour*,' Keith called, striding out to greet the French blokes, shaking hands and introducing them to Ross. I couldn't make out what they were saying, but there was a lot of gesturing and astonishment when Ross said something about flying from London. I don't think they could believe it.

'Benny,' I called. 'Let's get the water out of the radiators before it freezes.'

I could hear Ross and Keith using scrappy French and a lot of English to ask if a delivery of fuel was possible before daylight. Benny and I drained the scalding, spitting water before covering the engines with tarps. It was getting dark by then, so Ross organised for us to sleep in a hangar while he and Keith caught a lift into Lyons to send cables back to England and find themselves a place to stay.

From the air we'd seen an impressive town nearby, with a huge cathedral on a hill and a winding river. But that was the closest Benny and I would get to it. Back in Weybridge, Ross had spelt out the rules: us mechanics were in charge of keeping the machine running and the plane safely guarded; he and Keith were in charge of refilling the petrol and oil tanks, dealing with local inhabitants, sending communications back to England and resting up so they could concentrate in the air. If anyone was going to sleep rough with an empty stomach, it was us mechanics.

'I'll bring you something to eat in the morning, chaps,' Ross said as he and Keith peeled off their flying suits. In his uniform Ross looked almost like his old self.

★ ★ ★

True to his word, he arrived at 7 am carrying a long thin loaf of bread under his arm and some sticky cheese wrapped in paper. They'd both had a wash and a good tidy up. Their eyes looked better, too, but their faces were red raw and they were both unshaven. Benny and I had spent the night in our uniforms, curled up in old tarps. I was unwashed and starving, but I'd had a decent rest. After the war I could sleep anywhere.

'Where's the fuel?' asked Keith without saying hello.

Benny shook his head, sniffing warily at the cheese. 'Jesus, this Frog cheese smells like a dead man's feet.'

'Fuel should be here by now,' said Ross. 'Where the devil is it? Keith, take care of that, will you?'

'Right,' said Keith. 'I'll see if I can get a lift back into town.' And he was off, striding toward a couple of young blokes in the hangar.

Benny and I got to work repairing the manifold while Ross went to ask for some hot water to refill the radiators. An hour or so later, there was still no sign of Keith, no petrol and no hot water. Mist was swirling and snow was threatening, reducing the horizon to a flat grey gloom across the airfield. A dozen French mechanics were hanging around at the front of the hangar, chatting and laughing as they watched us work.

Benny nodded toward them and spoke in a low voice: 'Wonder if they're playing funny buggers to buy Poulet some more time.' He continued muttering as he secured the engine cowling. 'So much for

Australians dying in their tens of thousands to save the French.'

'Nah, Benny,' I said. 'You've heard Ross and Keith's lousy French. I'm sure they just don't understand what we need. Ross'll sort it.'

But I did wonder if he was right.

Poulet's Caudron G4 biplane was most likely built in Lyons. Lots of the big French aviation companies moved their headquarters out of Paris when the Germans looked like taking over the capital at the start of the war. Poulet's hero Jules Védrines, the French aviator who'd lost his life while planning to fly around the world, had died not far from here. There could well be deep sympathies for both men. And who could blame these people for wanting a Frenchman to win the first race across the world? For as long as I'd been reading about aviation, the French had been winning races and breaking records.

I didn't say any of that to Benny. But I did remind him that more than a million French lads had died in the war alongside our boys. It was only fair to say that.

A battered French army lorry rolled up with Keith glowering in the passenger seat.

'I've got the fuel,' he called. 'Three hundred lousy gallons.'

'Damn it!' said Ross. 'We'll need double that if we're going to make Rome.'

Benny and I unloaded nearly 80 four-gallon cans off the back of the lorry and stacked them beside Ross. He in turn handed each can up to Keith, who stood on the lower wing to pour the fuel into the tanks between our two cockpits. All fuel was poured through a leather chamois and funnel, to stop water getting into the tanks. Ross had a rule that only he or

Keith could pour the fuel, to ensure he knew exactly what was going into the tanks.

A while later, Benny and I were tying down our tools and rearranging our cockpit when we suddenly heard Keith raising his voice. 'Is this some kind of joke?' he said angrily, glaring down from the wing. 'That's not enough!'

A young French bloke with a mop of dark hair and a lopsided grin was standing beside Ross with a small jug of hot water.

'Sorry, Buck,' said Ross. 'I should have made myself clearer.' He turned to the Frenchman, speaking very slowly. 'We need 24 … *deux quatre* — ' Ross held up two fingers as he spoke, followed by four fingers, ' — *litres* of hot water for the radiators. I think the French word for more is '*plus*'.' He smiled at the young man. 'We need *plus*.'

'*Plus!*' yelled Keith, pointing at one engine and then the other. '*Plus! Pour* radiators. *Pour* engines. *Seal voo play. Plus!*'

'Jesus, Buck, your French is worse than mine,' said Ross. 'It's *s'il vous plaît*. So much for that Queen's College education.' He held up another fuel can for Keith, waiting to receive an empty in return.

The young Frenchman placed the jug carefully on the wing beside Keith and hurried off. In a few minutes he was back. Holding another small jug of hot water.

'Oh dear,' muttered Ross.

'You stupid bloody fool!' roared Keith. 'What does a man need to do to get some fucking hot water around here?'

The Frenchman started gabbling something like 'razor', pointing from the jug to his cheek and then to

221

Ross's cheek.

'Shave,' said Ross. 'He thinks we want to shave.'

'I don't want to bloody shave,' yelled Keith, shaking his head and waving his arms furiously at the two engines. 'I want to fill the fucking radiators and fly out of this forsaken fucking country. *Plus! Plus!*'

'Calm down, Buck,' said Ross. 'It's not their fault our French is so bad.'

I jumped down from the back cockpit and grabbed two of the empty four-gallon fuel cans at Ross's feet. 'Benny,' I said, 'grab some more empty tins.'

I walked over to the young Frenchman, held out a can and said *'plus'* like Keith had said it. The lad smiled his lopsided grin and nodded excitedly, emptying the two small jugs onto the snow as he led the way and chatted in French like we were old friends. I enjoyed the sound of their language, the way the words rose up and fell all the time like waves. While he filled our tins, Benny and I searched around and found a large blow lamp. A couple of Frenchmen helped us get it set up, and brought us strong black coffee to drink while we waited for the water to heat. By 10 o'clock we'd refilled the radiators and were heading into the sun to Italy.

★ ★ ★

OVER FRANCE, NOVEMBER 13th 1919

There was a young girl from Narrandera

I'd decided to write a poem. Maybe have it cabled to Helena. A poem so loving and clever, I'd win her back forever.

222

But from the French Alps to the Mediterranean coast, I got stuck on seven words.

I wrote them, and then I crossed them out. Over and over and over.

Chewing on my pencil, agonising over the next line, panicking that it wasn't just a matter of application like Colonel Borton had said. Not for a bloke like me, anyway.

Not far from the sea, Benny carefully placed his Kodak camera at his feet, took the pencil and notebook from my hands and scrawled across the page ...

There was a young girl from Narrandera
Whose boyfriend was quite the philanderer

Underneath he wrote ...

Get better at writing limericks or find new girl!

WATCH BELOW!!

He underlined everything three times, then handed back my notepad and damp pencil stub.

And the view of the French countryside was worth watching. Golden stone villages carved into hillsides. Dark, winding rivers lined with green. Neat slabs of forest and farmland rolling toward the blue Mediterranean. Its beauty made my heart hurt for my brother, buried somewhere in a French grave I'd probably never see. I'd never even cried for Bill. Barely thought about him now. My favourite brother. What did that say about me?

Ross started dropping altitude as we approached the coast, and when we got a bit lower I began to

223

notice the white country roads and village streets speckled with people looking up at us as we flew over. Keith had told us he was setting a compass course for Nice, before heading north-east around the coast into Italy.

So it must have been Nice where Ross flew at a couple of thousand feet over a promenade lined with palm trees beside the water, and thousands and thousands of doll-like figures came spilling out of grand buildings to watch and wave as we passed. Tiny bright ladies with parasols. Tiny neat men with black top hats. Even tinier children running along the beach, trying to keep up. I wondered if they knew who we were, or if the sight of a peace-time aircraft so large was still something special. The same thing happened over Monte Carlo. Ross circled above the casino and its pretty terraced gardens, and within minutes there was a crowd so large I thought there must be something wrong. But they were all looking up, waving, pointing, cheering. That great sea of people was honouring us – four Australian blokes they didn't know, trying to beat the French hero Poulet to Australia.

★ ★ ★

PISA, ITALY, NOVEMBER 15th 1919

It was before dawn and we were eating breakfast in the near-empty dining room of Pisa's Royal Victoria Hotel. I yawned, tore apart some bread and mopped up the last of my white beans, tomato and egg.

'Hey,' said Benny, 'didn't your mother teach you any manners?'

I nodded at two smartly dressed men on the next

table, wiping their plates clean as they continued a loud debate in Italian. One of them noticed I was copying him with the bread, and he smiled and winked with food stuffed in his cheeks.

Benny scowled, dropped his fork and followed suit. 'Been here two nights and we're turning into bloody Macaronis.'

I leaned back in my chair and sipped the strong coffee, watching Benny as he wiped his plate clean. A hotel waiter walked among the empty tables, his shoes clicking on the black-and-white marble floor as he checked the cutlery on starched white cloths. Through an open window I could hear a horse and cart on the cobblestones outside, and the far-off cry of a gull.

'Why do you do that?' I asked quietly.

'Do what?' Benny said.

I nodded toward the Italians. 'You know — Macaronis? And Frenchies. Frenchy bastards.'

He screwed up his face. 'I'm only jokin', Wal.'

'Yeah.' I fiddled with my knife.

It was our second morning in Pisa. We'd arrived from Lyons late in the afternoon on the 13th of November. Ross decided the manifold was making too much racket again and it was unlikely we'd get all the way to Rome with the limited amount of fuel we'd been able to secure in Lyons. Besides, Ross hated flying on the 13th.

The Leaning Tower was right across the fields from the aerodrome, poking up behind the old city walls. Seemed to me the architect had drunk too much Johnnie Walker.

Biffy Borton had stopped here on his flight to Cairo in the Handley Page, and he'd given Ross the name

225

of a British officer to contact when we arrived. Captain Horne was his name. Jolly chap – whistled a lot. He drove straight out to lend a hand and arranged to have the Vimy put under military guard so Benny and I could get a good night's sleep at a hotel in town. Then he booked us all into the fancy Royal Victoria Hotel, right on the River Arno.

The rain had started falling as we drove away from the aerodrome, and it didn't let up most of the night. When we'd returned early yesterday morning the whole airfield was under water. We'd refuelled the plane and replaced the manifold, but by 11 am the rain was pelting down and an angry wind was blowing in from the south.

It was matched by Ross's mood.

'We can forget flying today,' he said, standing in the door of a hangar, soaked through and filthy with mud like the rest of us. He folded his arms across his chest and scowled at the grey European winter, muttering under his breath about Poulet winging toward Australia through cloudless blue skies.

The 30-day deadline was already a curse. We'd aimed to be in Rome at the end of day one. We didn't look like getting there until at least day three, so one tenth of our race time would be gone, just like that.

With the rain coming down in sheets and the Vimy's wheels under water, Keith convinced Ross to head back to the hotel to go over the maps again; try to work out where we might make up some time.

It was Captain Horne who offered a ray of hope. He'd heard the aerodrome on the island of Crete was still open. That meant a quick hop down to Cairo in Africa, instead of flying across to Athens like they'd recommended back in London. If that was true, we'd

226

make up some time.

'Finally, some decent bloody news, Horne,' said Ross. It was the first time since Hounslow I'd seen him look happy.

Ross walked across the dining room toward our table. 'Let's go, lads,' he said. 'Sun'll be up soon.'

The two Italian men were rising to leave and both reached out to shake hands with Ross as he passed their table. One of them made the sound of an engine roaring and moved his hand through the air like a plane. The other crossed himself and put his hand on Ross's shoulder, and Ross nodded and said '*Grazie ... Grazie tante*'.

It had been the same wherever we went yesterday. There was an election going on, with crowds marching and people making rowdy speeches we couldn't understand, but many of them stopped to wave and whisper when they saw our uniforms. Captain Horne said the newspapers had been covering Poulet's journey for weeks, and when the Vimy was spotted in the skies over Pisa, word had spread that we were in the same race to Australia.

Out at the aerodrome, the rain was holding off but the ground still looked like a lake. As the Leaning Tower began to emerge with the first light, Ross and Keith pulled off their boots and socks, rolled up their trousers and began splashing through the icy water to find the highest patch of airstrip for take-off.

'Over here!' shouted Keith finally, locating an area where the water barely covered his ankles.

'Right-o,' said Ross, wading quickly back to the Vimy. 'Prepare to depart, please!'

We got ourselves sorted and said our goodbyes to happy Captain Horne. Benny yelled 'Contact,' and he and I cranked the machine to life with the small crank handles on the side of each engine. Then we jumped in the back cockpit and Ross eased her forward.

And within two feet we were bogged. Badly.

It took 30 Italian mechanics to dig us out, using wooden planks for traction in the thick, black mud.

Then off we went again.

'Contact!'

Engines roared. Forward on the throttle.

The Vimy rolled a few feet.

Bogged.

Three times it happened. Finally, after being both cheerful and patient, the 30 mechanics threw up their hands and began a furious argument among themselves.

The four of us jumped down to take another look. The Italians stood in a ring around us, still in angry debate, pointing, gesturing, fighting over where to place the wooden planks.

'I'm sick of this,' said Benny suddenly. 'Fucking Macaronis.' He grabbed a plank of wood off two arguing mechanics and stomped over to a wheel, talking a mix of Arabic, jibberish and profanity as he tried to lever it from behind.

Keith took a deep breath and folded his arms. 'I think we're here for another day.'

'No!' snapped Ross. 'You think Poulet's sitting somewhere for another day? I just need five minutes' peace to think.' He stomped through the water for 50 yards and stood with his hands on his hips, looking back at the plane.

Benny threw the plank of wood to one side and walked away from the plane to light a smoke, offering me one too. Our flying suits, pulled over our uniforms for take-off, were spattered with mud.

'Thanks mate,' I said, taking the smoke.

A small crowd of locals had gathered by the hangar. The children hid behind their mothers' skirts when I looked over.

'Hey, Benny,' I said, 'I didn't know you could speak Arabic.'

'Me neither,' he said. 'Must have learnt it off the bloody Gypos.'

I hesitated for a moment. 'I've been meaning to ask if you remember that day we went out to fix the truck near Rafa during the war, and you started getting sick with enteric fever?'

'Oh God,' he said, taking a drag. 'I remember it coming out both ends.'

'Do you remember the ride back to the base? You were collapsed in the back of the lorry and an Egyptian bloke took off his headscarf and put it under your head.'

Benny exhaled. Raised an eyebrow at me. 'Really?'

'Yeah.'

'What did you do?'

'I tried to thank him by saying *Shukran*.'

I turned my face to the sun, forcing its way through the clouds. I could hear cows in a nearby paddock.

'Benny! Got a job for you.' Ross was walking back toward the tail of plane. 'Right,' he said when we were all gathered around. 'Each time we're trying to take off, the nose drops which forces the wheels down into the mud.'

'Yes,' said Benny.

'So what I need you to do — ' Ross threw his arm across the aircraft, ' — is put all your weight on the fuselage near the tail here while I'm taxiing. Once I've

229

got up some speed and we're about to take off, you'll have to let go — ' Ross demonstrated as he talked, ' —and run like hell to climb aboard the plane.'

Benny scratched his head, looking uncertainly from the tail to the little foothold below our cockpit, a distance of over 15 ft. 'Umm ...' he said slowly.

'Yes, I realise it's a bit risky,' said Ross impatiently, 'but it's the only way we're going to get out of Pisa.'

Benny looked around. 'Could Horne do it, maybe? Or one of the Italians?'

'Sorry, no,' Ross said, rubbing at a spot of mud on his neck. 'I can't afford any damage. Not near the tail.'

'Come on, Benny,' I said, trying to sound encouraging. 'I'll pull you in, mate.'

Benny looked at me. Then he began rubbing his hands and rolling his shoulders. 'Right-o,' he said.

Ross slapped him on the back. 'That's the way. And if you don't manage to scramble on board, get Horne to race you to the station and catch the first train to Rome. We'll meet you there.'

While we worked to free the Vimy again from the mud, Benny studied how best to hold down the tail, pacing out the distance he had to run and the height he had to jump to make it into our cockpit. He was struggling to take off his sodden flying suit over his muddy boots, so two Italian blokes got under his shoulders while another heaved his overalls by the cuffs. I could hear them all laughing as they stumbled around in the water.

Two Italian mechanics cranked the engines into life. As Ross prepared for take-off, I got myself ready in our aft cockpit, feet wedged and arms outstretched to grasp Benny's hands. Half a dozen mechanics stood at each wing tip to help inch the Vimy forward when

Ross gave the command. The other men stood clear with Captain Horne. Some crossed themselves. Some whispered and shook their heads. Others watched silently with hands over their mouths.

Ross eased up the throttle.

The Vimy resisted for a second or two. More throttle, and then she lunged forward. Suddenly she was rolling and picking up speed. Benny was running alongside her, holding onto the fuselage and pulling it down to the ground as the port propeller's draft showered him with water.

I felt the wheels start to lift off and screamed, 'C'mon, Benny!'

He let go and started sprinting. The Italians ran screaming and clapping alongside.

'Come on! Come on!'

The Italians were shouting, the engines were thundering and Benny's eyes were wide as saucers as he pumped his arms furiously, racing to catch up with me in the cockpit.

The plane lifted right off the ground and he sprang upwards, grabbing the edge of the cockpit with one hand as his left boot found the foothold. I latched onto the scruff of his uniform and hauled him in with all my might.

Keith turned around to see what had happened and I pointed at Benny's muddy boots poking up beside me. He laughed and nudged Ross with his shoulder and gave a thumbs-up. Once we were a few hundred feet in the air, Ross circled back to test the engines a little longer over the safety of the airfield — a chance also to wave farewell to Captain Horne and our Italian helpers.

Benny untangled himself, stood up in the cockpit

and raised his arms in a victory salute as we flew past, and down below they all jumped about and threw their hats in the air.

Then Benny fell back down onto his seat, gasping for breath. As he pulled on his goggles, I was sure he wiped away tears.

Watching all those people below us, still waving as they grew tiny with distance, I thought maybe this race wasn't plane against plane or crew against crew. It was man against world. That's why people were so quick to cheer, or whisper excitedly behind their hands as we walked by. After all those years at war, we were all on the same side.

Chapter 18

ADELAIDE, 1968

'Wait a second,' says a new bloke along the bar, spilling his beer in his eagerness to interrupt. 'So you're telling us the crews didn't all take off from England at the same time? What kind of race is that?' I haven't seen this lad before, so I reach out my hand to introduce myself. But another bloke cuts in: 'Hey, hey, hey. Don't you be talking to Wal like that,' he says, jabbing an angry finger. 'Show some respect.' I raise a hand to calm things down. 'S'alright mate,' I say, 'It's not the first time I've been asked that.' I smile across at the new lad, lift my glass in welcome. 'Really, we were racing against time and that thirty-day deadline. And for the glory of being the first men to fly across the planet.' Delvene rests her elbows on the bar. 'Must have been so excitin', Wal, seeing all those wonderful places you only ever read about.' I nod. Respond with the usual 'Mmmm,' into my scotch. But in my mind I think, 'No. It was not exciting.' Very quickly it became terrifying and dull and exhausting and bloody hard work. Sometimes I couldn't even think straight.

★ ★ ★

RAMADIE, NOVEMBER 20th 1919

There was a Jonah on the plane. His name was Keith Macpherson Smith.

The curse of Keith nearly smashed us into rocks

233

off the coast of Greece. It almost hurled us against a jagged mountainside on the island of Crete. It bogged us. It delayed us. It broke a drought over Palestine with torrential rain so hard it scrubbed our faces raw.

When a desert wind began whipping up the orange dirt of Ramadie, I couldn't look at Keith for the bitterness I felt. His flat tone of voice. His dark glaring eyes. His constant questioning and running me down. He was not a nice man. He was a negative force.

In the first week of the race, we'd somehow made it down the boot of Italy and over the Mediterranean via Crete to Cairo and into Mesopotamia.

Ramadie was less than 60 miles short of Baghdad, and we'd come in to land right near some old trenches and machine gun posts from the war. We'd flown over a lot of the old battlefields since leaving Cairo two days earlier. Romani. Gaza. Ramleh. I had mixed feelings about seeing it all. Sadness, yes, lots of that. Remembering the screams of that poor young bloke who'd lost both his legs but could feel his feet on fire. But I also felt an odd kind of bond with the place, because of the friends I'd made down there. Young Bernie, who had so much life ahead of him, all lost at Gallipoli. Ando the young aircraft rigger who showed me around on my first day with No. 1 Squadron and became a good mate, mostly because he was single and enjoyed hearing Helena's news almost as much as I did. And then there was Westy. Westy with his stammer, always going on about the Saints. I promised myself I'd turn up at a St Kilda footy match one day and push through the crowd until I found him. We'd drink ourselves stupid. I'd thank him for changing my life when he told me to t-t-t-toughen up and apply for the Flying Corps job, even after Copping said I'd fail. An Indian cavalry regiment was stationed at Ramadie now. Tough as nails, they were, too. We anchored the Vimy with ropes and organised to have two men guard her near the workshop.

A huge red sun was nearing the horizon when we left the mess, our bellies stuffed with curry and rice. We'd all been savaged by bed bugs a few nights earlier on Crete, and I was desperate to splash myself with cool water to calm the itching before I collapsed into a bunk. But as we walked across the aerodrome for a quick check of the aircraft, the wind started picking up and little squalls of dust rose across the plain. Then a gust blew through, nearly knocking us off our feet, and we realised the wind had changed direction. The Vimy was facing the wrong way. If we didn't turn her around she might flip over.

We sprinted toward her in the rising gale, sand whipping at our faces still raw from the hours of flying through torrential rain over Palestine.

As the two guards shouted the alarm, a wire on the Vimy broke with an almighty twang and the ailerons began flapping so wildly I thought they might tear right off the wings. Dozens of men appeared from across the base, holding the ailerons down while Ross had us fire up the engines so he could turn the Vimy into the wind.

Ross rubbed Marmaduke II's tiny head for luck and jumped down from the cockpit, yelling something that got lost to the wind. He was still wearing his goggles to shield his eyes from the swirling sand, and handed Keith his pair too. He bellowed in Benny's ear for us to do the same, and then told us to get a few Indian blokes to help lash tarps

235

over the cockpits and engines.

The wind was howling. The wires were shrieking. Men were running in all directions, bodies bent into the gale. Somewhere a door banged furiously.

I ran into the workshop to find more rope, and heard Keith yelling to Ross: 'How do we keep her down? Ropes won't hold her.'

I grabbed Ross and shouted in his ear. 'El Mejdel! We used men to weigh down the planes ...'

That miserable Christmas Eve, when Benny and I sat hunkered down, back to back in the mud, trying to stop an RE8 from getting whisked away to Jerusalem.

'Yes!' Ross thumped my back before turning to shout into the ear of the CO. Within minutes, 50 men were weighing down the wings and lower fuselage. Scarves shielding faces, heads buried in arms as they settled in to wait out the storm.

Benny and I squeezed in along the fuselage to take up our positions. Ross and that bloody Jonah Keith were already hunkered down near the tail-plane to do the same. I covered my head with a spare bit of tarp, trying to wipe some of the dust from the angry bites and sores on my hands, and as the night turned pitch black I felt the sand start to bank against my boots.

There was a time I'd have played the Helena game, beating back the dread, boredom or loneliness with happy memories of her.

Now I played the game of cursing Keith, even though I knew it was dangerous and nothing good would come of it.

* * *

My stoush with Keith had blown up quicker than the Ramadie storm. It had started in Rome, five days earlier.

Ross received a telegram from Prime Minister Billy Hughes, saying the entire nation hoped an Australian crew would be first home, but urging us not to do anything foolhardy. It was almost exactly the same telegram Hughes had sent a month earlier to Matthews in Cologne, except for one little detail: he'd started referring to the race as a flight from 'Europe to Australia'.

'That's interesting,' I said, peering at the telegram in Keith's hands. 'Before now, the Australian government has always referred to the race starting in England.' I pointed at the words. 'See how Billy Hughes has started talking about Europe?'

'So?' said Keith, folding his arms and turning to stare at me so intensely I almost took a step back.

I looked across at Benny for moral support, but he'd returned to unscrewing the cowling from his port engine.

'Well ...' I pointed back at the telegram. 'It means they think Poulet's probably going to win, don't you think? He left from Europe.'

Keith raised his eyebrows and kept his voice low and slow, like he was talking to a child. 'Well then, it's our job to make sure Poulet doesn't win. No?'

'Yes. Of course.' I rubbed my eye. It was after midnight. 'I didn't mean ...'

'Sounds like you've written us off.' He folded the telegram very precisely and put it in his pocket. 'Don't know if I'd want you on my Cricket XI.'

I couldn't tell if he was serious or having a lend of me. He was impossible to read.

I shook my head. 'It's not like that at all ...'

'Good.' He cut me off, swatted me away like an annoying bug, and stared at me for a second longer before stepping up into the front cockpit to get his cylinder of maps.

I must have replayed that conversation a thousand times in my head since then, in the long days and hours on the Vimy when we couldn't see the earth for heavy mist or driving rain, or were getting thrown around and dropped thousands of feet in the air. Every jolt reminded me of the Jonah's words — questioning my loyalty after everything I'd done for Ross. After everything I'd given up.

On Crete I was in no mood for taking his lip. Bed bugs got me good and proper. I was itching all over, tired and cranky. I was also spooked at the idea of flying hundreds of miles over deep, dark Mediterranean waters to North Africa.

That was when Benny and I hatched a plan: we'd inflate our four spare wheel inner tubes, to use as life rafts if we pitched into the Med.

Ross thought it was a great lark. Keith rolled his eyes.

'Inflatable tyres won't save us from sharks if we go down,' he said, scratching at a red welt on his neck. The beg bugs had spared no one. 'And when we increase altitude and the air pressure drops, those inner tubes are going to start inflating again.'

I told Benny to ignore him, and shoved the inner tubes at our feet in the cockpit. 'They've all got valves,' I said. 'If they inflate, we'll just open them up and let the air right out. What's the problem?'

But as Ross took us above 6,000 ft to pass over the mountain range running the length of Crete, we must have hit some critical point in altitude because the four inner tubes started inflating so quickly I thought they might lift us out of the cockpit. And they got so fat so fast we couldn't reach the valves. Panic set in until Benny grabbed his jack knife and punctured them all before they could do any damage.

I spent the rest of the flight to Egypt scratching at the bites on my hands, desperate to come up with just one line of my poem for Helena but unable to think of anything but the superior look on Keith's face when he found out about the shredded bits of rubber at our feet.

Cairo was the worst.

We landed to a heroes' welcome; a huge mob of our old RAF mates crowding in around the plane, cheering and shouting hellos as the engines shut off.

Ross stood in the front cockpit, giving Marmaduke II his customary pat for helping us to a safe landing, before shouting, 'Well, aren't you ugly bastards a sight for sore eyes?'

If there was a roof he would have raised it.

Jeez I felt proud, standing up there in my cockpit, returning to Cairo in the Vimy with one of Australia's finest airmen. We were triumphant at the end of stage one. Exhausted and elated and ready to celebrate. We bantered with the blokes below as we peeled off our flying suits, then climbed down to shake hands and be thumped on the back by the gathered crowd. For the first time, it felt like we were really in a race and excitement was building – hell, we might even catch that bloody Poulet.

In the middle of all that, Keith pushed through and tapped me on the shoulder and announced: 'Shiers, your engine's sick.'

The noise died and it felt like everyone was staring at me — the mechanic standing between the legendary Ross Smith and victory in the Great Air Race from England to Australia.

I looked back at Keith, weighing up my words while I rubbed an angry bite on my wrist. I knew the engine was running too hot. We all did. That's what our temperature gauges were for. Ross had throttled her back not long after we hit the African coast, letting Benny's engine get us across the desert to Cairo.

'I'm aware of that,' I said, dropping my gaze and looking back at the plane. 'I'll have a look at it now.'

Someone yelled out, 'Plenty of us lads here to give you a hand, Wal!' And I was grateful for that. But we had the Vimy routine down pat, so Ross told them to keep the beers cold and we'd catch up later.

Turned out it was a crack in the induction pipe. Worse, the pipe was aluminium and impossible to fix. Jonah had cursed us again.

'Think, lads!' Ross ran his hands through his hair. Looked like he was close to tearing it out. For the past two hours he'd sent telegrams to everyone he could think of from England to India. He'd paced around the Vimy, sprinting off to make a call or send a telegram every time he'd thought of another possible remedy. No luck. There wasn't a spare on any aerodrome in Egypt, despite the small fleet of Vimy bombers stationed out there since the war. Vickers said it would be two weeks before the part arrived from Weybridge. Rolls-Royce said we'd need a new engine and that might take a month.

'There must be some other way,' Ross said. 'Something we haven't thought of.'

I looked at Benny, racking my brains for an idea.

He was standing in the aft cockpit, tapping the shifting spanner in his hand while he thought.

'Isn't there some way to plug that crack?' said Ross.

Benny shook his head. 'Runs too hot. She'd burn.'

Ross clasped his hands behind his neck. 'What about wrapping something around it?'

Keith looked doubtful. 'That'd burn too, wouldn't it?'

'Shit!' Ross kicked a wheel, hard, his boot thwacking against the rubber.

'Wait a minute,' I said. 'You might be onto something there, Ross.'

He turned to me, still fuming, waiting to hear what I had to say.

'What about a poultice that wrapped around the pipe and plugged the crack without burning?' I called up to Benny. 'Mate, hand me the chewing gum from the emergency rations.'

'Is that the Wrigley's from Weybridge,' said Keith, frowning and folding his arms as Benny handed me down a small brown cardboard box.

I didn't answer that. Didn't look at him.

'Not sure where it came from, Keith,' said Benny, climbing out of the cockpit. 'Good thing it's here, though, eh?'

I rested the box on the lower wing of the plane and folded back the top to reveal two neat rows of gum in thin, white packs reading 'Wrigley's Spearmint, the perfect gum'.

'Over the top with Wrigley's,' Benny said, mimicking the war ad.

I took a pack of five strips and handed it to him. 'Chew these Benny,' I said. 'All of them.'

Then I took a second pack, pulling out a few strips

and letting the white paper sheaths and silver tinfoil fall to the floor as I shoved the gum into my mouth.

As the gum softened, the sharp spearmint taste took me back to my early training days in Egypt, sitting in Bobby's shade among all the hot, patient Walers, reading one of Helena's first letters and chewing the gum she'd sent me.

'Ross?' I held out the half empty pack.

He took the gum warily. 'What are you thinking, Wal?'

'Create a poultice.' I spat out the gum and held out my hand to take Benny's, too, before pressing the sticky ball into a pad. 'Wrap it around the pipe. Seal it with tape and shellac.'

I looked at the engine uncertainly. 'It's a bit of a long shot.'

'Indeed,' said Keith.

Fighting the desire to flatten him, I looked directly at Ross. 'We'll know if it's worked in the morning.'

Benny took another pack and started peeling back the layers of paper and tinfoil. Little piles of rubbish were collecting at our feet. 'How much do you reckon, Wal?' he asked. ''Bout the size of a golf ball?'

'Yeah, about that.'

Ross leaned in to grab another pack. 'It's not like we have any better ideas,' he said, chewing furiously with his mouth open.

Across the aerodrome two Bristols came in to land, their engines roaring as they taxied past us to a waiting group of air mechanics.

'That's a sound I miss,' said Ross, spitting a ball of wet gum onto the palm of his hand before placing it on a piece of discarded tinfoil on the wing of the plane.

I held out some gum to Keith. 'How about you, Keith?'

'I don't eat chewing gum,' he said. 'Can't stand the stuff.'

'Right, good work lads,' Ross said, oblivious to his brother. He checked his watch. 'Lord, it's past 6 o'clock. I need to chase up that fuel delivery in case we can actually fly out of here tomorrow.' He thumped Keith's shoulder. 'Then I'll treat you to Shepheard's Hotel, Keith. Need to send some telegrams back to England.'

Off in the distance I heard the call to prayer. The vast sky was turning pink. We'd need to organise some spotlights.

'Jesus, Wal,' said Benny as we watched the brothers depart across the airfield. 'What's going on with Keith?'

'Nothing,' I said, holding out my hand. 'Your gum, sir?'

He frowned. 'Nothing? Doesn't look like nothing. Watch yourself, Wal.'

I combined the gum into a two-inch ball, rolling it between my palms. 'Yeah.' I sighed, looking at all the wrappers strewn at my feet. 'He's just so bloody ...'

'I know, mate,' Benny said. 'I know. Did you hear him telling me to stop standing up in our cockpit because I'm slowing down the plane?' He rolled his eyes.

Benny washed down the aluminium induction pipe while I pressed the gum out flat and cut it into long thin strips, keeping it moist with lots of spit. Then I wound the strips around and around the cracked pipe, being careful to smooth over any bubbles and holes and cracks with a wet thumb.

243

Working under spotlights set up around the air-craft, and in a mobile workshop pulled up alongside, we finished the job with layers of ignition tape and thin coats of quick-drying black shellac. Then we left it to dry, and walked out into the cool, smoky night to see if any RAF mates were still awake to shout us a drink.

★ ★ ★

I breathed in the familiar smell of grilled chicken as we settled onto low stools beside our RAF mate, Taff. The cafe was just outside the base, and had become a favourite haunt when we were modifying the Handley Page for the flight to India. Despite the year's absence, nothing had changed when we walked through the heavy wooden door. The yellow walls were grimy, brass star lanterns hung from the ceiling and a faded blue-and-white striped curtain led back to the kitchen. Two white-haired Egyptian blokes hadn't moved since I was last there – they were still drinking coffee and arguing over backgammon in the corner.

A hunched woman in a black dress and a navy apron emerged from the back with a tray carrying three long-neck beers and hand-painted glasses. She gave me her usual toothy grin when she saw me, and I was just wondering if she knew I'd been missing for 12 months when she leaned across and took my hand in both of hers.

'Ahlan wa sahlan,' she said.

'Ahlan bik,' I said, nodding. 'Hello old friend.'

She held my hand a moment longer, rubbing my palm with her bony fingers as she looked into my eyes and chatted away. I couldn't understand another

244

word she said, but I got the feeling she was happy I was alive. She'd have seen lots of airmen come and go these past years of the war.

'The other blokes gave up,' said Taff, glancing at his watch. It was well after midnight. 'Said they'll see you in the morning.' He picked up a bottle and filled our glasses with frothy beer. 'We just heard the news earlier about your two boys. Dreadful business, eh?'

And that's how we heard air race competitors Roger Douglas and James Ross were dead.

Their Alliance Endeavour had taken off from Hounslow a day after us on the 13th of November and crashed into an orchard a few minutes later. An official inquiry was under way. That's all the newspaper report said.

'Jesus,' said Benny. 'Poor Dodger.'

'He had a new fiancée too,' I said. 'Poor girl.'

I'd met Roger 'Dodger' Douglas briefly at the Air Ministry meeting, and thought he seemed shy behind his big smile. I told him Endeavour was a clever name for his plane, like Captain Cook's ship, and he winked and said the Australian press were fond of it, too. Douglas had survived Gallipoli, Pozières and Polygon Wood before joining the Flying Corps, winning the Military Cross and the Distinguished Conduct Medal in the process. If a man like that could crash out so quickly, what hope was there for a bloke like me?

We all fell silent, remembering two more fallen airmen. Pondering life and death. I wondered about Dodger's final thoughts as he hurtled toward the earth. I wondered what mine would be. Would I be sad or angry? Grateful for times past, or bitter about moments that would never be?

I could hear someone singing in the kitchen.

The old woman reappeared with two small plates of chopped grilled chicken with tomato and cucumber. I realised the only thing I'd eaten all day was a corned beef sandwich somewhere over the Mediterranean, just as we flew over that pair of warships sweeping for mines.

'Bugger it,' said Benny under his breath. 'Let's enjoy this.' He rubbed his brow and smiled weakly at Taff. 'So, how are you, Taffy?'

Ron 'Taff' Pepper had served with the RAF's No. 111 Squadron during the war. We worked alongside those blokes a lot. Played a lot of cricket against them, too. Taff was the only man I knew who'd lost his wife at the Front. She was a hospital nurse, killed in a bomb blast. The night Taff heard, we all gathered outside his tent to keep him company in his grief. No one spoke. No one tried to go inside to see him. There was nothing anyone could say to make it better. When it came time to leave, we put packs of cigarettes by the door as a token of sympathy. There were 126 packets when he woke up the next morning.

'I'm doing fine,' Taff said. 'Better for seeing you two safe and well.' He took a sip of his beer. 'They say you've got to be crazy to fly from London to Cairo.'

'Yeah,' Benny said. 'You've got to be pretty good at ducking Wal's breakfast, too.'

I grinned sheepishly at Taff and toyed with my beer glass, rubbing my thumb over the gold detail. 'What do you reckon happened to Douglas, Benny?' I asked. 'Too much weight?'

'Who knows, Wal,' Benny said wearily, stretching out his legs beside the table. 'Plenty of Alliance aircraft have flown perfectly well over long distances.' He rubbed an eye. 'Taff, I'm losing track of the days. Did you say Douglas left Hounslow on the 13th of November?'

Taff nodded grimly and we all shook our heads, staring into our beers.

Plenty of pilots avoided flying on the 13th if they could help it — Ross included. Might sound odd that some of the bravest men on the planet could be so superstitious, but these blokes were all about calculating risk. If something as simple as a lucky leather cap or a toy black cat could increase your sense of calm and help you concentrate at the controls, why wouldn't you trust in its charms? I'd heard about experienced pilots during the war who wouldn't fly unless their plane was painted with a particular name or mascot. The Red Baron never flew without his lucky scarf and jacket. Held good for him — until the day our boys shot him down.

'Yep,' Benny sighed. 'Maybe it was just bad luck.'

I gulped my beer and poured another. 'Plenty of that around.'

There was a tired edge to Benny's voice. 'What?' He stared at me over the rim of his beer. 'What are you on about, Wal?'

Lots of blokes thought it was bad luck to even talk about bad luck.

'Nothing mate. Sorry.' I shook my head to drive out the demons, and raised my glass. I wasn't wasting tonight on the Jonah. 'To Lieutenant Roger Douglas.'

'To Lieutenant James Ross,' said Benny, raising his glass.

Then the three of us recited the words of an old No. 1 Squadron poem I hadn't heard since Palestine.

There let me be beside the river;
There will I rest for e'er and ever,
There will I be in one hundred years from now,
One hundred years from now,
Hundred years from now,
Years from now,
From now,
Now.

★ ★ ★

In Ramadie, our luck blew away in the night. The whirling winds died down sometime in the early hours, and as dawn lightened the eastern sky we could finally survey the damage. It wasn't good. The Vimy was buried up to her wings in sand. The aileron control wires were broken or stretched. The Jonah had struck again.

'Dig, men!' The CO's deep voice boomed across the desert as his Indian regiment worked furiously to unearth the plane. 'Dig!'

All morning I kept to myself. Head down, methodically replacing the aileron wires while Benny assessed the engines for any signs of sand or damage. I was exhausted, like everyone else, and I'd scratched the top off an insect bite near the corner of my eye.

I tried to be polite. But on the inside, I was seething. I'd only ever loathed one man more than I loathed the Jonah right now: that bastard Sergeant Copping. I silently dared Keith to have a go at me; to tell me I wasn't securing the wires tight enough. I'd tell him exactly what I thought of him. I'd knock his bloody block off. I'd throttle him right then and there.

'Wal!' It was Benny, standing next to me on the

248

wing. 'Christ, mate, didn't you hear me calling you?'

The digging was close to being finished and Ross and Keith were about to start refuelling the plane.

'You right, lads?' asked Ross, looking up at us. 'Where are we with those control wires?'

'Almost done, Ross.' I smiled through gritted teeth until he turned back to his fuel cans.

'Have you done this wire, Wal?' asked Benny.

'Yep,' I said, not looking at him.

'You sure?'

'*Yes!*' I'd knock Benny's block off, too, if he wasn't bloody careful.

Ross glanced up again.

Benny dropped his voice almost to a whisper. 'Wal, mate, this wire is frayed. If we go up in the air with it like this and hit more rain, she'll snap.'

'What?' I tensed my shoulders, clenched my fists.

'Hey, Ross!' Benny was calling across to the boss. Oh Christ.

Ross turned, rubbing his brow with the back of his wrist. 'What now?'

Benny put a hand on my shoulder. 'We'll be back in a bit — just going to get some more wire.' Then he turned to me and hissed, 'You, with me.'

I followed him around the side of the workshop. The sun seemed brighter here, beating down on my stinging face. I put up a hand to shield my eyes.

'Right,' said Benny, folding his arms across his chest. His greasy hair was on end. He hadn't shaved, his face was blistered below the line of his goggles. 'Out with it before you fucking kill us all.'

'It's nothing,' I said, holding his gaze for a moment before looking away. In the distance, kids were playing in the bombed ruins of a stone hut.

Benny rubbed his chin, looking a hundred years old. 'Bullshit. I know when a bloke's scrapping for a fight.'

'It's nothing. Really.' I rubbed at the sore near my eye, then forced myself to stop. 'I'm just sick of Keith.'

He frowned. Shifted his weight. 'So that's what this is about?'

Kids' sing-song voices drifted across the desert. Benny watched them, sucking at the inside of his cheek. 'Now listen,' he said, turning back to face me. 'You're my best mate, Wal, so I'm going to give you some free advice. Whatever's going on inside that head of yours, it has to stop ...'

I started to apologise for missing the frayed aileron wire and he raised a hand. 'I'm not talking about that. You're on the way to saying something, or doing something that can't be undone. Keith will hate you. Ross won't forgive you. You won't forgive yourself.'

'He keeps running me down.' I scratched at a bite on the back of my hand. 'The Billy Hughes telegram. The spare inner tubes. Remember the chewing gum?'

'Wal, for Christ's sake!' He had his hands on his hips again. 'Okay, he did think the chewing gum was a stupid idea ...'

'Exactly!'

'But when it worked and you fixed the induction pipe, what did he *say*, Wal?'

I folded my arms, scowling.

His voice was raised. 'What did he say, Wal?'

'He said it was a job well done.'

'No!' Benny's eyes were bulging. 'He said you were one of the cleverest bastards he'd ever met. And then what did he say?'

I stared at him.

'What else did he say, Wal?'

'He said the two of us deserved a promotion when we got to Australia. But then he …'

Benny threw his hands in the air. 'Yes, he said we deserve a fucking promotion! So what are you on about?'

I pressed a closed fist into my eye socket, trying to calm the angry bite. Almost whispered. 'He's a Jonah, Benny. I'm sure of it.'

He stared at the sand and shook his head. Then he leaned his shoulder against the shed. 'Mate, you're exhausted.' He let out a long sigh. 'We're all exhausted. But have you ever stopped to think maybe Keith's bringing us good luck, like Marmaduke?'

'I'm serious!' I said. 'We've almost crashed a dozen times. We get bogged everywhere we fucking land. It won't stop raining when we're in the air. Look at us!'

'Yes, look at us, Wal! We haven't crashed. We're on the way to India, nearly halfway home. We're starting to make up ground on Poulet. And you're too fucking miserable to enjoy it.'

I slumped against the shed wall beside him. Every inch of me was screaming for sleep. The bug bite near my eye was throbbing.

A child squealed with delight in the distance. The CO boomed an order about stacking empty fuel cans onto the tray of the lorry.

'You're right,' I sighed. 'Y'bastard.'

He rested a hand on my shoulder. 'Enjoy it, mate. We're gonna be home soon.' He turned to stare at the sky. 'Well – home or dead.'

251

Chapter 19

BANDAR ABBAS, NOVEMBER 24th 1919

Ross pushed the pith helmet off his forehead and cupped his hands around his eyes, staring into the blinding desert.

'Both hacked to pieces, I'm afraid,' the British Consul said. I looked across at Benny, who was busy checking wires on the port wing. He made his usual face of mock terror as the British Consul continued, 'We never did find Lieutenant Harris's left foot. Why the blazes they'd want a left foot is anyone's guess.'

I turned and peered east, too, wondering if Ross was searching for Poulet's Caudron in the blue above, or the marauding tribes in the yellow below.

An ambulance vehicle was parked off to the left on an otherwise empty, flat horizon. A big cross was painted on the side of the vehicle's canvas tarp. Blue sky. White tarp. Red cross. It made for a striking picture, but there was something not right about it, too. The vehicle didn't belong. It shouldn't be there.

I forced myself to stop fretting about the flight ahead and concentrate on the aileron wires of the starboard wing, using the tips of my fingers to feel for fraying.

Two Persian kids stood in the shade of the barracks, snotty-nosed, wiry-haired. One had his arms crossed, the other had a leg tucked up like a flamingo. They'd been standing there, perfectly still, for more than two hours, four eyes following every move Ross made. Eyes

252

were always following Ross. He never seemed to notice.

We were in Bandar Abbas on the Persian Gulf. Poulet had passed through a fortnight earlier. After flying around the northern coast of the Mediterranean, he'd finally dropped south onto the same route as us.

So now we knew exactly where he was.

We also knew he had a two-week lead. And we knew he'd already crossed this dangerous, desolate part of the planet and arrived safely in Karachi 730 miles further east. I glanced back to the desert and imagined a group of bearded tribesmen on camelback, dark robes flowing and daggers at the ready, watching the tiny French Caudron buzzing through the cloudless sky. I prayed that we'd pass overhead, too, and not crash into a desert canyon in a ball of flames so high it would draw marauding tribes from afar.

'Take this, Captain,' the British Consul said, offering Ross a piece of paper. 'It's a message commanding the tribal chiefs to grant you safe passage.' He stared east, too, smoothing down his moustache before slapping Ross on the back.

From my spot on the wing, I glanced down at the document before Ross folded it and put it in his pocket. It was handwritten in something like Arabic. Farsi, maybe. The British Consul's seal was in the bottom left corner.

'Thank you, Mr MunGavin,' Ross said. 'I appreciate it.' They'd met earlier in the year on our flight down to Calcutta in the Handley Page. Got on well. Last night they'd chatted over dinner about the Paris talks, Colonel Lawrence and the British and French carve-up of Mesopotamia.

The British Consul took his leave. Ross and Keith watched him go.

'Do you think his piece of paper is going to save us?' Keith asked quietly.

Ross shook his head. 'No. He's just doing what's in his power to do.'

They turned back to the map spread out on the wing. Keith ran a palm over the expanse of brown. 'Are you sure there's not one spot to land between here and Karachi?'

'No,' said Ross. 'It's all clay ridges and canyons and cliffs dropping into the gulf.'

'So if we ditch, and survive, we've got to show the murderous tribes a handwritten letter?'

'Yes.' Ross smiled. 'Well, that and my pistol.' He wiped his brow with the back of his hand. 'The trick is to get the engines as perfect as they can be before take-off, so we remain in the air. Focus on what you can control. All else is folly.'

Keith cocked his head to one side, scratching his shoulder. 'Where'd you hear that?'

'I just made it up.' Ross looked up at me and Benny. 'Lads, let's give those engines one final check, to be on the safe side. And Wal, grab me a couple of packs of that Wrigley's, would you?'

Before we took off, he walked over to the two boys in the shade, crouched down to shake their hands and gave them each some chewing gum.

* * *

DELHI, NOVEMBER 26th 1919

The woman's voice startled me. It was soft and suggestive. Very British. Out of place on the sweaty Delhi aerodrome.

254

'Thank heavens you're back, Ross. It's been so dull!'

Then a man. 'Don't you have coolies to do that work for you?'

I poked my head out of the aft cockpit, where I'd been searching for my spare packet of cigarettes.

There were three of them, smiling up at Ross from the side of the Vimy. They'd turned up unannounced, with their white linen outfits and straw hats and tight buttoned collars. Their father must have been important enough for the guards to let them through the gate.

It was about 11 in the morning and Ross and I had just finished refuelling the plane. Keith was meeting with a RAF observer who had some new maps for the route to Burma, and Benny was over in the workshop.

Ross jumped down, apologising for not shaking hands as he wiped his palms on his filthy overalls, and introduced them to me as I climbed down, too. Peter, Dora and Viola Fairweather. Peter had the square jaw and straight back of a wealthy young man. His sisters didn't look like sisters. The older one, Viola, was short and thick-waisted with wire-rimmed glasses. The other one, Dora, was all white teeth and blue eyes, with wispy blonde hair falling to her shoulders beneath a wide-brimmed boater. Seemed like they'd become quite chummy with Ross when we were here at Christmas in the Handley Page.

Ross stank of petrol. So did I. It suited me fine, but he hated it. Not the work — he relished getting his hands dirty — but if there was a choice between a laundered shirt and overalls he'd always choose to be presentable, especially in mixed company. He'd be annoyed at having to greet them like this, for sure, but his guests wouldn't know it. The guards who let them

255

through the gate were in for a quiet word, though.

'Captain Smith ...' It was the older sister this time, Viola.

'Oh, Viola,' said Dora, 'can't you just call him Ross?'

Viola turned to her sister. 'I can call the Captain whatever I want.' She turned back to Ross. 'Has anyone made the Phileas Fogg connection?'

'Viola!' said Dora, flicking a strand of hair from her face. There were small freckles on her nose. 'What a daft question.'

Ross smiled. 'I wish I had Phileas Fogg's London bank account, Miss Fairweather.'

'Do call me Viola.'

Dora rolled her eyes. 'Well, he might if you called him Ross.'

Peter grunted. 'Oh shut up, you two.'

My stomach rumbled. It had been hours since breakfast in the RAF mess. I glanced at all the empty fuel tins that needed carrying back to the lorry.

Ross bent to wipe his hands again on the legs of his overalls. 'I wish I had Phileas Fogg's deadline, too. He had the luxury of getting around the world in 80 days. We've only got 30 days to get to Australia.'

Viola smiled, adjusting her glasses on her nose. 'You see?' she said to Dora. 'I just knew there was a Jules Verne feel to it all!'

Ross rubbed his forehead with the back of his hand. It made his hair stick out at the side.

Dora clasped her hands together beneath her chin. She was wearing short white gloves. 'I do hope you get to meet Captain Poulet, Ross,' she said.

'Now there's a curious chap,' said Peter. 'Larger than life. Quite the hero. Quite the ...'

'Quite handsome!' giggled Dora.

Ross raised an eyebrow. He spoke slowly, and I thought there was an edge to his voice. 'Well, let's hope I get to meet him sometime very soon.'

A hawk screeched in tall trees by the fence. I swatted away a fly before jumping down from the aft cockpit. 'Captain,' I said, trying to sound enthusiastic, 'would you like me to show your guests around the Vimy?'

'What a fine idea, Shiers!' He patted me on the back, nodding to the others. 'I have to get myself cleaned up. Please excuse me, Peter, ladies. I won't be long. And then we can leave for the reception.'

'Oh yes,' said Dora. 'It's going to be awfully fun, Ross. I heard Mrs Agnew is going to perform a song she's written for you.'

'Well,' said Ross, giving me a quick look, 'how marvellous.'

We'd touched down in Delhi yesterday, 13 days after departing London. Poulet had left the aerodrome just hours before, 42 days after leaving Paris. 'His Gallic goose is cooked,' said Keith, when he heard how close we were.

'We've got the French bastard,' said Benny at exactly the same time.

And I felt the tiniest twinge of sympathy for the man, determinedly pressing on across the skies as our big bomber bore down relentlessly behind him.

Ross had flown 1,450 miles in 18 hours over two days from Bandar Abbas to Delhi, wrestling with the controls to keep the Vimy steady in fierce head winds and turbulence. He was wiped out, almost falling from the cockpit when we landed before tens of thousands of people. He'd been deafened by the engines, too. General McEwan, the RAF chief in India, and dozens of others were lined up to tell Ross what a

257

hero he was, but he couldn't hear a word they said for three hours.

With Poulet's lead all but gone and the 30-day target on track, Ross decided to stay an extra night in Delhi to give the engines a good going over, and rest up for the final half of the race.

Benny and I caught up with a lot of old RAF air mechanic mates, too, some from the war and some from the Handley Page flight. They were the kind of men who drift out of your thoughts and into the past, but when you're together it's as if time has stood still and your chest fills in a way it never quite does with anyone else. We worked under spotlights on the Vimy with half a dozen blokes gathered around, passing a spanner or a screwdriver while we reminisced about the war years – about who'd made it through and who hadn't.

Meanwhile, Ross and Keith were in demand with the British Raj. That's why the Fairweathers had been dispatched to collect them for a reception at Government House.

As Ross disappeared inside the barracks, I clapped my hands together. 'Right-o,' I said. 'Who'd like to see the cockpit first?'

Peter put his hands in his pockets and turned to look out across the aerodrome. 'I think we'll wait for the Captain to show us around. But thanks all the same, old chap.'

I looked at the women. Dora wouldn't meet my eyes. Viola gave me a thin-lipped smile. I nodded. 'No problem. Captain Smith won't be long.'

The hawk screeched again, and a flock of small birds lifted from the trees before settling back down.

I collected up the empty fuel tins and ferried them

258

to the lorry while the Fairweathers strolled around the Vimy, watching and whispering.

Half an hour later, Ross still wasn't back. I stood reading the signatures and messages people had been leaving in the white G-EAOU letters painted along the fuselage. Then I gazed out across the aerodrome to the white marble dome – a tomb – in the distance, deciding what to do next. The Fairweathers had wandered back to their vehicle, and were standing in the shade beside the barracks. Peter and Dora were sharing a cigarillo, leaning against the car. The rich cinnamon smell of the expensive tobacco wafted toward the Vimy and reminded me of the Bengal Club in Calcutta, and the elderly Sikh waiter with his fine turban. The most magnificent man in the room.

I knew Ross wouldn't want me to leave the Vimy, so I peeled off my overalls and hung them over the fuselage to air out, straightened up my uniform and retrieved my diary from the aft cockpit. Then I sat on an old wooden chair in the sun, found my page and set to scribbling.

'Are you a writer?' It was Viola. She'd come up behind me and was peering over my shoulder.

'Ha!' I shut the book, embarrassed by my chewed pencil, my scratchy writing, my words. 'I'm no writer.'

In the distance I thought I could hear drums. There was a procession near the tomb.

Viola straightened her hat, following my gaze. 'Gandhi followers and their non-violent protest, no doubt,' she said, almost to herself. 'As if there can be such a thing.'

I'd read about Gandhi. If I had to put up with the likes of Peter Fairweather on a daily basis, I'd probably be protesting too.

She cleared her throat and clasped her hands in front of her skirt. 'Sorry about my brother,' she said. 'He can be thoughtless sometimes.'

I pressed my hand onto the black cover of my book, shocked at how leathery my skin looked. 'Didn't notice.'

A horn honked in the street. Someone yelled in Hindi.

'What was that you were writing?' asked Viola. 'Poetry?'

'No, no,' I said. 'Nothing like that.'

'Don't be so modest, Sergeant Shiers,' she said. 'It's lovely to see a man writing poetry.' She recited what I'd written:

> *I broke a vow,*
> *I broke your heart,*
> *Look what I've done to you …*

It sounded even worse out loud. And that's all I'd managed to come up with since Crete. It really was hopeless.

'So who's the heartbroken damsel?' Viola's voice was all fun and light as she poked me in the shoulder.

I stared at my lap, my cheeks flashing crimson.

'Oh!' She'd seen the look on my face. 'She's real.' Then all her words ran together. 'I'm so sorry, it's really none of my business.'

'Viola, what are you up to with Sergeant Shiers?' Jesus, it was the other one.

Viola snapped. 'We're just *talking*, Dora.'

'I can see that. What are you talking *about*?'

I rose from my seat with my diary held behind me.

'Oh,' said Viola. 'I was just asking Captain Shiers if

260

he knew the Australian airmen who died in the crash in London.'

'Wasn't that simply awful?' said Dora. 'Those poor men. Did you know them well, Sergeant Shiers? Roger Douglas and James Ross?'

Poor buggers. I'd thought about them often since Cairo. Every take-off, I imagined what it must have been like to be hurtling back to earth. You can dredge up a lot of memories, good and bad and downright sad, in a few moments.

'I didn't know them well,' I said, shaking my head. 'Douglas won the Military Cross for bravery at Polygon Wood.' I paused, not knowing what else to say. 'He didn't deserve to die like that.'

Ross finally reappeared, looking clean and refreshed in his uniform and hat. 'Keith won't be a jiff,' he said. 'How'd you like the Vimy, ladies? Isn't she a marvel?'

'Marvellous,' said Viola.

Dora beamed. 'Peter thought we should wait for the hero's tour.'

I twisted my mouth. 'Well, Captain, I'll leave you ...'

Ross turned his gaze on Dora, frowning. 'You're far too kind, Dora,' he said. 'Though I tend to think heroes are the invention of idle men and mourning women.'

Peter sauntered over, cigarillo in hand. Ross waited, hands on hips, until he was in earshot. 'Pity Sergeant Shiers didn't get to tell you how he fixed one of the engines with chewing gum. You three could have dined out on that for months.'

He turned to clasp Peter's shoulder. 'So good to see you again, old sport.' He nodded at the cigarillo. 'Don't suppose you can spare one of those beauties?'

Peter reached into the inside pocket of his linen

261

jacket and threw Ross the pack. 'Take the lot,' he said. 'Anything for the man of the hour.'

That tiny pack was worth more than I earned in a week.

'Thanks, champ,' said Ross. 'Man of the hour is Sergeant Shiers.' He tossed me the pack. 'He's the only reason we're still in the air.' Peter gaped like a carp on a river bank. 'Enjoy, Shiers,' said Ross. 'Save me one for the night we catch Poulet.'

★ ★ ★

CALCUTTA, NOVEMBER 29th 1919

I was 11 years old when the Commonwealth of Australia was born. There was a big Federation parade through the streets of Adelaide and a monster picnic in the dusty parklands for us kids, with running events and sack races and patriotic songs. There was special Federation chocolate, too, with wrapping that said 'January 1st 1901. One People. One Destiny.' I gobbled mine down a bit fast in the hot sun and threw it straight back up, on my sister Mabel's new blue dress. Mum hissed, 'You wait till I get you home, Walter Shiers!' and I spent the rest of the day petrified and being extra nice to Mabel, and by the time we got home all tired and sunburned, it was forgotten. Mum could never hold on to her anger.

The Australian flag wasn't ready for Federation. There was a national competition and five winners were announced later that same year — they'd basically all come up with the same design.

So there I was in Calcutta, 18 years later on a different continent, holding that flag for the very first

262

time. A pretty young woman had reached out and pressed it into my hands as we were doing a final check of the plane. Benny and I were standing behind the starboard wing, waiting to crank the engines and studying the flag while Ross finished showing Lord Ronaldshay the controls in the front cockpit. The flag was hand-sewn in silk, maybe three feet by one and a half feet, and as I ran my fingers across the stars of the Southern Cross I felt a pang of homesickness so strong it was almost like being walloped.

I leaned against the wing and looked out across the Maidan. Must have been 100,000 people there, easy. Their voices surged across the huge park like white-caps on the ocean. There was a smell of cooking oil and burning incense, and damp grass on the race-track, which had been cordoned off for take-off. My mind drifted to everything that had happened since that night in the Bengal Club. Hard to believe that was only four months ago.

Benny nudged my shoulder and nodded toward the front. 'The great aviator and the Governor of Bengal,' he said quietly. 'I don't how Ross does it.'

'What?' I asked. 'You mean finding the right things to say to important people? Ross is pretty impressive like that.'

'Nah,' Benny said. 'I mean being patient and not telling the bloke to fuck off out of the cockpit. We might finally catch Poulet today — if we ever take off.'

It was two days since we'd left Delhi on our final quest to track down the Frenchman. From Delhi to Agra to Allahabad and Calcutta, over the marble dome of the Taj Mahal, dazzling in the sunlight, to the peaceful Jumna River and over patchwork farmland in a thousand shades of brown and green. On we flew at 3,000 ft, searching, hunting for Poulet.

He wasn't in Allahabad. And his Caudron wasn't on the racetrack when we came in to land at Calcutta.

Ross had circled the sprawling city a couple of times to herald our arrival, but we were still astounded by the tens of thousands of people already assembled at the Maidan in anticipation of our landing. Turned out they'd been there since morning, when Poulet had taken off, and they were in such a state of excitement by the time we arrived that they broke through the barriers and were threatening to tear strips off the Vimy as souvenirs. It took hundreds of police and army guards to drive them back.

'The Governor is *still* bloody talking,' whispered Benny. 'Poulet will be doing a victory lap of Australia before we get across the Ganges.' Just then Benny noticed something. He jumped up on the wing and pointed down the race track. 'Here, Wal!' He shielded his eyes with his hand. 'You seen that flock of birds down there?'

I jumped up to take a look. 'Where?' I asked.

He pointed again down the far end of the track. Must have been a few dozen of them, some on the ground, others circling overhead.

'Jesus,' I said, eyeing the length of the runway. 'This track's always worried me, too.'

'Yeah,' said Benny. 'Betcha Ross'll give her everything she's got, or else we'll run out of grass.'

Just then Lord Ronaldshay shook hands with Ross and presented him with two official-looking envelopes before being assisted off the wing by Keith. The crowd applauded as he stepped back down to earth.

'More mail,' groaned Benny. 'Bloody piles of the stuff. How many envelopes we got now, y'reckon?'

'Dunno,' I said. 'Couple of hundred?'

Complete strangers had been shoving mail into our hands since Weybridge. They wanted their envelopes to be among the first post to arrive in Australia by air. Made you realise how many people scattered across the Empire had ties to Australia. Made me feel guilty for not being a better correspondent.

'Ready men?' yelled Ross, as Keith climbed into the cockpit.

'Captain!' Benny pointed down the far end of the track. 'Birds!'

Ross and Keith turned to look, then Ross gestured for one of the RAF chiefs to come over and leaned down to chat. Next thing a motorbike was dispatched down the racecourse into the flock's midst, trying to scare them off.

'Nice one, Benny,' I said as he ducked under the fuselage to start the port engine.

The engines roared to life, we climbed into our cockpit and Ross taxied to the end of the track. I waved my new flag and played to the crowd, enjoying the novelty. The Brits cheered, waved their hats. A few Indian men and boys waved, too, but the women stood perfectly still in their colourful saris, wide-eyed, silent, not at all sure about this monstrous green bird.

We turned and Ross steadied the Vimy for a minute. I pulled the flag inside the cockpit and stared down the track.

The motorbike was tearing around in circles, still trying to clear the flock. Damn those birds.

We sat there a moment longer, engines booming, crowd waving.

The birds were cleared.

I relaxed my shoulders a bit.

Ross throttled forward hard and we were off: bouncing, then racing, then hurtling past the screaming sea of people, building speed, getting ever closer to the end of the straight.

Benny was right. We were running out of grass. Those trees were beginning to look huge.

The wheels lifted off the ground and I could feel Ross trying to pull up her nose as hard as he could.

My hands clutched the silk folds of the flag. There was no way we were going to clear those trees.

Suddenly a white bird flashed past my starboard wing. Another — and another. They were everywhere, flying in panic.

Then a bird flew straight into the port propeller.

There was a mighty thud, and I clutched at Benny's arm as the plane shuddered violently.

The trees were looming, less than 20 yards away. We were headed for the middle of the canopy.

The port wing dipped. My heart stopped. We were goners.

But suddenly Ross was wrenching her up, up. The propeller was holding firm. The dead hawk was wedged in the wiring of the port wing, its feathers shedding into the slipstream.

Ross eased to starboard to avoid more birds and we scraped over the trees, the rubber wheels just inches from the leaves.

We circled back, flying low over the Victoria Memorial building with its heavy scaffolding and the Maidan with its waving masses.

Benny and I were laughing and rapping the top of the fuselage with our knuckles, and then I held the Australian flag aloft and wondered how many thousands of people were seeing my country's flag for

266

the first time — because of us, because of this race, because of Ross Smith and his incredible capacity to save the day, every day.

That was 8.30 in the morning. Four and a half hours later, we'd flown over the Ganges Delta. We'd passed over Chittagong, where Ross and Biffy had nearly blown themselves up on the *Sphinx*. We'd passed over hundreds of miles of Burmese coastline, too, with nothing but blue sea out to one side of the Vimy and thick green jungle out the other.

Then, finally, the seaside port of Akyab came into view, and in the middle of a makeshift aerodrome surrounded by hundreds of people, I saw it.

A tiny Caudron twin-engine biplane.

We'd caught him.

In the forward cockpit Keith started punching the air. He turned around to me and Benny, pointing like a madman at the ground and at us. I thought he was going to fall out of the plane, he was so excited. Then he gave Marmaduke II a little pat on the head and sat back down and I saw his shoulders sag with relief.

I felt it, too. Relief. Exhilaration. Hope. We'd caught Poulet — anything was possible now.

As we came in to land, I scanned the faces for my first real look at him. A man who'd become almost mythical in my mind for his daring and his cunning. How would he be feeling, seeing this huge aircraft circling and swooping down? He must know it was over.

The Vimy's wheels had barely rolled to a stop when a lanky bloke with a wide forehead and an easy smile came striding out to meet us. It's exactly how Ross would have done it. Gallant, sporting, big-hearted.

It was an honour to be there when they met.

267

★ ★ ★

RANGOON, NOVEMBER 30th 1919

'*Bonne chance!*' Poulet raised his arm in the air and champagne sloshed out of his tin mug. '*Bonne chance* and good luck!'

I downed my mug of fizz in a single gulp, topping up on the plonk I'd just drunk at the reception, and felt a rush of affection for the tall, crazy Frenchman.

The six of us stood in a tiny circle in the centre of the Rangoon racetrack. Ross, Keith, Benny, me, Etienne Poulet and his mechanic, Jean Benoist.

Beside us was the Vimy, a giant eagle next to Poulet's tiny sparrow of a Caudron G4. I liked the way the names 'Poulet' and 'Benoist' were painted on its two propeller cowlings.

About 50 yards away on three sides, Burmese troops manned barricades holding back mums cradling babies, dads scolding children, old men with no teeth and young women with golden circles painted on their cheeks and sleek black hair that looked too shiny to be real. From the air we'd seen tens of thousands of people, perhaps as many as 40,000, who'd travelled hundreds of miles over jungle tracks to see the first plane to ever land in Rangoon.

Down here on the racecourse I could still hear the excited babble, but all I could see was the front of the crowd pressing in against the barriers, standing and staring like they were watching a performance, or a ritual maybe.

And I suppose they were.

Beyond the masses, beyond the tall trees, soaring 300 ft into the brilliant blue sky was the shimmering golden Shwedagon Pagoda — a Buddhist stupa so massive we'd spotted it rising above the jungle from 40 miles away on the flight east from Akyab. I hoped there was time to take photos, or no one would ever believe it. It struck me: if I couldn't tell Helena, who would I want to tell?

'*Merci*, Lieutenant,' said Ross, returning his empty mug to Poulet and looking at me and Benny. 'Right, lads. Let's get this done.'

We had 12 days left to get to Australia, across 4,000 miles with only one known airfield and two racetracks large enough to land on. We would be crossing mountains and jungles and oceans that no man had ever flown across before. It was the riskiest stage of the route and the hardest stage to plan for — the stage where British assistance ended and ever more danger lurked.

We'd arrived in Rangoon early that afternoon, an hour in advance of Poulet despite his head start from Akyab. British and French expats had been out in force, with excitement heightened by the fact two planes racing from the other side of the planet were appearing out of the sky on the very same day.

The expats had all cleared off after the welcome toast, to prepare themselves for the Governor's dinner. We honoured guests were to follow them into town after the engines had been checked and tanks refuelled.

'Wait,' said Poulet, grabbing Ross's arm. 'Captain Smith. You and me.' He pointed to Ross and back to himself. 'We drink. We talk.'

Poulet liked to talk. And when he talked, in his thick French accent, he was either throwing his arms around like a conductor, or hugging himself tightly, holding his chin like a professor deep in thought.

269

Ross shook his head. 'Sorry, old son, that'll have to wait for the Governor's dinner.' He pointed to the fuel lorry, parked over near the stables. 'We need to be in the air tomorrow before it gets too hot, so the plane's got to be refuelled now.'

Poulet grabbed his mechanic by the shoulders and steered him toward Ross. 'Benoist will do it,' he said, before gabbling something in French.

'*Oui, d'accord.*' Benoist shrugged his shoulders. I reckon he'd have walked on hot coals for his boss. No different to me and Benny, really.

Ross looked at the tiny Caudron and raised his eyebrows. 'What about your own aircraft?' he said. 'Surely you check it and refuel?'

'Look at her!' said Poulet, nearly collecting me in the face as he waved toward his plane. '*Le petit* Caudron. Very quick to refuel. We check in the morning.' He clasped Ross's shoulder and looked down at the second bottle of champagne he'd borrowed from the reception. 'Now we drink. Talk!'

Ross looked at Keith.

Keith shrugged his shoulders. 'I'm sure Benoist knows how to pass a fuel can.'

Benny raised his hand. 'I'm happy to drink and talk if you'd prefer to work, boss.'

'Thank you, Sergeant,' said Ross dryly. He placed a hand on Poulet's shoulder. 'Okay, maybe one more.'

Benny and I collected our tools from the aft cockpit and got ourselves assembled on our respective wings.

Benoist already had a dozen fuel cans stacked at the front of the Vimy. He was trotting between the fuel lorry and the plane, a man possessed, passing up tins to Keith between laps. The man knew how to work. He'd served as a mechanic to the famous French airman Roland Garros during the war, but before and since he'd only worked for Poulet.

Their 160-horsepower Caudron biplane was designed back in 1916 and had been flown for two years over the Western Front before Poulet bought it for a song at the end of the war. It was the weirdest-looking machine, normal from the front but with no fuselage out the back — just four rather flimsy-looking uncovered steel bars running out to the tail wing. Poulet had test-flown hundreds of Caudrons during the war. When he'd decided to fly across the world in honour of his fallen friend Védrines, it was the only plane he trusted to make the distance. You could still see the Hun bullet holes in the fuselage.

With his broken English, Benoist had told us how the Indian newspapers were convinced Poulet had a small boy hidden on the plane as a mascot, because some French magazine had run a photograph of them with a child before they left Paris. He told us how they'd been forced to land in a fierce storm in a remote part of India, and the villagers thought they were devils coming out of the tempest to eat them. Benoist had pleaded with Poulet to fire his pistol, but he'd walked toward the villagers instead, to show he meant no harm.

Poulet poured two mugs of champagne and settled back onto one of the chairs Ross had carried across from the stables. The Frenchman was over six feet tall and his legs seemed to sprawl in all directions. He was constantly fidgeting.

I looked across the crowds to the pagoda, feeling lightheaded and proud, and suddenly a bit sentimental about being right there in the middle of it all.

'So, Captain Ross Smith,' Poulet began, 'You were

271

a pilot in the war, yes? What aircraft did you fly?'

Ross sipped his champagne. 'Bristol fighters, mainly, toward the end. And a Handley Page 0/400 bomber.' He nodded to the Vimy. 'A third bigger again than this old bus. How about you?'

Poulet shook his head. 'I was a merely a test pilot for Caudron.'

Benoist trotted past carrying two more fuel cans. 'He test 1,000 aircraft in war!' He was wheezing as he spoke, still suffering from the malaria he'd caught in Karachi. 'One *thousand*!'

Poulet shook his head modestly and held up a hand to silence his mechanic. 'Thank you, thank you, my friend. Captain Smith, did you fly before the war?'

'No,' said Ross. 'I didn't get my licence until 1917. You?'

Poulet smiled. '1912.'

Ross let out a low whistle. 'You must have been a small boy!'

'I was 22.'

I did a quick calculation. He was born in 1890, same year as Keith, two years before Ross.

Poulet poured more champagne into their mugs, and held out a hand to the aircraft and people beyond. 'What will you do when this is over?'

Benny called out. 'Spend the winnings!'

Ross smiled over at Benny and shrugged. 'That's a very good question.'

'You will be heroes, no?' asked Poulet.

Ross frowned. 'I'm not interested in any of that.' He sipped his drink. 'Might go back to London, get a job in the RAF. You?'

Poulet thought for a moment, tapping the side of his mug with his fingers while he studied the golden stupa. 'I fly east and I am happy.' He took a long sip of his drink. 'I am in no hurry to return to France.'

'It's very generous, what you're doing for Védrines's widow and her children. I read you've raised tens of thousands of francs?'

'It's true,' said Poulet. 'Thank you. I do not need the money as she does. I just want to fly, so I do not have to …' he waved a hand in the air '… work.'

'Ha!' said Ross. 'That's you and me both.' I noticed he was starting to slur his words. 'I aim to show the potential of aviation in peacetime, so I can continue to be an aviator now the war's over. Doesn't get much more self-serving than that.'

'But Ross,' I said, from up on my wing. 'And pardon me for interrupting, Lieutenant Poulet. Ross – wouldn't it be heroic to be the first man to fly from London to Australia?'

'It would certainly be a splendid achievement, Wal, but we're trained for this. It's not heroic.' Ross stared up at me. 'Are you doing this to be a hero, Wal?'

'No,' I said, looking at the grease on my hands. 'I'm doing it to get back … to get back home.'

'And I'm doing it to get back to my mum.' Ross laughed, finished his mug and held it out for a refill. 'A hero I am not.' He rubbed the scar on his forehead.

Poulet pointed at Ross's face. 'Battle scars, no?'

'Yes.' Ross tapped his cheek. 'Bullet went through here and knocked out some teeth.' He tapped the part in his hair. 'Another bullet smashed my goggles and grazed my head here. Drawing-room scars, really.'

Poulet rolled up the left sleeve of his shirt. 'Accident in Lyons. 1917.' A white scar ran like a train line from his elbow to his wrist.

'Jesus,' said Benny. 'I can see that one from here!'

273

Poulet crossed himself. 'The aircraft not so good.'

Ross rose from his chair and took off his jacket. He unbuttoned his shirt and pulled it off his shoulder to reveal a dozen quarter-inch scars near his shoulder blade. 'Hun shrapnel, I think. Not even sure how I got some of them.'

'But what is this?' Poulet pointed at the small butterfly tattoo near the top of Ross's arm. 'In French we say *papillon*.'

'*Oui*,' said Ross, smiling at Keith. 'It's a butterfly tattoo.'

I craned over the wing's edge to get a better look. I'd forgotten all about it.

'Got it when I was a lad,' said Ross, 'travelling to Britain and America with the mounted cadets. Dad went berserk.'

'This *papillon*. This … butterfly,' said Poulet, waving a hand at Ross's shoulder. 'Do all Australian men have this tattoo?'

'Ha!' Ross shook his head, pulling his shirt back over this shoulder and sitting heavily in his chair. 'No. Just a few of us idiots.' He downed the last of his champagne and held out his mug for a refill. 'There was a tiny tattoo parlour on the pier in San Francisco and I asked the old guy to choose me a symbol.' He rubbed his shoulder as he spoke. 'He said the butterfly's existence is short but extraordinary.'

Ross sat silent for a few moments, then turned in his seat and pointed his mug at the Shwedagon Pagoda. 'It's certainly extraordinary today.'

Poulet sat forward, resting his elbows on his knees and cradling his mug in his hands. 'My hero Jules Védrines was a *papillon*.' He nodded to himself, staring into his mug. 'A short, extraordinary life. You

274

remind me of Védrines, Captain Smith.'

I looked over toward Benny, feeling uneasy about where this talk was going.

'Excuse me, gentlemen,' said Keith, 'there's an uncharted mountain range between here and Siam, so let's not talk about butterflies and short lives, shall we?'

'Keith!' said Ross, screwing up his face. 'It's a tiny bit of ink!'

For the first time, he sounded like a kid talking to his older brother.

Poulet stood and raised his mug to the pagoda. 'To Védrines. And to you, Captain.'

Ross stood too, and Poulet threw a lanky arm around his shoulders. 'To Védrines,' Ross said. 'And to loyal friends.'

'Live long, *le petit papillon* Ross Smith,' said Poulet.

Those two men, those giants of men, stood arm in arm, swaying slightly, with the four of us watching silently and 40,000 others just over there, drawn to their light like moths to flame. Forty thousand people momentarily more captivated by two aviators than a 300-ft shrine plastered in gold. I screwed the engine cowling back into place and started carefully checking my aileron wires, suddenly anxious to get Ross far away from Poulet.

★　★　★

Ross held up a hand, silencing his brother. 'I'll say this just one more time. We are not leaving without Poulet.'

He'd made a pact with the Frenchman the night before, to fly in tandem over the high ranges and dense

275

jungle between here and Bangkok. It wouldn't be easy, given we had more than four times the horsepower, but Ross was convinced that by throttling down and manoeuvring it would be possible to keep together.

I didn't really like the sound of it, containing the natural rhythm of our own engines to suit a far smaller, slower plane. But Ross was the boss – and in no mood for mutiny.

'For Christ's sake,' Keith muttered under his breath, and stormed off to fume by the Vimy.

The two aircraft were still surrounded by tens of thousands of people at the base of the Shwedagon Pagoda.

It was half-past six in the morning and already steaming hot. Every minute we waited would make it harder to rise quickly and clear the trees when we took off.

And Poulet and Benoist were having engine trouble. Benny and I had tried to help, but neither of us could see what the problem was without taking the machine apart.

Finally, Ross caved in, offering his farewells to the dignitaries and telling Poulet we'd see him in Bangkok that afternoon. We started the engines and waited at the end of the track to see if Poulet looked any closer to starting. When the Frenchman waved us on, Ross increased the throttle and we were off — clearing a fence by less than a foot and once again brushing tree-tops with the undercarriage of the bomber's fuselage.

Ross circled the racecourse for 20 minutes, waiting for signs of movement below. Then we saw Poulet step away from the Caudron, look up to the Vimy with his arms spread wide and wave us on. Ross dipped the Vimy's wings, once, twice, and Poulet saluted. One hero to another.

Chapter 20

SINGORA, DECEMBER 2nd 1919

Just for a second, I closed my eyes. Folded my arms and leaned back against the workbench. My head sagged forward and my chin rested on my chest. Sleep washed over me. Just for a second I felt blissfully happy, on a soft Sydney mattress beside Helena, drifting off. Drifting.

In the distance I could still hear Ross's voice, encouraging, cajoling, like a parent persuading a child. It wasn't working. The four Malays who'd been turning the heavy pulley-wheel, transmitting power by belt to the lathe, were on strike. They didn't want more money. It was after dark, they'd been working since dawn, and they wanted to go home to their families. I wanted to go home, too. Drifting. On the mattress I rolled over and touched Helena's bare arm.

Something moved. I woke with a start. My eye was throbbing again. I rubbed it gently and felt a crust in the corner. Could barely see out of it now.

In the eerie gloom, the foreman stepped forward and delivered a vicious blow with a long, thin piece of bamboo, striking a worker's bare arm with a nasty crack.

'Whoa. Hang on, old boy!' Benny's voice rang out through the rice mill.

The four Malays stood with heads bowed beside the pulley wheel. Sulky, stubborn.

The foreman raised his stick to strike another.

'Wait!' Ross held out a hand. 'I've got more money. If you could just explain …'

The foreman shook his head, delivering another sharp blow to the man's lower thigh below his shorts. The welt turned white before blood beaded along it.

'No, Captain Smith.' The foreman spoke in a thick Yorkshire accent. 'Can't have you wasting good money on coolies.'

'Jesus,' I muttered. I looked away and noticed a small, faded photograph nailed to the wall, of a young white woman with a full belly and a fat toddler standing in a perambulator. The woman had a protective hand on the boy's shoulder and another on her stomach, and she was staring past the camera with a worried look on her face. She looked hot, overdressed and out of place. I wondered if she was out here, too, trapped in the middle of a jungle. Trapped with a man like this.

'Is this necessary?' asked Keith, frowning.

'Depends,' said the foreman, scratching his neck and waving his cane toward the lump of steel in the lathe. 'On whether you want to fly your aircraft to Australia, or walk home?'

We'd left Poulet a day and a half ago. I'd vomited most of the way from Rangoon to Bangkok. Keith had warned us there was a mountain range to cross, and when mist descended Ross had climbed higher and higher in case the peaks were hidden in the clouds. I got as crook as a dog again, throwing up stale champagne and rice and egg and milky tea. Benny took a leak in his piss bottle and the plane jerked suddenly and it spilled down the front of my flying suit. It stank. I didn't have the energy to shove my head out of the cockpit, so I retched bile into my mitt and used it to wipe away Benny's piss. And right then I knew, with absolute certainty, I would never, ever do anything like this again. Not for ten thousand quid. Not for a hundred thousand. Not even if Ross said I was the only man for the job.

Then the engine noise dimmed and I really did think we were dead. Wind whipped past the struts and squealed through the wires, like a siren's song calling us into the mountain. I pressed my mitts over my ears and buried my head in my knees to block it all out. Benny thumped my leg and gestured with his hand like a glider. We weren't falling, we were drifting down. Ross had throttled back the engines to pull our speed right back, which probably meant we'd used a lot of petrol and he was being forced to descend blindly through cloud, without knowing if we'd passed the mountains. He was slowing us down to lessen the impact if we hit anything.

It was like playing blind-man's bluff as a kid, only you're about to crash into the side of a mountain and you might get splattered into a thousand pieces, or you might end up half-dead in agony waiting for birds to peck your eyeballs out of their sockets. I could feel my own sweat. Even if we survived, I knew I'd stink of death.

When the engines finally roared back to life, I poked my head out of the cockpit and saw we'd come through the clouds, and below us a glorious green carpet of jungle stretched to the horizon in all directions. We were at 1,500 ft, low enough to see a flock of white birds lift from trees, cruise in a circle above a dense outcrop of bright-green vine and settle back down again. It was magical, and the mountains were behind us. I slumped back on my seat and fell asleep until we bounced to earth at Don Muang aerodrome.

That was the last time I slept. Benny and I had worked all night under lights, regrinding the valves on two of the cylinders of my starboard engine and carrying out the usual machine checks beside the Don Muang workshops. The Siamese Flying Corps had one of the most advanced aerodromes in the world. Before the war, Siam had invested in French aircraft and sent three of their finest army officers to train as pilots in Paris. They'd even sent a Flying Corps to aid the allies on the Western Front in 1918.

What they also had was bugs. Every insect and flying ant in Siam was flickering under our spotlights. About 2 am something flew into my left eye and bit me under the lid, right in the corner. Stung like a bastard.

'I am never doing this again,' I said to Benny, as I tried to lift my swelling eyelid with a clean bit of my wrist.

Benny replied flatly, without looking up. 'I know.'

I stared at him, anger rising in my chest. 'What does that mean?'

'What does what mean, Wal?' He was busy with the valve — grinding, checking, grinding again.

'You said 'I know'.' My eye was screaming at me. 'What does that mean?'

'It means I know. You've had enough. I get it.'

I poked around at the nuts and bolts from the cowling, soaking in an oil bath. 'Thanks for the sympathetic ear.' My words sounded more sarcastic than I'd intended.

'Mate,' he said, shaking his head, 'I'm so fucking knackered, I don't give a shit if you don't want to do this again. No one's asking you to, as far as I can tell.'

'Right.' I stared at the oil bath.

'Now, how about we fix this fucking engine before Ross arrives in the morning?'

We didn't speak again that night. Just grunted a lot, cursing at insects. I decided he probably thought less of me for saying I'd had enough.

A Siamese prince and three other fighter pilots escorted us out of Bangkok. I caught the prince's eye and exchanged a wave just as he banked and headed for home. I thought maybe it was a sign. Today was going to be better.

It wasn't.

It was one of the worst days of the flight. From an hour in, torrential rain nailed us. Ross sat at 1,000 ft just off the coast, and I could not for the life of me understand how he could see where we were going. Goggles were useless, and the rain pained my one good eye. Within minutes of hitting the storm, Benny and I were soaked to the bone, and using our piss bottles to bail water. We shoved a tarp over our heads and sat in miserable darkness, with the plane buffeted from angry headland winds. Ross suddenly pulled the machine around sharply into a climbing turn. I crashed the top of my head into the rim of the cockpit and was drenched in the water that had pooled on the tarp. I poked my head out into the rain and saw a jagged cliff face disappearing into the gloom off the port wing behind us. We must have just missed it.

We'd planned to fly straight to Singapore from Bangkok, but some genius told us Singora had a freshly cleared aerodrome with a good supply of aircraft fuel. They failed to mention it was 500 litres of aircraft fuel, not 500 gallons, so we needed to wait a day while more fuel was transported by rail from Penang. And

281

they failed to mention the cleared aerodrome had not been cleared of tree stumps. Ross circled the machine above the clearing. Then he circled again. Then he must have said a prayer and we went in to land.

Miraculously, we only hit one stump. That's what wrenched off the back tail-skid. That's why we'd spent hours crawling over a local Chinaman's scrap heap in search of a bit of steel. That's why we were waiting around in a rice mill well after dark, trying to use the biggest lathe in Singora to grind the steel into a workable new tail-skid. But the lathe was powered by four Malays, and the Malays had already worked a full day for a man they didn't like.

'What's the Malay word for 'please'?' asked Ross, stepping between the foreman and his workers.

'Words don't cure indolence,' the foreman said, scratching his ankle with the tip of his bamboo cane before pointing it at Ross. 'The only language they understand is this.'

He was like Copping. Not the sharpest tool in the shed, but the only man with the bamboo cane. I should have said something. I should have stood up for those poor little fellas who'd already been turning that huge pulley-wheel in stinking heat for hours before going on strike. I should have offered to turn the pulley-wheel myself, like Benny did. But I was so tired. I just wanted to get the plane fixed and fly away.

The foreman scratched at his neck again and I noticed insect bites thick like welts.

'Yes, old son,' said Ross, nodding. 'You've certainly shown them who's boss.' He rubbed his chin. 'Humour me.'

'*Sila*,' the foreman said, shaking his head. 'My wife says the Malay word for please is *sila*.'

Ross turned to the men and pressed his palms together, like we'd seen the Malays do earlier that day. 'Sila!' he said. He pointed to the steel shafting in the lathe and to the wing badge sewn onto his chest, and then he held out his arms like he was flying. 'Sila.'

I stepped forward and pressed my palms together in front of my chest. '*Sila.*'

'*Sila,*' said Keith, nodding.

Benny stepped forward. '*Sila,*' he said. '*Sila,* I bloody beg you.'

The workers stared at the ground. The foreman grunted. 'Told ya.'

Then the man who'd been caned said something in Malay and the four of them returned to their positions around the pulley-wheel, grunting with the effort of getting it turning again.

The foreman started cursing and threatening and ordering them to push harder.

'Thank you, my good man,' said Ross, clapping the foreman's shoulder. 'You have been singularly helpful. Now, why don't we let these chaps do their jobs while you show me around this fascinating mill of yours.'

A dozen Malays sweated in relays for five hours until we finally had a piece of steel resembling the tail-skid. We walked out into the night not long before midnight, calling 'Thank you, thank you.' The bloke who'd been caned stood silhouetted in the doorway of the mill and put his arms out to fly like Ross had done, then shouted out in Malay as he pressed his palms together in front of his chest. Ross put his arms out like he was flying, too, then he raised his hands to the heavens to thank his own God.

I was desperate to go to bed and close my eye, but on the buggy ride back to the aerodrome, the monsoon we'd flown through earlier that day caught up with us again. All four of us spent the night huddled under the wings of the plane, soaked through as 10 inches of rain fell in a few hours, holding her down during the worst of the squalls.

I kept myself awake by saying 'never again'. Must have said it 10,000 times.

★ ★ ★

SINGAPORE, DECEMBER 5th 1919

'Listen to this, Ross.' Benny was lying on top of his cream floral bedspread, in freshly pressed army shorts and socks, in our twin room of the Europe Hotel in Singapore. The top half of his body was hidden behind a pressed copy of the *Straits Times*, and he was reading aloud in a British colonial accent. 'Ladies may be interested to know that Captain Ross Smith is 26 and unmarried. It has been remarked that he bears a striking resemblance to Major Norman Black, MC.'

Ross groaned, sinking further into his armchair and checking the bottom of his boots before propping them up on my bed. 'Newsmen do write the most awful balls, don't they?'

I looked up from my diary. 'Who's Norman Black?'

Benny spoke from behind the paper, still assuming his accent. 'A fine specimen of a chap, I'd wager.'

'I'm 27, for one thing,' said Ross, loosening his tie and unbuttoning his collar. 'Although, granted, only by one day.'

He'd turned 27 in Singora. Keith said his birthday gift was 200 convicts arriving from the local gaol to dig out the stumps on the aerodrome.

I was sitting on the other twin bed with my back against the wall, rolling my ankles over the side of the mattress and enjoying the feeling of clean, dry socks on my feet. Benny and I had been chauffeured from the Singapore Racecourse to the Europe Hotel the evening before, and our first order of business had been to hand over our sodden, stinking kit bags. Leaning over to the window, I pulled back the lace curtain and looked across the alley to a red brick wall dotted with tiny windows. A woman stared down from one of them, dabbing her forehead as she watched the scene in the street below. She must have seen me from the corner of her eye, because she looked across and smiled the smallest of smiles before stepping back and away.

I let the curtain drop and sat back, frowning down at the blank page of my diary. A hawker yelled, and I could hear the squeaking wheels of his cart.

Ross reached out and whacked Benny's foot. 'What else does it say?'

Benny folded the paper and handed it to Ross. 'All the usual. Dreadful flying weather. Marvellous welcome. Couldn't have done it without my trusty mechanics. Yes, yes. What, what.'

'Ha!' Ross shot him a look. 'Am I that repetitive?'

'Well,' said Benny, lying back on the pillow with his hands tucked behind his head, 'there's not a lot else to say, is there? Unless you want to mention that bastard whipping his workers in Singora.'

Ross frowned and shook his head as he began rifling through the paper. 'Coolies and convicts — lifeblood of the British Empire.'

Benny grunted in agreement, and turned his head to look at me. 'Short, swarthy bloke like you'd have some convict blood, wouldn't ya, Wal?'

I blinked, a bit surprised at the question. Wasn't something polite people asked. Then I smiled, thinking about Mum proudly retelling the Shiers story on special occasions like we had royal blood. 'I don't know how much is true, but Mum used to tell us the first Shiers to arrive in Australia was a convict transported to Van Diemen's Land.'

'Really?' said Ross, raising his eyebrows.

'Knew it!' Benny pointed at finger at me. 'I've got a knack for guessing convict blood.'

'That's not the best bit,' I said, pausing to add some drama. I could see why Mum liked telling this story. 'Old man Shiers was one of a dozen convicts to escape Van Diemen's Land in a small stolen ship. He got all the way to Chile before he was caught.'

'You're just making this up now!' Benny waved a dismissive hand.

'No, it's true,' I said. 'Well, Mum always said it was true. They were taken back and charged with piracy, but the judge let them off on some technicality, and they only served a few more years. That's how old man Shiers managed to get to South Australia after it was settled.'

'That is a fine story, Wal,' said Ross. 'My father emigrated from Scotland, and mother had Scottish parents too – rather dull, now, in comparison. How about you, Benny?'

'Yeah, same,' said Benny. 'Granddad McKendrick emigrated from Scotland to South Australia – had a big shipbuilding yard out there.'

We were all quiet for a while, then. I thought about old man Shiers crossing a huge ocean in that tiny ship, probably running out of food and water. Made my own journey seem easy.

Ross started rifling through the paper again. 'Any word in here on Matthews or Rendle?'

'No,' I said. 'I've got a bad feeling about Matthews.' He and Tom Kay were likely still snowbound in Germany, unless they'd got desperate and tried to fly in that foul European winter and crashed somewhere over the Alps. He'd made a poor choice, heading to Cologne from Hounslow.

In the top right-hand corner of my blank page, I drew a square, and then carefully shaded inside the lines. 'It mentions Poulet,' I said. 'He's been forced back to Rangoon twice. Been having all kinds of trouble. Sounds like Val Rendle and Hubert Wilkins are the only ones who might stop us from being first to Darwin now.'

'Yeah,' said Benny. 'Just Rendle and Wilkins and 2,500 miles of jungle and ocean.'

A telegram had been waiting for Ross in Singapore, to say Rendle and Wilkins had departed Hounslow on November 21st, and Rome on December 1st. As expected, the Blackburn Kangaroo was making sure and steady progress across Europe, but there was no way they could catch us unless we crashed or were delayed. Ross was more worried about meeting the 30-day deadline than staking our claim to the prize money.

We had seven days to get to Darwin. We'd stayed an extra night in Singapore to rest up and give me and Benny a solid day on the engines. We'd been working on the Vimy at the racecourse all day, in 95-degree heat and the sort of humidity I'd never experienced. This couple of hours at the hotel was like a holiday.

Ross leaned his head back on the armchair and closed his eyes. 'You blokes don't know how lucky you are, hiding away in here. You should see how many people are hanging around at the house where we're staying. I've left Keith playing croquet with the Colonial Secretary's wife.'

Benny snorted.

Ross stared up at the ceiling. 'Everyone's always so bloody accommodating. It's exhausting.'

He didn't sound like the decorated airman Captain Ross Smith. He sounded like me.

I looked at Benny, expecting him to be as shocked as I was. He didn't move. He didn't even open his eyes. 'I know,' he said, in the same flat tone he'd used with me in the workshop at Bangkok.

And then I realised Benny wasn't judging anyone. He understood, because he felt the same way.

'Me too,' I said, admiring the neat little square on my blank page.

Ross sighed and closed his eyes. 'There's a bloody ball in our honour tonight. Hunkered down in a monsoon one night. Drinking champagne under chandeliers the next.'

Out in the hotel hallway I heard a man and woman talking softly, and then a door opening and closing sharply.

Ross's mouth sagged open and he started snoring, loud like a motorbike engine. From this angle I could see how much weight he'd lost. His face was gaunt and his lips were chapped and sore. He looked 90.

I chewed the end of my pencil for a minute and wrote 'Love you I do' before closing the diary and resting it quietly on the bed beside me. I gently touched my puffy eye. After a cool bath it was feeling better.

★ ★ ★

SURABAYA, DECEMBER 7th 1919

We flew into Surabaya at noon on a sweltering December day. By Ross's reckoning, we only had two more stops before Darwin, so close you could almost smell the eucalypts. For two days the weather had been glorious as we flew along the east coast of Sumatra and began hopping across a chain of turquoise-rimmed islands leading us east and home. Benny was so happy he'd sometimes stand in the cockpit and do a little jig.

From the air, the Surabaya aerodrome looked perfect — a half-decent stretch of flat, firm ground, clear of stumps and not so much as a puddle in sight. But the second the Vimy rolled to a stop, her four wheels dropped through a thick layer of crust and sank to the axles in mud.

It was land reclaimed from the sea, and for half a mile in all directions, liquid black sludge sat just below the surface.

After six hours in the boiling tropical sun, with help from 200 villagers and Dutch soldiers, we'd managed to haul the plane onto a little platform of bamboo matting at the end of the aerodrome. Ross knew there was no way he could take off. The wheels would sink the second we left the matting.

It was a lousy feeling, stuck in the mud just 1,200 miles from Darwin. A Dutch engineer from the Harbour Board suggested bringing in soil to lay a roadway, but that would take days, weeks maybe, and we only had four of our 30 days left. As the sun dropped in the sky, Ross said he'd sleep on the idea, and sent everyone home.

Working by the light of lamps from the engineer's motor car, he and Keith started refilling the tanks with petrol and oil while me and Benny checked the engines. Then the four of us turned our attention to the two tyres punctured by long nails in the matting, and realised we should have attended to them first, before refilling the tanks and adding the weight of hundreds of gallons of petrol. Just as we got one wheel jacked up, the ground sank underneath the Vimy's six-ton weight and the jack broke. So we dug her out and borrowed a jack from our new friend's motor car. The ground broke underneath us again and the Vimy sank to its axles, breaking that jack, too.

'To hell with this!' Keith was kneeling beside the wheel, thigh-deep in stinking mud.

'No more,' agreed Ross, flicking black sludge as he threw up his hands. 'If I spend one more minute on this aircraft tonight, I'll torch the damned thing.'

Benny and I set up a campfire by some nearby warehouses to ward off the bugs, and kept an ear out for anyone going near the Vimy. She was somewhere just out there in the blackness, forlorn and flat bellied. The engineer gave Ross and Keith a lift into town, to send a telegram ahead and share a meal with local dignitaries.

We were resting back on our kit bags, having a smoke after finishing the last of the bully beef in our emergency kit, when Ross and Keith turned up. The engineer had lent them his car.

Ross handed Benny a small bottle of scotch as he sat down and peered out into the darkness. 'If this is the day our race ends,' he said, 'this is where I want to be.'

We all sat silently for a while, watching the flickering fire.

Benny lit a smoke. 'What are we gonna do?'

'Dunno,' said Ross, biting a twig between his teeth.

'We'll think of something tomorrow,' said Keith.

'Always do,' I said, nodding into the flames.

'I dunno,' said Ross, shaking his head. 'Can't see a way out of this one. Not in four days.'

I walked over to our small pile of kindling and placed a few sticks on the fire. It crackled and sent out sparks. The smell of smoke took me back to Egypt, sitting around the fire with Westy and the lads. 'Maybe the mud will dry out in a few days?' I asked, settling back down.

'We don't have a few days,' said Ross.

'Besides,' said Keith. 'It's wet season — we're likely to be hit with more rain, not less.'

'Ever the optimist, eh Keith?' said Ross, shaking his head.

Keith frowned. 'You said it yourself in town, half-hour ago.'

'I know, Buck. Sorry.' Ross picked up another twig, cracked it in two. 'We could still be sitting here in another fortnight, watching Rendle and Wilkins fly right over us.'

We all stared at the fire. I thought about how close we were. How far.

'Fuck,' said Ross. 'I should have pushed her harder. Gone the extra 400 miles to Bima.'

'That's my fault,' I said, not taking my eyes off the flames. I'd been pretty forceful in persuading Ross to make smaller flights, now that the engines had been running so long without a total overhaul. I wouldn't have suggested landing in Surabaya if I'd known the

291

condition of the aerodrome.

'Bullshit, Wal,' said Benny. 'We both warned against long flights for this last bit. She's not up to it.' He opened the scotch bottle, had a swig and offered it to Ross.

'Thanks.' Ross said, taking his own swig and handing it to me. 'Bloody hell, Wal, I was so close to getting you home to your girl for Christmas.'

I coughed as the scotch burned my throat. 'Yeah,' I said, studying the label to avoid his eye. 'Ah, well.'

'You still haven't told him?' Benny was resting his elbows on his kit bag. I frowned at him and he stared back, eyebrows raised.

'Told me what?' asked Ross.

'Helena,' said Benny. 'She dumped him at the end of the war.'

'What?' Ross looked from Benny to me.

'Ahhh,' I said, my face burning. 'Nothing, it's, y'know …'

I handed Keith the bottle and he took a long swig, stared right through me in that way of his. 'Ross said you'd been together for years.'

'I thought you were engaged,' said Ross.

I was silent for a moment. 'I got a letter from her at Cheveney.'

Ross rifled through his pockets and got out a cigarette.

'You should have told me, Wal.' He took a stick from the fire to light his smoke. 'Must be hard for women back home, waiting for years on end.'

'Yeah,' I said, thinking that would be the last of it. I reached out my arm toward Keith. 'Can I have another swig of that scotch?'

'It was our fault,' said Benny.

292

I rolled my eyes. 'Leave it out, Benny, will you?'

'How was it our fault?' asked Keith, looking at Ross.

'Wal promised her he'd be home as soon as the war ended,' said Benny. 'She'd booked the church and everything. But by then me and Ross had talked Wal into flying to India. And then we signed up for the race.'

I picked up a handful of dirt. 'No one talked me into anything.' I stared at the fire, feeling stupid.

Somewhere nearby a frog croaked.

'Well, Wal,' said Ross, sitting up straight and resting his elbows on his knees. 'I am sincerely sorry to hear that.'

'Mmmm,' said Keith, nodding. I felt uneasy about him hearing all this.

'But you're gonna get her back. Right, Wal?' said Benny.

'Enough.' I pointed at him. 'I'm warning you now, Benny.'

'How?' asked Ross, drawing on his cigarette.

'Yes, how?' asked Keith.

'He's …'

I glared at Benny. He was grinning.

' … writing her a poem.'

'How about we just concentrate on the Vimy?' I said, knowing that's what Ross and Keith would be thinking too.

Ross shook his head. 'I am sick to the back teeth of the Vimy. And this flight. And our next landing site. And fuel and oil supplies. And wondering what the fuck I'm going to do with my life if we ever get back to Australia.' He took a pull of his cigarette. 'What have you written so far? And hand me that bottle, would you please?'

Benny cleared his throat. 'There was a young girl from Narrandera ...'

'Benny!' I said. There was a silence filled with frogs.

'Is that it?' asked Keith, frowning. 'A limerick?'

'No!' I said, my face burning with embarrassment.

'He couldn't think ...' Benny snorted.

'Please, mate,' I said, hating the whine in my voice.

'He couldn't think ...' He started to giggle.

'Mate!'

'Of a rhyming word ...' He laughed some more, '... for Narrandera.' He doubled over in the dirt.

I tried not to smile.

'How about ...' Keith rubbed his chin, deadly serious, 'philanderer?'

Benny roared with laughter. 'That's what I said!'

They were all laughing now. It was good to see Ross's eyes crinkling at the corners again.

'Okay, okay.' I grinned. 'You've had your fun.' I got up and grabbed another couple of twigs for the fire.

'So what else have you written?' asked Ross.

I placed the twigs on the embers and rubbed my palms on my shorts, watching the smoke rise into the night. 'Bugger all. Not that it matters. She'll either want me or she won't.'

'I actually like the idea of a poem, Wal,' Benny said quietly. 'It's something that a man of the world would do.'

It suddenly struck me how much I'd miss him when this was all over.

'Women love poetry,' said Ross. 'Don't they, Buck?'

Keith grunted. Stared blankly at the fire.

Ross took another swig, emptying the bottle. 'Wal, get us some paper and a pencil.'

I looked at him. 'What?'

'That's an order, Sergeant Shiers.'

I rummaged through my kit bag, handed him my diary and chewed pencil.

'Okay,' said Ross, smoothing down a blank page. 'I'll be Colonel Borton. Let's think of some pertinent words.'

Benny rubbed his hands together. 'Wally. Helena. Race. Promise. War. Narrandera.'

Ross shook his head. 'Let's forget Narrandera, shall we? How about ...' Ross drew a line down the side of the page. '... love?' He looked uncertainly at Benny.

'No, that's a good one,' said Benny, pointing at the page. 'Wal wants to marry this woman — a bit of romance is just the ticket.'

Keith was smoking a cigarette, staring at the fire. I stared at my hands in my lap.

'C'mon, Wal,' said Benny. 'What else?' He picked up a twig and threw it at me.

I shrugged and shook my head. 'I've been trying to write this bloody poem since Lyons.'

I stared at him.

He stared back, waiting.

Ross drew another line, parallel with the first one.

Keith was still watching the fire.

I took a deep breath and said, 'During the war, we used to write 'Love you I do'.'

Ross looked up. 'What was that?'

Benny pointed at the page. ''Love you I do'. Write that down, Ross.'

Ross smiled as he wrote it. 'Right, let's start with that ...'

The frog croaked again.

'Love you I do ...' said Ross, tapping the page with the pencil. 'Love you I do ...' He chewed his lip. 'What goes with that?'

Croak. Croak. Keith flicked his cigarette end into the fire. 'Love you I do,' said Ross again. He blew out through his cheeks. 'The Colonel and Biffy always made it look so easy.' 'Are you sure she wouldn't like a limerick?' asked Benny. Keith held up a hand. 'Shhh!' I felt the hairs rise up on my arms. Benny opened his mouth, but Keith raised a hand again to silence him. He stared at the fire, then started to speak:

> *I've raced through skies o'er half the globe*
> *And now I know it's true,*
> *The long flight home means nothing*
> *If there's no love you I do.*

★ ★ ★

I woke at first light with a bad feeling in my guts and a stiff, sunburned neck.

We were stuck. We wouldn't fly today. I glanced across at the Vimy, sad and helpless in the mud.

Lying flat on my back, I watched a thin line of campfire smoke drifting up into the sky and recited Keith's poem to the sound of Benny's Rolls-Royce snores. When he drew breath I heard voices. Lots of them. I flipped onto my side and nudged him with my boot, nodding toward the villagers streaming in from every direction bearing sheets of bamboo matting.

'Bloody hell,' said Benny, shaking his head in wonder. 'Keith's done it again.'

Sometime around midnight, Keith had come up with a plan. We'd ask for more matting from the villagers and lay an entire runway. Ross liked the idea so much they'd driven straight off to wake the engineer.

296

We needed to get away before the day got too hot. There wasn't a moment to lose.

As the sun rose they arrived in their hundreds. Smiling, shy, gracious. Generously offering sheets of bamboo matting they'd stripped from the walls of their own homes. While Benny and I worked with a team of Dutch soldiers to dig out the Vimy and replace the tyres, Keith and Ross worked with the villagers to lay two 300-yard bamboo runways — a barrier between our two sets of wheels and the mud. Matting Road, we called it.

I was beside the Vimy, waiting for Benny to hand me down a spare wheel, when Ross called me over to meet the British Consul and ask if I knew the telegram code for Narrandera. I stood there feeling witless while Ross went into far too much detail about how we'd flown straight to India after the war, and how I'd broken Helena's heart, and how Keith's poem was going to make everything right again.

'Could you possibly organise a telegram, my good man?' Ross finished 'It's a diplomatic emergency.'

The chap was about Ross's height, maybe 50, with a black handlebar moustache and a huge stomach trying to burst through the buttons of his cream jacket. He stood studying me with a serious expression, jingling coins or something in his left pocket, and for a moment I felt like saying the telegram wasn't my idea. Then he straightened his pith helmet and nodded toward a motor car parked under the trees nearby. A portly woman sat in the front passenger seat, surveying the scene as she fluttered a fan in the same pale-green silk as her dress.

'Twenty-five years, Sergeant,' the Consul said, 'and never a cross word.' He patted his belly. 'Finest puddings this side of the Indian Ocean.'

I cleared my throat. 'Helena's jam sponge is very nice, too, sir.'

He twirled his moustache, nodding thoughtfully. 'Gentlemen,' the Consul said, 'this will be the most important thing I do today.' He took the piece of paper from Ross and folded it delicately in half like he was handling some ancient parchment, and then folded it into quarters before tucking it away in his top pocket.

The first attempt at take-off was a disaster. The swirling propellers sucked up the bamboo matting, chewed the sheets to bits and spewed them out in all directions. I would have felt bad for all those people, watching their homes being torn to shreds, except the Vimy veered off course and got bogged again.

Without a word the villagers picked up the biggest pieces and started over. A lorry arrived with more sheets and this time we pegged it all down and interlaced the mats so they couldn't blow up in the slipstream.

And it worked.

We trundled along Matting Road and had one of our easiest take-offs of the race, circling back to fly low and wave our thanks. The British Consul stood in the shade beside his wife, waving his helmet and patting his stomach. I thought about Keith's poem, and how incredible it was that it would beat me back to Narrandera.

Out in the hot sun, hundreds of villagers were already bent over the job of removing the wooden pegs to take their walls away. I'd never forget the people of Surabaya laying down their homes for us.

Chapter 21

APPROACHING AUSTRALIA,
DECEMBER 10th 1919

I knelt in the bottom of the plane with my arms folded on the rim of the cockpit.

Australia. Please God, let us see it soon. Don't let anything happen now.

I wanted to climb down from this cockpit one more time and *be there*.

I wanted to close my eyes and hear Australian voices. Mate and missus and cobber and cooee.

The smell of dry summer heat. The bush. The dirt. Jam sponge, freshly made with sugar dusted on top.

I wanted chops. Gravy. Mash. Served on Mum's yellow china plates with the scalloped edges. I wondered where that crockery set was now.

Jesus. What was I doing thinking about crockery?

I flexed my fingers, glad I'd decided not to wear my mitts, then shifted my weight to get comfortable on my knees. Accidentally shoved Benny in the arm, and shot him a 'sorry, mate' look. Again. Christ, I wouldn't miss this coffin. He nodded, grinned, gave me a thumbs up and went back to concentrating on his Kodak.

Bloody hell, he was a patient bastard.

Big smile. Big day.

I took some deep breaths to stop the churning in my guts. Checked my starboard instrument gauges. Engines running like clockwork.

You had to hand it to Rolls-Royce. Twenty-eight

days, 11,000-odd miles. And still those engines boomed away like it was day one out of Hounslow.

Was that really only 28 days ago? Felt like a year. No wonder I was knackered.

Shaking my head, I gave the old girl a pat in the spot I'd rubbed a bit bare. Wondered what would happen to her when the dust settled.

I peered ahead to the horizon, remembering how much I'd hated Keith last time we were flying over the sea like this, from Crete to Cairo.

Australia. What then?

Family. Jack's kids. They'd be so grown up now, couldn't wait to see them. My heart ached at the thought of Bill left behind in France. Couldn't wait to see Alf and Arthur and Dick. Hug 'em tight. Beers all round. They'd be proud of me.

I was proud of them, getting through all that was thrown at them in France.

I wondered if it had changed them at all? Couldn't not, really.

I wondered if I'd ever lose my small knot of guilt for not serving on the Western Front, in the trenches. Did anyone back home even know there'd been a war in Egypt and Palestine?

Couldn't imagine not having served. How would you look another man in the eye?

Dad.

I took a deep breath. He'd be proud of us all, too. I hoped he was.

I took a few more deep breaths, lifted my goggles to wipe my eyes, clear the mist.

Couldn't think of Dad without welling up. It had been like that for days now. Funny. I hadn't ever missed him before. Hardly thought about him for years and years. Something about my having been away – or maybe it was just growing up a bit, or the thought of going home and Mum not being there. Anyway, it would be good to see him. Shout him a beer. Maybe get a couple of words out of him.

I turned to check if I could still see HMAS *Sydney*.

The smoke stacks, the cheering lads were gone. The horizon swallowed everything eventually.

I hoped they rescued Keith's pickle jar before it sank into the waves. The little parachute had worked a treat.

Australia. Jesus. I rapped the top of the plane with my knuckles. Benny smiled and rapped his knuckles too. It was our little joke. Hurry up! We've had enough now!

I wondered where Westy was. Wondered if he and the other blokes knew I was on the Vimy. Be great to see him if we flew to Melbourne. When we flew to Melbourne. That's where the cheque was.

I wanted to track down Bernie's parents in New South Wales, too. I'd been thinking about that for a long time now. I wanted to tell them that I knew so much about their farm I could practically draw them a map. The paddock where Bernie's dad had taught him to ride. The tree where he'd buried Blacky when he was bitten by a king brown. The couch on the porch with the red and yellow cushions, where Bernie and his sister took turns reading aloud to Mrs Ranford. I wanted to tell them he was a good lad. Brave and funny and thoughtful. That he'd made a mark despite dying so early. That it wasn't all for nothing. Bernie deserved better than that.

Australia. I stared out across the sky. It was so pale,

almost yellow-blue. Almost like a completely different sky.

Had to keep reminding myself that no man had ever flown into Australia before. No man had ever seen Australia on the horizon like we were about to see it.

Ross was always saying it was us mechanics who kept the plane in the air. But he was the bloke at the wheel. He was the man who decided to fly across the world and then made it happen. He was Christopher Columbus. He was Captain Cook. We were deckhands following orders.

I stared down at the rolling whitecaps, thinking it might make the time go quicker if I concentrated on the sea.

Made me think of that first voyage out of Australia on the way to war, when I was as crook as a dog and Copping kept barking orders anyway. I was so homesick for Helena back then. Could barely speak for missing her.

Would she agree to see me?

Christ, what if she was married? Why had I never thought of that? She might be Mrs Someone Else. Of somewhere else. She could even have a kid!

Australia. I had to get back. I had to know.

I rested my cheek on my arm and closed my eyes for a second.

Benny poked me in the ribs, hard. Clumsy lug.

I frowned at him, rubbing my side, but he was concentrating on the Kodak.

I peered ahead and noticed Keith almost standing in the front cockpit, twisting, pointing.

And there she was.

A thin brown haze where the dark sea met the

bleached sky.

The hairs rose on my neck.

Australia.

Home. Dear God, let it be a home with Helena.

I put my arm across Benny's shoulders and gave him a squeeze. He raised a fist. 'Yes.'

We'd done it. Flown from England to bloody Australia.

We'd done it.

We'd done it.

And I never had to do it again.

I took a deep breath. My eyes ached. I lifted my goggles to clear the mist again, then rubbed underneath my flying cap to scratch my temple.

As the blue sea became a muddy continental halo of swirling browns and greens and yellows, I crawled into the fuselage and retrieved the small flask of scotch Joan had given Benny as a present for the moment we saw Australia. We'd secretly wired the bottle to the frame deep inside the tail on our final day in Weybridge. I wriggled back into position, and opened the flask before Benny's huge grin. Every sip, one of us made a toast with words that flew up and away, unheard on the wind. Didn't matter. I knew what Benny was saying because it was exactly what I was saying, too. Thank you to everyone who helped us home, kept us alive and in the air. I liked the idea of their names flying on the wind, forever.

We passed over mangroves and low red cliffs and finally the Australian mainland was beneath our wings. Port Darwin's dirt roads were wide and dusty, cutting between rows of stone buildings with elegant verandahs, and shanties made of corrugated iron, all wonky and rusted. On its little peninsula ringed by mangroves and turquoise sea, the town looked more like Surabaya than Sydney. A simple place, an outpost through and through. There was no fancy Leaning Tower. No pyramids. No golden Shwedagon Pagoda. And no town had ever looked more beautiful from the air.

I was home.

Ross circled low in triumphant celebration and Benny and I waved like kings as people came running into the streets to shout and cheer and cry — they were actually crying. Kids and businessmen and women clambered aboard vehicles, horses and buggies racing north to the aerodrome, and Ross circled out wide over the water one more time to give them a headstart before we raced them north, flying low and letting the people guide us home.

A white flare marked the landing spot and indicated a pretty strong breeze.

Ross circled around to bring her into the wind.

As he came into land I held my breath, staring straight ahead at the scratched brown earth.

Closer.

Closer.

Just one more landing, please God.

One more time.

* * *

The wheels touched the earth with a bump and everywhere people were jumping about and running in, cheering and waving and throwing hats in the air.

I raised my fists in triumph, leaning against the back of the cockpit as the Vimy bounced along the runway.

As we came to a halt I told myself to stop searching

304

the faces for Helena. Would I even recognise her now?

Before the propellers stopped turning, Ross sat up on the fuselage in his flying suit and stretched back to shake my hand and Benny's, before we were even out of the cockpit. His goggles were pushed up untidily on his head and he was laughing with relief. There were tears in his eyes. They were in mine, too.

The crowd had rushed forward over the runway, but were keeping their distance. Apparently they'd been told they might catch some terrible disease being carried aboard the plane. The Vimy's seals were checked and Health and Customs blokes poked around in the cockpits and asked dozens of questions while 2,000 people started chanting demands that we be freed to speak.

Then all four of us were carried on the shoulders of men to the nearby Fannie Bay Gaol, where we stood on a raised verandah to give everyone a view, and Ross and Keith and Darwin dignitaries spoke between thundering applause and cries of three cheers.

Ross introduced me and Benny as 'the finest air mechanics in the world' and people started yelling 'Speech! Speech!'. I looked at Benny and he pointed back at me. I couldn't think of anything to say that hadn't already been said, so I cleared my throat and said I thought we might have to fall into Darwin because there was hardly any fuel left in the tanks. The whole crowd laughed. I laughed too. I felt lighter than I had in years.

A trail of dignitaries made their way onto the verandah to speak. One of them was Hudson Fysh, an old mate of Ross's from No. 1 Squadron who'd had the job of scratching aerodromes out of scrub and desert from Darwin to Brisbane in time to receive the air race crews.

The speeches all started blurring together until Ross made a joke that he'd be in trouble with his mum if he didn't tell her we were home. Suddenly we were being shoved into a vehicle and people were waving arms and yelling, 'Get out the way. Let 'em through!' and we were on our way to Government House. As we drove away, I turned to see people streaming back to admire the Vimy.

The dear old Vimy. She looked tired, triumphant, magnificent. It suddenly felt a bit wrong to leave her. Wished I could have shouted her a beer.

* * *

'Whacko,' said Benny, peering through the white verandah shutters to the tropical gardens and the sun setting over the sea beyond. 'Now that's a welcome-home view.'

Government House was home to the director of the Northern Territory, Mr Carey, and his family. The stone building was surrounded by pretty verandahs enclosed with white shutters. Benny, Keith and I had been deposited in the western verandah, with its potted palms and cane chairs, while Ross dispatched some telegrams.

I poured three frothy beers into tall glasses on the table, and handed them to Keith and Benny. 'Here's to being the first men to fly across the globe,' I said.

'Hear, hear,' said Benny, throwing it back.

Keith took a sip and glanced down at the book in his lap. 'After exactly …' he paused to add the final day's tally to his list, ' … 135 hours in the air. Twenty-seven days and 20 hours after leaving Hounslow.'

306

'Gee,' said Benny, looking down the long, empty verandah. 'We beat the deadline easy in the end, didn't we?'

'I still can't believe we've done it,' I said. I was feeling a bit numb, here in the quiet with nothing to do on the Vimy.

'Yes,' said Keith, rubbing his eyes. 'It will take a while to sink in, I think. It's almost an anticlimax.'

'Wonder if the Prime Minister knows we're here,' I said.

Keith nodded. 'The *Sydney* would have sent word when we flew over.'

I walked over to the shutters and looked at the orange sky, arching my back and digging my fingers into my shoulders.

I wondered how long before the news of our arrival reached Narrandera. Hours? Days? I wondered if she'd be proud of me. If she'd care. If she'd seen the telegram from Surabaya or refused to read it.

'I'm desperate for a wash,' said Benny, downing the last of his beer and loosening his collar.

Just then Ross walked in, waving a dozen pieces of paper. 'Lads,' he said. 'Telegrams. Here's one from the Prime Minister.'

'You beauty,' said Benny, as we crowded around to read over Ross's shoulder. 'Does it mention the £10,000 he owes us?'

Ross read aloud: ' "In the name of the Commonwealth I greet you and your gallant companions' …'

'Gallant,' I said. 'The Prime Minister called us gallant!'

'Shh,' said Keith.

'… 'on your safe arrival and most heartily congratulate you on your magnificent achievement. You have

307

covered the name of Australia with fresh laurels. You have broken all the world's records and have shown the world once more what manner of man the Australian is' ...'

'Jesus, this telegram must've cost a fortune,' muttered Benny.

'He can afford it,' I said, laughing.

'Fellas!' said Ross. 'Can we please let the bloody Prime Minister finish? 'You have given your country a world-wide advertisement and have proved that with relays of machines and men, Europe can be brought within 12 or 15 days of Australia'.'

Benny whistled. 'Twelve days to reach Australia!'

'You reckon that's really possible?' I asked.

'It will happen,' said Keith. 'Just a matter of time.'

'And when it does,' said Ross, looking at Keith, 'we'll be right in the pilot's seat.'

The door opened and Mr Carey strode in. 'Telegrams, Captain Smith.'

'There's more?' said Ross.

There were many more. They started arriving by the score every 15 minutes, from politicians and people we didn't know from across Australia. From around the world.

Ross scanned the messages. 'Here's one from Gilberton, Keith. Dear old Mum and Dad.' He paused to re-read before handing it over.

'Oh, and King George V says, 'Delighted at your safe arrival. Your success will bring Australia nearer to the Mother Country, and I warmly congratulate you and your crew."

'Strewth,' said Benny. 'The King knows we're home!'

Mr Carey looked over his glasses. 'You four are all

anyone's talked about for weeks.'

'Really?' I said.

'It's the biggest news story since the war, Sergeant,' said Mr Carey, taken aback. 'The newspapers have written about little else.'

He called for a houseboy to bring out back copies of the newspapers, and began rifling through them on the table to show us the articles. 'Our news is a bit old up here in Darwin, of course,' he said, 'but this gives you an idea.'

'The world's gone mad,' said Keith, picking up one of the newspapers. 'How do they get all these details without even talking to us?'

'I think we might be famous,' I said, picking up another paper.

'I think I'd better write a half-decent speech,' said Ross, frowning, still holding a stack of unread messages.

When the telegrams began coming in from more remote cities and towns across Australia, my palms started sweating. She must know by now.

I put my beer to one side. Tried to breathe slowly, tried to act normal.

The four of us were seated around the table now. As the telegrams piled up, Ross began scanning them.

'No,' he said, passing each one to Keith on his right. 'No. No. No. Oh — Winston Churchill!' He looked up and waved it at us. 'He says, 'Well done. Your great flight shows conclusively that the new element has been conquered for the use of man.' Jolly nice.' He continued scanning. 'No. No. No. No. Hey, it's from Biffy!'

We all cheered. 'What's he say?' I asked.

'He says: 'Never a doubt!'' And we cheered again.

Ross handed it on to Keith and picked up more telegrams. 'No, no, no.'

'What are you doing?' asked Keith, frowning.

'Looking for a message from our girl,' said Ross, looking at his watch. 'She must have heard by now.'

My face burned. I picked up my glass. Benny reached over and squeezed my shoulder.

'No,' said Ross, passing another sheet to Keith and adding a new batch to his pile. He sipped his beer and looked up. 'Let's not lose any of these, by the way. I've seen the names of some dear friends, and I'll want to read them again properly.'

'Well, this one's from the British Prime Minister ...' said Keith.

Ross shrugged and passed more telegrams. 'No, no, no ...'

The pile was nearly cleared. I was sitting directly opposite him, sipping my beer slowly and watching the expression on his face as he scanned each telegram.

'No, no, no ...'

He was about to pass another sheet to Keith when he stopped. 'Wait — it's Alford, isn't it?'

'Yes,' I said. A shiver ran up my spine. 'Is it from Narrandera?'

Benny leaned forward. 'What does it say?'

Maybe it was Fred, not Helena — she didn't want to know. I was too late.

'It says ...' Ross cleared his throat.

'Come on you old blow bag!' said Keith, leaning in. Christ.

Ross looked across the table at me. 'It's a message from Mr F. Alford of Narrandera. Do you know him?'

'Yes,' I said, my heart sinking. 'Helena's brother,

Fred.'

He kept staring straight at me. 'It says …' He cleared his throat again, holding the message to his chest.

'So help me, I'll clock you …' said Keith.

Ross smiled. 'It says, 'Yes' and 'Yes'.' He reached across and handed me the sheet.

I looked at the page …

YES. YES.

I looked back at Ross.

Benny snatched the paper from my hands. 'What does that mean? 'Yes. Yes.'?'

'Well,' said Ross, 'I may have made a small addition to the end of the poem.'

'What?' said Keith, his black eyes widening. 'You didn't …'

Ross raised his palm. 'I did nothing to ruin your exquisite wordsmithing, sir.' He sipped his beer. 'I told her it was my fault, and I said Wal adored her. Then I asked her to forgive me. And I asked her to marry him.'

★ ★ ★

SYDNEY, FEBRUARY 17th 1920

I turned my back on the garden party and watched three little sailing boats crisscrossing the harbour below. The red boat went over, arms waved and shouts carried across the water. I pointed, as if that would make a difference, and then the boat popped upright like a cork and the two blokes were back on board and in the race.

By God, Sydney Harbour was beautiful. As Benny said, man's quest for powered flight was worth it just

311

to see this one city from the air. We'd flown in through the Heads, with sun-drenched bays and growing suburbs sprawling out before us. We'd stood up in the back cockpit to get a better view as tiny figures raced to rocky shorelines and sandy inlets and out onto the decks of passenger ferries and military vessels to get a glimpse of the Vimy and her crew. To welcome us. To wave us home. We'd been a long time coming.

I smoothed down my hair and felt in my pocket for another cigarette.

Someone whacked my back and I stumbled forward into a yellow hibiscus. Looked like it had been planted just before the party.

'Congratulations, mate!' the bloke said.

I turned to say thanks but he'd walked away, another uniform blending into a garden party of military khaki.

One of the bands was set up on the tennis court, playing some new tune I didn't know. I was sure I could smell orange blossom. Made me think of the Sydney copper who'd changed my mind about orange trees and sent me to war instead. He'd tapped thousands of blokes on the shoulder. That's what he'd said. I wondered how many would thank him now.

I looked around for an orange tree, and sure enough there it stood, heavily clipped into a perfect lollipop beside one of the tables set up as a bar. I felt a rush of sympathy. It looked as out of place as me.

Drawing back on my smoke, I scraped dirt from my boot on the grass and scanned the garden for Benny or Ross and Keith. 'Sir' Ross and 'Sir' Keith, it was now. Had to keep reminding myself of that. No knighthoods for me and Benny. We got bars to our Air Force Medals instead. People kept asking me how I felt about that, given I'd kept the engines running. How was I meant to feel? It didn't matter to me and Benny that we didn't get a knighthood. What mattered to us was that the Smith boys got one. Countless times I'd stared at the backs of their heads, Ross at the wheel and Keith with his maps, and thanked God for them.

Benny was nowhere to be seen.

Ross and Keith were surrounded. They were always surrounded now. By their parents. By the Premier. By our host, Mr McIntosh. And by Brigadier-General Cox, who I knew from my Light Horse days. Ross leaned over to whisper something in his mum's ear and she touched his arm and laughed behind a black-gloved hand. There was something very decent and solid about her, with her mousy face and little round glasses. You could tell she doted on Ross by the way she'd clung to him when we landed at Mascot. Eventually Ross's father had to gently prise her off him. Ross wasn't just hers anymore. He was the most famous Australian in all the world. He'd made a speech with thousands of people hanging on his every word.

A seagull flew overhead, squawking rudely at the banquet table near the tennis court. A large group of officers stood near the service line, women in pretty frocks fussing around them, offering finger sandwiches and dainty cakes and pastries. One of the blokes, a swag of ribbon on his chest, smiled and nodded. Funny how things changed. I nodded back, took a drag and turned to face the harbour.

Sixty-eight days. That's how long it took for us to get from Darwin down to Sydney. We landed up there on December 10th 1919. We landed down here yesterday, on February 16th 1920. Silly, really, given it

313

had only taken 28 days to fly all the way from London.

Benny blamed the bastard who'd stolen Marmaduke II's head. Our lucky mascot's neck got bent somehow when we landed in Darwin, and Benny had unscrewed him to fix it the following day. He was working surrounded by sightseers and one of them pinched it. I thought Benny was going to blow a gasket. The police made an announcement, demanding it be given back immediately, but no one stepped forward. Tarnished the moment a bit.

But the port propeller was the real problem. We all knew it was damaged – a split in the wood had been growing since the incident with the hawk in Calcutta. But the wet season was coming and the Darwin aerodrome was on low-lying ground, so Ross decided to take our chances of reaching Sydney instead of getting stuck up north for three months. On the 13th of December, Ross's unlucky day, we headed south. And two days later, in mid-air, in the middle of nowhere, that port propeller split from the tip to the centre. Took us three days to fix it, in heat so intense the rubber on our goggles melted. Keith reckoned the temperature under the shade of the wings was 125°F.

Luckily, even way out there, some blokes had seen the Vimy overhead and came out to lend a hand. Benny was a bloody marvel, too, using wooden shavings from an old packing crate to plug the crack before smothering it with glue. We wrapped both blades in thin strips of galvanised iron fastened with old screws from the Vimy's floorboards.

The temporary fix got us all the way to Charleville, over west of Brisbane, when the Vimy and her Rolls-Royce engines finally said enough and carked it. We had a holed cylinder, two broken piston rods and a propeller in need of replacement. This time we were held up for seven weeks. Things looked so crook that Ross phoned Billy Hughes to talk about dismantling the aircraft and sending her by train to Melbourne. Glad we changed his mind on that. Australia deserved to see the Vimy in the air – and she deserved to be seen in all her glory.

Lads at the Ipswich Railway Workshops came good for us, slaving away for weeks on 460 quid's worth of repairs and a new propeller. Never charged Ross, either.

Everyone, everywhere we'd flown across Australia, had been so kind, elated to see us. It didn't sit naturally with me yet. You'd think fame would make you feel powerful, but it had the opposite effect on me. You couldn't turn it on or off. It was out of your control.

'Wal!' It was Benny. 'Wal! You look like you're away with the fairies there, mate.'

I frowned. 'Wotcha been doing?'

'Just getting some blokes organised,' he said, handing me a fancy glass of champagne. 'Someone's got to take charge.'

I looked around for somewhere to put down the champagne, clutching my stomach.

'Jesus, you're hopeless,' he said, throwing back his own drink and holding out his hand for mine. 'Best not waste it.'

The collar of my new uniform was scratchy. I rubbed my neck gently, careful not to leave a mark.

Benny nodded toward Ross and the others. 'You talked to Mr McIntosh yet?'

'Yeah,' I said, glancing at my watch. 'He and Mrs

McIntosh have been very generous, haven't they?'

'Well, yeah,' said Benny. 'But I'm sure they'll do alright out of it all. He's not called Huge Deal for nothing.'

Hugh D. 'Huge Deal' McIntosh was a big sports promoter who owned Sydney's Sunday Telegraph newspaper and the Tivoli theatre chain around Australia. He was as short as I was, with slicked-back hair and a closely trimmed moustache like Biffy's. He was already talking to Ross about a lecture tour, and down the other end of the garden I could see a dozen pressmen and photographers capturing the day's news. The sight of them made my stomach knot.

Benny lit himself a smoke, squinting at me through the blue haze. 'You look like you're about to shit yourself.'

'Yeah, thanks, mate.' I took a deep breath. Down on the harbour the little red sailboat had shot ahead of the others and was headed for the final orange buoy. Go, little red boat.

Just then the music stopped and Mrs McIntosh appeared under the pergola at the rear of the house. 'Almost ready, Sir Ross,' she called, before disappearing back inside.

'Ah shit,' said Benny, flicking away his cigarette. He raced off, tapping blokes on the shoulder as he went.

Ross glanced around the garden, finished his drink and handed it to a waiter. He found me and smiled. Waved me over. I looked back toward the water, just in time to see my little red mate streak past the finish line with its nose in front.

You can do this, Wal. You flew from England to bloody Australia. You can do this.

A tall, elegant woman in a fancy blue dress reached

out to touch my arm as I walked past.

You survived a war. You can do this.

Keith stepped forward as I approached, put his hand on my shoulder and guided me into position. 'He's in a flat spin,' he said loudly, to ripples of laughter.

I shot him a dark look. So now he'd developed a sense of humour?!

A press photographer yelled out. 'Oi, Sergeant Shiers! Mind turning this way a bit?'

I pressed my lips into a smile and turned slightly toward him. Then I looked at my feet; looked anywhere but all those cameras.

Deep breaths.

The music started and I looked up toward the pergola.

Captain Chaplain Wilson cleared his throat. 'Ready gentlemen?' Only he wasn't looking at me, he was looking at all the photographers.

I looked around for a familiar face. Benny had disappeared.

Christ. What was I thinking, doing it like this? This wasn't me.

A flurry of women with expensive frocks and immaculate faces emerged from inside, pouring out like champagne.

Then nothing. The music stopped. Oh God.

I went to step forward. Ross held my arm. 'Wait, Wal,' he whispered.

Benny appeared from the side of the house, leading 20 blokes in uniform. I counted five VC ribbons as they lined up in an honour guard between me and the back door. Five VCs lining up to honour me. Wally Shiers. Made me wish Dad was here. I hoped Mum was looking down. She'd think this garden was heavenly.

I put my hands in my pockets. Then took them out. Smoothed down my hair and heard a camera click. I clasped my hands behind my back and parted my feet a bit, rolling my shoulders and trying to remember what Ross had said in Weybridge about looking interesting for the cameras.

Suddenly I felt overwhelmed with gratitude. I turned to Ross, to thank him for everything he'd done for me, but the music started so I stopped and turned back to face the front.

Plenty of time for all that.

Would we stay mates? I wondered.

The honour guard was blocking my view of the back door now, but I could tell she was there by the 'oohs' and 'aahs'.

The music started. Breathe, Wal, breathe.

Ross leaned over. 'This is it, old boy,' he whispered. 'The big show.'

I could feel my heart beating against my rib cage.

Boom.

Boom.

Boom.

Every second an eternity.

Then she stepped into view, looking tiny behind her huge bouquet of garden flowers, and delighted with herself behind her pink veil. God, she was lovely.

She'd had to borrow it all, bless her. The white velvet wedding dress adorned with little pearls. The teeny white pointy shoes. The light-pink veil that flowed into a train sweeping along behind her on the lawn. She'd given up the chance to wear the gown she'd sewn so we could be married today and have a few days in the

318

Blue Mountains before I flew south to Melbourne. She'd given it up for me.

And there was Freddy Houdini, walking beside her in uniform, with his crook arm and weary soul. Dear old Fred. He gave me a nice big smile and a wink, too, and I wanted to walk forward and hug them both, to say how proud I was, to take away some of the sadness of losing their mum. They'd buried her the day I was in Delhi, dealing with those silly Fairweathers.

When Helena was at my side, Benny and the blokes came in behind us and everyone pressed in. I could feel them all at my back. Waiting. Wanting.

Photographers jostled for position, urging everyone to move in closer. A bit closer. A little more. I was hot in my uniform. My collar was too tight.

Then Helena tucked her hand into my arm, and looked up and whispered, 'Hello, Wally Shy-ers.'

I noticed her tiara was made of orange blossom. As I leaned in closer, the scent washed over me. 'Hello, my orange blossom girl,' I whispered.

Captain Chaplin Wilson started the ceremony and I stood there in a happy daze. Helena on my left. Ross on my right. My best man. The best of men.

The padre mentioned something about true love standing the test of time and distance, and then Benny piped up, 'Yes, about 11,000 miles!'

Before I knew it, the padre pronounced us man and wife. 'And may I suggest,' he said, glancing around at the crush of men in uniform, 'that you get in quick to secure the first kiss.'

And then it happened — quick as a flash.

Sir Ross leaned over and kissed my new wife.

Heroes roared and cameras clicked.

His mother gasped — 'Ross Macpherson Smith!' —

like he was a little boy in big trouble.

Then Helena had her tiny hand behind my head, pulling me into her huge blue eyes, and we were kissing and laughing and everyone was cheering and I was home.

Postscript:
What Happened Next

ADELAIDE, 1968

Every story has an ending. Some have two or three. I dig in my pocket for my old blue hanky, and remove my glasses to dab the moisture from my eyes. I sip the last of my scotch, enjoying the heat in the back of my throat, and picture Helena all shy smiles and secret curves in our swanky hotel room at the Jenolan Caves, where we spent four nights after the wedding. I catch Delvene's eye and stretch out my arm for a refill, giving thanks to that young Dunstan chap for bringing in 10 pm closing and giving a bloke time to tell a decent tale. Then I square my shoulders. And it only takes a moment for the questions to roll in like the tide on Bondi Beach.

'So what happened then, Wal?'

'Where's Benny now? And Ross? And Keith?'

'Did Poulet make it?'

'Who else got home?'

So I start at the beginning of the end …

How we flew into Melbourne and got the cheque from the Prime Minister, Billy Hughes. How Ross handed him the keys to the Vimy, as he'd been instructed to do, and then caused a controversy by asking for them straight back so we could fly across to Adelaide. There was no way Ross wasn't flying all the way home.

We landed north-east of the Adelaide city centre on March 23rd 1920. I told some young bloke to get his hands off the plane before I realised he was my younger brother

Arthur, all grown up. Jeez we polished off some South-wark bitter that night. Benny said he'd never seen a family drink like the Shiers mob.

Ross and Keith took us into Elder House in Currie Street to split the prize money into quarters, like they'd promised. For the next few months I made a few bob speaking at country shows and the like, too. Ross even did some talks in England, met King George and Prince Albert. He was as famous as any movie star but he didn't like it much. He was dying to get back in the air and away.

But it was a big story, for a while at least.

Only one other crew made it home. That was Ray Parer and John McIntosh in their Airco DH9 PD. They didn't leave England until a month after we landed in Darwin, but they wanted to do it anyway and set out on a journey that took them nearly seven months. We got to calling Ray Parer the 'Repairer', on account of how many times he needed to fix the old Dung Hunter during the flight.

Poor old Matthews and Kay did eventually escape the snow in Germany, but they were forced to land the Wallaby on a pig farm in Yugoslavia and ended up imprisoned for four days, suspected of being militant Bolsheviks. They made a break for freedom while their guards were sleeping off a night of heavy drinking, and took off in a blaze of bullets. They overcame sandstorms, survived dengue fever and spent weeks fashioning their own spare parts, only to crash out in Bali, just a day away from Australia. Poor bastards.

Hubert Wilkins, Val Rendle, David Williams and Garnsey Potts crashed out, too, with their Blackburn Kangaroo coming to rest in a ditch near a lunatic asylum on the island of Crete. They were keen to carry on despite major damage to one of their Rolls-Royce engines, but we'd already made it to Australia by then, so Blackburn pulled

322

the pin. They were a good bunch of blokes. I was sorry for them.

Cedric Howell and George Fraser crashed and died off the island of Corfu. People reported hearing their cries for help but the seas were too rough to send out a search boat that night. Howell's new wife was travelling home by sea at the time. They didn't have the heart to tell her until the ship docked in Adelaide. Howell's grieving dad campaigned for a long time that he'd met with foul play on Corfu, and even released a pamphlet accusing Ross of rigging the race to his advantage. Ross demanded a public trial to clear his name, but Dicky Williams — our CO at No. 1 Squadron who was later sent to London to oversee the air race – wrote a long rebuttal on the integrity of the process and that ended the matter.

There were two inquiries into how Roger 'Dodger' Douglas and Leslie Ross crashed to their deaths just six minutes after leaving Hounslow. Mabel Woolley, Douglas's fiancée, caused a stir in the press by claiming the Alliance Endeavour had been badly damaged two weeks earlier and hadn't been properly tested. Others blamed the enclosed cockpit — reckoned it might have impaired Dodger's vision — and in the end the crash was called an accident.

So six Australian crews left England. Two crews died. Two more crashed out. Only us and the Repairer made it home. His plane's in the Australian War Memorial. They took our Vimy for a while too, until the place got too full after World War II and they mothballed it because no Vimy actually flew in active service in the Great War. We were ropable when we heard about that — had the plane moved to Adelaide. She's still sitting pretty as a picture out at the airport, in a hangar the people of South Australia had specially built for her. That's despite some idiot flicking a cigarette butt and torching half the thing on the back of a truck on the way down from Canberra. An RAAF inquiry never proved it was a cigarette butt, but I reckon I know the truth.

One of the young lads at the bar stands up to stretch, says it's his round and asks who else wants another. 'Wal,' he says, 'I need to take a leak. Don't say anything until I get back. I want to hear about Poulet.' I nod, and another lad says: 'Yeah, and Biffy. What happened to Biffy?'

When everyone's settled back down, I tell them.

Poulet never did make it to Australia despite getting as far south as Batavia with Benoist in a second aircraft funded by his friends back in France. He lived and worked across Asia until he was well into his 60s, spending years as the aviation advisor to the Chinese government. He was a leader of the French underground in Asia during World War II and interned for a time in a Japanese prisoner-of-war camp. Died back on his home soil at the age of 70 in 1960, with a stack of French honours to his name but bugger all recognition outside aviation circles.

Good old Biffy has lived long and well, too. He'd be in his 80s now. Married a woman he met on our first flight from Cairo to Calcutta, and retired in 1933 as an Air Vice-Marshall with the RAF before setting out to lose the family fortune on failed business ventures. Bit by bit the estate was let go until eventually Cheveney was sold to a Texas oilman. You know, it wasn't until we got back to Australia that we learnt he and the Colonel had painted GODSPEED right across the main lawn for us at Cheveney — we'd missed it on account of the heavy fog the day we left Hounslow. A fine family, that one.

Delvene wipes up some spilt beer on the bar. 'What happened with you and Helena, Wal?'

I fall silent, rubbing the tip of my thumb on my wedding band. Could never bring myself to take it off.

Helena and I moved to Sydney like we planned. Thanks to my prize money we bought a little house in Dover Heights and a garage at Bondi Junction. It was just a stone's throw from the beach where we'd eat fish and chips on the rocks and watch the surfing on a Sunday afternoon. Fred moved up to Sydney, too. Found himself a lovely wife and was content, on and off, until his death in '29. We lost our Freddy Houdini far too early — for some blokes there was just no escaping that war.

Helena and I never did have kids, but we were happy, for the most part. Had lots of pets, Pomeranians mostly. And we always had lots of friends around, too, with Helena topping up the sherry while I recounted my tale. She never once told me she couldn't bear to hear the story again. Never once in 32 years, bless her.

I was formally discharged from the AIF in 1920 and granted the honorary rank of lieutenant – Benny was too. I eventually got my pilot's licence, even had a crack at flying back the other way from Australia to England in 1930 with a young chap by the name of Dave Smith — yet another Smith, would you believe? We made a forced landing in Western Australia, on the first day out from Sydney, and crashed again in Siam and called the whole thing off. Bloody daft idea, that was. I stuck with aviation, though. Got a job as chief engineer with Airlines of Australia. I tried to re-enlist in the Air Force in World War II, but they found me some work overseeing the manufacture of parachutes instead. Made me proud knowing I was making our boys a bit safer in the air.

Helena died in '51, but not without a damn good fight. We used to joke that cancer had never come across a woman so stubborn — it obviously hadn't seen the way she'd stood her ground when I flew to India with Ross Smith. And that's how I'll always remember her: the beautiful girl who *got me through a war and across the world to home. I was proud the Narrandera Argus ran a little obituary for her, talked about her work with a number of patriotic bodies during the Great War. But then they went and said I'd flown from England to Australia in the Southern Cross with Charles Kingsford Smith. Can you bloody believe that? Old King Dick was as famous as Phar Lap by then for flying across the Pacific.*

Not too long after I lost Helena, I got smashed up in a motor car. That's when I moved to Adelaide, to live just around the corner from here with my brother Arthur — in Bennett Street, funnily enough. Been with Dorothy for a few years now.

'I want to hear about Benny and the others!' the new lad says.

'I know, son,' I say. 'Almost there.' Suddenly I'm bone weary. Feel a bit woozy too. I reach out to put down my scotch, and the glass nearly topples off the bar.

'You right, Wal?' There's a familiar note of concern in Delvene's voice. 'Maybe that's enough for one day …'

I shake my head, give her a reassuring wink. 'S'oright Delvie. We're nearly done.'

Keith married Anita Crawford in 1924. They never had kids either. He was the Vickers representative in Australia and was on a stack of aviation company boards including Qantas until cancer got him too, in '55. Left me a hundred quid in his will. I was touched by that. Only saw him rarely after the race and what came after, but from afar I was always proud of what he went on to do. Given what happened.

I take a deep breath.

'As for Ross and Benny …'

I rub the watch given to me by Rolls-Royce after the race. Get out my hanky again, just in case.

Ross, Benny and Keith returned to Weybridge in 1922. They hoped to circumnavigate the globe in another Vickers aircraft — this time the amphibious Vickers Viking. I didn't go on account of me being a married man by then.

It was all going so well. The press loved them. The route was all planned. Excitement was building across the globe.

Then Ross and Benny did a test flight – right over the Brooklands racing circuit.

At first, everyone thought Ross was doing one of his stunts, but the Viking got into a spin at 1,000 ft and he never regained control.

I pause. Along the bar there's silence. 'They dropped out of the sky and crashed behind trees lining the track ...'

A cry goes up. 'Nooooo!' And again I feel the unbearable weight of people learning the truth for the first time. It's a burden I've carried for 48 years.

I nod my head slowly, staring at my old man's hands. 'Yeah. Sorry.' I wish I could end it another way, but the lie wouldn't be fair to Ross and Benny.

Ross and Benny. I reach for my drink and take a sip to stop the sob rising in my chest.

'Both of them?' asks a quiet voice.

I nod again. Crushed from head to foot.

Keith had been delayed on a train that morning, and got to Weybridge just in time to see the plane spiralling to the ground. Can't imagine how he must have felt cradling his broken younger brother in his arms. Very alone, I suspect. And a long way from home.

I was repairing a busted hub on a motorcycle at Bondi Junction when I heard. Pulled the roller door closed behind me and wandered off God knows where.

Helena and Fred found me on Bondi Beach, sitting on the sand, staring at the horizon. She wrapped her arms around me and held me tight.

I said I should have been there with them. With my hero and my friend.

She said the greatest men always leave one good man behind, to keep their story alive.

* * *

Author's Note

Wally Shiers died of heart failure in his brother's Bennett Street home on June 2nd 1968. His death was reported on the front page of the Advertiser the following day, with a small photograph and seven paragraphs under the headline, 'Last Flier In Pioneer Crew Dies'.

Notes

Chapter 1

When I reached the house, I stopped and leaned my overnight bag against the fence.

Although there's no exact street address, records show Helena lived on Arthur Street with her mother and Fred before World War I. The Narrandera Railway Station is at the top of Arthur Street, so it's where Murrumbidgee Irrigation Area (MIA) workers like Wally would have arrived every Saturday for a weekend of sport and drinking. Alcohol was prohibited in the MIA, and trains returning workers home of a Sunday evening were known as 'The Drunks' Express'. I like to imagine Wally got off the train one Saturday in late 1914 and was wandering down Arthur Street when fate brought him to Helena. The egg-throwing incident is fiction. Helena's father was born in Germany, but obituaries in the *Narrandera Argus* reveal both parents were highly respected, and John Alford was a 'staunch Britisher'. He'd arrived in the district in the 1870s, making him one of the earliest pioneer wheat growers.

The Narrandera boys must have got a wicket.

In the early years, 'Narrandera' (pronounced Narran-dra) was sometimes spelt with one 'r'. I've used the double 'r' throughout for consistency. The cricket oval, with its white picket fence, is still on Cadell Street.

I thought I'd miss the red dust when I left the mine in Broken Hill, but the Riverina suited me fine.

The Murrumbidgee Irrigation Trust actively sought to capitalise on miner unrest in Broken Hill by recruiting miners to the district after 1910. Wally would have been among scores of mine workers who made the hot and dusty journey across New South Wales by horse and wagon.

He was positive the magician Harry Houdini had been the first man to fly over Australian soil in 1910, but I knew for a fact that a South Australian by the name of Custance had beaten Houdini by a day.

In *Charles Kingsford Smith and Those Magnificent Men*, biographer Peter FitzSimons explains that a number of Australians including South Australia's Fred Custance had fleetingly left the ground before Harry Houdini, 'but it was some time before these feats became widely known'. In the meantime, master self-promoter Ehrich Weiss, aka Harry Houdini the magician, stole the glory as the first man to fly in Australia.

And then it happened — my run-in with the Sydney copper.

In a taped interview with Hazel de Berg in 1966 (held in the National Library of Australia's oral history collection), Wally talked about travelling to Sydney to buy some fruit trees and how a Sydney policeman handed

him the Kitchener postcard. Wally recalled the policeman saying to him, 'There's thousands more like you,
my lad, I've issued it to.'

Chapter 2

**Blokes heading off to the Front figure their
sweethearts might as well be listed to receive a
widow's pension.**

Wally's Soldier's Pay Book, issued on April 19th
1915 and now held in the National Library of Australia (NLA), lists Helena as the 'Person to whom
Allotment or Compulsory Stoppage is payable'.
Curiously, it also lists Wally's age of enlistment as
'23 and three quarters', which suggests he was born
in 1891. His birth certificate, also held in the NLA,
shows he was born on May 17th 1889, or two years
earlier. Even some of the most basic truths can be
hard to pin down.

**'Walter Shiers, sir,' I said, nice as pie, back
straight and eyes forward like they taught us in
the Barrier Boys' Brigade, my old cadet group
back in Broken Hill.**

The Boys' Brigade movement had its origins in 1883,
when a Scot by the name of William Smith started the
first group to motivate his Sunday school students
with training drills. He believed that by challenging
them physically and mentally, he could help them
thrive in all areas of their lives.

Chapter 3

Because there's no cover in the desert, we taught the horses to lie down in front of us for protection.

Wally's horse Bobby is fictional. According to the Australian Light Horse Studies Centre, the 4th Light Horse Brigade actually shipped to Egypt without horses. There would have been a surplus of mounts in Egypt because all the Light Horse boys who served in Gallipoli had to leave their horses behind. I learned about horses being trained to lie down and shield soldiers in a newspaper article on Susan Brocker, author of *Brave Bess and the ANZAC Horses: A true story of courage and loyalty.*

Chapter 4

During the evacuation in December 1915, the last soldiers were ordered to wear socks and old rags on their feet so the Turks wouldn't hear them leaving.

This was one of many strategies used to successfully evacuate thousands of troops without casualty. Digitised letters held in the Australian War Memorial collection show it's also true that soldiers felt troubled by leaving their dead mates behind on the peninsula.

I told the recruiter bits and pieces that I knew ... the fact we were the only country in the British Empire to demand its own separate Flying Corps in the war.

In *Australian Flying Corps*, Ian Hodges explores why Australia was alone among the British dominions to establish its own Flying Corps in World War I. 'On such a vast but sparsely populated continent aviation's potential was obvious and the idea of using aircraft to help in the country's defence appealed to many military and political figures.' *In Fire in the Sky: The Australian Flying Corps in the First World War*, Michael Molkentin explains that until January 1918, No. 1 Squadron AFC was officially named No. 67 (Australian) Squadron, Royal Flying Corps. (I refer to it as No. 1 Squadron throughout for simplicity's sake.) 'The British would supply the higher command, organisation and equipment. The Australians only needed to send pilots and ground crews.'

'It's remarkable, the number of men who mention horses the first time they get up close to a plane ... It's no accident that we're recruiting cavalrymen from the Light Horse.'

Official war historian F.M. Cutlack noted this in *The Australian Flying Corps in the Western and Eastern Theatres of War 1914–1918*. 'Both Britain and Germany found that the best raw material for the making of an air pilot was the accomplished horseman. The demand for good heart, good hands, and a quick eye is the same in each case.'

I've been seeing quite a bit of John of late — we're working together on the conscription committee.

Press clippings and a 1951 obituary in the *Narrandera Argus* show Helena was 'associated with a number of patriotic bodies' during the war. She served on the local ladies' branch of the National Referendum Committee to generate support for conscription, raised money for the Red Cross and worked on campaigns to support soldiers' wives and children.

Fred would be in France by now — we're hoping for a letter any day to hear he's safe and settling in as well as can be expected.

Frederick William Albert Alford's service records show he embarked at Sydney with the 6/55th Battalion on October 7th 1916. Throughout 1917 (and until he suffered gunshot wounds to his left arm, breast and leg in late 1918) his service records show he was in and out of the trenches in France, either wounded in action or suffering from trench fever or 'gassed'. He was twice hospitalised for a lengthy period after being listed as 'absent from duty … V.D.'. Venereal disease was common among troops both overseas and in Australia, and without antibiotics was basically incurable. As Peter Stanley explains in *The Crying Years: Australia's Great War*, VD 'put out of commission hundreds of soldiers at any time, and about a fifth of the force through the war'. A 1929 obituary in the *Narrandera Argus* shows Fred returned from war 'practically deprived of the use of one of his arms'. He married after moving to Sydney, and died at the age of 38 'after an illness of only a few days'.

Chapter 5

My seat was a wooden crate, but the table had a white cloth on it, and there were candlesticks wedged into old wine bottles.

Though it's unlikely that the ranks' mess would have had candlesticks, Australian airmen were apparently particularly proud of their mess arrangements. In *Aces and Kings*, Les Sutherland wrote that No. 1 Squadron's alcohol-fuelled mess nights were extremely popular with all units. 'In furniture, ours was an excellent show — for a war mess. Souveniring had helped considerably, but the pride of the mess and of the anterooms were the home-made settees and arm-chairs, made by members of the mess out of sandbags.'

Egyptian labour crews put 'em up mostly, but I once saw a pilot attach the canvas to the back of his plane and fly the covering right over the frame.

I heard this anecdote while interviewing the late Chas Schaedel, a South Australian historian who did a tremendous amount of research on our early wartime aviators. Chas was careful to say he'd heard the anecdote only once, and he couldn't corroborate it, but I loved the story so much I had to use it.

'But let's not chance it, eh? We'll be in all sorts of trouble if Dicky hears we're not in the trench.'

'Dicky' was how the men of No. 1 Squadron referred to their Flight Commander Richard Williams. In *Aces and Kings*, Les Sutherland writes: 'Dicky was an unusual chap. He did not smoke, swear or drink. His most dashing expletive was 'darn me!' ... Also, his sense of humour was markedly underdeveloped.' For all that, Sutherland also notes that Williams was 'the soul of fairness'. 'Dicky was not only popular, but he was also deeply respected throughout his squadron.' Born in the South Australian town of Moonta, Williams was the first military pilot trained in Australia and is widely regarded as the father of the Royal Australian Air Force.

One in six British and dominion airmen died, making their odds of surviving even worse than a soldier in the trenches.

In *Fire in the Sky*, Michael Molkentin notes that 'flying corps squadrons suffered the highest casualty rates of any service in the British Army during World War I. In No. 4 Squadron, an airman was killed or wounded every week on average'. In *Flight: 100 Years of Aviation*, R.G. Grant notes that British-trained pilots arriving on the Western Front in 1917 had an average life expectancy of a little over a fortnight.

'I stowed away on a ship as a kid,' Benny said.

On the 13th March 1909, Melbourne's *Age* newspaper reported a 15-year-old boy by the name of James Mallett Bennett was missing from his Hawthorn home. It noted that 'ships had a strong attraction for him'. Subsequent reports — including an interview with his sister Brenda in the wake of Jim Bennett's death in 1922 — reveal he'd stowed away on a ship to Fremantle in a bid to get out of his apprenticeship with printing firm Sands and McDougall.

Chapter 6

I stood to leave and noticed another bloke just up the beach ... I'd met him briefly earlier in

the year with some Light Horse boys passing through Kantara. Ross Smith was his name.

On the issue of Wally's relationship with Ross, everything I've read (with one exception) suggests they shared a mutual professional respect. The only time I've seen it suggested they didn't get along was an interview with former No. 1 Squadron observer George Mills, who was interviewed late in life for *The 14–18 Journal*, published by the Australian Society of World War 1 Aero Historians in 1968. In that interview Mills said Wally had been serving as his batman (or servant) and initially did not take to Ross. Service records show that Mills and Wally did join the AFC on the same day, but there's no record to suggest Wally was serving as his batman. At any rate, by war's end Wally was working with Benny on the giant Handley Page flown by Ross, and invited on the flight down to India. In a private letter to Biffy Borton (after the race), held in the A. Grenfell Price collection in the State Library of South Australia, Ross wrote: 'We had practically no engine trouble at all thanks to Bennett & Shiers. They were really wonderful & I'm seeing that they get their fair share of any credit that is due to us.' In speech notes for a touring moving picture show in 1920, now held at the National Library of Australia, Wally wrote that Ross Smith was 'our gallant leader, one of the world's foremost airmen and a great Australian'.

There was a tattoo of a butterfly on his upper left arm. I wondered why he had it.

According to Ross Smith's enlistment papers from 1914, one of his 'distinctive marks' was a tattoo of a butterfly crest on his left arm (and another was an appendicitis scar).

By Christmas Eve 1917 we'd endured three days of determined drizzle.

The fierce pre-Christmas storm in which an officer died and No. 1 Squadron aircraft were destroyed did actually happen, as highlighted in the book *One Airman's War: Aircraft Mechanic Joe Bull's personal diaries 1916–1919*, edited by Mark Lax. I invented Wally's plan to use their body weight to anchor the planes, as a precursor to the true event in the air race when Indian cavalrymen held down the Vimy in a raging sandstorm in Ramadie.

Chapter 7

Captain Ross Smith. He was fearless in his Bristol Fighter that final year of the war ... He was the most decent man I ever met, but he wasn't above the thrill of killing.

The Australian War Memorial lists Ross Smith as Australia's most decorated airman of World War I. By war's end he'd been awarded the Military Cross twice and the Distinguished Flying Cross three times. In the official history of Australian air operations in World War I, F.M. Cutlack wrote that 'there was probably no better example of what a fighting pilot should be than the Australian, Ross Smith'.

In letters home to his mother, which have been digitised and transcribed by the State Library of

South Australia, Ross had no qualms about killing the enemy. 'We are taught to believe that vengeance belongs to the Lord I know, but ever since Colin went I've felt like killing every Turk I see,' he wrote. 'That's also why I want to meet a few Huns. You'll think me very bloodthirsty Maw but I can't help it, it must be some of your Highland blood I think.' He did, however, believe there was a certain nobility among pilots. Towards the end of the war, Ross won a Distinguished Flying Cross for bringing down an enemy two-seater, before landing beside it, shooting over the heads of the airmen to scare them off and setting the plane alight.

'Takes you up to his rank when he's speaking to you, if you know what I mean? Maybe because he started out at the bottom like the rest of us.'

Ross Smith did start out at the bottom, but he wasn't there very long. He enlisted as a private with the 3rd Light Horse Regiment in Adelaide in August 1914, and within two months was promoted to sergeant. He landed on Gallipoli in May 1915, and by October had been invalided to England with scarlet fever. (On the back of his medical evacuation certificate, now held in the Sir Keith Macpherson Smith collection in the Barr Smith Library at the University of Adelaide, Ross wrote: 'My ticket when I left Anzac. RS.') After returning to Egypt he served with the 1st Light Horse Brigade, 1st Machine-Gun Squadron, including in the battle of Romani in August 1916. By the time he joined the AFC as an observer in late 1916, he held the rank of lieutenant.

Joe Bull's angry blisters coincided with the formation of a special British air detachment, called 'X Flight, RAF' formed to work in the desert with Colonel Lawrence and his Arabs.

Wally and Jim's service records show they were both part of this 'special air detachment', which is detailed in F.M. Cutlack's official war record: *The Australian Flying Corps in the Western and Eastern Theatres of War 1914–1918.*

Within an hour we got word from a recco crew that a massive column of Turks was trying to retreat through the narrow Wadi Fara gorge towards the Jordan River.

This two-day bombing campaign is well-documented, including a first-hand account by No. 1 Squadron pilot Lieutenant L.W. 'Les' Sutherland in his book *Aces and Kings*. Lieutenant Sutherland wrote that the assault on fleeing Turkish troops 'was the kind of stunt that every red-blooded flying man longed for; an open go for guns and bombs; a chance to revenge fallen comrades; an opportunity to thrash the enemy into defeat'. Sutherland also wrote that 'it was not so much war as cold-blooded, scientific butchery. I feel sick even now when I think of it'. Many World War I airmen wrote of vomiting after killing ground troops, however the scene here involving Les Sutherland is fictional.

Chapter 8

'Chivas Regal, sir,' he said. 'Compliments of Brigadier-General Borton. Enjoy your evening at the Bengal Club.'

There are conflicting reports about whether Ross, Biffy and the mechanics learned about the air race when they were in Singapore or India. Interviewed in later years, Wally and Biffy both said it was Singapore. And given the race was announced by the Australian government in March 1919, they could well have heard the news during those months of travelling by ship to scout possible landing sites between Calcutta and Timor (with Ross and Biffy deciding nevertheless to continue with their plans to fly the Handley Page down to Australia from India). In *14,000 Miles through the Air*, now republished by Wakefield Press as *Flight to Fame*, Ross wrote that he heard the news in India. I've chosen this version because it fits with the timing of the Handley Page being destroyed on the North West Frontier (and the three Aussies being seconded to fight with No. 31 Squadron RAF at Risalpur — as shown on their service records). It also fits with the men immediately jumping on the next ship to get back to England, which is what I think Ross would have done. And I must admit, for the purposes of writing this story, India works better as a full point on that year between the Armistice and the race.

I've been up all night having a high old time in East Street — the party is still going on over there.

In *Narrandera Shire*, Bill Gammage explains how an Argus journalist convinced a friend at the post office to intercept and decode any telegram carrying news of the Armistice, and then arranged to tell the mayor. 'On the night of 11 November, district people thus heard earlier than most Australians that the long years were over. The mayor said it was too bloody late to start celebrating, but church and fire bells were ringing, railway sirens sounding, skyrockets sailing into the air, and people crowding into East Street ... All that night people rejoiced, and next day shops and offices stayed closed to let them continue.'

Mr McCaughey from North Yanco Station made the funniest speech. He said the plane he donated to your No. 1 Squadron was court-martialled for cowardice for continually breaking down when approaching the enemy!

A number of Australian individuals and groups raised private funds or simply bought military aircraft for the new Australian Flying Corps squadrons. As Bill Gammage explains in *Narrandera Shire*, Sam McCaughey was a wealthy pastoralist and one of the most patriotic philanthropists in the district, donating £500,000 to the war effort in 1914 alone. 'McCaughey's plane was a 'perverse devil' which kept breaking down, especially when approaching the enemy, for which it was solemnly court-martialled for cowardice by No. 1 Squadron of the Australian Flying Corps,' Gammage writes. 'On 20 January 1918 its engines stopped over Turkish lines in Palestine, and its crew burnt it before being captured.'

Brigadier-General Amyas Borton was the very picture of a charming British gentleman.

Les Sutherland writes a beautiful summary of Biffy: 'He was good to the eye, was Biffy; and good to the ear; and to the soldier's heart. With his easy, straight-backed carriage, set off by a perfect tunic; with breeches cut as only an English cutter can cut, and field boots that would grace a field marshal, he looked the perfect gentleman-soldier. His voice was the kind one would have expected of him, although it sounded rather 'what-whatish' until we got used to it. But when he used to refer to us as 'my Australians', and said it in a way which meant 'and I'm damn proud of 'em', we were Biffy's to a man.'

Biffy's father, who we know as the Colonel, kept a comprehensive diary during World War I that included his own day-to-day activities, newspaper clippings and letters from his two sons (the other being Lieutenant Colonel Arthur 'Bosky' Borton who was awarded a Victoria Cross for bravery in Palestine in 1917). In 1973, Biffy's step-grandson Guy Slater edited the diaries into the book *My Warrior Sons*, which provides a terrific insight into the family and the war. Slater, who remembers the formal dining arrangements that endured at Cheveney well past World War II, kindly gave me some additional insights into the family home and also his blessing to use my own creative licence where necessary.

'Lads, you won't believe this, but our government has announced an air race from England to Australia.'

On March 19th 1919, Adelaide's *Observer* newspaper recorded the news with a small article on page 36:

COMMONWEALTH PRIZE OF £10,000.
MELBOURNE, March 19.

The Acting Prime Minister (Mr. Watt) announced to-day that with a view to stimulating aerial activity the Commonwealth Government had decided to offer a prize of £10.000 for the first successful flight to Australia from Great Britain on a machine manned by Australians.

Secret cablegrams held in the Australian Archives (copies of which are held in the National Library of Australia) show Prime Minister Billy Hughes first proposed a race from Paris a month earlier, on 18 February: 'Australian Aviators are desirous of attempting flight London to Australia in Handley-Page machine,' the cablegram states. 'They are all first class men and very keen ... In view of existing possibilities and advantages aerial communication between Australia and Europe, it would be a great advertisement for Australia and concentrate eyes of world on us if flight was undertaken.'

'Alcock and Brown received £10,000 in prize money for their first flight across the Atlantic in June. Must be the going rate.'

Britain's *Daily Mail* proprietor Lord Rothermere first offered this prize in April 1913 (well before World War I), and reignited interest in the race in the wake of the war. John Alcock and Arthur Brown won the race with a 16.5-hour flight on 14–15 June 1919.

The Captain leaned over to chink Biffy's whisky tumbler. 'Here's hoping the rules allow you to come along, General. You're almost an honorary Australian these days.'

Ross and Biffy were the best of mates, but Ross only ever addressed him as 'General', including in letters sent after the race. This is completely normal when addressing superiors in the armed forces – as weird as it might sound to the rest of us. Their deep friendship was never more evident than in a condolence letter to Mrs Jessie Smith after Ross's death. Biffy writes that he had come to regard his friend 'in the light of a favourite brother; his was such a lovable character, so essentially upright and straightforward and as unaffected by distinction and success as he was by dangers and difficulties which he regarded merely as incidents to be met and overcome'.

Chapter 9

'I know a thing or two about gardening, sir,' I said. 'Feel free to use me while I'm here.'

Letters written in the 1960s from Biffy to Smith brothers biographer Grenfell A. Price, author of *The Skies Remember*, reveal the friendship that developed between Wally and the Colonel. 'During the weeks they were waiting for their Vimy, they made my home theirs,' Biffy wrote. 'Shiers endeared himself to my father who admired his head for heights when put on to prune the top branches of the tallest trees.' Price's book also notes that 'the mechanics attempted to repay the General's kindness by rehabilitating his electric power plant and two of his motor cars'. The National Library of Australia also holds a letter from Laura Borton to Wally, sent before the flight with some photos of the crew and the Borton family in the Cheveney garden. It ends: 'Thank you again so much for all you did for us while you were here.'

Chapter 10

'Welcome to a Borton breakfast tradition, chaps,' Biffy said.

I got the idea for this little breakfast poetry competition from Guy Slater's book *My Warrior Sons*. It notes numerous poems jotted down by the Colonel, including one written on the back of an envelope 'on seeing the marriage of a Day to a Miss Week in the *Morning Post*'. As for other poems featured, I learned about hopping and the little hopper ditty in J.M. Maloney's *The Sisters of Battle Road*. The two poems about dying airmen are from L.W. Sutherland's Australian Flying Corps memoir Aces and Kings.

I had no papers from India — none of us did.

The service records of Ross, Wally and Benny all state, in the same handwriting, 'Not considered necessary to apply to India for documents' before briefly recounting their service since the war. Interestingly, the records suggest that Wally and Jim arrived in London from Bombay, India, a few days before Ross. I've always wondered whether he stopped off briefly in Europe to visit the war grave of his younger brother Colin, who was buried at Belgium's Lijssenthoek

Military Cemetery after dying of wounds at Passchendaele in October 1917.

**Biffy lit a cigarette, settled back into his seat
and nodded to the open notebook on the table.
'Right, who are we up against?'**

Considering it was written decades before the won-
ders of the internet, *The Greatest Air Race* by Nelson
Eustis contains a treasure trove of facts about the
other competitors, including Etienne Poulet. For
other sources, see the bibliography.

Chapter 11

**'How much they asking for one of those Avro
biplanes?'**

There was a huge glut of surplus aircraft in Britain
after the war. Many were gifted to dominions such as
Australia for the purpose of establishing independent
air forces throughout the Empire. This included 128
aircraft for Australia, according to George Odgers in
his *Pictorial History of the Royal Australian Air Force*.
In *Smithy: The life of Sir Charles Kingsford Smith*, Ian
Mackersey highlights a letter from Kingsford Smith
to his parents in Sydney in 1919, which shows just
how cheap the aircraft were: '... we are getting three
or four machines for about £50 each and, after paying
freight to Australia, they will have cost us somewhere
about £100 each.'

**Christmas Hams piped up. 'You're the reason
they've delayed the bloody race.'**

This bar scene — and the pre-race angst about Ross Smith gaining an unfair advantage against his competitors — is fictional. However, the frustration of both Bert Hinkler and Charles Kingsford Smith at not being able to race is well documented. Kingsford Smith later famously referred to Prime Minister Billy Hughes as a 'nigger in the woodpile' for standing in his way. Hinkler also held a grudge for years at being denied the chance to race the route solo. 'I get wild whenever I think of that time,' he wrote years later. 'I was all dressed up and no place to go.'

The drama surrounding the delay generally – and Kingsford Smith's removal more specifically – is recounted in *These Are Facts*, the autobiography of Air Marshal Sir Richard Williams. Sir Richard (or 'Dicky') was asked to represent the Australian government in matters relating to the race. According to his autobiography, he made the decision to delay the departure because conversations with Val Rendle (of the Blackburn Kangaroo team) and George Matthews (Sopwith Wallaby) led him to believe crews were planning to set out 'without adequate arrangements being made, taking risks and perhaps not informing us fully about their route'. He believed the result could be 'much loss of life' and a 'great deal of harm' to the aviation industry. According to Sir Richard, it was the manager of the Blackburn Aircraft Company in London who replaced Kingsford Smith. 'I was interested to know why the Blackburn Aircraft Company desired a change and was informed that the pilot concerned had, with his friends, purchased an aircraft from government disposals and was barnstorming in the country and contrary to civil air regulations was landing in fields not approved for that purpose,' Sir

Richard wrote. 'I was also told that he had found that he could insure his aircraft for an amount in excess of that for which he could replace it and there had been some crashes. The Blackburn Company's view was that this was undermining not only civil aviation control ... but it was also damaging aviation insurance which was just getting established.'

Secret cablegrams held in the Australian Archives (copies of which are held in the Crome collection in the National Library of Australia) show Prime Minister Billy Hughes, in Paris, was eager for race crews to start as early as April, but Acting Prime Minister William Watt, in Melbourne, urged a delay to give airmen in Australia time to get to London to compete. Watt feared a 'great clamour' if they were denied the opportunity. In June, Hughes wrote to say that after speaking with Richard Williams and British Air Ministry officials, he'd changed his mind about starting immediately. He now proposed to postpone the flight 'until we have information that depots are established [to provide fuel and oil along the route], landing places marked out, and all arrangements made'. The race rules were formally announced by the Royal Aero Club of the United Kingdom on May 22nd 1919, with supplementary regulations announced in June stating that no aircraft could start until September 8th.

To create a sense of tension between Ross Smith and the other competitors, I used a booklet printed and widely distributed by the grieving father of Cedric Howell in the wake of the young aviator's death off the island of Corfu. The pamphlet, held among the papers of A. Grenfell Price in the State Library of South Australia, is titled *The Last Flight of the Late*

Capt. C.E. Howell DSO, MC, DFC, RAF and his mysterious death at Corfu. AN APPEAL and goes to great lengths to raise questions about the race process and the circumstances in which Howell died. On the final page of the 20-page pamphlet, Mr Howell says an enquiry into the race would clear up the following four questions: 'Was the race postponed to allow Ross Smith to compete? Was the race made to suit Ross Smith, regardless of the interests and lives of the other competitors? Were the alterations ordered on all machines as a result of Ross Smith's report necessary, and were they the cause of the death of four of the competitors? Were the conditions fair to all competitors, or all in favour of one?'

Three related documents are also contained among the papers of A. Grenfell Price. The first is a letter dated September 9th 1920 from race competitor George Matthews, debunking allegations raised by Mr Howell and offering unqualified support to Ross Smith. 'As one of the unsuccessful competitors I deeply regret that the brilliant success of yourself and the Vimy crew should meet with such unjust criticism as embodied in the above pamphlet and in the event of an enquiry taking place shall be only too pleased to attend in support of the foregoing statements,' Matthews wrote.

The second related document is a letter dated 10th September 1920 from Ross Smith to the Minister for Defence, in which he too demands a public enquiry to clear his name. 'I need hardly to say that there is absolutely no truth in or foundation for these charges; but they so seriously reflect upon my character and are made so publicly that I feel that some step ought to be taken to prevent a repetition of the charges and to secure their public refutation,' Ross wrote. 'I make every allowance for Mr Howell's grief and mental disturbances due to the tragic loss of his son and have no wish to punish him by the bringing of a libel action against him, which indeed is not a satisfactory method of settling a matter of this kind. Mr Howell has demanded a public enquiry, and I too feel that a public enquiry is the proper means of putting a stop to these calumnies and of clearing me from the imputations made against me and incidentally against the government.'

The third related document, dated October 12th 1920, is a response to Ross from the Department of Defence, in the form of a statement supplied by then Lieutenant Colonel Richard Williams and confirmed by another official who helped to oversee the race. The letter states that it is not proposed to institute a public enquiry. In his four-page statement, Williams categorically denies the allegations made by Mr Howell, including favouritism being shown to Ross Smith. 'The Prime Minister was influenced by no-body when delaying the flight to the 8th September and at that time, neither he nor anybody else knew of Captain Ross Smith as a possible entrant for the flight ...'

Two days later we were in London again, Benny and me sitting at the back of a room filled with officials from the British Air Ministry, the Royal Aero Club and the Australian government.

British aviation publications including the *Aeroplane* reported on this September meeting. In his letter to Ross Smith, dated September 9th 1920, George Matthews also confirms a meeting at 'Air Ministry H.Q.' in which 'General Borton and yourself reported at length on aerodromes and conditions generally throughout the stage Calcutta — Darwin.'

Chapter 12

We stood watching the hop-pickers for a bit.

I got the idea for the hop-picking scene from *My Warrior Sons*. During the war, the Colonel and Mrs Borton turned their local village hall into a makeshift hospital for injured soldiers, who were referred to throughout the diaries as 'the Colonel's cripples'. In one diary entry in August 1916, the Colonel talked of taking them hop-picking as part of their convalescence.

Then Biffy brought in the heavy artillery: Major-General Salmond, who was back briefly in Britain from Cairo.

A. Grenfell Price writes about the September 1919 meeting between Vickers heavyweights and Salmond in *The Skies Remember*, noting that everyone got 'very enthusiastic' and that the Vickers' Board later offered 'warm and interested approval' and 'the warmest recommendation to use Ross Smith and his men'. In a letter to Biffy Borton after the race, dated January 25th 1919, Ross Smith gives all the kudos to his friend: 'I think [then Vickers Aviation second in command, Walter] Caddell must have felt very bucked at your persuading him to let us have the Vimy.'

Chapter 13

I couldn't help but compare her, and she didn't stack up.

Wally spoke at length about his life, the air race and his first impressions of the Vickers Vimy in a taped interview with Hazel de Berg in 1966 (held in the National Library of Australia's oral history collection). Given the plane was state-of-the-art at the time and only recently off the production line, chances are Wally's recollections tend to exaggerate his initial view that the Vimy was incapable of making the flight. In later life I think Wally developed a reputation as a bit of a raconteur. In the late 1960s, Smith brothers biographer A. Grenfell Price asked Biffy Borton to read a draft of his book The Skies Remember. In responding, Biffy wrote: 'I agree that Shiers' contribution [by way of the taped interview with Hazel de Berg] is inimitable. I have not attempted to modify his occasional slight exaggerations, to do so would mar the delightful atmosphere. I should so much like to hear his version of how I got my nickname. It goes back 60 years, so I don't know the answer; but I've no doubt Shiers has invented a good one!'

The Vickers Vimy came too late for war.

In *Vickers Aircraft Since 1908*, C.F. Andrews writes: 'Behind the scenes in official quarters a controversy had raged between the protagonists of tactical and strategic bombing. This seems to have been resolved because of the need to retaliate against the night bombing of targets in Britain by German aeroplanes, which began in September 1917. In consequence, the Vimy was one of the new heavy bombers selected for production.' Initial contracts of 150 and 200 aircraft were received, with subsequent contracts taking the total to 1,130. 'Production during 1918 was to be reserved for aircraft for anti-submarine duties (carrying two torpedoes) and subsequent deliveries for night-bombing aircraft.' By war's end, when the government drastically cut orders, Vickers Crayford had made only seven aircraft and Weybridge six. 'In October 1918 one Vimy bomber was flown to Nancy, in northeast France, to stand by for a series of long-range raids deep into Germany, including Berlin. The Armistice of 11 November 1918 cancelled this plan, and consequently the Vimy was not used operationally in the First Word War.'

Then three months earlier, Alcock and Brown flew a Vimy into the record books across the Atlantic, and suddenly everyone had heard of them.

Alcock and Brown's Vickers Vimy (one of only two surviving original Vickers Vimy aircraft in the world – the other being the Smith crew's Vimy housed at Adelaide Airport in South Australia) has been a centrepiece of Britain's Science Museum since December 1919. A 1969 article in *Vickers News* notes the plane was taken back to Weybridge to be reconstructed and cleaned of mud from its illustrious landing in an Irish bog, before being transported up to the museum in London. One worker recalled that the windows had to be taken out of the building so they could get the Vimy inside. The museum's collection numbers 200,000 objects, and in 2013 the

Vimy was numbered among the top 112 key developments in science, technology and medicine that have shaped the modern world.

'Men still do the specialist mechanical work, of course, but we had 25 girls dedicated to the build of each and every machine,' Rex said.

This conversation is lifted largely from Wally's interview with Hazel de Berg in 1966. In May 1969, Vickers News published an article on 'Vimy veterans' to celebrate the 50th anniversary of Alcock and Brown's 1919 trans-Atlantic flight. Mrs Anne Boultwood spoke of her work as forewoman in the erecting and doping shop at Weybridge during the war, managing 300 girls sewing fabric on the planes and repairing damage to the fabric. They were part of an estimated 1.6 million British women who entered civilian employment during the war, taking over previously male roles in arms factories but also as bus crews, postal workers, farmhands and in many other areas of employment. In *The Crying Years*, Peter Stanley explains that the experience was vastly different in Australia. 'While the war created work for some women in shops and offices, the lack of manufacturing or war industry, and the rejection of conscription, failed to bring about the widespread economic changes that occurred in Britain (and which Australian troops there noted with unease).'

It was a story you couldn't forget: dubious workers had christened the poor airship the *Mayfly*, because they thought it may fly, but it may not.

According to C.F. Andrews in Vickers Aircraft Since 1908, Vickers was awarded the £30,000 contract to build HMA (His Majesty's Airship) No. 1 in 1909, and it wasn't long before a series of delays and design changes led to its 'opprobrious nickname'. The 512-ft airship, which cost more than twice the original allocation, was struck by a squall on launch and broke in two.

Chapter 14

'You'll get used to him fellas,' he said. 'He's the blunt one.'

Ross Smith makes a direct reference to Keith's blunt nature in *14,000 Miles through the Air,* as he recalls his brother's frustration with the French in Lyons: 'My brother's [whisker] growth, like his temper, is much more bristly than mine.' A former Vickers Weybridge worker by the name of Charles Tullett, interviewed in 1969, told a similar story: 'I knew both the Smith brothers ... I think Keith (the navigator) was the more forceful of the two.'

'It's not right,' I said, tapping angrily at my cigarette to drop its ash. 'Should be Pard.'

Throughout his life, Wally maintained the view that Ross's former No. 1 Squadron observer Pard Mustard was 'very disappointed' at not being on the Vimy crew. In Wally's interview with Hazel de Berg in 1966, he said that after being introduced to Keith in London, he said to Ross: 'Well now you've broken the party up, Ross. You'd better let Mustard know.'

Pard (who changed his surname from Mustard to Mustar after the war) debunks the myth. In *D'Air Devil: The story of 'Pard' Mustar*, author Frank Clune explains that Ross did ask Mustar to travel to England after the war, to take up aviation as a career, but he declined because he wanted to return to Australia. The pair spoke again after the 1919 flight, with Ross asking why Pard hadn't come to England, as he'd wanted him on the trip. 'Oh well, bad luck! thought Mustar,' Clune writes. 'It was just another of life's little jokes that, after so many adventurous flights with Ross Smith, he should have missed the chance of taking part in the greatest flight of all.'

'He tried to enlist a couple of times in Australia but was knocked back on medical grounds.'

Papers held in the Keith Macpherson Smith collection at the Barr Smith Library, University of Adelaide, show he was twice rejected for military service in Adelaide on the grounds of 'physical unfitness', in July and October 1916. No reason is given, however I once read a reference to Keith having an operation for varicose veins (a common reason for rejection in World War I) before recuperating on a ship en route to England. I should reinforce that there's no proof the medical condition was varicose veins. The Barr Smith Library collection includes a Royal Flying Corps certificate, showing Keith qualified to become a pilot on February 24th 1918. His RFC service records held in the National Archives in Britain show Keith served as an instructor in the final year of the war, which was no mean feat. In Australian Flying Corps, Ian Hodges states that the average trainee pilot in the Royal Flying Corps destroyed two aircraft and wrecked six undercarriages. Instructors like Keith, who were up in the aircraft with them, risked their lives daily to train these unskilled young men.

Ross peeled off his overalls. 'I'm buying us all dinner at the Hand & Spear and you two can fill Keith in on the Vimy.'

Letters written by Ross Smith to family and friends just before the flight, and which subsequently became some of the first international airmail to reach Australia, reference the Hand & Spear as his address. The pub is still operating just outside Brooklands Museum in Weybridge.

'Gee, Keith, you've got even more like Dad,' said Ross, nodding at the open notebook. 'His station records were more thorough than the Holy Bible.'

Ross and Keith's father Andrew Smith ran Mutooroo Station, on the South Australian border near Broken Hill, for pioneer pastoralist Peter Waite. Smith senior was credited with converting the waterless, 3,000 sqm property into productive wool country supporting nearly 130,000 sheep. Waite's great-grandson Jim Morgan writes in his essay *Knights of the Air* that Smith and Waite established 'giant earth tanks, pipelines as long as thirty miles, the buildings necessary to such an enterprise and, above all, fencing'. The result was 300 paddocks where there had been nothing. 'I've held in my hand his little black notebook, maybe only three inches by four or five, covering several years in the early 1890s, showing woolclips, total income and expenses both capital and running ... full of facts and disciplined activity recorded by the day.'

'It was worse in South Australia,' said Ross. 'We had the highest 'No' vote of any state. Lousy lot.'

A letter to Keith in June 1916, held in the State Library of South Australia, illustrates Ross's disgust at the apathy of Australian men towards enlistment, and his support for conscription. '... for goodness sake try to get them to stop wasting money in sending those idiotic, recruiting trains about the country,' he writes. 'Everyone over here is positively disgusted with the idea, and I feel positively ashamed to think we have to stoop to such levels to get men ... What must the Germans think of us? It's all a ridiculous farce, and the sooner compulsion is passed the sooner do we stop making fools of ourselves.'

Australians voted against conscription in October 1916 and again in December 1917 (joining India and South Africa as the only participating countries not to introduce subscription in World War I). In the first referendum, South Australia joined New South Wales with the largest 'No' votes of around 57 per cent. 'Yes' majorities were recorded in Victoria, Tasmania, Western Australia and the federal territories. In *The Crying Years*, Paul Stanley notes that in the second referendum, all states and territories except Tasmania and Western Australia voted 'No'.

Rex Pierson had shown us a newspaper clipping from the *New York Times* that said Christopher

Columbus didn't take one tenth of the risks the air pioneers would face on the race to Australia.

The *New York Times* article, published on October 18th 1919, offered a sobering view of the task facing air race competitors: 'Columbus in his caravel did not take a tenth of the risks that these bold air pioneers will have to face. Luck be with them, but they will be throwing dice with Death.'

Chapter 15

I think Keith Murdoch took one look at Ross and knew if any pilot was going to make it home to Australia, it was him.

It's unknown how the Smith brothers met Keith Murdoch, but given their shared Scottish Australian heritage and Keith's work in London on the 1917 conscription referendum, it's not beyond the realms of possibility that the two Keiths had met well before the air race. Documents held in the Royal Archives at Windsor Castle, England, include a letter dated December 9th 1919 from Keith Murdoch to the Rt.-Hon. Lord Stamfordham, Private Secretary to His Majesty the King, which confirms that the then United Cable Service managing editor was receiving telegrams from Ross during the race. 'Sir,' it says, 'We understand that His Majesty has expressed some interest in the superb flight of Captain Ross Smith ... to Australia. As we have received the enclosed personal wires from Captain Ross Smith, we have pleasure in forwarding them to you in case they may be of further interest to His

Majesty.' Throughout the race, Australian news-papers including the *Herald* and the *Weekly Times* in Melbourne, the Sydney Sun and other papers signed up to the wire service splashed 'Exclusive Messages' directly quoting Ross from landing spots along the route. Just before their record-breaking flight, the Smith brothers also dined with Murdoch in London. In *If I Remember Rightly: The memoirs of W.S. Robinson 1876–1963*, industrialist William Sydney Robinson recalls the dinner with the Smith brothers and his friend Keith Murdoch at the British Empire Club in St James's Square.

'Do you reckon you can survive the Blazing Trail?'

By late 1919, Australian newspapers including the Melbourne *Herald* were also reporting on the large number of deaths occurring among airmen on 'The Blazing Trail' from London to Cairo. Colonel Lawrence crashed near Rome's Centocelle aerodrome, where the Smith crew landed on their way through Italy.

Two boxes had arrived that morning. One was from Kodak Ltd.

The March 1920 edition of the Australasian Photo Review reveals all four men had a Kodak and a supply of Kodak Speed Film, and took some of the first aerial photos ever captured along parts of the route. The £800 cheque for first prize was awarded to Ross, although Keith took most of the photos and the prize money was split between the four men.

Chapter 17

Lyons, France, November 12th 1919

Many place names along the route have changed since the air race – or differ from Ross Smith's Anglicised spelling. However, I have stuck with 1919 references for consistency with earlier non-fiction books on the race. Also, I am not going into vast detail here about the facts of the race, because I'd simply be repeating fantastic resources already available (as noted in the bibliography).

'Wonder if they're playing funny buggers to buy Poulet some more time.'

The scene in Lyons is largely drawn from Ross's recollection in *14,000 Miles through the Air*, with embellishment for dramatic effect. However, I do think it's entirely plausible that the French airmen would have favoured Poulet over any English crews —especially given that he entered the race to honour the revered French aviator Jules Védrines, who had died in an accident not far from Lyons.

The Leaning Tower was right across the fields from the aerodrome.

A photograph taken by Biffy Borton on his 1918 flight from London to Cairo in the Handley Page, and featured in Clive Semple's *Airway to the East*, shows the Pisa aerodrome was once located in sight of the Leaning Tower. It's true that on landing, Wally said it looked like the architect had drunk too much Johnnie Walker.

Chapter 18

In the middle of all that, Keith pushed through and tapped me on the shoulder and announced: 'Shiers, your engine's sick.'

According to Wally's interview with Hazel de Berg, this actually happened, although I've ramped up the animosity for dramatic effect. In the same scene I mention Benny rolling his eyes at being told by Keith to sit down in the aft cockpit because he was slowing down the plane. This is taken from a line in Keith's flight diary, now held in the State Library of South Australia, in which he makes a note to himself and/ or Ross: 'I would tell Bennett not to stand up for too long at a time, it must take at least 5 mph off our speed.'

'What about a poultice that wrapped around the pipe and plugged the crack without burning?' I called up to Benny. 'Mate, hand me the chewing gum from the emergency rations.'

Ross Smith's *14,000 Miles through the Air* makes no mention of Wally's chewing gum idea, and I wonder if this was part of a deliberate strategy immediately after the flight to understate any real trouble with the Rolls-Royce engines. This is reinforced by a confidential letter from Ross Smith to Vickers (held in the State Library of South Australia) after the crew's arrival in Australia and the subsequent breakdown of the aircraft. 'I have made certain guarded statements to the Press about our trouble and sent a wire to the Sydney Sun,' Ross writes. 'I thought that the best course as otherwise all sorts of rumours get about. I think that our best way will be to partially blame the vibration caused by the mended propeller and the fact of not being able to give the engines overhaul before. As I have said I do not think the latter reason had anything to do with it, but we do not want the Vimy's reputation or Rolls Royce to suffer in any way.' The first published reference to the chewing gum incident appeared in A. Grenfell Price's *The Skies Remember*, in which he quotes from Wally's 1966 taped interview with Hazel de Berg and confirms it is 'vouched for by Lady Smith and friends of the family'.

Chapter 19

The Vimy's wheels had barely rolled to a stop when a lanky bloke with a wide forehead and an easy smile came striding out to meet us.

This long-awaited meeting with Poulet in Akyab is recorded as it happened. 'Poulet was the first to greet us on landing,' Ross Smith writes in *14,000 Miles through the Air*. 'He came forward with a cheery smile and outstretched hand – a true sportsman, the hero of a gallant and daring enterprise.' Newspaper clippings from the time also describe Poulet as a likeable character.

Ross held up a hand, silencing his brother. 'I'll say this just one more time. We are not leaving without Poulet.'

In truth, it's unlikely there was any opposition from the crew to Ross's idea of flying to Bangkok in tandem with Poulet. As Ross notes in *14,000 Miles*, 'The way to Bangkok lay across high ranges and dense jungle, and the mutual advantage in making the journey together over this unfrequented and practically unknown country, should a forced landing have to be made by one of us, was obvious.'

Chapter 20

In the eerie gloom, the foreman stepped forward and delivered a vicious blow with a long, thin piece of bamboo, striking a worker's bare arm with a nasty crack.

It's only fair to note that the Smith crew weren't quite as kind-hearted as I make them out to be in this scene. It was, after all, 1919 and they were on a tight schedule to reach Australia within 30 days. In *14,000 Miles through the Air*, Ross explains that the 'coolies' were given a pay increase to do the work, but when they went on strike again within 15 minutes he called the foreman. 'There was a different kind of strike, and so the work proceeded.'

I slumped back on my seat and fell asleep until we bounced to earth at Don Muang aerodrome.

During the 1919 flight, Ross Smith told Bangkok's *Siam Observer* that the Don Muang aerodrome was the best he'd struck since England 'and expressed himself as delighted with the arrangements made and the very efficient administration'. During my Churchill Fellowship in 2017, I visited the National Aviation Museum of the Royal Thai Air Force in Bangkok and learned that the Thai Royal Family was an early adopter of aviation technology. In 1912 three officers were sent to France for flight training, before returning to create the Royal Thai Air Force. In June 1918, Thailand sent an aviation regiment to support the Allies in France, and by 1919 airmail services had begun and the 'Army Air Division' was well advanced. When the Vimy flew out of Bangkok, four aircraft formed a military escort for 50 miles.

'Old man Shiers was one of a dozen convicts to escape Van Diemen's Land in a small stolen ship. he got all the way to Chile before he was caught.'

True story, as told in Adam Courtenay's 2018 book *The Ship That Never Was: The greatest escape story of Australian colonial history.*

Sometime around midnight, Keith had come up with a plan. We'd ask for more matting from the villagers and lay an entire runway.

This is a true story, but it's not so clear whether all local villagers gave up the walls of their homes willingly, or were coerced to help out. However, the crew did take many photographs of villagers happily pitching in that morning to lay 'Matting Road' and get the crew on their way.

Chapter 21

I turned to check if I could still see the HMAS *Sydney* ... I hoped they rescued Keith's pickle jar before it sank into the waves.

The final leg of the flight over the Timor Sea into Port Darwin was one of the most dangerous, so you can imagine how happy the Vimy crew were to sight the HMAS *Sydney* about 180 miles off the coast. With no radio on board, Keith dropped an Escoffier pickle jar complete with a parachute tied with string. The pencil message read 'The Air, 10/12/19, Vickers Vimy, The Commander, H.M.A.S., Very glad to see you. Many thanks for looking after us. Going strong. Keith Smith, Ross Smith, Sgt J. Bennett, Sgt W.H. Shiers.' The jar and message were donated to the Library of New South Wales by the Captain H. Cayley, Commander of HMAS *Sydney*, in 1922.

One of them was Hudson Fysh, an old mate of Ross's from No. 1 Squadron who'd had the job of scratching aerodromes out of scrub and desert from Darwin to Brisbane in time to receive the air race crews.

Hudson Fysh and fellow Australian Flying Corps pilot Paul McGinness founded Qantas as a result of carving out the airfields across northern Australia for air race competitors in 1919. In his autobiography *Qantas Rising*, Sir Hudson describes seeing the Vimy appear as a little speck over the Timor Sea before coming in to land in Darwin. 'It was one of the most moving sights I can remember — the termination of one of the greatest flights, if not the greatest, in the history of aviation, and a great fillip for civil aviation in Australia, for no one had ever flown across the world before.'

'Sir' Ross and 'Sir' Keith, it was now.

Ross and Keith were knighted by King George V within weeks of the Darwin landing, and the accolade didn't sit easily with Ross. In January 1920 he writes to Biffy Borton, lamenting 'I'm afraid it will only be a nuisance to me'. He continues: 'All the 'sharks' in the country are doing their best to get us into companies & all sorts of things but we have survived so far.'

Benny blamed the bastard who'd stolen Marmaduke II's head.

In the same letter to Biffy Borton sent in January 1920, Ross reveals the fate of the crew's little mascot. 'At Darwin his 'neck' got bent and the spring pulled out a bit. Bennett was mending him surrounded by a crowd of sightseers, one of whom stole Marmaduke's head. The united efforts of ourselves & the police failed to recover the missing piece & I'm very sorry about him.' Ross also confirms the Colonel's wife Laura Borton donated the mascot, saying '… please tell Mrs Borton that I will write & thank her for Marmaduke later on when things get quieter, it is almost impossible at present to do anything except listen to hot air & silly speeches'.

The temporary fix got us all the way to Charleville, over west of Brisbane, when the Vimy and her Rolls-Royce engines finally said enough and carked it.

In *The Skies Remember*, A. Grenfell Price gives an insight into the damage that occurred after the take-off at Charleville, when Wally heard 'a terrific bang, and a flash of fire came out past Benny and me, and we wondered, and thought we were gone'. According to Price, the port engine was taken to Ipswich and needed 'one new cylinder, two pistons, all the big ends, two connecting rods, six new valves, a new manifold, and the sump patched'. While a new propeller was being made of Queensland maple, the Vimy back in Charleville was redoped, varnished and fitted with a new set of control wires. The repairs took 'some fifty days', nearly twice as long as the flight from London to Darwin.

Sir Ross leaned over and kissed my new wife.

A detailed article and photograph in Sydney's the *Sunday Times* on February 22nd 1920 tells the story of Wally and Helena's wedding. The garden party was hosted by prominent politician and theatre promoter Hugh McIntosh in honour of the Smith crew, and 'was made intensely interesting' by the fact that it doubled as Wally and Helena's marriage ceremony. Guests included the New South Wales Premier William Holman and other politicians, Sydney socialites and highly distinguished soldiers. 'As Capt. Chaplain Wilson remarked, the wedding was arranged by the photographers and not by the clergyman,' the article says. 'Sir Ross Smith was best man, and incidentally hastened to kiss the bride after the Chaplain had warned the bridegroom that he had better be quick if he wished to secure the first kiss.'

Postscript

'So what happened then, Wal?'

The events unfolded largely as Wally describes, and the facts are widely documented in non-fiction books and resources.

Hubert Wilkins, Val Rendle, David Williams and Garnsey Potts crashed out, too, with their Blackburn Kangaroo coming to rest in a ditch near a lunatic asylum on the island of Crete.

In *The Last Explorer*, Simon Nasht details the trials faced by the Blackburn Kangaroo crew and suggests sabotage may have occurred first in France and later on Crete. 'For the rest of his life Rendle remained convinced that the Blackburn had been deliberately sabotaged and, though less certain, Wilkins agreed there was evidence that someone had tried to prevent them continuing,' Nasht writes. 'If so, it amounted to attempted murder, but none of the pilots would ever know who was responsible.'

Keith married Anita Crawford in 1924.

Anita Crawford (nee Schmidt) had previously been married to England cricketer Jack Crawford. In *Flick of the Fingers*, biographer Michael Burns describes the 'talented and glamorous' Anita as a prominent figure in 'Roaring Twenties' London. 'She had her portrait painted by the distinguished Australian artist Marion Jones, she designed a collection of flapper-girl clothes for Adelaide's fashionable ladies, and she was appointed the conductor of a Shakespearean orchestra ...' When Lady Anita died in 1986, she bequeathed her entire estate to the development of the Sir Ross and Sir Keith Smith Fund, which to this day remains dedicated to encouraging the advancement of aeronautics and aerospace technology in South Australia.

I pause. Along the bar there's silence. 'They dropped out of the sky and crashed behind trees lining the track ...'

Ross and Benny died in Weybridge on April 13th 1922. An inquest found that the accident was caused by Ross's lack of training in handling the new single-engine amphibian Vickers Viking, and the fact that he'd not been flying for many months. A large memorial service was held at St Clement Danes, the church of the Royal Air Force, in London, before Keith Smith escorted the bodies home to Australia. Ross lay in state at St Peter's Cathedral in Adelaide, while Benny lay in state in the Queen's Hall of Parliament House, Melbourne. Ross was buried on June 15th 1922, with an estimated 100,000 people (one fifth of South Australia's population) lining the streets to watch the funeral procession from St Peter's Cathedral to North Road Cemetery. As his mother Jessie continued to receive messages of condolence from across the globe, she noted: 'Before Ross died he belonged to us, but now he belongs to the Empire.'

Acknowledgements

Huge thanks to everyone who's been on the Long Flight Home with me.

To old schoolmate Nigel Parsons, who called me up in 2009 (after reading about South Australia's Smith brothers in Peter FitzSimons's Charles Kingsford Smith and Those Magnificent Men) and demanded I write a column on the largely forgotten Vickers Vimy at Adelaide Airport. Nige, you have the honour of turning me into the crazy plane lady.

To Nigel Daw at the South Australian Aviation Museum, who was so very generous with his time and expertise when I began my book research in the wonderful museum library at Port Adelaide. Nigel later joined with my News Corporation boss Melvin Mansell in supporting my application for a Churchill Fellowship. That application was life-changing, and I am sincerely grateful to the Winston Churchill Memorial Trust, both for the research trip and my new Churchill Fellows family.

To those I met overseas: Alex Spencer at the Smithsonian's National Air and Space Museum; Doug Millard at Britain's Science Museum; Brian Riddle at the National Aerospace Library; Royal Aero Club trustee Andrew Dawrant; Andrew Lewis at Brooklands (and Phil and Marianne in the museum library); Lionel Dufaux at the Museum of Arts and Trades in Paris; Pierre Lussignol, Jacques Baillet and Pierre Biard from the Lyon Aviation History and Aeronautics Documentation Society; and Chamnong

Sripho from the Royal Thai Air Force Museum. Even taxi drivers (from Jaspal Singh in Delhi, to George in Crete and Tedy Try in Surabaya) were so inspired by the story that they'd bail up random elderly people on the streets to ask if they'd heard of the air race as children.

To Claire Kingston from Allen & Unwin, who was super encouraging when only a third of the book was written and kept me motivated all the way (and to South Australian author Liz Harfull who made the connection for me). And to Susan Harrington, Alicia Ranford and Kate Jordan-Moore who read early and earnestly and all said exactly the right thing at exactly the right time.

To Australian adventurer Lang Kidby, who built and flew a replica Vimy from England to Australia in 1994, for pointing out mistakes that would make me look really stupid, and then telling me not to sweat the rest. The advice I received from Lang and his wife Bev was priceless.

To Ross Smith biographer Michael Molkentin, a genuine, generous soul whose talent for non-fiction makes me glad I chose to tackle the air race as a novel.

To my book club girls, who unknowingly inspired me to write the kind of book they'd (hopefully) want to read.

To my partners in crime on the epic flight centenary, who make sharing this story a joy: Greg Mackie, Greg Weller, David Byrne, Jim Whalley and the rest of our EFC2019 Committee.

To those who offered tiny gems that had a big impact: Smith family descendent Gary Lloyd; Smith family friend Judith Rischbieth; Shiers family descendent Gary Shiers; Guy Slater, step-grandson to Biffy

Borton; Carolyn Spooner from the State Library of South Australia; Cecile Cutler and Peter Speck from Flinders University; Vimy enthusiast Stephen Heading; Richard Green, my London man on the ground; aviation historians Mike Milln, Peter Ingman, the late Chas Schaedel and the late Paul Daw; Helen Stein at North Road Cemetery; and Narrandera historian Geoffrey Sullivan.

This book is in print because Michael Bollen from Wakefield Press is a bloody nice bloke who believes in good stories, even if they don't quite fit the marketing mould of one genre or another. Thanks also to his small but superb team including Jo Case, Liz Nicholson, Margot Lloyd, Michael Deves and Maddy Sexton.

To my little family, sometimes a bit neglected but always much loved: Harry and Jack, Mum, Pete, Meryl and Ron, Ian and Barb. And darling Dad; he'd be proud.

But if I could only thank one person, it would be the one and only Max: my husband, my pain-in-the-arse editor, my Wally.

Bibliography and Sources

Andrews, C.F., *Vickers Aircraft Since 1908*, Putman & Company, 1969

Barnaby, Jane, *Australian Aviators*, Cassell Astralia, 1973

Blainey, Geoffrey, *If I Remember Righty: The mem-oirs of W.S. Robinson 1876–1963*, F.W. Cheshire Publishing, 1967

Bowyer, Chaz, *History of the RAF*, The Hamlyn Publishing Group, 1977

Brearley, Sir Norman, *Australian Aviator*, Rigby Limited, 1971

Brocker, Susan, *Brave Bess and the ANZAC Horses*, HarperCollins New Zealand, 2010

Canby, Courtland, *A History of Flight*, Editions Rencontre and Erik Nitsche International, 1962

Clune, Frank, *D'Air Devil: The story of 'Pard' Mustar*, Angus & Robertson, 1941

Cutlack, F.M., *The Australian Flying Corps in the Western and Eastern Theatres of War 1914–1918*, Angus & Robertson 1938

Dowie, John, *A Life in the Round*, Wakefield Press, 2001

Eustis, Nelson, *The Greatest Air Race: England–Australia 1919*, Rigby Limited 1969

FitzSimons, Peter, *Charles Kingsford Smith and Those Magnificent Men*, HarperCollinsPublishers, 2009

Fysh, Sir Hudson, *Qantas Rising*, Angus & Robertson, 1965

Gammage, Bill, *Narrandera Shire*, Bill Gammage, 1986

Grant, R.G., Flight: *100 Years of Aviation*, Dorling Kindersley, 2002

Gunn, John, *The Defeat of Distance: Qantas 1919–1939*, University of Queensland Press, 1985

Gwynn-Jones, Terry, *Aviation's Magnificent Gamblers*, Lansdowne Press, 1981

Gwynn-Jones, Terry, *On a Wing and a Prayer*, University of Queensland Press, 1989

Gwynn-Jones, Terry, *By the Seat of Their Pants*, University of Queensland Press, 1992

Gwynn-Jones, Terry, *Wild Blue Yonder*, University of Queensland Press, 1996

Hamilton, John, *The Price of Valour*, Pan Macmillan Australia, 2012

Haynes, Jim & Dellit, Jillian, *Great Australian Aviation Stories*, ABC Books, 2006

Hodges, Ian, *Australian Flying Corps*, Department of Veterans' Affairs, Canberra, 2010

Hyde, Andrew P., *The First Blitz*, Leo Cooper, 2002

Kabaila, Peter, *Leeton, a Thematic History*, Canprint Publishing, 2013

Kieza, Grantlee, Bert Hinkler: *The Most daring man in the world*, HarperCollins Publishers, 2012

Lawrence, T.E., *Revolt in the Desert*, Jonathan Cape, 1927

Lax, Mark, *One Airman's War: Aircraft Mechanic Joe Bull's personal diaries 1916–1919*, Banner Books, 1997

Livesey, Anthony, *Great Battles of World War I*, Marshall Editions, 1989

Mackersey, Ian, *Smithy*, Little, Brown and Company, 1998

Maguire, Marie, *Living Memories: Tales of Leeton and its pioneers*, BH Maguire, 1984

Maiden, Peter, *The Sky Racers*, Central Queensland University Press, 2010

McCoy, J.P. and Keohane, *The 14–18 Journal*, The Australian Society of World War 1 Aero Historians, 1968

Miller, H.C., *Early Birds*, Rigby Limited 1968

Molkentin, Michael, *Fire in the Sky: The Australian Flying Corps in the First World War*, Allen & Unwin, 2010

Nasht, Simon, *The Last Explorer: Hubert Wilkins, Australia's unknown hero*, Hachette Australia, 2007

Odgers, George, *Pictorial History of the Royal Australian Air Force*, Paul Hanlyn, 1978

Price, A. Grenfell, *The Skies Remember*, Angus & Robertson, 1969

Rendall, Ivan, *Reaching for the Skies*, BBC Books, 1988

Roberts, Tom D.C., *Before Rupert: Keith Murdoch and the birth of a dynasty*, University of Queensland Press, 2015

Robinson, Derek, *Goshawk Squadron*, Cassell Military Paperbacks, 1971

Schaedel, Chas, *South Australian Airmen of the Great War*, South Australian Aviation Museum, 2015

Semple, Clive, *Airway to the East 1918–1920: And the collapse of No. 1 Aerial Route RAF*, Pen & Sword Aviation 2011

Slater, Guy, *My Warrior Sons*, Peter Davies, 1973

Smith, Sir Ross, *14,000 Miles through the Air*, Macmillan & Co, 1922

Stanley, Peter, *The Crying Years: Australia's Great War*, National Library of Australia, 2017

Sutherland, L.W., *Aces and Kings*, Angus & Robertson, 1935

Verne, Jules, *Great Works of Jules Verne*, Projapoti, 2011

Williams, Sir Richard, *These Are Facts*, The Australian War Memorial and the Australian Government Publishing Service, 1977

Sources

Australian War Memorial: www.awm.gov.au

Flight magazine archives: www.flightglobal.com/pdfarchive/

National Archives of Australia RecordSearch for World War I service records: recordsearch.naa.gov.au

National Library of Australia: Walter Henry Shiers interviewed by Hazel de Berg in the Hazel de Berg collection [Oral trc 1/182–184]

National Library of Australia: Album of Walter (Wally) Shiers memorabilia relating to the 1919 Ross Smith flight, 1919–1986 [NLA MS 8627]

National Library of Australia: Papers of Ernest and Virtie Crome, 1784–2005, relating to Ross Smith and Wally Shiers [MS 1925, MS Acc11.005]

National Library of Australia: trove.nla.gov.au (particularly archive copies of the *Narrandera Argus*, Adelaide's Advertiser and Observer newspapers and Broken Hill's Barrier Miner)

The State Library of South Australia has digitised its collection of Sir Ross and Sir Keith Smith's personal papers and other material relating to the brothers from throughout the SLSA collection. https://digital.collections.slsa.sa.gov.au/pages/ smith-brothers

State Library of South Australia: Ross Smith letters to his mother Jessie Smith and father Andrew Smith [SLSA PRG 18/17/1–56]

State Library of South Australia: A. Grenfell Price

collection [SLSA PRG 1067]

The University of Adelaide Rare Books and Special Collections: Sir Keith Smith and Sir Ross Smith certificates, pamphlets, photographs and miscellanea 1916–1956 [MSS 92 S653]

We do hope that you have enjoyed
reading this large print book.

Did you know that all of our titles
are available for purchase?

We publish a wide range of high
quality large print books including:
Romances, Mysteries, Classics
General Fiction
Non Fiction and Westerns

Special interest titles available in
large print are:
The Little Oxford Dictionary
Music Book, Song Book
Hymn Book, Service Book

Also available from us courtesy of
Oxford University Press:
Young Readers' Dictionary
(large print edition)
Young Readers' Thesaurus
(large print edition)

For further information or a free
brochure, please contact us at:
Ulverscroft Large Print Books Ltd.,
The Green, Bradgate Road, Anstey,
Leicester, LE7 7FU, England.
Tel: (00 44) 0116 236 4325
Fax: (00 44) 0116 234 0205

Other titles published by Ulverscroft:

ALCHEMY AND ROSE

Sarah Maine

1866. Will Stewart is one of many who have left their old lives behind to seek their fortunes in New Zealand's last great gold rush. Rose is about to arrive on the shores of South Island when a storm hits and her ship is wrecked. She is snatched from the jaws of death by Will. Drawn together by circumstance, they stay together. But after a terrible misunderstanding they are cruelly separated, and their new-found happiness is shattered. As Will chases Rose across oceans and continents, he must come to terms with the possibility that he might never see her again. And if he does, he will have to face the man who took her ...